Detective Iceheart
Twin Crowns

A Detective Runewall Novel

Detective Iceheart
Twin Crowns

A Detective Runewall Novel

B.T. Frost

COPYRIGHT

Other works by B.T. Frost

Detective Runewall Series:

Book 1: Detective Runewall: Uncut Gems

Book 2: Detective Runewall: Grave Secrets

Acknowledgements

As it was with *Uncut Gems* and *Grave Secrets*, I must first thank my family and friends for all their enthusiastic support and encouragement.

To McKenzie Spies, I thank you again for turning my mess of a manuscript into something publishable and for helping me to better edit my own writing.

Last, but not least, I must thank my mother for excitedly reading every single chapter after I wrote it.

Chapter 1

Amelia Iceheart didn't awaken. Awakening suggested she slept. She lost consciousness and slowly regained it. Recovering from a drinking sickness was never pleasant or easy. Her memory was jumbled at best, and she couldn't recall how she had gotten home. Thankfully, Blueregard had tended to her needs throughout the night.

His presence was constant throughout the brief moments that she was cognizant. She hoped he had at least gotten some sleep of his own. She didn't need much attention, if any. A glass of water and a strong bitter tonic did most of the work. She didn't remember drinking any of it, but the familiar aftertaste of the tonic lingered on her tongue.

Drinking was not something she was accustomed to. When attending the funeral of a dwarf, one was expected to divulge in drinking games until one couldn't stand. She had undeniably succeeded in that aspect.

Any attempt to call for her lifelong companion came out as little more than a whimpered murmur. Yet, he somehow always heard her.

Blueregard entered her room with a graceful ghostliness; she hadn't heard him at all. It was also entirely possible that she had been unconscious and entirely incapable of hearing anything when he arrived.

"You called, ma'am?" He had a strong, rumbling voice, but he managed to keep his tone low and soft.

With her head pounding rhythmically against the sides of her head and her stomach rolling like a rowboat on stormy seas, she didn't trust herself to speak. Instead, she let out another grumbled whimper and lazily pointed to the back of her neck as she buried her face into her pillow.

"At once, Ms. Iceheart," his voice just as gentle as before. Blueregard turned on the spot and silently stepped from her room. Again, he was a ghost and didn't make a sound.

You are a blessing.

As a result of the many years that Mr. Blueregard had served her family, then her exclusively, the man had learned many of her wants and needs without her even having to vocalize them.

In short time – or perhaps she lost consciousness again – Blueregard returned. She almost jumped from the sudden touch of a soft cool cloth on the base of her skull beneath her hairline.

"Gods…" She couldn't help but curl her toes a bit and sigh in relief from the familiarity and ache-easing coolness. She breathed in deeply and exhaled the heat from her body.

"I take it the anti-toxin tablet didn't hold out against the might of dwarven ale?" Amelia couldn't see it, but by the tone of his voice, she was almost certain Blueregard was raising his eyebrow in his 'I told you so' sort of way.

The aforementioned tablet was often ingested prior to attending drinking parties, designed to help absorb the alcoholic toxins. Sadly, they only lasted a few hours.

The entombing ceremony lasted far longer than she

expected. She'd never attended a proper dwarven funeral before and had no idea how much was involved.

Part of the ceremony included turning the deceased into a statue. That meant that they needed dwarven wizards with transformative or polymorphic abilities. Only a few of them existed, and they were in high demand. Due to the exhaustive nature of the work, they had to take turns, and there were only two of them last night. The laborious difficulties of the endeavor didn't even include the over-exaggerated necessity for dwarven chest-thumping heroism. Officer Dromvil Anvilhearth was positioned so that he appeared to be roaring and flexing.

According to tradition, nobody was allowed to drink a drop until the transformation was complete. By the time they had finally finished, the tablet had long since been digested and she was both starving and thirsty. Dwarven ale and heavily-spiced meats were all that was served. Drinking sickness wasn't exactly something that could have been avoided in that particular scenario.

Her answer to his rhetorical question was to grumble and curl up under the blankets as she pulled them over her head. There wasn't much light in the room, so she mostly did so in order to hide from his scrutinizing gaze.

"Shall I draw you a bath, Ms. Iceheart?"

Amelia stuck a hand out from the corner of the bed and lazily waved him toward the water closet. It was her way of saying 'yes'.

It didn't take long for her to hear the familiar squeak of the taps, the rattling of the pipes, and the muffled rush of water. The lack of footsteps wasn't surprising as her bedroom was carpeted.

With her magic slowly returning to her senses, she could feel the shifting warmth in her room. Through it, she could tell that Blueregard had returned from the water closet. "Your bath shall be ready momentarily, ma'am. Would you care for assistance in getting to the tub, or would you prefer I begin brewing a tea to help settle your stomach?"

She lifted her dangling arm from the side of the bed and pointed to the kitchens.

"Very well. If you require any assistance, I am always within earshot." His warm presence slipped from the room, and her door shut behind him.

Amelia took in a deep breath through her nose and released another breath of hot air. Lowering her core temperature helped to ease her stomach and temper some of her pounding headache.

Despite all her gifts as a wizard, snapping her fingers and banishing a drinking sickness was not one of them. She could, however, use her talents to combat some of the symptoms until her body could recover normally.

She took in another deep breath and lowered her temperature yet again. The thunderous pounding that sat behind her eyes and squeezed the sides of her head slowly eased to a dull thrum. It would have to do.

Amelia groaned and slowly pushed away the bed sheets, then gingerly stuck one foot at a time out from the bed. Sitting upright was to be the true test of her rolling stomach.

She opened one eye and peered about the room. Her vision wasn't tilting, rolling, or swaying.

That's always a good sign.

Not taking any risks, she kept the other eye closed and eased herself up from the bed. Her hair stuck to the pillow, and the pillow came up with her.

That's never a good sign.

She couldn't smell any vomit or ale. There was at least that good news. She swatted the pillow back onto the bed. Her hair stayed exactly as it had been while stuck to the pillow – everywhere. It stuck up at odd angles and remained plastered to the side of her face.

Afraid of examining her hair and learning what she could have possibly gotten into it, she opted for ignoring its existence and focused on getting to the tub.

She was about to test her legs and stand up from the

bed when she noticed she was wearing her white trousers. Further tilting her chin downwards, she couldn't help but notice that she was still in her detective's garb. Her trench coat was on the floor beside her bed, but she was wearing her enchanted vest.

Mortifyingly, the vest was unbuttoned down to her navel, and so was her shirt. The only thing that had kept her decent was her brazier. "Oh, gods!"

Amelia rubbed her eyes with the palms of her hands and prayed that whatever unbuttoning had taken place was done once she had gotten home to bed. Her stomach rolled from the anxiety of having done something publically inappropriate. A quick strengthening of her will and a calming breath settled the storming sea in her gut.

By the sounds of the water filling the tub, it was nearly ready.

One problem at a time.

Amelia put one hand on the bed and held the other out before her for balance, then slowly pushed off to begin the perilous and nauseating journey to the water closet.

It didn't take her long, and she managed to finish stripping down along the way. It didn't take much effort to undress either, as she was nearly undressed to begin with; that bothered her deeply.

The water was exactly as she liked it, only a touch warm. She shivered a little as she dipped one foot in, then eased into the waters and soon acclimatized to it. Once in the tub, she was able to push her body heat out into the waters and breathe in cooler air. The water began to steam as she pushed out the stresses and cooled herself down. The pounding behind her eyes alleviated itself. Her stomach was still a bit floppy, but it would be dealt with in time.

With the water at the right temperature, she got to investigating why her hair was so stiff. A few dunks of her head and several vigorous brushings of her hair revealed thick white clumps of wax.

Why in the storming devils do I have wax in my hair?

She truly hoped that she hadn't made some unsightly scene at Anvilhearth's funeral. As much as dwarven funeral rituals involved excessive drinking and vulgar obscenities, she didn't feel like being lumped in with that sort of lot.

A few more furious combings of her hair resulted in a length of wick. One end was burned.

Oh... I fell asleep by a candle.

The funeral had been held in a traditional dwarven grand hall, where lantern lights had never been installed. Everything was lit by candles. She must have passed out on the table and a candle melted into her hair.

With a clean scrub and well-combed hair, she took a minute to soak her stresses away into the water before emerging to get ready for the day.

She unplugged the tub and allowed it to drain. Once the tub was emptied, she breathed in deeply and released all the heat from the surface of her skin. The water droplets that had clung to her flesh quickly solidified into crystals of frost, ice, and snow.

A gentle shake, pat, or brush was all she needed to knock it all free from her body; she could then step out of the tub without the need for a towel.

The full-length mirror beside her sink allowed her to examine herself. It revealed that she hadn't suffered any injuries or bruises from the night before. Nothing suggested that she had stumbled home drunk. That was a slight relief.

The mirror above her sink revealed that her stark white hair had combed out straight, and there didn't appear to be any leftover wax.

A quick check revealed no blemishes either. Despite what many women thought, Amelia didn't apply much makeup. A moisturizing cream and a touch of Stormbay Gray eye shadow was all she ever used. Her white eyelashes, eyebrows, hair, and lips were all a result of her ice magic.

Magic, in all its wondrous incarnations, altered the form of the human body. The more frequently a type of magic was used, the more it altered the body. It wasn't always an apparent difference, but her use of magic clearly made an impact.

She opened a jewelry box she kept beside the sink and perused her earrings before deciding on a small set of spiraling snowflakes. Thankfully, they didn't require her ears to be pierced; they simply latched onto her earlobes with the smallest string of magic.

Once set for the day, she turned to her bedroom and the fuzzy white carpet upon which she had tossed her clothing. Amelia pulled her blue detective's vest from the rest and gave it a quick flick to shake off anything that might have possibly settled on it. The vest had enchantments that protected her from harm. Subsequently, the vest never got soiled or dirtied. She could wear it endlessly without the need to ever clean it.

Amelia turned to her closet and the clothing within. Her apparel never truly changed except for outside of work, so it was merely a matter of grabbing a pair of white slacks and a blouse to go with her vest and trench coat.

She appreciated simplicity, and so her room had been decorated in a stark white design. The walls, baseboards, ceiling, doors, carpet, bed, bed frame, night stand, and night lantern were all painted white. The only thing that she left unpainted was the dark walnut lectern that held aloft her spell-tome.

Amelia wasn't one for nuances. Simplicity appealed to her far more readily than anything else did. That wasn't to say she couldn't understand nuance. She likely understood it far better than some others; she merely preferred simplicity.

Clean and dressed, minus her trench coat, she was as ready as she was going to be to face the aftermath and horrors of the drunken dwarven funeral. She also couldn't seem to find her staff, so she had no choice but to head for the kitchens.

Amelia snapped her fingers to shrink her spell-tome down to pocket size, picked it up off the lectern, and stuffed it in her trouser pocket. She then stepped up to the door to the kitchens and prepared herself for the onslaught of questions she was about to receive.

Opening the door proved to be a horrible mistake; the sunlight that assaulted her eyes near reawakened the headache she had earlier banished. "Oh, gods."

Amelia shut her eyes and raised her arm to block out the morning sun that was penetrating the kitchen windows to her immediate right.

A fog of cold air billowed into existence in the doorway as the two climates collided around her. She preferred a much colder bedroom. That differential, too, threatened to reawaken her headache.

"Mornin', sunshine!" Her fellow resident, Ms. Betty Hopper, was as cheery as a child with a handful of sweets. The volume level at which the woman spoke caused Amelia's hair to squeeze her head.

Ms. Betty dressed in bright, patterned dresses. Her hair never stayed the same color from one moon to the next, and it was pixie pink that morning.

The loudness of her appearance threatened to make Amelia's stomach upheave in absolute mutiny. In response, Amelia shut her eyes and breathed steadily.

Betty was only a little younger than Amelia, and the youngest child of an engineer and factory owner. The two of them split the cost of their loft residence. The poor woman also routinely scared away young men with her overly zealous attempts to land a husband, while Amelia deliberately scared men away.

"Where's—"

"On the table, Ms. Iceheart." Blueregard noted.

Amelia peered out of her left eye and noted that her tinted spectacles sat upon her empty plate. "And my—"

"It is leaning in the corner by the door. You dropped it on the kitchen floor this morning, ma'am."

Amelia squinted and peered at the corner by the door to the hall. Her staff was indeed leaning there. Her belt, gun, and holster were similarly in the corner.

Truly a blessing.

Amelia set her trench coat over the back of the chair, picked up her spectacles to put them on, and sat down. "My hat?"

Blueregard turned away from the kitchen stove and used a pair of metal tongs to place two pieces of toast on her plate. "It is hanging on the rack by the door." The toast was perfectly browned, and she could smell a hint of ginger spice. For the first time that morning, her stomach rumbled in a good way.

Following the toast, a mug of steaming tea was placed on a saucer just north of her plate, its aroma a mixture of mint and ginger. It too helped to settle the flopping in her stomach. She was truly touched by his care and the effortless way in which he exhibited it. "Thank you, Blue."

"You are eternally welcome, Ms. Iceheart."

Amelia turned to Betty and greeted her in turn. "Morning, Betty." The woman absolutely beamed and clapped excitedly, as she did every morning.

With the pleasantries aside, she took a hearty bite of her toast and curled her toes again in joy and the relief of finally getting something into her system to help aid in her recovery.

"Sooo… who did you meet last night, puddin'?" Betty routinely used endearing terms when trying to coax gossip from Amelia. It never worked, but she also never told her to stop trying.

Amelia finished chewing and swallowed before speaking. "It was a funeral for a fellow fallen officer, Betty. I met my colleagues at the precinct." She picked up her tea and sipped it to test. It warmed her throat and stomach, and she shut her eyes to revel in it for a moment.

"And… who else was there?" The woman was endlessly and doggedly determined to see Amelia find someone. Amelia was just as determined not to.

A quick puff from her breath cooled the brew so that she could greedily drink from it. "There were a great many dwarves there. It was a dwarven funeral." She proceeded to take in a mouthful of tea so to cleanse her palette before taking another bite of toast.

"Oh! I heard they're passionate lovers!"

Amelia choked on her tea, sucked it in, and shot it out her nose and back into her cup. She proceeded to cough and water from the eyes as she thumped her chest with her fist.

Gods, woman!

Blueregard was quick to offer a towel so that Amelia could clean herself up. She put down her teacup, took the towel, and coughed into it as she wiped her face.

"Oh dear! Honey, you have to be more careful with your tea. All that huffing and blowing you do with your magic is bound to cause you to suck it down into your lungs. That can't be good for you." Betty got up from the table and hurried over to pat Amelia on the back as she continued coughing.

Passionate lovers?

The thought of a dwarven man yanking on a dwarven woman's beard caused her stomach to turn. Her coughing eased up quickly as she felt a deep-pitted burp rise to the surface. It was horrible and tasted of dwarven ale, spiced meats, and regret.

Having stifled her coughing fit, she dabbed her eyes and grimaced at the toast in front of her. She didn't feel like eating any more. Not after the horrible image that Betty had inadvertently stuck in her head. "Blue, do you have more–"

As she turned to look at Blueregard, she gladly spotted her favorite cylindrical heating container in his hands. "More tea, ma'am, in your favorite travel container."

She sighed and thanked him under her ragged breath. "Thank you."

"As always, Ms. Iceheart, you are eternally welcome." He offered the briefest of smiles before bowing in the old court fashion.

Amelia stood, went up on her toes, and kissed the old man on the cheek. "You truly are a blessing."

He tilted his head a bit higher in acceptance of her praise and strode across the room so that he might open the door for her.

"Puddin', you're not done your breakfast; do you have to go so soon?"

Amelia checked the time on her watch and sighed, "Yes, sadly." She had a few minutes to spare, but the conversation had turned far too uncomfortable far too quickly. She grabbed her trench coat as she headed for the door.

She picked her hat up off the rack and placed it on her head. She adorned her belt and holster as each was handed to her by Blueregard. Once buckled in, she shrugged on her trench coat. Lastly, she accepted her staff.

A thought then occurred to her and she quickly turned back to him. "When I got home... was my... vest..." She cleared her throat and made a brief and quick gesture up and down.

"You were decent, I assure you. You did not attempt to disrobe until you were already in your room."

Thank the merciful goddess.

She dared to follow up that question with another. "How did I get home?"

"Master Stonehand brought you home."

Thank again the merciful goddess. John's always respectable.

"Well that's—"

"Limp as a fresh corpse and swung over his shoulder like a carcass on a meat hook."

Betty giggled.

Amelia sighed and stared at Blueregard for a moment. "Thank you for that degrading and completely unnecessary description."

"You're quite welcome." She could see the slightest glint of joy in his eye. He took pleasure in humbling her from time to time. It was rare, but it certainly showed he had a sense of humor.

"Good day, Mr. Blueregard."

"Good day, Ms. Iceheart. I will see to it that there is a hearty meal prepared for you upon your return home."

"That would be lovely." She turned to leave but was quickly stopped by his hand on her arm. He didn't grab her, but he did grab her attention.

"One last thing, Ms. Iceheart."

She turned back and raised an eyebrow. "Yes?" Her voice croaked a bit from the coughing fit earlier. She cleared her throat and repeated, "Yes?"

Mr. Blueregard reached into his inner vest pocket and produced a letter envelope. It was stamped with a familiar red seal.

Blast it all. Not today.

"Burn it." She knew who it was from and had no time for them. Amelia turned to head out the door when she heard something she wasn't expecting.

"I already tried, ma'am… The letter is protected this time." He was sincerely apologetic as he said it.

That can't be good.

She slowly turned back and sneered at the envelope being proffered to her. "I hate family."

Chapter 2

Amelia lived on the second level of a three-level abode. Blueregard, Amelia, and Betty all lived on the same level in separate rooms. She descended the stairs to the main floor and out the door to the cobblestone streets.

It was a drizzly day but there were rays of sunshine piercing the clouds. Many people were already out and about, heading to work, as she was.

She affixed her tinted spectacles on her nose and did her best not to look at anything too bright. The air was fresh, so the walk would hopefully help ease the slight headache she had redeveloped from the sudden coughing fit.

The envelope – the current object of her ire – was in the inner breast pocket of her trench coat. Blueregard had placed it there for her. She feared touching it with her hands, as it might trigger some form of blood-bound binding magic. It wouldn't be the first time her family had used such underhanded methods to get her to the table.

Advocates used to use a binding magic in their legal

documentation, making it so that the recipient was bound to appear on a specific day and time. Any attempts to refuse would result in that person being bewitched. Their body would walk them to the destination, no matter how far away it was.

A professor at the Arcanum had warned students of several instances in which binding magic got the recipient killed. If the person was on a boat, the spellwork didn't care if they couldn't swim. If they were leagues away, they would march the poor victim to death. Due to those mishaps, the utilization of that particular form of binding spell was deemed illegal.

As far as Amelia was concerned, legality was beneath her family. Thus, she didn't want to touch the envelope until someone else had examined it.

She didn't want to have to ask him, but Joseph Runewall – Rook, the rookie – was her best choice. The man had a unique talent when it came to barriers, traps, locks, and the like. He would certainly be able to give the envelope a thorough once-over and determine if it was safe for her to handle.

Amelia shrunk her staff to the size of a wand and pointed it skyward to use its magic to deflect any rain droplets. With her heating container in the other hand, she set off for work. Hopefully, she would arrive before Joe did, and she'd be able to have him examine the envelope before he began work.

A squeeze of a button on the side of her heating container caused a small flap to open on the top. The strong scent of ginger and mint rose up in a wafting steam.

Amelia wove her way around a gentleman in a raincoat – he was heading the opposite direction down the cobblestone walk – and took a sip of her tea. Her stomach thanked her for it. Her nose still burned from the earlier violent expulsion.

The walk helped to clear her head a bit and ease some of the drinking sickness. She even managed to enjoy a ray of sunshine for a brief moment.

It was a peaceful morning… *was*.

She was halfway to the precinct when a sudden eruption of glass and shouting came from a storefront window half a block back. Amelia rounded on the spot to try and locate the source. Unfortunately, there was a wall of pedestrians between her and the storefront. All of them had turned, same as she had, and blocked her view.

Based on the distance and general location, she guessed it to be Mr. Greenthumb's Flower Boutique.

"Get back 'ere, ye filthy rascal!" A booming explosion of gunfire followed the shouting. It was undeniably Mr. Greenthumb.

Men and women screamed, turned, and began running past her in a panic. They gave no care for who they shoved out of their way in the process. A squat and stout dwarven woman in a flowery raincoat had the audacity to shove Amelia aside and against a brick building.

She grunted from the shove and gripped the building. Sadly, she had to let go of her heating container in order to hold on. Dropping her wand wasn't an option. Her tea had to be sacrificed. The heating container clattered across the cobblestones and out of sight. "Blast it!"

The panic and shoving only lasted for a brief moment, but it was long enough to give the assailant a head start.

As soon as Amelia was able to peer through the crowd, she spotted him. A thin and wiry man was etching history into the soles of his shoes and putting as much distance between himself and the storefront as one possibly could. He had a flat cap, a patched jacket, worn brown trousers, suspenders, and a yellowed and dirty button-up shirt.

"Freeze!" Amelia released her wand into a staff and pointed it directly at him. The many glistening facets refracted the dozens of raindrops that struck it, causing her crystalline staff to appear as though it were glowing with great power in the drizzly morning sunlight. It was, but the power wasn't readily visible.

The man peered over his shoulder and spun about mid-stride in order to see who had yelled at him and from where. Amelia noted that he carried plants, herbs, and brown bags.

Their eyes locked, and even from the great distance between them, she could tell he was about to rabbit. His body language said it all. He thought he had enough of a headstart, and he was going to risk it. The man jolted on the spot, turned, and ran full-tilt down the cobblestone road, beelining for a nearby alleyway across the street.

"Blast it!" She pointed the tip of her staff to the cobblestones and used a touch of magic to summon up all the water and moisture that had collected throughout the drizzling rainfall. A sizeable puddle quickly formed around her feet.

With her staff in hand, she didn't need to breathe in or out in order to alter the temperature of the water. The staff had been invested with countless hours of energy by her and those that came before her. It had energy of its own and responded to her will.

A focused bit of energy flowing down her arm and extending through the core of her staff allowed her to reach out and push the heat from the water. It immediately froze around her feet and turned into a sheet of ice, locking her legs in place.

Another quick motion of her staff brought the water beneath the ice rolling and pushed her along. In less than four shakes of a stiff drink, she was sliding across the cobblestones. She picked up speed and was soon gliding along far quicker than most could run.

She passed Mr. Greenthumb's storefront just as he emerged from the door with a smoking long-barrel. "Get 'im, Ms. Iceheart!"

Amelia pointed a finger back at him and hollered over the wind whipping past her ears, "Put that away!"

The culprit managed to make it to the alley just as she was closing in on him. A reeling in of her staff and a twisting motion made it so that the ice sheet around her feet tilted up on one side. It brought her into a turn and curved toward the mouth of the alley.

A quick focusing of her mind allowed her to reach out and search. All she could sense was the ambient chill of the morning rain. She couldn't see any warm bodies or significant masses of heat anywhere near the mouth of the alley. He wasn't waiting to ambush her; he didn't seem like the type to do so anyway. Amelia made the corner and bent deep at the knees so that she might better absorb the forces associated with the sudden change in direction.

As soon as she rounded into the mouth of the alley, she realized it was a dead end and brought her ice-sheet to an immediate stop. Bits of snow and ice scraped off the bottom of her makeshift transportation and sailed out into the alley. The cast-off quickly melted back into water. Releasing the magic that held the ice together resulted in an almost immediate melting. A pressing of heat into the ice caused it to melt even faster and release her boots.

A quick scan of the alley revealed that there were only two doors. A sturdy door to the right led into a smoke shop. The door on the left led to the back end of a respectable tea shop. She couldn't hear any commotion from either building, there didn't appear to be any ladders in the alley leading to the rooftops, and the far end was a flat brick wall. They were hiding.

Coward.

Trash littered the alley, and there was a metal trash bin just beyond the door on the right. Her bets were on the suspect hiding behind the trash bin.

She rolled her wrist a little and made a circle with the butt end of her staff. A large puddle of water quickly formed around her at the entrance of the alley.

Amelia took a moment to calm her hammering heart and prepare her mind to open to the greater 'verse. It didn't take her very long, as she had spent years practicing. With only two deep breaths, she was ready. A blink was all that was needed to open her mind and expose the world around her in all its temperate glory.

She saw everything in shades instead of lines and colors. The darker the shade meant the object was colder to the touch. The brighter the shade meant the object was warmer. People tended to be brighter than the room they stood in or the world around them. It wasn't always accurate, as there were days when the hot sun made everything bright. On a drizzly day, a person would stand out like a lantern light in a darkly lit room.

She saw a brief cloud of light billowing up from a storm grate, and a bit of heat emanating from the lantern lights above the doors. Otherwise, she didn't see any body heat.

With her eyes open to the 'verse, she slowly reached into her trench coat with one hand and drew her six-shooter. She eased her way into the alley, stepping wide of the bin. It didn't take her long to realize that nobody was hiding behind it. There simply wasn't any body heat.

Amelia was about to begin cursing her luck when she noticed tendrils of concentrated heat curling up from the cracks, crevices, and seams of the trash bin. There was too much heat for simple garbage.

"I hate it when people run." She intentionally raised her voice so that the perpetrator would hear her.

There was a clattering noise from inside of the bin. They heard.

"Especially when I yell–"

The culprit burst from the trash bin, throwing the lid up and open. He leaped over the edge with one hand on the rim. His sights were set on the mouth of the alley. The eyes were wide as tea saucers, and he looked as pale as the dead.

"–Freeze!" Amelia slammed the butt end of her staff on the cobblestone. The puddle of water she had earlier gathered jumped up and snatched the thief from the air.

The man found himself encased in a prison of ice shards and tendrils and suspended two steps off the ground. He screamed and began shivering violently, "P-p-p-please d-d-d-don't k-k-kill m-m-m-me!"

Amelia blinked away her arcane vision and looked at her six-shooter before holstering it. "I'm not going to kill you, you whimpering ninny!" She made her way back to the mouth of the alley, set her staff to stand on its own, crossed her arms, and glowered at him. "I'm arresting you for theft, numbskull."

He seemed to mutter something under his breath as his teeth chattered. He also seemed to calm a bit.

Amelia thought nothing of it. Criminals muttered curses about their bad luck and others tended to exhibit signs of relief when caught. She couldn't imagine that running from an officer of the law wasn't stressful.

Running from a blue coat was one thing; they didn't have magic, or at least weren't legally allowed to use it. Trying to escape a detective was something else altogether. All detectives were wizards; they all had specialties, and they were legally charged with using those abilities to catch criminals. It made them into living nightmares for the lawless.

She sighed and pulled a set of irons from her back belt pouch. "I'm going to release you from the ice, and you're going to let me put these on you, right?"

The man couldn't get out a single word. He was shivering too violently and was simply too cold. Instead, he nodded his head as best he could, sniffed, and continued to shake.

"Good."

~~

Amelia made her way back to Mr. Greenthumb's storefront with a handful of the stolen goods. The culprit, known to her then as Garrick Jenkins, had been about the dumbest thief she'd ever met. He had attempted to steal dried herbs, a potted flower, and a small brown bag of fertilizer.

"Hi, Allen," Amelia hefted the armful into the bigger man's arms. "I believe these belong to you."

Mr. Allen Greenthumb had a farmer's frame with the shoulders of an ox. He also had the body hair of a werewolf dwarf during a full moon. The armful that Amelia had unloaded filled only one of his massive meaty hands.

He wore a soil-stained green apron and hearty gardening gloves with holes in a few of the fingers. The handles of sheers poked out of one of his apron pockets and a spade out of the other. His massive eyebrows looked like two rabid weasels kissing at the nose. They entirely covered his eyes and made it impossible to determine what the man was looking at.

"Did ye get 'im?" His voice was deep, and he had a touch of a farmer's accent; it wasn't an attractive accent.

Amelia shut her eyes and nodded, "Yes, Allen, I got him. I wouldn't have brought all this back to you if I hadn't." She gestured to the returned items she had just handed him.

Allen lifted his head and looked up and down the cobblestone street. "Where?"

"A blue coat came and escorted him back to the precinct. They headed up the street while you were sweeping up the broken glass." She pointed toward the precinct in the distance. She could see the top of it peering over the buildings a block over.

"Now," she took out her notepad and stylus, "can you tell me what happened, prior to you shooting and shouting at him?"

As slow as the shop owner seemed at times, he was practiced at delving out specific details. He had been robbed before, but the criminals had always been after his transactional station, never his plants.

Amelia took her time jotting down notes and asking

follow-up questions to make sure she had gotten everything correctly.

Mr. Jenkins had apparently entered the shop and had looked a bit jittery and ragged, as if he'd seen a ghost. The man proceeded to frantically search about the store and had inquired as to whether Mr. Greenthumb carried any blood lotuses.

That small detail caught Amelia's attention. "Blood lotus… isn't that used in healing potions?"

The big man slowly nodded his balding head. "Among other things."

"Like what?" The crime had suddenly taken an interesting twist.

The big man looked around his store, as if making sure nobody else was listening in.

Amelia, puzzled, glanced about the empty flower shop as well. Nobody else had stepped inside, and it didn't look like he'd be getting any business until he had his front window fixed.

Allen lowered his voice and cupped one side of his mouth, "Brewin' 'alf-moon." He had trouble enunciating his 'h's.

She was taken aback by the sudden mention of an illicit substance. "You know about half-moon?"

He nodded his head. "I get the odd dirtblood in 'ere, asking if I 'ave any dried blood lotus petals or 'owler root." 'Dirtblood' was a derogatory term for werebeasts, commonly known as Lycans.

Half-moon was an alchemical accident. A student at the Arcanum had recently attempted to discover a means by which to activate certain lycanthropic properties without physical changes. Lycans have accelerated healing – a desired trait for many. The student attempted to extract that one ability and bottle it. Instead, they developed a drug that could trigger a transformation without the need for a full moon. If wrongly administered, a single dose could drive a lycanthrope into a blood-craze, or kill them. Newly-bitten

Lycans were sometimes too lazy to learn how to control the animal spirit within, and turned to alternatives.

Half-moon had been on the street for a year, and Amelia hadn't managed to track down the alchemist making it.

"Next time you have someone asking you about those ingredients, you bring it to my attention, understand?" She made sure to give him a stern glare.

He nodded his head in understanding.

"Good. Then what happened?"

Allen continued to describe the interaction in the store. Mr. Jenkins became impatient and simply started grabbing things off the shelf and bolted for the door. That was when Allen had pulled his long-barrel from beneath the counter and fired.

Thankfully, the man had purchased and utilized non-lethal ammunition. He used pea-rocks and salt; it packed a hearty wallop but didn't do any more than leave a nasty bruise... and break windows.

Amelia sighed, flipped closed her notepad, and thanked the big man for his cooperation. She left the man to clean up his store and began heading back toward the precinct.

She paused momentarily to search the cobblestones. Eventually, she found her heating container and the puddle of tea it sat in. Amelia grumbled and used a touch of magic to rinse off the container with some drizzle collected from the sky. Once emptied and cleaned, she stuffed it into her outside trench coat pocket.

It only took a few brief minutes to reach the steps; she hadn't been that far away. As she began climbing the steps to the main doors, John Stonehand began descending them. "Hurry up, we'll need your help."

John was a detective, like her, and had a good bit of height on her. He had massive broad shoulders and dark skin. Like the dwarven wizards at the funeral, he had polymorphic and transformative abilities.

Amelia stopped and turned on the spot as John stepped past her. "Help with what?"

"There's a bunch of bodies over by a warehouse in the industrial district. I hope your stomach is settled because I heard there's a bunch of murder and mayhem to clean up today." John marched on as though he hadn't even touched a single drop of dwarven ale from the night before. Despite not remembering how she got home, she definitely remembered him drinking far more than a drop.

As much as she decidedly wanted to shout some angry quip at him for being so damned cheery, she couldn't. He had carried her home and had made sure she had gotten home safely. She owed him. He had perhaps carried her in an undignified way, but she couldn't be sure that he had done it the whole way. It was possible he had only carried her in that fashion in order to get her up the steps.

"Morning." The voice was horribly gravelly, but it sounded like Joseph.

Amelia turned and near shrieked upon spotting the man. His metallic silver eyes were bloodshot, his left eye had a black ring around it, and he was as pale as the walking dead. His hair was disheveled, he shuffled by with a limp and a hunched back, and one arm was tucked to his side. "Good gods!" His trousers even looked dirty and wrinkled. Mind, his clothing always looked dirty and wrinkled.

Petals – Wadnar Pettlebottom – their precinct training officer and trickster gnome extraordinaire, happily and mirthfully chuckled, "Hahaha! That's what I said when I saw him this morning. Looks like a valiant crusader mistook him for a zombie and beat him with a club, doesn't he?" The little man looked just as cheery as John did – he hadn't had enough to drink. Or if he had, he'd clearly found some means by which to combat the drinking sickness that she hadn't.

Amelia scowled at Petals, then looked up at Joe and couldn't help but scrunch her nose a little.

I'll ask him later.

Chapter 3

Amelia removed her tinted spectacles and greeted the lobby clerk, Ms. Mistwind. She then ascended the spiral metal steps to the detectives' bullpen. It was mostly empty, thankfully; she didn't feel like having any pleasant conversations that morning.

As soon as she got to her desk, she hung up her trench coat and hat and set to generating her report for the morning's arrest. She was momentarily delayed when she had to replace the ink cartridge in her arcane mechanical typographer and was also interrupted by Blue Coat Argen Tannen.

The young man had graduated from the Academy at the same time as Amelia, but he didn't have any mystical talents. He would forever be a blue coat. Despite that, he was a skilled officer. The man was smart, quick, strong, and respectable.

"Ms. Iceheart?" Mr. Tannen stepped up to the side

of her desk and removed his hat as he spoke.

"Yes, Officer?" Amelia turned her full attention to the young man.

"The thief you arrested this morning…"

She eased back in her chair and crossed one leg over the other. "The plant thief. What about him?"

"He keeps shouting 'She's going to kill us all.' I…"

Amelia shut her eyes and let out an irritated sigh, "I didn't threaten the man. I have no idea what he's on about."

Mr. Tannen took her word for it, nodded in acceptance, and excused himself before putting his hat back on and leaving.

Her stomach gurgled a little, announcing its displeasure at having missed most of breakfast. She soothed her tummy by patting it. "Don't worry, we'll stop by a pastry shop on the way over."

Amelia refocused her efforts and finished the remainder of the report. It didn't take her more than fifteen minutes in total, including the interruption and ink cartridge exchange.

She set aside the two pages of the report so that the ink could dry. While waiting for that, she plucked the heating container from her trench coat pocket and made her way to the tea table at the far end of the office.

There wasn't any ginger mint tea left. "Blast." She snatched up a regular red leaf packet and dropped it in her container. A quick glance at the temperature crystal on the back of the kettle showed that the water was tepid at best. "Double blast!" Lifting the kettle then revealed it had barely any water in it. "Blasted thundering–!"

"Detective?" Captain Adragan 'Bolt' Thunderhowl's rumbling voice carried across the bullpen, startling her. Amelia almost jumped out of fright. She let out a calming sigh, released the tension, put down the kettle, and turned to face the dragon kin.

The captain of her precinct was a storm variant of dragon kin. He stood two heads taller than her and had the frame of a brick building. Storm gray scales covered his entire body and translucent electric blue horns jutted from his head and chin.

While it was fitting to find such a creature in a stormy seaside city, it was no less surprising, and he was no less intimidating.

"Yes, Captain?" Outwardly, she kept a cold and calm appearance. Inwardly, she screamed like a little girl whenever the captain caught her off guard. Despite the years she had worked at the precinct, the captain always set her at unease.

She never feared that the captain was untrustworthy or incapable; she simply feared him. The man was a mythical beast and had unparalleled strength and power. Like the ever mysterious trickster gnome, she didn't have any idea as to how old the captain was or what all he was capable of doing.

"Why are you not with the others?" Despite the extraordinary depth of his voice, he didn't need to raise it in order to be heard. It rolled across the room.

"Sir, I made an arrest this morning while on my way into work." She pointed at her desk. "It's there; I was just getting some tea while waiting for the ink to set."

The massive lumbering beast of myth slowly turned to look upon her desk. He nodded in approval before heading back to his glass-paned office. "Very good, Detective. Bring it to me when it is ready."

Amelia watched the dragon kin lumber back to his office and slowly shut the door behind him. She let out a deep sigh before turning back to the kettle. Grumbling, she picked it up, walked it over to the tap, and filled it. Once full, she set it back onto the heating plate and flicked the switch.

It would take a minute to heat, so she headed back to her desk, organized her report into a file, and hurried back when the kettle startled to whistle.

With a new container of tea, she quickly made her way back to her desk, picked up the report and her trench coat, and put on her hat. Once ready, she prepared herself to step into the captain's office.

She knocked on the glass pane, then opened the door. The captain lazily waved her inside as his eyes slowly scanned a report. It never ceased to amaze her how he managed to hold the reports in his massive clawed hands.

Amelia stepped inside, closed the door behind her, and took up position in the middle of the room before his desk. She held her report at the ready in one hand with her trench coat draped over the other arm. Her heating container was stuffed in her coat pocket again.

The captain set down the file and closed it before turning his attention to her. Amelia briefly stepped closer to hand him the file and promptly returned to stand at attention. Through her time at the precinct, she had learned that the captain praised order and militaristic discipline. One could only assume that the captain had served at some point in time. Unfortunately, natural curiosity could not be appeased. It was against regulations for one officer to pull another's records.

The captain opened the file and scanned through it with a slow yet discerning eye. It only took a minute, but it was a very unnerving minute. Dragon kin had the natural ability to radiate intimidation magic, and it was working. Amelia had grown accustomed to its overpowering presence, but was never able to fully hold it at bay. The longer she stood in the office, the more it chewed away at her mental faculties and set her stomach churning.

He closed the file, gave her his nod of approval, and stamped the document. "The others have already left for the crime scene. The lobby clerk has the address."

Amelia nodded in understanding and waited for her formal dismissal. A cold sweat was threatening to break out on her brow if she didn't get out soon.

The captain leaned forward, placed his elbows on the desk, and entwined his scaly clawed hands. "Considering the past night's festivities, and the sore state of some of my detectives," – Joseph's ragged appearance came to mind, and the cold sweat emerged – "I feel it is pertinent that I ask you to take your time, steady any sickness you may be feeling this morning, and focus on your duties."

The warning was as clear as a dinner bell. "Yes, sir."

"You are dismissed, Detective."

Amelia turned on the spot and almost threw herself out the door. She closed the door behind her and breathed out a deep and slightly nauseated sigh. A few more deep breaths helped to steady her stomach and banish the cold sweat. Her stomach gurgled a little more loudly. If she didn't get something into her stomach, she'd be no good to anyone.

She marched her way to the steps, descended to the lobby, and made her way over to Ms. Mistwind. "Hi Maggie, the captain said you have the address to where all the others are heading?"

"Of course." She gave Amelia a tight-lipped smile, and turned to pull the report from a tray while fixing her horn-rimmed spectacles on her nose.

Margaret Mistwind was a recent addition to the precinct. She transferred over shortly after the Bloodvault Incident. The finance officer, Ms. Penelope Rosewater, had been arrested for secreting personnel files to her half-brother, a criminal. Ms. Rosewater's vacant position was then filled by the lobby clerk that Ms. Mistwind replaced.

"The report says you're heading for the industrial district just south of Red Lightning Boulevard; Iron Way, Warehouse 57." She smiled a little more broadly and lifted a parchment baggie out to Amelia. "And make sure you give these to Johnny." She was rather smitten with Detective Stonehand.

Amelia couldn't help but immediately sense the heat emanating from the bag and raised a curious eyebrow alongside a smirk. "And what's in this?"

Maggie absolutely beamed, "Breakfast biscuits! I baked them myself. They're my grandmother's secret recipe. She'd make them whenever grandpappy had the drinking sickness."

Amelia couldn't help but perk up at the mention and pull the bag a bit closer so she might breathe in the intoxicating aroma. "Oh my gods."

The woman closed her eyes and nodded in understanding. "Grandpappy was a sailor... he had the drinking sickness a lot."

Despite her best efforts, her stomach gurgled in greed. "Maggie, I hate to ask, but can I have one?"

"Of course! Just don't eat them all and make sure Johnny gets them, and don't go giving any to that Runewall putz!" She pointed a rather stern finger in Amelia's face.

"You really don't like him, do you?"

"He's a putz! He made me take care of his landlady like I'm some damn maid!" She shook her finger a bit more vigorously, "Promise me that he won't get a single biscuit!"

Amelia raised her hand and swore, "I promise he won't get any."

"Thank you." Maggie sat back down upon her chair with a bit of a harrumph.

Amelia glanced at the drizzle outside and began to throw on her coat. She set down the parchment bag before turning to put the coat on. "He's not all that bad. He's just an idiot when it comes to talking to women."

"He can't be all dumb."

She chuckled and heartily disagreed, "Oh, he's very dumb when it comes to women."

Maggie shook her head and crossed her arms. "Can't be that dumb if he's spending time with that nurse."

Amelia paused from straightening out her trench coat to rerun what was said back through her head. "Nurse?"

Maggie nodded. "Uh-huh; she's a looker too."

"No!"

"Yes!" Maggie said it as though it was the most unbelievably delectable gossip she'd ever heard.

Amelia gaped, "Thun–"

"Detective?" Captain Bolt's rumbling voice carried

out from overhead.

Amelia almost shrieked. She jumped a little on the spot and turned to peer up at the detective's bullpen. The captain was standing at the railing and peering down at her with his hands clasped behind his back. "I take it you've learned of the address."

"Leaving now, sir!" Amelia snatched up the bag and made a mad dash for the door.

~~

Amelia quickly devoured one of the biscuits while waiting for the gnome cart; it was salty and savory. From what she could tell, there was some form of cured ham or bacon chunks mixed into the dough. It was buttery, greasy, and hefty.

It did exactly what Ms. Mistwind said it would – it helped to cure a bit of her drinking sickness and settled her stomach significantly.

When the gnome cart arrived, she squeezed into the back, provided the destination, and dropped the appropriate coin into the tray.

The trip would likely take her a few minutes, so she decided to take the time to pull her personal spell-tome from her trouser pocket and study. Thankfully, her sensitivity to light had abated enough that she no longer needed her tinted spectacles.

The tome was compressed and no bigger than a notepad, so she first had to release it. A snap of the fingers was all that was needed. It expanded significantly and thumped weightily into her lap. It was of standard size; one and a quarter steps in height and one in width. The leather binding was white with flaked frost and snow covering it.

In typical wizardly paranoid fashion, she kept it locked. Students from the Arcanum were repeatedly taught to keep their spellcraft locked and protected from non-magical eyes.

The metal binding and lock on her tome was made from dwarven dark iron. The key, however, no longer existed; she had destroyed it. Amelia lifted her wand and pointed the tip at the palm of her hand. A focused bit of magic and a recalled memory resulted in the creation of a solid key of ice.

Unlike Joseph, she couldn't fully partition her mind. She did, however, have the ability to lock away certain thoughts and memories and recall them when needed, but that was the extent of her mental magic abilities. By destroying the original key and recrafting it from ice when she needed it, she was able to keep her spell-tome much more secure.

The key fit perfectly into the lock, as it always did. She gave it a twisting jerk and the metal binding released. A second touch of magic melted the key back down and it evaporated into the air.

She shifted the tome in her lap and opened it to the first page. Like any professional wizard should, she refreshed her memory on spell structure and arcane frameworks. The first half of the tome covered the basics and fundamentals, and she was able to breeze through it quite quickly. Any practiced wizard would be able to do the same.

The latter half of her tome focused on specific spells she favored and their frameworks. The further to the back she went, the more complex the spell structure became. Elemental magic at its core wasn't very difficult to summon. Controlling the magic was the difficult part.

Much of Amelia's concentration in ice magic was in controlling the temperature of objects and the surfaces surrounding them. She had graduated from the Arcanum at the top of her class in Combative Elements.

The most common spells in her arsenal consisted of ice shards and temperature manipulation. There was a shield spell she had learned while at the Arcanum, but she barely ever used it or needed it. Despite that, she spent a minute memorizing the framework and necessary steps to summon and tether the free-floating block of ice so that it followed her without her having to hold it or lift it.

Ice was heavy. Having to lift it up with her own hands was a non-starter. To that end, she needed to know how to connect objects with tethers and levitation.

The most difficult of spells consisted of freezing auras and mass manipulations. Given appropriate time and preparation, she could utilize one or the other but not both.

"Ma'am? I'm afraid this is as far as I can take you." The gnome cart came to a rumbling and puttering stop in the middle of the cobblestone street.

Amelia lifted her head from her reading to give the driver a piece of her mind. That was when she saw the thing that had caused the little gnome to stop. "Holy thundering fireballs!"

The street was blocked by a veritable icefield. It stretched from one side to the other and even crawled up the brick buildings. Great white and blue shards of solidified water jutted up into the sky at jagged and tilted angles. Amelia couldn't help but gape at the stunning display. "I think you're right."

A frozen body looked to be impaled from behind and the arms and legs were dangling from one of the jutting ice spears. Only the tip of the ice was red; otherwise, there didn't appear to be any more blood.

She slammed her spell-tome shut, flicked the metal binding closed and pressed until she heard it click and lock into place. Practice made it so that she didn't even have to look while doing so; her entire focus was fixated on the jutting spires of ice.

A quick snap of her fingers made the tome shrink again. She blindly stuffed it in her trouser pocket and stared out the front window at the horrible display of power before the cart.

A brief moment passed, then her cart door opened. "Amelia." It was John's voice. She glanced away from the chaotic scene in front of them and noted that John was holding the door open for her.

The gnome cart driver mumbled a prayer in the gnomish tongue as Amelia exited the cart; he seemed to be terrified, and she didn't blame him. The amount of power required to turn an entire cobblestone street into a field of sharpened icicles was staggering.

Amelia lifted the parchment bag and held it out for John. "Maggie made these for you."

"I... uh... thank you." John took the bag from her hand.

She shut the cart door and slowly stepped toward the extraordinary feat that was before them. "Who... how?"

"That's what we're trying–" She heard a brief sniff and the crinkling of the parchment bag. "–Oh!" There was a louder and longer sniff. "Oh gods, yes. These are exactly what I need this morning."

Amelia took in a deep and steadying breath and did her best to ignore the sudden screeching of tires as the gnome cart driver made a decidedly expedient exit. She took in another deep breath and ignored the happy mouthful-moaning of John. With her heart a bit more settled, she closed her eyes and reopened them to the greater power of the 'verse.

The world shifted into shades, and revealed to her the disturbing truth of the ice magic. Some of the jutting shards weren't just being utilized as spear barricades. They were also ice tombs. She could see the outlines of bodies, and they were just as cold as the ice that encased them.

"Sweet Goddess of Mercy..." she said under her breath.

John stepped up to her side and stuffed the remnants of a biscuit into his mouth. She didn't bother asking him any questions, as he wouldn't be able to effectively answer.

Petals, their senior officer, stepped up to her other side. "What do you see?" He sounded genuinely interested and entirely somber. His usual joviality wasn't present.

"Bodies."

The little man nodded his head. "At least we'll be able to gather evidence from these ones when they thaw out."

She figured there were more. "What happened to the others?"

"Incinerated."

Chapter 4

She blinked to return her vision to normal, turned to look down upon her superior, and blinked again. "Incinerated?"

"That's what I said, my dear." Petals looked troubled. He was gazing off into the ice field with his hands clasped behind his back.

The fact that there were both an ice field and incineration suggested some serious clashing between rival wizards. Based on the numerous bodies, she was leaning toward rival gangs. The problem was that she'd never heard of any ice or fire-themed groups.

One would think them to be a popular trope, but they weren't. Elemental magic was difficult to master and had numerous uses in the modern world. Few chances that someone of significant skill or power couldn't find work or would make it through the Arcanum without being questioned for certain behaviors.

It was possible that the gangs were not from Stormbay, and had moved to the city in order to establish some form of criminal enterprise.

Amelia shook her head free of the theories and inquired, "What is it you need me to do first?"

"Examine the ice, thoroughly. Once that is done, confer with Joseph. He's examining the incinerated remains inside the warehouse."

She turned and looked back over her shoulder to spot John stuffing another biscuit into his face. "Uh-huh... and what are you two doing?"

John paused with a biscuit poking out his mouth and his cheeks puffed. He had the 'caught with his hand in the cookie jar' look.

Amelia fired a disapproving glare his way and doubled down by narrowing her eyes and putting her hands on her hips.

"Mr. Stonehand has already aided in the investigation by solidifying the dusty warehouse floor. We can now tread upon its surface without worry of disturbing the existing prints." She shot a look back over her shoulder and noticed that Petals was still gazing upon the ice field.

"And you?" She didn't put as much spice on the question. He was her superior.

Petals took one hand from behind his back and stroked his long white beard. "I have some hunches I would like to eliminate."

"And–"

Petals slid his fingers from his beard and snapped them. A cloud of sparkling blue powder instantaneously engulfed the trickster gnome.

Amelia jumped from the sudden explosion of powder and took a step back. A brief breeze brushed past them, and the cloud dissipated into nothingness. Petals had utilized a teleportation and vanished.

"That little–" She fumed at having been ignored so off-handedly.

John swallowed and cleared his throat before speaking. "Petals was scared."

Amelia turned to him with a raised eyebrow. "Petals? Scared?"

John nodded. "Yes. Something about what he's seen here has him rattled."

She lifted her right hand and gestured at the field of ice shards. "This doesn't frighten you?"

He turned his head to gaze upon the glistening ice. "It does. What frightens me more is that Petals has a hunch–" He turned his gaze back upon Amelia, "–and was so concerned by it that he immediately teleported to go and check on it… personally."

She caught on to what John was saying and felt her stomach drop a bit from the implications. "Okay, now I'm worried."

John waved her toward the ice field. "Apply your expertise as Petals suggested. I'll follow the tracks and see where they take me." The man pulled his wand from his pocket and released it into a staff.

The staff was similar to Amelia's in that it had many faces and facets to it; it differed in that it was carved from various veins of raw ore and stone. It had an earthy color and warmth to it.

He shut his eyes and breathed deeply. Amelia steadied herself in preparation for it and jumped only a little when she felt a tremor go through the ground. She couldn't help the primal instinct to jump when the ground shook beneath her feet.

The man opened his eyes, and instead of the warm deep brown, they were a golden sand tone. It always made her skin crawl when she saw his eyes like that. It looked as though someone had replaced his eyes with balls of sand. The thought of it grating against the inside of her eyelids made her eyes water a bit.

John looked about the ground around them and began following something that only he could possibly see.

She watched him for a bit as he circled around and tapped the ground with the butt of his staff. She always wondered what it was he saw and how he saw it.

"Get to the ice!" He barked it as he wandered off, following something she couldn't see.

Amelia realized she'd been staring and quickly turned back around to the ice field. "I'm on it!"

As she had done earlier, she closed her eyes, breathed deeply, and opened herself to the greater 'verse. Her vision shifted and everything turned to a world of shades. She took a better look around and noticed that the warehouse on her left was much warmer than the other buildings. It was clear which warehouse had the incinerated bodies in it.

The ice that was climbing up the wall of that building was much shorter than the ice on the opposing side. That stood to reason; ice didn't stand up well against heat.

Walking across the cobblestone road helped her get a better idea as to how the ice expanded and from where. There was a subtle curve in the middle of the ice wall. It had expanded further than it had near the buildings.

The brick could have simply held that much more heat and stunted the growth of the ice, but the more obvious answer was that the wave of shards had been pointed down the middle of the road, and she was merely standing at the tail end of it.

The only way to confirm her theory was to see it all from above. Amelia pulled her wand from one of her many vest pockets and began swirling the tip about her upturned palm.

She pulled water from the air and nearby puddles and concentrated it. The compressed water began to solidify into an orb of ice. She mouthed out the appropriate wording while recalling the necessary runic sequences and trigonometric symbols to complete the framework of the Seeing Eye spell. With the Seeing Eye, she would be able to view the world through the lens of the ice orb. Naturally, being a more difficult and complex spell, it took a bit more time to conjure and construct.

The orb finished growing and solidifying, and floated a finger-width above her palm. Its surface was smooth and frosted. One end had an iris of light blue arcane runes.

With great care, she proceeded with the final step. Amelia closed her eyes, pointed the tip of her wand to her forehead, and released a touch of magic. A tether of sorts snapped into existence and gently pulled on the skin just above the bridge of her nose; the other end was connected to her wand.

Blindly, she brought the wand down and touched the tip to the floating ice ball. Breathing out, she gently twisted her wrist and made the necessary connection. Thankfully, the spellwork was successful.

She had heard of students at the Arcanum that had attempted to utilize the same spell in order to spy on friends or love interests. They weren't careful enough and wound up blinding themselves. Through improper tethering, they either ripped their eyes out of the sockets or caused the Seeing Eye to slam into their real one.

Amelia was practiced enough not to make that mistake, but the memory of those incidents always made her a little nervous when casting it. Otherwise, the spell was extremely useful.

With the connection completed, Amelia blinked and opened her eyes. The disorientation was immediate. She wasn't looking through her own eyes anymore; she was seeing through the ice orb and was floating at chest height.

Knowing better than to move too quickly, she slowly turned to face the ice field and tested moving it about: up, down, left, and right. Once she was orientated and steady, the ice orb began to ascend and observe.

Her body remained as still as possible throughout the use of the Seeing Eye. As dictated by the spellwork, a wizard was charged with locking their body in place. It was mostly for their safety. Walking about while one's vision was externalized was never a wise decision.

As the orb ascended above the cobblestone streets, she was pleasantly rewarded with a wondrous view of the greater city. She could see rooftops and streets stretching out into the distance to the north and to the east. She knew better than to get lost in sightseeing and halted the orb once an acceptable aerial view had been attained.

A slight tilt allowed her to visualize the world below at a gentle angle. She turned the orb back around and faced her own self, far down upon the ground. It made her feel a bit easier knowing that she could see if anyone tried to sneak up on her from behind. She doubted anyone would try, as John was still nearby searching the ground while two blue coats stood at attention. One was near to her and keeping an eye on things, the other was further down the street, redirecting people and carts. It was also broad daylight.

She slowly began moving the orb back and away from where she stood so that she could better see the entirety of the ice field as it led to where she stood.

As predicted, the further back she went, the smaller the ice shards got. Eventually it all came to a point. The ice field was only as large as the cobblestone street that sat directly out front of the warehouse to her left.

Lowering the Seeing Eye brought her back down to street-level. From there, she was able to get a person's perspective.

It seemed awfully wasteful to her to use such a grand spell for only a few bodies. Opening herself back up to the greater 'verse, she shifted her vision in order to reveal the shades of temperature.

The reasoning became a little clearer. The few bodies she had noted earlier were only the tail end of the corpses. Four more bodies were buried under the ice field. She hadn't noticed them earlier because they were curled up on the ground or desperately crawling away from the source. Whoever these people were, they weren't wizards, or at least not good enough ones to protect themselves from the wave of cold that overtook them.

Amelia noticed an oddity amongst the bodies. One of them looked to be fragmented. It wasn't until she floated a bit closer that she realized why; the body was fragmented in her vision because it had shattered upon impact with the ground.

"Oh, gods," Her stomach turned a bit, but she was able to settle it with a steadying breath. The body wasn't only shattered – the boots and feet were still upright. The body had snapped off at the shins while trying to turn and run. They hadn't been fast enough. A closer examination revealed that many of the bodies had been shattered, either through the fast freezing or through attempts to flee while in the process of freezing.

The wave of ice wasn't meant to just kill. It was meant to terrify as well.

Whoever had conjured the overwhelmingly powerful elemental forces could have easily done away with all nine of the people with a few well-tethered ice lances and an ice wall. Summon the wall for cover, tether some shards of ice to the intended targets, and release them. Clearly, that wasn't good enough. They wanted to terrify their enemy.

A gang war was looking far more likely.

Amelia blinked away her arcane vision and began moving the Seeing Eye back to her body. She wasn't going to learn any more from the aerial view.

Knowing that there was some slight disorientation that followed releasing the Seeing Eye spell, she waited until the ice orb was well in hand before releasing it and returning her vision fully to normal.

There was a little wobbliness and mild nausea, but it quickly dissipated when she pulled the corpse cloth from her vest pocket and used it to cover her mouth and nose. She'd enchanted it with some stomach-soothing aromas. It worked well when dealing with stinking corpses. It worked even better against mild disorientation.

A few more blinks and a moment to steady her vision aided in the quick recovery. Once settled, she turned to melting the ice orb and deconstructing the magic within it. Leaving an object of that nature lying about, ice or not, was unwise.

After melting the orb, she turned to examining the ice shards a bit closer. She stepped up to the tallest one she could see and wiggled on her silk arcane gloves. Despite the caster no longer being present, it was more than plausible that there was some residual magic. If it had been Amelia, she would have made it so that a secondary discharge of ice would attack whoever tried to free the encased bodies. The gloves would help to protect her from such things.

Being familiar with elemental energies – especially ice – she was able to determine quite quickly that there were no such traps within the giant blue spike. There were, however, secondary micro-shards on the surface of the ice. If anyone tried to grab the ice, their hands would have been shredded. The small snowflakes that covered the surface of the ice acted like teeth.

Good gods, you are talented.

She took off her hat, leaned closer, and breathed on the surface of the ice with a touch of magic to her breath. The miniature snowflake-blades melted away, leaving a clean and water-slicked surface of blue ice.

A touch of one finger was all she needed to get a better and intimate understanding of the magic that created it. Amelia shut her eyes and felt out the energies surrounding the ice. Confusingly, it felt natural. It felt as if the ice hadn't been constructed at all. The framework was near flawlessly natural. It was if it had always been there.

She opened her eyes and took her finger away, only to furrow her brow and tilt her head in confusion. "How?" As much as she wanted to glare at the ice and demand an answer of it, it wasn't going to give one.

Recalling lectures at the Arcanum, she did remember one professor speaking about innate or instinctive magic being much closer to that of the natural elements.

We're dealing with a sorcerer... fireballs.

Having finished her examination, she pulled out her stylus and notepad and began jotting down her observations. Caution concerning the abrasive surface of the ice was underlined multiple times.

Amelia turned to the nearby blue coat. "Hank?"

The man was only a touch taller than her, had a dimpled chin, green eyes, and a bright red mustache. "Yes?"

"Make sure nobody touches the ice. It's designed to cut you if you try."

The man turned a bit to look over his shoulder at the wall. "Aye, ma'am, that's good to know... and what if we have to touch it?"

"Well, you can try to melt the surface first, but then that would make it that much more slick and slippery. It could cause you to slide your hand directly into the sharp stuff." She shrugged. "Sorry, wish I had better news."

The man blew out a sigh of frustration, "Got it, don't touch."

"Good man." She turned and headed to the warehouse.

It was a fairly small warehouse, perhaps one hundred by fifty paces. During her aerial view, she had noted that there were two man-doors. The first was located directly to her left; the other was on the opposite end of the ice field. They both faced the street. The roof was gray clay tile like many of the other warehouses in the area. Unlike the others, it had a long series of skylight windows for natural light. Her best guess was that the building had been used as a botanical nursery in the past.

That thought unnerved her. She made a mental note to check in on Mr. Jenkins again when she got back to the precinct.

Knowing that she'd be stepping into a brick room full of incinerated bodies, she pulled her corpse cloth from her pocket and tied it around her face and over her nose.

The man-door had been left wide open, and the inside of the building looked to have a dirt floor. There was no natural light coming in through the skylight windows. They were blackened with soot. She could only hope it was a result of whatever industry had last taken up residence in the building, and not from the scorched bodies.

She stepped over the lip of the doorway and peered into the darkness. "Joseph?" She looked back down to her boot when she noticed that the dirt wasn't giving way to her weight. It felt like she was stepping on hardened concrete.

Right, John hardened the dirt.

"Over here." Joe's voice still sounded a bit gravelly, and was slightly muffled as it echoed off the interior walls.

Amelia stepped further into the warehouse and peered around. It wasn't until her eyes adjusted that she spotted him. He was floating two steps off the ground in the middle of the room. "What are you doing?"

Joe turned a little on the spot and looked to her as he held his staff in hand. His staff was far simpler than hers or John's. It was made from a standard length of marbled iron maple and headed with a shield pin.

"I needed a better view." He was wearing a cloth over his nose and mouth, just as she was.

"Why not use a Seeing Eye?"

Amelia couldn't help but smirk a little when Joseph gave a whole body shiver in reply. "No thanks."

She couldn't blame him. He had also studied at the Arcanum and had likely heard the same stories. That didn't mean she couldn't tease him and watch him squirm a little. He was the rookie. It was her job to poke him from time to time.

A glance about the room revealed nothing of interest. She couldn't even make out any bodies. There was just dirt, four walls, and a roof.

"Figure anything out?"

Joseph looked back down upon the ground around him and nodded slowly. "I think I have an idea as to what happened here."

"Mind sharing your wondrous insights?"

"Certainly." He floated toward her and lowered down to the ground. Amelia didn't notice it until he stepped off of them, but Joe had been standing on top of the iron manacles that he had enchanted to float and encircle the head of his staff.

The two dark iron rings suddenly jumped up several steps as they were released from holding the man's weight. Once stabilized, they floated up and over the head of Joe's staff and floated there freely. "After John hardened the dirt, I went to floating over the scene in order to get an aerial view. I then used my track-finding lens and charted out the movements of each individual."

Amelia held up her hand to halt him. "Not in so many details. Give me a brief summary, Rook."

He scrunched his nose and turned to look back into the room. "It was a trap." He pointed to the two man-doors on the front side of the building, then off into the darkness to the two opposite corners of the back of the building. "They came in through the four doors."

"Four?"

Joe stopped and turned to look back at her with his bloodshot eyes. "Yes, four. The two at the back are hard to see through all the corpse soot."

"Corpse… soot?"

Joe nodded again. "Yep… whoever blasted them, blasted them to dust. I haven't even found so much as a single charred bone."

Sweet merciful goddess.

C h a p t e r 5

"Keep going." She wanted his full assessment.

Joe turned back to the darkened room and began pointing out the finer details. "Based on the tracks and the burn patterns, it looks like the one who threw the fire came in through that far door." He pointed to the door closest to the origin point of the ice.

"That stands to reason. It looks like all the ice originated over on that side of the street as well. Maybe they were running away from whoever was throwing around the ice magic."

Joe nodded in agreement. "That would make sense." He continued and pointed to the four doors again, "He was followed inside and ambushed by the poor souls that are now painting the walls with their ashes."

"Anything else?"

The taller man shook his head. "That's all I can determine from the examination I gave. There's quite literally nothing left and the footprints are chaotic and overlapping.

Whoever did this has frightening abilities with fire magic."

"Same goes for the ice sorcerer."

"A sorcerer?" He stood a bit straighter upon hearing the word.

"Yes. They're extremely rare and just as dangerous. You can usually spot them because of their unusual physical traits."

"Right... Petals mentioned them." He seemed unnerved.

Good, you should be scared. A sorcerer is not something to take lightly.

She nodded in understanding. "Petals taught me about them in far greater detail than the damn professors at the Arcanum ever did." There were a great many lessons she learned outside of the Arcanum that could have easily been taught within its walls.

Learning how to bond with a staff would have been one of those important lessons. Petals enlightened her on that and on how the Arcanum professors selfishly kept a great deal of information to themselves.

"Professors taught you about sorcerers?" Joe looked genuinely surprised and a bit angered.

"More mentioned in passing than anything."

Joe breathed a frustrated sigh out his nose. "I like the Arcanum less and less every day."

Amelia reached over and patted him on the arm, "It's okay, Rook. We were all fed the bare minimum."

The talk of sorcerers made her think of the envelope and Joe's expertise. "Before you start on your notes..." She pulled a pair of long metal tweezers from one of her vest pockets, opened her trench coat, and removed the envelope. "Could you take a look at this?"

She used the tweezers to hold the red wax-stamped envelope out to Joe. He looked down at it with a furrowed brow and took it with his gloved hand.

Amelia couldn't help but squirm on the inside. She wasn't a fan of her personal life being rummaged through publically. Worse yet, there was nothing she could do to hide her family name from being on the face of the letter. Thankfully, Joe hadn't turned it over to see what it was.

Joe shrugged and turned to hand it back to her. "It's an envelope."

Oh... good... god!

Amelia punched his arm. "I *know* it's an envelope, dummy!"

"Haaaa!" Joe doubled over, cradling his arm. His staff stood on its own.

"Oh, don't be such a ninny! I didn't punch you that hard!" As broad-shouldered and as muscular as he was, he seemed to crumple rather easily.

Joe shook his head and sucked on his teeth to grit through the pain. "Not you!"

"What? What do you mean not me?" She put her hands on her hips and glared down at him as he dropped to a knee.

Her envelope dropped to the dirt floor as Joe flexed his hand open and shut several times. His eyes were squeezed shut and he looked to be in considerable pain.

I swear I didn't punch him that hard.

He let out a ragged breath and groaned, "I went three rounds with Anvilhearth's family last night."

Amelia shook her head to try and get the wax from her ears. "Pardon, you did what?"

"I felt guilty... about Dromvil." Joe struggled to his feet and stood there for a bit while wobbling through the pain. "I confessed my guilt to them. I apologized profusely."

Oh... you idiot.

"They roped you into an honor brawl, didn't they."

Joe nodded and slowly rubbed his punched arm.

"No wonder you looked like the dead this morning." Honor brawls were ancient traditions amongst dwarves. If an individual felt as though that they had done something dishonorable or unforgivable, they could request an honor brawl. The offended family, or families, would pit their strongest fighters against the offender, and they would straight up beat on one another for as long as the offending party could withstand it. The goal was to survive at least one round in order to regain their honor. It sounded easy enough if the odds were fair, but the honor brawls were never fair. It was always three on one.

"Did you seriously take a beating for three rounds?" If he had, it would have been more than acceptable to the Anvilhearth family to forgive him of any plausible wrongdoings.

In the case of Dromvil's death, Joe was not in the wrong. Dromvil, if anything, had earned even more honor. He had successfully killed his killer while in the throes of death. Dwarves would consider such an end to be more than worthy of song.

Joe turned his head away in embarrassment. "I'm not proud of it."

A quick glance at his knuckles provided her with even more insight. They weren't bloodied, bruised, scratched, or even blemished. He hadn't fought back. Joe had gone in and taken a beating for the sake of letting them beat on him.

You really are a soft-hearted idiot. May you ever be in the good graces of the Goddess of Mercy.

"Uh-huh…" Amelia bent down, picked up the envelope with her tweezers again, and handed it back to Joe. "Now examine the damn envelope this time."

"I did!" He looked at her like she was some crazed witch.

"No, you didn't! You looked it over like it was a piece of paper and tried to hand it back to me!"

Joe scowled furiously. "I did not! I examined it and determined it was enchanted with a standard eyes-only revelation trigger. It also bares a simple destruction ward to prevent someone from shredding it or burning it."

Amelia was taken aback. "How did– You couldn't have!" There was simply no means by which he could have examined the envelope that quickly and with so little effort.

"Fine!" Joe grabbed his staff, shrunk it down to a wand, and pointed it at the envelope. Arcane runes immediately burst alight across the parchment. "Here," he pointed to a segment with the tip of his wand, "Self-ignition framework and revelation runes." He pointed to another section, "Here is the eyes-only proclamation."

Thundering fireballs.

Amelia gaped at the obvious, then turned her gaze upon Joe. "How?"

"What do you mean 'How?'" His furrow softened.

"How did you do that so quickly?"

"I– it's my thing. I'm good with barriers and wards."

He was. It was the very reason she had turned to him in the first place. How he managed to get so good was what bothered her. As much as she liked Joe Runewall, he was keeping secrets. "She pushed the envelope back at him. Look deeper."

"I–" He looked like he was about to protest, but gave up. "Fine." He took the envelope from her tweezers and pocketed his wand.

She watched as he slowed his breathing and focused on the envelope. It only took a moment before a blink resulted in a shift. His eyes transformed into polished silver orbs of light.

Magic manifested in a metaphorical representation of one's ideals and wills. Joe was one of those 'knight in shining armor' types. Nothing said barrier, wall, or armor like solid metal.

The man was always ready to jump into the line of fire to protect those around him. Thankfully, he treated everyone fairly and never considered her to be anything less than capable. She'd warned him against such thoughts when she first met him. It was nice to see that the warning had been completely unnecessary.

At first, she thought he was only humoring her and not really looking. When he didn't notice the presence above them, she knew he was focused.

She hadn't noticed it right away. It was more of a feeling that she was being watched. The hairs on the back of her neck stood up. She then felt the subtle shift in ambient temperature. Whoever it was, they were directly above and peering in through the soot-smudged skylight windows.

"Rook," she kept her voice to a whisper.

He didn't even budge. His eyes were locked onto the envelope.

"Rook!" She said it a bit louder and tugged on the sleeve of his jacket.

"Huh? What?" He blinked several times and his eyes suddenly reverted back to the bloodshot silver irises they were before. "What is it?"

She kept her eyes locked on his, then cleared her throat and briefly glanced up.

Joe's eyebrows shot up in recognition of what she was saying. He looked back down at her envelope, closed his eyes, tilted his head, then tensed. "I feel their eyes on me." He thankfully kept his voice low.

She cleared her throat again and spoke normally, "So, did you finish examining it or not?"

He opened his eyes and glanced to her while handing over the envelope. "It's clean. Some odd magic at play, but there's nothing you need to worry about." His other hand pulled out his wand.

Amelia began recalling any spells that might be of use to her. Nothing worked for the distance they were dealing with. The skylight windows were easily fifty steps above their heads. Anything she threw up there wouldn't make it to the intended target in time.

She took the envelope, stuffed it back into the inner breast pocket of her jacket, and removed her wand from her vest pocket. "So, how do we plan on catching this culprit?"

Joe, thankfully, wasn't all that dumb. He had the wherewithal to understand who she wasn't so subtly hinting at. "The good old-fashioned way–" He released his wand back into a staff. "We run them down." The manacles on his staff began to swirl about in a way that was far livelier than she'd ever noticed them at rest.

Smart thinking, Rook.

Releasing her wand back into a staff, she felt far less worried about who was observing them from above. She couldn't help but smirk, "You think you'll catch them before I can?"

He raised one eyebrow quizzically. "Is it a race now?"

"So long as it helps to get the job done." Amelia pulled some water from outside the warehouse and snaked it along the wall behind her. The fire magic that had been used to incinerate everything in the room had also sapped it of any moisture.

Joe perked up a bit and even smiled a little. "On the count of three then?"

Amelia accepted the terms by nodding. She pulled the water through the dirt in order to hide any reflective surface from view.

"One." Joe gripped his staff all the tighter and flexed his jaw.

"Two." Amelia pulled enough water to her feet that she'd be able to lift off again with a hovering ice sheet.

Joe furrowed his brow. "Wait."

Amelia sighed, "What now, Rook?"

"Do we go on three, or after three?"

She tilted her head and eyed him. "What?"

"You know, one, two, three, *go*. Or is it one, two, *three*, where we go on three?" He made a forward gesture on 'go' and 'three'.

She hung her head and pinched the bridge of her nose. "Why does this matter?"

"If one of us jumps on three and the other doesn't, then one of us gets a headstart on the other."

"How do you know one of us would get a headstart on the other? What if we *both* jump on three? Did you ever consider that?" She looked back up only to see that Joe was looking up at the skylight.

"He's running! Three! THREE!" Joe turned and bolted for one of the far doors. For a man that took a three-round beating the night prior, he could run. He must have visited the doc.

Amelia roared her anger and frustration and slammed the butt of her staff against the solid dirt floor. The water welled up around her feet and quickly solidified into a hardened frozen disk around her boots. "This is your fault!"

Joe kicked open one of the far doors and screamed as he exited, "We need to organize our counting!" He looked skyward, cursed the sun in his eyes, and cast his staff like a fishing rod, shooting out the manacles.

Amelia lifted her staff a bit higher and began levitating off the dirt floor of the warehouse. With a forward tilt, she began gliding toward the open door that Joe had kicked open.

"Blast it!" Joe reeled in his staff. Both iron manacles returned to him in an instant. He had missed.

"Move it!"

Joe glanced in Amelia's direction and immediately flattened himself to the cobblestones as she sailed out the door and over his head. The back-end alleys of the warehouses were thankfully spacious and provided her with ample room to glide through.

She didn't realize how dark and bleak the warehouse had been until she was struck by the blinding mid-morning sunlight. Amelia covered her eyes with her free arm and quickly glanced about.

Blue coats had been stationed in the back alleys as well as on the main street. One of them was at the mouth of the alley and pointing to a nearby rooftop. "He jumped to that one, Ms. Iceheart!"

Amelia nodded in thanks and lifted her staff higher. She quickly ascended to rooftop level and briefly spotted their suspect. The figure dropped down into the alley opposite; they were wearing a dark trench coat, dark slacks, gloves, and a hat. She couldn't make out anything more beyond that. Her glimpse was far too brief.

"Where did he go?" Joe was yelling it from ground level.

Amelia pointed with her staff and began gliding toward the alley in question. "Next over!"

She wanted to catch the culprit but also feared getting into a confrontation with them. What if they were the ones to incinerate or freeze the corpses?

The warehouse she glided overtop of was much longer than the one they had just left and one of many in the area. She didn't want to get into a game of cat-and-mouse in the industrial district. There were far too many workers that could potentially get dragged into the crossfire. Hopefully, with the aid of the blue coats, they would be able to corner the suspect. She also had a worrying hope that they didn't. People were most dangerous when cornered.

She glided along the slanted rooftop and gray clay tiles as she headed toward the other end. She wanted to push herself to go faster, but that required more will than she wanted to give. She'd already expended far too much energy earlier that morning and again in her examinations and use of the Seeing Eye.

There was a very real chance that they would get into an arcane duel. Based on her waning strength, she didn't like her odds of surviving that battle.

Amelia reached the edge of the rooftop and peered down into the alleyway below. She couldn't see them anywhere.

Blast!

Tires squealed and screeched off to her right. She turned to the cobblestone street and watched as a cart rumbled passed the mouth of the alley. The culprit must have ran to the street and stolen a cart in order to double back.

Amelia turned and pushed her ice disc in the

opposite direction and followed the cart from above. She leaned into it and bent low at the knees, accelerating as she did so.

With a clear view from above, she was able to make detailed observations. The cart she followed was a private model. The driver's cabin was full-sized and the rear passenger box was shaded to block the sunlight. The wheel covers were robust and so was the suspension.

It clearly had a powerful engine, as it was easily pulling away. Thankfully, there were few to no pedestrians or gnome carts about. The warehouse district strictly catered to workers and large transport carts. Few of them were on the road.

It was both a blessing and a curse. Nobody could possibly get hurt by the reckless speed their suspect was utilizing, but neither was anybody in the way for the suspect to slow down and avoid.

Amelia reached the other end of the rooftop and jumped. With a touch of magic and a great deal of forward momentum, she easily cleared the alley and made it to the next rooftop. Her legs shook with the effort of absorbing the impact, and she almost lost her balance, but she was able to hold herself upright by gripping her staff tight.

The cart was easily two warehouses ahead of her and nearing an intersection.

Blast it all!

She couldn't keep up, and her waning energy was about to give out.

"Amelia!"

She turned her attention to the road on the left and was surprised to see a large transport hauler rumbling up to her side. It had a wooden flat-bed with a squat and square driver's cabin. The flat-bed was empty, and Joe was yelling at her from the inside, "Jump!"

You marvelous idiot.

The cart they were chasing made a sharp turn to the left and headed toward Red Lightning Boulevard.

Amelia timed her jump with the edge of the next warehouse and leaped off it toward the flat-bed. She released the magic that held the ice sheet and her feet in place and softened her landing with a brief gust of wind.

The ice sheet shattered on contact with the flat-bed, and she rolled with the impact. Unfortunately, she slammed into the wooden side rails with a grunt; she hadn't been able to fully stop her sideways momentum. It wasn't the softest landing, but it was better than breaking her legs or falling off the cart.

Joe must have heard her land in the back, because as soon as she was down, he hit the accelerator and screamed out the window, "WAHOO!"

The sudden jump in speed made her scream in panic as she nearly slid off the back. Had she not stuck the butt of her staff through the side wooden railing, she would have.

I'm going to kill that marvelous idiot!

Chapter 6

Amelia kept the staff lodged in the side rail and hauled herself to her feet.

Joe was clearly enjoying himself. The man-child was laughing maniacally as the engine of the flat-bed roared. They accelerated all that much more.

A gentle tethering was the only thing that was keeping her hat on her head. The wind from their forward momentum was whipping at her hair, hat, and coat. She gripped the railing that framed out the back of the driver's cabin and pulled her staff free from where she had wedged it.

Her heart was thundering in panic and excitement. She didn't know whether to scream at Joe to slow down or go faster. Admittedly, she wasn't being very safe, but it was a bit exhilarating at the same time.

They made it to the corner and Joe slowed down.

He'd clearly paid enough attention to gnome cart drivers to know at least some of what he was doing. That said, the turn was a bit scary. The tires screeched and one side of the cart lifted slightly off the ground, causing her to screech, "JOSEPH!"

"I got it!"

The cart thumped back down to all four wheels as they straightened out. Joe hit the accelerator again; they lurched forward, rumbled, and roared down the road toward their target. The cart was making another left turn, which would lead to Red Lightning Boulevard.

Fireballs!

Amelia slapped the hood of the cabin with her gloved hand.

Joe yelled out the window, "I see it!"

Neither of them wanted to go to Red Lightning Boulevard. Dark dwarf and bloodling businesses were concentrated on that road, and they hated the law. They expressed that hatred fervently. The law avoided going there unless they had someone to watch their back, and contacted dispatch first.

Amelia shrunk her staff into a wand, then released it again once she had wedged it between the cabin and the railing. With a firm grip on her staff, she let go of the railing and pulled her crystalline network box free from her belt.

"Detective Amelia Iceheart to dispatch, come in!" She had no idea how well her voice would carry through with all the wind rustling in her face.

"Dispatch to Iceheart. Go ahead, Detective." It sounded frazzled. The wind was undoubtedly having a negative effect on communication.

"In pursuit of a suspect driving private cart, heading to Red Lightning Boulevard. Send blue coats immediately!"

"Stonehand responding!" John was always reliable.

"Confirmed, sending blue coats to Red Lightning Boulevard."

They reached the same corner where their target had

turned. Joe slowed, more than he did at the first corner, and brought them around in a sharp turn. He then slammed his foot on the accelerator, and Amelia gripped her staff for dear life.

The engine in the flat-bed roared, and they gained ground on the private cart. It wasn't more than a block ahead of them.

Amelia crouched low and widened her stance so as to steady herself. She blindly clipped her network box back onto her belt and prepared to do whatever she could when they got closer. She still had no idea how they were going to stop the other cart.

Dark dwarf and bloodling men and women watched in a mix of curiosity and agitation as the flat-bed roared and rumbled past. It likely wasn't every day that they saw a detective standing in the back of an empty flat-bed as another detective drove it at reckless speeds.

They passed numerous shops and establishments as they hurried to catch up. Cinderbeard's Smokes and Pipes was directly to her right, and the Bloodvault Bank was ahead on the left. Other establishments included the Charred Bone Bistro, Targrog's Tinkering, and The Smelter. The latter was a rough pub. It catered only to dark dwarves.

Each of the establishments in the district was covered in dingy grime from lack of care or maintenance. The red brick was more of a gray; trash and refuse littered the cobblestones. It only added to the poor reputation and lack of appeal.

They made quite the headway against the cart. They managed to almost catch up to it by the time they had passed the massive structure of the Bloodvault Bank off to the left.

Amelia gripped the railing again in preparation for any more idiotically marvelous maneuvers that Joe might get in his head to try.

For reasons she couldn't fathom, the denizens of Red Lightning Boulevard deemed it pertinent to cross the street, despite the fast-approaching cart and flat-bed chasing it. They simply stepped out onto the cobblestones with their sneers set and chins up.

The cart slammed on its decelerator in order to avoid striking those crossing the cobblestones.

Interesting.

Thankfully, Amelia was holding on, because Joe slammed on the decelerator as well. She slammed into the railing and her staff. If it hadn't been there, she would have gone over the cabin railing and flown into the rear of the suspect's cart.

Sadly, Joe hadn't reacted quickly enough, and they slammed into the back of the private cart. Thankfully, it didn't push the cart into those that were crossing – they did start cursing though.

Dark dwarves and bloodlings alike began yelling and shouting in their mother tongues – you know you've angered a dwarf when they no longer use Common. The guttural language of the dwarves was not one that was spoken softly or quietly; it was often shouted and growled. Bloodlings had a quickly-spoken jittering language. It reminded her of squirrels that had gotten ahold of a potent bag of spiced tea.

Amongst the yelling, shouting, and foot stomping was a series of excessively suggestive and crude hand gestures that Amelia didn't think were necessary given that the suspect's cart was hardly damaged and nobody had gotten hurt. At least, she hoped that Joe was all right.

"Joe?"

"I'm alive." He groaned it.

The cart door swung wide, their suspect bolted, and Amelia was finally able to get a good look. Her glimpse was brief but telling.

As before, she noted that the individual was wearing a dark trench coat, dark slacks, gloves, and a hat. With a much closer view, she was able to tell that they were well-tailored, dark gray, and fitted to a small frame. Her first guess was their suspect was a small woman or a young man. She could only guess, because the face was entirely covered.

They were wearing some sort of black sock over their head, and their eyes were protected by tinted goggles. Even stranger, she couldn't make out a nose or any other typical facial features.

The masked suspect stepped out of the cart and vaulted over the roof of it to the other side. The motion was nearly flawless. There wasn't even a second's breath to shake off the cart crash.

Whoever it was landed on their feet on the right side of the cart and immediately dashed for the nearest alley. A dark dwarven couple stepped in the way and looked to be ready to get into a scrap and grapple the one trying to flee. Only, the masked suspect vaulted over them, tumbled through the air, and landed with the grace of a professional dancer. They quite literally hit the ground running.

Joe was just as quick to respond. He kicked open the passenger side door and jumped from the seat to begin chasing their target.

Amelia shrunk her staff in order to unwedge it, then released it again before vaulting over the side rail of the flat-bed. A thrust of her staff and a brief gust of chilling wind helped to carry her over the heads of the stubborn dwarven couple and into the alley.

Joe dove over their heads and landed with an Academy-approved shoulder roll.

Despite having a few paces headstart, Joe overtook her. He had the longer legs and the athleticism. They both ran down the alley after their target as the person dashed to the other end and toward the adjacent road.

Amelia pulled her crystalline network box and updated dispatch, "Amelia to dispatch. Suspect is heading north of Red Lightning Boulevard!" She huffed as she ran and cursed the drinking sickness. It wasn't even lunch and she was sapped of strength.

Joe finally did what he should have done from the start. He took a grand leap, drew back his staff, and cast forth the iron manacles with a hearty and visceral grunt. The black iron rings shot out from the head of his staff, screamed through the air, and clamped onto the ankles of their fleeing suspect.

FINALLY!

The person's feet flew forward and out from under them. They dropped hard onto their back and directly into a puddle. They had nearly made it to the alley exit on the other end.

Joe stopped running altogether and bent over at the waist with his staff across his knees. He was breathing heavily and looked like he was about ready to fall over.

Amelia slowed to a jog, eased to a walk, and then to a halt as she bent over at the waist and leaned on her staff beside Joe. "About… time!" She was out of breath and absolutely exhausted.

Damned drinking sickness.

Joe nodded his head and groaned as he slowly stood and shuffled toward their suspect. He had no fears that the person would run away. They couldn't escape his manacles. Or so she had thought.

The suspect in question sat bolt upright, lifted their leg, examined the manacle, and popped their foot off.

Joe halted on the spot in obvious surprise and confusion.

Amelia gaped. "How?"

The culprit pushed and popped the manacle off their ankle and reattached their foot as though it had been merely a slight inconvenience. Then they turned to the other foot.

Amelia yelled at Joe, "Stop them!"

He seemed to jolt out of his state of shock and reeled on his staff. The suspect spun on the spot and slid across the cobblestones toward Joe.

Amelia grunted, straightened, and hurried over to his side with her staff at the ready. She didn't have much of anything left in her, but if their suspect could remove their limbs, then they would need something else to restrain them.

Ice did a wonderful job of restraining people if they were fully encased in it. She didn't know if she had anywhere near the necessary strength to fully encase them, but she would have to try.

The culprit suddenly slammed the heel of their shoe against a bump in the cobblestones and used it as leverage to vault themselves up into a hopping position. They hopped toward the both of them, then jumped into the air and spun about like a wind-up toy.

Amelia realized what was about to happen and ducked in time. Joe didn't. She both heard and saw the clap of foot to face. Joe's head snapped to the left, and he staggered wildly, dropping his staff.

Amelia turned her attention back to the culprit, only to see a spinning mass of limbs on the ground. She felt her feet sweep out from under her, her stomach lurched, and her back struck cobblestone – she'd been hit with a leg sweep.

Her drill instructor at the Academy would be disappointed in her. To make matters worse, she landed in a grungy puddle, and the water was running down the back of her trench coat and soaking her blouse and trousers. She would have made a disgusted noise, but she was busy wheezing and trying to get air back into her lungs. She dropped her staff as well.

The spinning and flailing combatant made a brief and expert removal of their foot and popped off the second manacle, all while spinning on their back. With the other foot free, they made a quick adjustment of their limbs, and with a wheel of their arms and legs, were standing again.

Joe returned from shaking off the kick and threw a quick couple of jabs while advancing in a standard fisticuffs stance. The suspect dodged each well-thrown jab as though they were dodging the wild flailings of a drunkard.

Amelia rolled out of the disgusting puddle, coughed and sucked in a lungful, and picked up her fallen staff. While picking up her staff, she noticed the other problem. A handful of dark dwarves were marching their way, and they were all carrying some sort of improvised weapon. There were clubs, broken whiskey bottles, and even a few knives.

Blasted thundering fireballs.

She turned back only to watch as the suspect retaliated. They snatched one of Joe's wrists with one flowing hand, twisted his arm, and jabbed into Joe's side ribs with the tip of his gloved fingers. It did something more she couldn't see, because Joe dropped to his knees and howled at the top of his lungs.

Amelia threw herself up out of the puddle and swung with her staff.

Thankfully, it caused their suspect to let go of Joe and leap back. She brought her staff around in a wide overhead circle and swung again. She swung and stepped forward, protecting Joe by placing herself between them.

That, apparently, was all they needed to learn her movements. Despite her best efforts and a third swing, she was quickly beaten down.

They lunged at her and struck her in the gut with a single outstretched finger. It didn't cause anywhere near the same pain that Joe experienced, but it definitely caused her to double over.

A second flat-fingered jab struck her in the right side just under her arm. The twist was what did her in. It felt like she'd been struck by lightning. Cold twinging pain shot through her body and almost the entire right half felt like it had been struck by numbing pins and needles.

She screamed and dropped. Her staff fell to the cobblestones nearby, and they were both left defenseless. Joe was doubled over, and she was laid out on her side. A rising panic began to overtake her as she couldn't feel the right side of her body, and she couldn't move it either.

The guttural swearing and jittering grew closer as she heard the footsteps of the dark dwarves and bloodlings drawing nearer.

"That's right, beat 'em down so we don't have 'em in our side of town again!" said a dwarven man.

"Cut 'em!" came from a woman.

"Let's bleed them!" That was undeniably a bloodling.

Amelia couldn't see them. All she could see was the legs and feet of the culprit and the bright daylight at the other end of the alley.

Is this how it ends? Where is John?

Panic was gripping her heart, and she could feel it choking her. There wasn't an ounce of strength left in her body, and Joe wasn't jumping up to save them either.

The footsteps were getting ever closer. The hairs on the back of her neck were starting to stand on end. She didn't want to know what they were going to do, and funnily enough, she appreciated not being able to feel half of her body in that instant.

"Quick! Kill 'em before their friends arrive!"

The feet that stood before her vanished in a quick leap and a scraping of shoe on cobblestone.

Oh, gods!

Amelia shut her eyes and began praying as she never had before. She let the tears flow as she heard a grunt and the sounds of thrashing and beating.

Gods… I'm so sorry, Joseph.

"Hey – Hngh!" It was a dwarf yelling.

"Get – Hrmph!" That was a bloodling.

A roar of confusion and angry shouting erupted in the alley, and the mob suddenly turned to panicked screams, shuffling feet, and clop-footed running.

"What's going on?" She breathed it through the panic. She couldn't roll over to look – not that she wanted to.

Someone grunted, crawled across the cobblestone, and dropped in front of her. She dared to open an eye, and nearly cried out when she saw that it was Joe, and he wasn't beaten to a bloody pulp. "Joseph?"

Joe was looking over her head and down to the opposite side of the alley. He had a look of pain and bewilderment. "They're protecting us… but why?"

There was the sound of a wet and meaty crunch, immediately followed by a sickening scream.

Joe cringed and sucked on his teeth, "Oh! That's going to need a doctor."

"What?"

Joe shook his head. "You don't want to know, and you don't want to see it." His eyes widened and he threw himself over her, blocking her from seeing anything but his vest and neck.

She heard the clopping of shoes on cobblestone. It started from far behind her, paused, then started again in front of her and on the other side of Joe. "Did he just run and jump over us?"

"Yes."

She sniffed back the tears and scrunched her nose as she felt his breath on her neck. "Hey, Rook?"

"Yeah?"

"If you want to keep breathing and live to see another day, I suggest you move your head and look somewhere else." She felt his gaze shift to directly where she didn't want it.

"Oh. Right. Sorry." He grunted and rolled away to lay on his back beside her.

She hated awkward silences, so she focused on the job as she stared at him, unable to look elsewhere. "Are they all limp like us?"

Joe lifted and turned his head to look over her, winced, and dropped it again. "Yes. Whoever that was, they did the same thing to them that they did to you and me."

"Why would they help us, after we tried to arrest them?"

"No idea."

She still couldn't move her right side, and she was laying on it. She could drunkenly lift her left leg and arm, but that didn't help her any. "I contacted dispatch before we got here; John should be arriving any moment now."

Please hurry up, John.

"Fantastic."

She finally managed to roll so as to partially lay on her back. Thankfully, it meant that she wasn't looking directly at him anymore. It made life a little less uncomfortable.

She sniffed back the tears and pretended that they had never existed to start with. "Hey... Rook?"

"Yeah?"

"You... dating a nurse?"

"I– uh, I guess I am... why?"

"You guess you are? Wow, I bet she feels special."

"I– It's– Fine, yes, I'm dating a nurse."

She let out a sigh. "Blast it."

"What?"

"I owe a coin."

Chapter 7

John arrived shortly, followed by half a dozen blue coats. He promptly secured the scene and contacted dispatch in order to get medical teams to the alley. Joe had managed to help Amelia sit up and back against the brick wall.

"Rook, how in the blasted thundering blazes are you able to move while I'm not?" The thought was irritating her to no end.

He grunted and slumped to the cobblestones beside her and stretched his feet out. "I don't know. Maybe it's 'cause I'm bigger?"

She scowled at that thought and did her best to shoot him a look without falling over. "Are you saying I'm a frail little woman?"

"I– It– No! Quit putting words in my mouth!" He shot a frustrated scowl right back at her while he cradled his side.

A massive frame towered over the two of them and

blocked out what little sun had managed to penetrate into the alley. "Children! Do I have to separate the two of you or are you going to stop bickering?" John put his hands on his hips. She couldn't tell if he was glaring, as the sun was directly behind him. Based on her experience, she guessed he was glaring. He rarely made jokes, and was usually fairly responsible and focused.

"Now, what all happened? One moment you're at the crime scene, the next you're on the crystalline network shouting about a suspect." He lifted his hands from his hips and raised a notepad and stylus to the ready.

Joe looked to Amelia. "You start. You sensed them first."

Amelia let out a pained sigh, then got to work detailing the events that had led them to the alley.

Joe finished by filling in the blanks from his end. "Just after we first spotted the suspect, I jumped out the back door of the warehouse and sent my manacles after them. I swear I had them by the wrist, but they kept going like I hadn't." He pointed to the other end of the alley. "Then I hit them in both ankles... and they just popped off their feet and knocked the manacles off."

John grunted and continued to scribble notes.

"Have you ever heard of anyone being able to take off their limbs like that?"

John shook his head. "I haven't, not like that. There are a few stores that sell arcane puppet hands for amputees, but nothing like what you're describing."

Amelia recalled meeting a noblewoman that had a porcelain hand. She always wore a silk glove over it, but it functioned just as her other hand did. "This was more than just limbs."

"Oh?" John turned his attention back to her. "What do you mean?"

"Their face was wrong."

Joe jumped in, "It was too... round."

"Round?" John looked back and forth between the

two of them.

Amelia agreed, "There were no curves or bumps, nothing that resembled a nose or ears. The eyes were covered by goggles."

John raised an eyebrow, shrugged, and scribbled the details into his notes.

"I think it might have been a puppet and not a person at all." It looked as though Joe was in deep thought. He was staring at his feet, and his brow was furrowed.

Puppets, in the arcane world, were constructs that could be controlled remotely. More often than not, they were used by assassins, and were deemed illegal within the kingdom.

Amelia could follow his line of thinking. "When you knocked the feet out from under them, there wasn't so much as a single sound. No cursing, no shouts of surprise, nothing. Not a peep, not even when they hit the ground — and they hit hard."

Joe sat a bit straighter, winced, and doubled over, clutching his side and grunting, "Right!" He took a few deep breaths to calm the pain in his side. In that moment, Amelia thanked the gods that most of her body was numb and the pain she did feel was tingling pins and needles. Joe was in worse shape than she was.

He took breaths between his words to grit through the pain. "I forgot... about that part... I was thinking more... about how they fought."

There was that as well. Amelia filled in for Joe so that he didn't have to try and talk. "They weren't just skilled, they were perfectly precise. They dismantled us both with little to no effort, then they turned and attacked them."

John stopped scribbling to lift his head and look at them both. "Attack whom?"

Amelia couldn't tilt her head — she was still numb and unable to move most of her body — so she darted her eyes to the right to the pile of groaning and grumbling residents of Red Lightning Boulevard. "Them."

"Them?" John pointed to the dark dwarves and bloodlings with the back of his stylus.

Joe let out a deep groaning sigh and nodded. "Yep, them."

"Why in the blazes would the person controlling the puppet attack them?" John looked back to Joe. "I thought this might have been *your* handiwork."

Amelia couldn't shake her head, so she cleared her throat "No. They were all taken down with good old-fashioned fists… or puppet fists. Joe isn't in any condition to take on that many people, fists or magic."

Joe grunted, "I also wouldn't attack innocents."

John shook his head as he scribbled more notes. "I know how you think, Joe. You wouldn't hesitate to immobilize a mob if it meant protecting other innocents."

She agreed with that assessment, but it wasn't the correct answer. "While true, that's not what happened here. We were both beaten down, then protected."

"Protected?" John raised an eyebrow.

Joe grunted and nodded, "Whether it's a puppet or an extremely resilient amputee, they spent considerable energy making sure nobody got killed, including us."

Amelia added, "To their own detriment. They could have gotten away from us much faster if they hadn't stopped to protect us."

"Be glad that they did!" Doctor Alexander Broom had finally arrived. He wore the typical white trench, vest, trousers, and shirt of the medical corps. All of it was emblazoned with the red droplet and enchanted with stain resistance. The man was in his middle age but looked older. He had a thin, gaunt frame with a long face. A pair of magnifying spectacles somehow managed to balance on his hooked nose.

The doctor marched his way through the grumbling and groaning bodies as a team of nurses and assistants followed behind him. They were sent from the hospital, tasked with helping the citizens. Broom was their precinct doctor and had the single task of keeping detectives and blue coats on their feet, when he wasn't examining corpses.

Amelia decided to quip, "What are you suggesting, Doc? We can't handle ourselves?"

He stepped free of the grumbling and groaning mass and briskly made his way to Amelia and Joe. "My dear, I have examined the cold bodies of stronger and smarter detectives than you," he said in a very disapproving way. She felt like she was being scolded by her grandfather. "They were killed by arrogance and ego."

The panic she had experienced earlier rose back up to choke her.

"By the looks of the both of you, I'd say the only thing that spared you today was the hands of the Fates... but what do I know? I'm not a soldier... I'm just a doctor." He dropped to a knee and yanked opened his black leather medical bag in anger and frustration.

Amelia had to fight back tears. The man was right. She'd been close to death before, but not in an alley and at the hands of a mob of people she was sworn to protect. It was frightening and frustrating at the same time.

"Hey... Doc?" Joe was speaking. Amelia didn't have the courage to test her voice at the moment.

"No, Joseph, I don't have any more rations! You ate the last of them!" Doctor Broom angrily rummaged around inside his leather bag.

"I– I wasn't about to ask that. I was going to ask if you've ever heard of arcane puppet hands for amputees."

The doctor let out a deeply frustrated sigh, stopped rummaging through his bag, and pinched the bridge of his angular nose. "Yes... yes, Joseph, I have." He kneeled on the cobblestones and shut his eyes.

"Could someone load them with paralyzation spells or would that interrupt the framework that makes them nimble?"

Everyone turned their attention to Joe. Doctor Broom opened his eyes and frowned in thought. "I don't rightly know." He paused in thought. "I'm not a wizard like you, Joseph. You'd be better able to answer that question on your own. Though I suppose it is possible."

That got Amelia contemplating the possibilities as well. If they could examine a replacement hand and how it was constructed, it might provide them with the answer.

While an interesting inquiry, she quickly realized that Joe was getting ahead of himself. There was no point in investigating if a false hand could hold a paralyzation spell. They had no idea what they had been afflicted with yet.

Then she realized that they couldn't have been afflicted by any spell. Their trench coats and vests should have protected them from any form of touch magic.

She glanced out the side of her eye to see Joe smirking. He'd thrown out a wild speculation in order to confuse the lot of them and force a change in subject.

Bless your idiotic brain.

She looked up at John and noticed he was covering a smile by stroking his mustache.

Bless both of you.

Amelia tried to raise her right hand, remembered it wasn't responsive, and barely managed to use her left hand to wipe her face with her sleeve. She sniffed back any possible tears and did her best to sit still and rest.

The tingles and pains seemed to be dissipating. Not very quickly, but they were easing. There was hope that whatever had been done to both of them was temporary… or she was simply getting used to it.

Doctor Broom pulled a large cylindrical spyglass from his bag. It was sheathed in black leather and had multiple lenses that were framed in silver and hinged to a parallel brass rod. One could peer through the spyglass and slide lenses in and out of place in order to adjust the focus. Each silver frame had a unique set of arcane runes etched into its surface.

It was a medical instrument that could examine the layers of the mortal form. Amelia didn't know what it was called and had never bothered to ask, but the doc often utilized it when examining injuries of a curious nature.

The doc shifted his spectacles so they sat on his head, shut his left eye, and peered through the spyglass while eyeballing Amelia. She hated the sensation that followed. Bumps formed across her skin and the hair on the back of her neck stood on end again. She could feel the invasiveness of the spyglass.

"My my, this is interesting." Doc blindly rolled a finger across one of the hinges and raised a lens out of the way. "Hmm…"

"What? What is it?"

Goddess of Mercy, please don't let it be permanent.

"It appears as though your energies have been disrupted." The doctor shifted and turned his gaze upon Joe. He frowned, raised a different lens, dropped it, then raised another. His frown deepened alongside the furrow of his brow.

Joe visibly shivered. "What is that thing?"

"It's my Arcane Examination Tool… now stop whatever it is you're doing! You're futzing with my sight!"

"Sorry," Joe grumbled under his breath and looked to turn inwards in concentration.

The doctor peered back through the spyglass and settled a bit. "Ah, that's better. Now, it appears as though you both have been afflicted with the same ailment. Your energies have been disrupted, though Mr. Runewall is a little less so than Ms. Iceheart."

"What does that mean? Will it go away? Will I get feeling back?" She desperately wanted control of her body again.

"It means that your magic won't respond to you, or at least, not very well. You'll also be temporarily paralyzed where you were struck." He collapsed all the lenses of his arcane examination tool and stuffed it back into his leather medical bag. "I know of someone that can resolve the issue with a single treatment. I'll contact them and have them meet you at the precinct."

"Not the hospital?" Joe was the one posing the question.

Amelia couldn't tell if he was eager to go there or to avoid it. He had strong cases for both. Joe, like others, didn't have a particular joy for visiting places of sickness, injury, and death. The nurse he was dating, on the other hand, seemed to possibly make it worth the trip.

Doctor Broom stood up with a grunt and balanced his spectacles back on his nose. "No, not the hospital." He pointed to the pile of dwarves and bloodlings. "They will, and if you'll excuse me, I have to present my findings to my colleagues and assist them in whatever way that I can."

Amelia felt an immediate embarrassing dread and a flush came to her face. "Wait, how am I supposed to get back to the precinct? I can't walk."

Doctor Broom waved off the question as he turned to the pile of overly dramatic groaning, "Ask your colleagues!"

She turned her eyes back to Joe and John and gave them her best glare. "If either of you gets the idea in your head to carry me like some damsel in distress—" she specifically glared at John, "—or a slab of meat, I swear I will make you suffer for it."

John raised an eyebrow and smirked. "I could always grab you by the belt and haul you around like dead luggage?"

Joe, for once, was the one to offer a reasonable alternative. "We'll each take an arm and carry you between us to the gnome cart."

Amelia let out a sigh through her nose. "Fine."

~~

The trip back to the precinct proved extremely uncomfortable. Besides the tingles and pains throughout the right half of her body, her trousers, blouse, undergarments, and hair were soaked with grungy puddle water from the alley. Sitting in cold damp clothing was horribly uncomfortable, especially when she had no means by which to access her magic and remove the water.

Annoyingly, no access to magic also meant that their staffs had to ride in the cart with them. They almost didn't fit and had to cross at odd angles.

Thankfully, the men had done as Joe suggested. John and Joe had each taken one of Amelia's arms and helped her to the gnome cart instead of carrying her. She was a colleague and deserved the respect of being treated as such.

The trip back mostly consisted of silent exhaustion. They both quickly agreed to rest. Neither of them had any new information to provide to the other or anything that needed discussion. As much as she appreciated it, she didn't get much rest. Her level of discomfort was far too high. Instead, she spent the trip contemplating the case, and occasionally wondering what her family wanted.

Upon arrival, Joe was the first to exit the cart. He would have to help her out and up the steps. John hadn't travelled with them – not that he would have fit. Two was the maximum capacity for any given gnome cart. John had the added responsibility of taking notes, collecting evidence, and taking statements from all those injured in the alley. There was also the original crime scene and bodies that needed to be thawed out.

Before leaving, Joe had suggested that the suspect's private cart be examined. Maybe they would get lucky and find a plaque or registration that suggested who it belonged to. They left a lot on John's plate.

Joe, thankfully, helped her out of the cart like a gentleman. He pulled her out and wrapped her numb arm around his neck and hauled her to stand on her one good leg. Together, they limped their way up the steps with their staffs for aid.

They'd nearly made it to the door when there was a sudden and loud pop in the air. The two of them jumped, and Joe turned them round to see what caused it.

A detective from the Northwest precinct was standing on the walkway at the bottom of the steps. She could tell he was from the Northwest because of the color of his trench coat: a warm brown, nearly red. His vest, like all detectives', was the standard vibrant blue.

The pop they had heard must have been a teleportation event. There were no carts about, and a passerby looked startled by the detective's sudden appearance.

The detective was middle-aged with salt-and-pepper hair and a patch of fuzz beneath his bottom lip. His chin was tilted up a bit, and his eyes focused on nothing in particular. They were clouded and white, suggesting the man was blind. Both of his hands lightly held a gnarled wooden staff that rested against his chest. The wood curiously looked as though it had grown up and around chunks of broken stained glass.

That can't be rainbow glasswood... can it?

"Howard!" Joe genuinely sounded happy.

The man's head tilted, and his eyes pointed more specifically in their direction. "Ah, Joseph. I was wondering if you'd made it back yet. I only recently got word from Doctor Broom." He had a comfortingly gentle and calming voice.

Howard tapped his staff against the steps and slowly made his way up them. Joe, surprisingly, didn't jump to help the man and dump her on the ground. He stood his ground and continued to talk, "How are things in the Northwest?"

"Peculiar, to say the least." Howard tilted his head a bit to the side, as if using his hearing to guide him up the steps and toward the two of them.

That was when she noticed a slight point to his ears. He had fey blood. It more readily explained the staff. Rainbow glasswood was only found in the fey realm, and it was extremely difficult to harvest, let alone control. If the right magic was infused through it, it could enchant almost anyone into doing almost anything, or it could blind everyone that happened to be looking in its general direction. That revelation made her question how the man lost his sight. Was he born that way, or did he make a mistake at some point while learning to use the staff?

"Peculiar?" Joe shifted his weight to better hold her up.

"Yes, but I'll explain later, when we're indoors." Howard eventually reached them and offered his hand to Amelia. "And you are?"

She rested her staff against her shoulder, took his hand, and gave it the best squeeze and shake that she could in her weakened state. "Amelia Iceheart."

He smiled while looking up at nothing in particular. "Pleasure, Ms. Iceheart. My name is Howard Truesight. I'm the Senior Detective in the Northwest precinct." He left his staff to stand on its own, lifted his hat – exposing more of his slightly pointed ears – and gently shook her hand in turn.

Amelia couldn't help but notice his flawless features. The man definitely had fey blood.

"Shall we? I'd like to change into cleaner clothes." Amelia didn't want to spend any more time in damp garments than she absolutely had to.

Howard nodded in understanding. "Certainly, you'll need to take them off anyway in order for me to resolve the issue you're both suffering from."

"Pardon?" She couldn't help but feel the sudden warmth on her face.

"No need to worry, I'm blind." He smiled in a disarming way.

It didn't make her feel any better.

"Besides," he picked up and tapped his staff against the stone steps, and made his way around the both of them toward the precinct doors, "I *see* in other ways."

That made her feel worse.

Chapter 8

They followed Howard inside. He seemed to know the way. That seemed odd, as she never remembered seeing him visit the station in her years at the precinct.

They made their way through the lobby and precariously down the stairs to the doc's office. It was a cramped square room nestled in the bowels of the precinct.

Despite the ancient walls, it had been refurbished to match a modern hospital's surgery room. The walls and floors were gray granite tile. Tall metal cabinets framed the far wall and were filled with medical supplies and potions. A cold metal examination table sat in the middle of the room, illuminated by a powerful overhead sun-lantern. To the right were the doc's desk and chair.

Preservation cabinets were built into the left wall. When a fresh body dropped, it was placed in the cabinets for storage until it could be examined.

Joe helped her over to the table as Howard stood by

with both hands on his staff. They had left their staffs by the door.

Amelia hated the examination table. It didn't matter how much the doc said he cleaned it; she didn't like laying on anything a corpse had been on. Despite her grievances, there were no other tables available.

She was able to put her left hand on the table and pull herself most of the way up onto it. Joe lifted her right side and swung her around so that she could sit upright. It didn't last, as she immediately began tipping over onto her right.

Thankfully, Joe had good enough reflexes to catch her and ease her down onto her side. He then grabbed her legs and lifted them up onto the table.

She hated feeling so useless, and merely grumbled her thanks.

"I mean no disrespect, Ms. Iceheart, but I will be examining Joseph first." Howard tapped his staff on the tile floor and summoned a three-legged wooden stool from the corner. It rubbed loudly against the floor and skidded to a halt directly in front of him.

"I– Uh– Why am I going first?" Joe had a slight wide-eyed look. He seemed just as unnerved as she was to be examined.

Howard tapped the chair with the bottom half of his staff. "Sit. I'll explain."

Joe sheepishly made his way over to sit on the stool. He sat facing Howard and looked a bit jittery. The blind fey-born detective set his staff aside; it stood on its own. He then reached out and placed his fingers on Joe's face. His head tilted, and he turned his unseeing eyes up and off to the side, as though in thought. "Hmm."

Amelia couldn't help but smirk at Joe's discomfort.

"What do you mean 'Hmm'? What is it? Why are you examining me first?" Joe looked like he was about to squirm away from Howard's hands.

The older detective cupped Joe's face to hold him

still and keep him from moving. "I'm examining you first because I have a feeling that resolving whatever was done to you will be quicker than what was done to her. You can still move, while she is half-paralyzed. The quicker I get you back on your feet, the quicker you can get back to finding this assailant."

Amelia couldn't argue with the logic, but she desperately didn't want to be tingling, helpless, or wet any more.

"And I said 'hmm' because I believe I understand the source of the problem." He took his hands from Joe's face and gestured. "Please remove your shirt."

"What?" Joe's eyebrows leaped up.

Howard let out an exasperated sigh. "You're not deaf, you heard me just fine. And I told you earlier you'd need to remove your clothing. Now, take your shirt off. I need to examine exactly where this thing hit you."

Joe glanced to Amelia with a flushed look of embarrassed worry.

She scoffed, "Oh don't be such a ninny. We see dead bodies all the time. A shirtless living one is hardly anything special."

He seemed a bit taken aback by her comment but accepted it and shrugged off his trench coat. He let it fall to the floor. Joe then began unbuttoning his vest.

Amelia couldn't help but feel slight irritation as he looked to move with much less pain than she was in. Why had he been spared from the paralyzation?

Joe removed his belt and holster with ease, but when he went to shrug off the vest, he winced in pain.

Big baby.

After the vest, he unbuttoned his shirt, and squeezed his eyes shut in pain as he shrugged that off as well. At first, she was impressed by his physique. He was undeniably fit. His muscles had muscles. There wasn't a pinch of fat on him. She could imagine why a nurse would take fondly to him. He was an impressive model of a man, but not her type. Then she saw the bruises.

Amelia was suddenly very happy to only be paralyzed. Joe's body was covered in bruises. They weren't little red blotches – they were black, purple, and green... and sizable. "Good gods, Rook." She then remembered what he had said earlier. He had taken a three-round beating at the hands of the Anvilhearth family.

"Ah... yes... that would explain why you weren't paralyzed like Ms. Iceheart." Howard was scratching the patch of salt-and-pepper fuzz on his chin.

Joe bunched up his shoulders a bit and absentmindedly rubbed the arm where Amelia had punched him earlier. It was blotched with a giant dark bruise. It started at the round of his shoulder, and stretched halfway to the elbow. That memory made her feel a bit guilty.

Okay, definitely not a baby. How in the thundering blue pixies is he still standing? How did he even make it into work?

"So, what is it that's exactly wrong with me, and why didn't it affect me the same way as Amelia?" He vaguely gestured to her.

Howard put his hands behind his back and calmly explained to them, "The mortal form consists of the physical and the metaphysical – the metaphysical being the spirit, or the energy that drives your body. If one studies long enough, one can learn to disrupt the energy lines in others."

"Energy lines?" Amelia had already learned most of what was explained, but she'd never heard of lines before.

The blind half-fey tilted his chin in her direction, "Yes, lines. Many who utilize their 'sight' to visualize the ever vast energies of the 'verse tend to see what they refer to as 'auras'. In truth, the auras are just blurred and unfocused concepts of the energies flowing through our bodies."

Joe postulated, "Like... veins?"

The elder detective turned his attention back to Joe and nodded in the affirmative. "Correct. Your body requires a proper flow of energy in order to utilize magic. Yours is disrupted, which is why you can't use your magic. The person that attacked you was well-educated. They undeniably studied one of the few martial forms that teach those skills." Howard took on a graver tone, "These martial forms were crafted for a single purpose – killing wizards. The two of you are exceedingly lucky to be alive."

Joe shut his eyes and shivered at the concept.

Amelia felt her skin crawl. "And the paralyzation?"

Howard reached out, lifted Joe's right arm, and pointed directly to the bruised ribs. "The assailant struck here, correct?"

Joe winced in pain and nodded.

Amelia verbally confirmed, as she couldn't effectively nod. "Yes."

"The paralyzation is a side-effect of the energy disruption. Joseph's body was already injured, and so the paralyzation wasn't able to spread or take."

It made sense, but it was still irritating. "Can you fix us?"

"Luckily, yes. I studied some of these martial forms." Howard politely smiled, then made several successive finger jabs into Joe's ribs.

Joe went wide-eyed, grunted with each strike, and turned ghastly pale. "Ahh! Hnngh! Haa!"

"I can imagine that this is extremely painful." Howard lifted Joe's arm up even higher, then finally stuck his pointing finger right into the center of a massive bruise and twisted.

Joe let out a howl of wide-eyed pain. His eyes rolled back, and he dropped.

Howard, thankfully, caught the young man.

Amelia looked on in horror as Howard slowly eased Joe to lay face down on the cold gray floor.

"Don't worry," Howard grunted with the effort of lowering Joe. "He'll be fine when he wakes up."

The frighteningly dangerous and blind half-fey stood upright and dusted off his hands. "Now, I'm afraid you'll have to remove your shirt, Ms. Iceheart."

"No thanks, I'll wait for it to go away on its own!" She wildly flailed her left arm in an attempt to roll away, but it was futile.

Howard let out an aggravated sigh and struck out with his right finger. It landed directly in the meat of her right thigh and caused her tingling foot to kick and twitch. She barked out a scream of surprise, but he didn't seem to care or mind.

"If we waited for this to 'go away on its own', we would be waiting near half a moon, if not more."

Blast it all!

"Now, would you like for me to continue to do this blindly... pardon the humor... or will you allow me to assist you in removing your clothing so that I can better administer the appropriate adjustments?" His finger remained jabbed into the top of her right thigh. Despite the pain it caused, she was starting to regain the feeling in the sole of her foot and her toes.

The thought of lying naked before a blind colleague while Joe lay unconscious on the floor was absolutely unappealing to her. "Fine! But you better get me a sheet from the cabinet! I don't want that putz waking up and seeing me naked!"

He rolled his blind eyes and took his finger from her thigh. The tingling and numbness crept back down through the sole of her foot and into her toes. It itched something awful. She ground her teeth and tried to shut it out, but it was of no use. She couldn't reach her foot to itch it or rub it.

Howard turned toward one of the far cabinets, stepped over Joe's prone form, picked up his staff, and tapped his way over to them. "You don't need to be completely naked. You can wear your undergarments and trousers. I merely need your vest, coat, and blouse out of the way. The majority of the adjustments I need to make are around where you were stricken."

That hardly made her feel any better. "I still don't want him seeing my undergarments!"

"I heard you the first time, Detective." He tapped his way over to the cabinets and began banging them with his staff. He'd smack one, listen, then smack the next and listen. He continued until he struck the fourth cabinet. "Ah, here they are." He ran his hand along the metal surface, found the handle, and turned the knob to open it.

Amelia gaped. The cabinet had a small stack of clean white sheets. "How?"

The man seemed far too exasperated to answer at that point. He simply reached in, grabbed the top sheet, and tossed it over his shoulder. It lazily sailed across the room and landed directly on top of her head, blinding her.

She was only able to grab it with the one arm. She tried to shake it out, but it seemed pointless.

Howard quickly returned. He took the sheet from her and unfolded it before flicking it out over top of her legs. Once done, he put a hand under her neck and helped her sit up. "Shall we get this over with?"

She hated being helped, but there was no means by which to help herself. "Please."

~~

The undressing proved to be horrifically awkward and unsettling but sadly necessary. Once it was over, she lay back down and allowed Howard to continue with his adjustments.

They weren't anywhere near as painful for her as they appeared to have been for Joe. Howard started at opposite ends of her body. One finger was jabbed into her thigh while the other poked deep into the side of her neck. He then made his way higher up her thigh until he was jamming a finger into her inner hip, and the other was deep into the pit of her arm. None of it could possibly be considered pleasant or intimate. It was simply painful and uncomfortable.

With each successive adjustment or movement of

his fingers, she regained more feeling. The stinging return of sensation was awful but welcome.

He made his way down her shoulder and up her hip to her side. From there he made a series of quick and successive jabs in ever narrowing points along her ribs. Eventually, it all ended when he drove a finger into her side and twisted. It was enough to make her gasp, clench her fists, and curl her toes in order to grit through the pain. It left a lingering sore spot in her ribs, but she otherwise was able to regain the feeling in all her extremities and was even able to sit up on her own.

She was halfway done buttoning up her detective's vest when she heard Joe grumble something from the floor. "You finally awake, Rook?"

"Hrrmph!"

Howard tilted his head and 'looked' down upon the ground. "Would you prefer to enjoy the floor for a bit longer?"

"Yes, please... the cold tile is kind of nice on my bruises..."

Howard slowly shook his head. "You truly are an odd man." He turned his attention back to Amelia and picked up his staff. "I'm certain this goes without saying, but knowing the stubbornness of youth, I shall say it anyway. Go home and rest, both of you."

Rest sounded wonderful, but she had a job to do. So she replied with a joyless tight-lipped smile, "We have reports to generate." She looked down, hopped off the table, and shook out her leg. The pins and tingles were still lingering, but she could walk.

She poked Joe with her boot. "Get up, Rook. Our day isn't done yet."

He let out a pained and whimpering groan.

I know the feeling.

Howard let out a deep sigh. "I tried." He then turned to the office door and headed toward it while tapping his staff. "Your magic will fully return in a few hours. Try not to get into any more trouble before then."

"Hey, Howard?" Joe let out a long groan as he slowly pushed himself up off the stone tile and grabbed his shirt.

"Yes, Joseph?"

"You said something about a peculiar day earlier." He shook out his white button-up, then proceeded to stiff-arm his way into it. He undoubtedly needed more than one night's rest in order to heal up properly.

Howard stopped with his hand on the door. "You're right, I did." He turned back to the two of them and put both hands on his staff, resting it against his chest and shoulder. "Should either of you two catch word of a missing dock warden, be sure to send it my way."

"Dock warden?" Amelia finished buttoning up her vest and grabbed her belt and holster.

"Yes. A very strange thing happened this morning. I'm sure there will be mention of it all over town and in letters of news."

Joe grabbed the stool, grunted, and struggled to pull himself to his feet.

Howard listened to Joe's struggles for a brief moment before continuing, "A merfolk was spotted on the northwest end of the docks earlier today."

Amelia reeled on her feet. "A merfolk? They haven't been spotted in decades!"

The elder detective stroked his chin in thought. "Yes. Even more troubling is that she threw something at a dock warden and knocked him unconscious."

"Something?" Joe wobbled to his feet and began buttoning up his shirt.

"That was what the dock warden's partner said, 'Something'. She couldn't describe it, because all she saw was her partner's head whip back from the impact. She never found what hit him."

"What did the merfolk have to say for their actions? I mean, Stormbay and the Kingdom of Greencoast have a standing peace treaty with the merfolk. Why now engage in hostilities?" Joe finished buttoning his shirt and tucked it into his trousers as he spoke. He was already moving a bit more freely and seemed to be in a bit less pain.

How do you keep going?

"Again, you are correct, Mr. Runewall. Strangely, the merfolk immediately left the scene and hasn't surfaced since. There have been no other incidents along the coast, and no communication. Delegates have descended into the depths in an attempt to discern what prompted the attack."

"And the missing dock warden?"

Amelia started to sense the shifting temperatures in the room.

Finally.

Her magic was returning, and she'd hopefully soon be able to pull the water from her clothing. Knowing her luck, she'd be done her reports and halfway back to her residence before she'd be able to do so.

"The injured dock warden was taken aside to rest and await a doctor. When the doctor arrived, they couldn't find the warden. He'd vanished." Howard lifted his hands and flicked them, as if gesturing a sudden puff of smoke.

Amelia glanced out the corner of her eye and noticed Joe glancing at her while buttoning up his vest. He was clearly thinking the same thing as her – how did an injured warden just vanish? They weren't wizards and had no magic to hide their tracks.

Joe looked to Howard and asked the dumbest question. "Could he have been enchanted to go to the water?"

Amelia blinked and turned her full attention on him. "Did you seriously just ask that question?"

Howard closed his eyes and shook his head in obvious disappointment. "This wasn't a siren attack. The warden would know the difference between a merfolk and a siren; they're trained to. Also, sirens are not found in these waters, and they don't hurl things at people's heads in order to enchant them; they sing."

She pinched the bridge of her nose and shook her head. "Rook, only you could think being hit in the head would be considered a form of enchantment."

"Hey! I wasn't suggesting it was a siren! I'm suggesting the warden was hit with a spell!"

Amelia was honestly surprised by the suggestion. "Wait. What's your thinking on this? They popped out of the water to enchant a random warden with a spell? Why would it hit them in the head like that?"

Joe shrugged. "We don't know the motivations of a lone merfolk, so there could be many reasons as to why. We also don't know how magic differentiates in functionality between water and land. Maybe there was a pressure difference that the merfolk didn't account for? It just hit harder than they expected it to because they hadn't compensated properly."

Amelia frowned in thought. She attempted to recall any classes that covered casting while underwater and couldn't remember anything concerning the concept. Joe's suggestion was actually plausible.

Howard tilted his head and stood a bit straighter. He seemed to be just as surprised by the suggestion as her. "Huh. That's certainly a plausible and interesting theory. I'll have to suggest it to the lead investigator." He turned and placed a hand on the door handle to the doc's office. "In the meantime, I suggest you both get something to eat and rest for the remainder of the day."

Amelia was about to reiterate that they had reports to finish when Howard pulled open the door. A cacophony of noise came down the stairs from the blue coats' bullpen.

Howard jumped from the sudden ruckus. "What in the blazes is going on up there?"

Chapter 9

The door to any given doctor's office was typically spelled with some form of muffling or noise cancellation. Privacy was respected, and a doctor needed to concentrate. Nobody wanted a slip-up, especially if a scalpel was involved. It explained why they hadn't heard any of the noise coming from the blue coats' bullpen until the door was opened.

There were muffled shouts coming from above, and the most notable sounded to be coming from Blue Coat officer Bob Johnson: "Jump 'im and hold 'im down! We don't need 'em floppin' like a fish on deck!" The man was a sailor before he turned to upholding the law, and he sometimes utilized the mannerisms of his previous trade.

The shouting was rounded out with grunting, cursing, and the sounds of a struggle. A chair rubbed violently across the wooden floor, and by the sounds of it, so did a desk.

Howard hurried out the door and tapped the butt of his staff against each step before ascending. It made for an interesting audible climactic click and clatter.

Amelia was in no immediate rush and wasn't even sure she could if she wanted to. Joe didn't look like he could rush if he tried.

He tried.

The idiot lunged and took two lumbering steps forward, went weak in the knees, shuffle-tripped, and tried to catch the door on his way down. He flailed and missed. Joe hit the ground in the doorway and grunted from the impact.

She cringed, shut her eyes, shook her head, and let out a disappointed sigh. "Do you ever stop?"

Joe let out a forlorn groan. "No…"

"You don't think that the Northwest's senior detective is capable of handling it?" She looked to the wall beside the doorway. "And you forgot your staff, you bumbling oaf."

He grunted in reply and simply lay there.

Amelia reached out to the wall beside the door and summoned her staff. It turned to a crystalline cloud of ice and snow before rematerializing in her hand. With her connection to her magic restoring, she was able to summon it and lean on its power.

Perhaps I can dry off?

She shrunk her staff into a wand and pointed the tip of it at her left arm. She first attempted to draw the moisture out of the sleeve of her blouse. If anything went wrong, the sleeve would suffer the consequences. Better safe than sorry.

Unfortunately, a curl of white smoke immediately appeared on the cuff. She released the magic, stuck her wand in her vest pocket, and slapped the cotton to put out any potential flares. The cloth was definitely dry and slightly browned. "Blast it!" She would undeniably have to wait for later.

Amelia pulled her wand from her pocket, released it back into a staff, and carefully stepped over Joe's prone form. Her staff acted as a bit of walking stick and source of stability, physically and mentally. It felt good to be back on two feet, no longer at the mercy of others.

Once safely out the door of the doctor's office, she turned and poked Joe with the butt of her staff. "Get up, we have work to do."

He grunted again and lazily waved her off.

It reminded her of that morning when Blueregard was trying to get her up for the day.

"You want the captain to catch you snoring on the job again?"

His head suddenly lifted up off the ground. "I'm up."

Thought so.

She used her staff for leverage and grabbed the rail to help pull her way up the steps. The exhaustion was down to her bones, and she needed to reserve every bit of energy she could.

By the time she had made it far enough up the steps to see what was going on, the struggle had ended. Tannen, Johnson, and a handful of other blue coats were all huffing and puffing. Howard was standing with his hand on the shoulder of Garrick Jenkins, the flower shop thief, who was sitting in a chair.

The thief looked to be the one that had caused the fuss. He was disheveled, his clothing all rumpled, and there was a sheen of sweat across his face. Fortunately, he was calm. The only reason he was calm was because Howard had him hypnotized and staring into the glass facets of his staff.

"He put up a thundering fight." Tannen was doubled over with his hands on his knees, breathing heavily.

Howard tilted his head a bit. "Why wasn't he in irons when you arrested him?"

Amelia answered, "I arrested him earlier today, and he was in irons." She turned her attention to the blue coats. "Bob… why was he out of holding?"

Johnson looked to be just as out of breath. His hands shook as he straightened out his mustache with his fingers. "The scallywag was pitchin' a fit and attacking the others." He took a deep calming breath and gestured to the lot of them. "We all had to jump 'im and drag 'im out of there before he killed someone."

"Well... I'm glad I was able to help. Can you handle him from here?" Howard patted Mr. Jenkins on the shoulder. The man was fixated and stared lifelessly into the colored glass of Howard's staff.

Bob nodded his head and lifted a pair of irons. "Soon as we clap these on 'im, we'll be good to go."

Tannen stood straight, took the manacles from Johnson, and stepped over to take Mr. Jenkins' wrists. He only managed get one wrist shackled. As soon as the band clacked shut, Jenkins broke free of the hypnosis.

She wasn't sure if she was seeing things, but she thought there was a flickering flare of red in his brown eyes.

"No! Let me go!" The would-be flower shop thief turned his attention immediately to her and screamed even louder. "NOOO! She's here! She'll freeze us all to death! The Ice Queen will kill us all!" He immediately began flailing and caught Tannen off guard.

The young officer whipped his head back and clapped a hand over his eye. "Ach! Blast it!"

Howard – naturally – reacted in an instant. He released his staff and slapped aside the flailing arms of Jenkins. Then he struck the edge of one hand directly into the shoulder and neck of Jenkins. The man went wide-eyed and momentarily stiffened. His eyes rolled into the back of his head and he limply toppled off the chair onto the floor.

Nobody bothered to try catch him from falling. So he hit the ground with a weighty *thump*.

Johnson stepped up to Tannen and put a hand on his shoulder. "Ye all right, boy?"

Tannen looked only slightly irritated. "Yeah, I'm good. He poked me in the eye with his finger. That's all." He removed his hand and blinked repeatedly while opening the one eye.

Johnson clapped him on the back. "Good ta' hear." The old man bent down, rolled Jenkins over, and finished clapping him in irons. "Now, let's get this deranged menace to a cell of his own before he wakes up."

Amelia had a few more questions. "Hold on."

Howard appeared to have the same concerns. "Wait."

They looked to each other. Or more specifically, she looked at him, and he tilted his head in her direction. Howard bowed respectfully and offered her the chance to go first.

She accepted. "I thought I saw a flicker in his eye as he was breaking free. I'm too exhausted to tell what, but there might be some magic at play."

"He shouldn't have broken free from my hypnosis to begin with," the half-fey detective looked exceedingly troubled. "I'd like to examine and question him."

"This isn't the first time he's mentioned you, Ms. Iceheart. He's been grumbling it all morning." Tannen was intermittently rubbing his eye and blinking it.

Howard turned his blind eyes and a raised eyebrow in her general direction. "Is that so?"

She had a different theory. "I don't think it's me he's afraid of."

Tannen frowned. "He looked right at you though."

"We came from a crime scene." They all turned to face the stairs. Joe was grunting and climbing his way up them. "Fire and ice were clashing there."

Amelia continued the train of thought. "The warehouse where the clash took place looked as though it could have been used as a greenhouse." She pointed to the unconscious and gangly form of Mr. Jenkins. "And I caught him frantically trying to rob a flower shop this morning… where he was asking about blood lotuses."

That raised all the eyebrows in the room.

"I think he is a survivor from the clash. I used ice magic to catch him this morning. It explains why he's terrified of me, and keeps saying we'll all freeze to death. His traumatized mind keeps connecting me to what happened to him earlier."

Howard returned to frowning. "That is certainly a sound theory, but I'd still like to know how he broke free of the enchantment I placed on him. Is there a room where we can hold him for questioning?"

Amelia nodded. "Of course." She turned to Johnson and asked, "Do you mind?"

The wiry old man grunted as he rolled Jenkins over onto his back. "Of course." He tipped his hat to her before turning to Tannen. "Some assistance?"

The young man's eye was a bit red and teary, but he looked no worse for the wear. Tannen nodded and got to helping. They managed to get the unconscious man to stand, then Tannen swung him over one shoulder.

Johnson dusted his hands off and introduced himself to Howard before suggesting the man follow. The three of them headed further back into the precinct, toward the solitary cells and interrogation rooms.

The remaining blue coats were already busy correcting their desks and picking up fallen stationary and knocked-over chairs.

Joe looked like he was ready to fall asleep where he stood. "Rook?"

"Huh?" He almost jumped to attention. "What? What is it?"

She couldn't help but empathize with the poor man. "Reports, then straight to bed with you."

He let out a longing sigh. "A bed sounds wonderful right now."

"Reports first."

He nodded in understanding, then looked up at the detectives' bullpen and let out a slight whine. "Why does there have to be more stairs?"

She couldn't help but smirk and throw in a jab. "You want me to carry you up the steps like a little baby?"

"Ha. Ha. Ha. Real funny." Joe slumped in the shoulders and took the brow beating as she had intended it: motivation.

The climb up the steps was worse than the climb from the doctor's office. The spiraling metal staircase was a bit narrower, and the stairs were a little steeper. One needed to lift their legs a little higher to climb each step. Joe slogged behind. She couldn't blame him; he was in far worse shape than she was.

Eventually, they made it and headed to their respective desks. She set aside her staff and hung up her trench coat and hat. As much as she wanted to change out of the damp clothing, she didn't have a spare set of undergarments, nor could she utilize any spellwork to switch out clothing.

With a moment to rest, and her watch telling her it was noon, she decided to grab a bite to eat. Amelia opened the bottom drawer of her desk and pulled out the arcane metal delivery box.

The box wasn't anything special. It was crafted in a production factory from thin sheets of metal. It was coated in a medium gray paint and was as large as a standard lunchbox. All the edges had been rounded off, and the hinges were of quality material. A dial on the front of the box was labeled with two settings: *Send* and *Receive*.

An identical box remained at her residence. Blueregard would prepare a meal at lunch time, place it in the second box, and set his dial to *Send*. Amelia would set her dial to *Receive*. The meal would transport between one box and the other. When she was done her meal, she could return the dishes to Blueregard by setting her dial to *Send*. The boxes were a common luxury among the middle and upper classes.

Amelia set her box on her desk and turned the dial to *Receive*. A hum of energy built from within the box. It quickly climaxed with a low and soft thump to the air. She flicked the latch and opened the box to a delightful surprise:

Blueregard had prepared her favorite.

Four sections of a delicate pork belly sandwich sat upon a white plate. She lifted it out of the box, and examined her meal. The bread was thin, light, and fluffy. The meat was moderately sliced, basted in a spiced peach glaze and topped with fresh greens.

Delightful!

An obnoxiously loud and satisfying groan emanated from the other end of the bullpen. Amelia glanced, only to immediately regret it. Joe was slumped in his chair and eating a military ration. There was a massive semi-circle chunk missing from the rusty brown slab.

A rite of passage at the Academy In the girls' dorm was to eat a piece of a military ration and not vomit. She passed… barely. It had a revolting taste and texture to it and sat in the stomach like a brick. As much as she hated it, it admittedly fed her and warmed her bones. There had to be some form of alcohol in it.

Seeing and hearing Joe revel in the ration nearly turned her off from eating. Thankfully, the smell of the spiced peach glaze and the warmth emanating from the meat immediately made her mouth water.

She hungrily devoured the first quarter of her sandwich, then set to organizing her desk so she could work and eat at the same time. Remembering her heating container, she pulled it from her trench coat pocket and greedily drank the hot tea to help wash down the sandwich.

Sadly, the events of the day required numerous pages of reports to be filed. She had to cross-reference her notes with Joseph's, detail her findings, and explain the decisions and subsequent actions. Since it was an open case, she would need to create a case file that herself, John, and Joe could all access and add their notes to. Thankfully, the sandwich and tea had reinvigorated her a bit.

In all, it took her most of the afternoon. By the time she finished, it was a little past three. Her clothes were drier than earlier, but every fresh movement reminded her of how damp they were. It left her in a sour mood.

She stood and gathered all her freshly-dried papers and prepared to take them to the captain when she turned to find Petals standing on a chair beside Joe's desk.

"Where have you been all day?" She shouted it a little louder than she needed to, but it felt necessary. They could have used his help in examining the crime scene and capturing the unknown puppet-handed suspect. She left her papers, marched over, and glared down upon the little gnome.

He slowly turned on the chair and looked slightly up at her with a sad half-smile.

She recognized the look on his face. It was not one of his usual smiles of mischievous glee. It was worry.

"I was chasing a lead, my dear." He was trying to sound amused, but she could hear the slight difference in his voice. He had been her training officer when she was first promoted to detective. She'd spent enough time with him to learn his more subtle expressions.

Amelia softened her tone and eased a little off the glare. "What lead?"

Petals turned to stand so that he could face them both. "I feared I knew who the fire-throwing menace may have been, so I paid a visit and investigated."

Joe asked before she could, "Who did you visit?"

Petals shook his head. "I swore to keep their secret, so long as they stayed out of trouble."

Amelia frowned in thought and tried to recall anyone that could possibly fit the necessary skillset. She couldn't think of anyone. "Sounds like this someone caused trouble before. How are you so sure it wasn't them, and why are you keeping their secret?"

Petals' fake half-smile turned to a dangerous glower. He raised a single finger and pointed it directly at her. "Ask nothing more."

She took an immediate step back while eying his finger. She knew exactly what he was capable of, and he was capable of so much more that she didn't know about. What she didn't know was what terrified her the most.

He took away the threat of the finger and crossed his arms while staring straight ahead. "I have good news and bad news."

Amelia and Joe exchanged a look, and Joe decided to ask first. "What's the good news?"

"It wasn't who I thought it was."

She inquired next, "What's the bad news?"

Petals' answer was slow in coming, and he looked all the more haunted by it. "It wasn't who I thought it was."

A distant clanging sound pulled their collective attention to the spiral stairs. Howard called out from below, "You need to come down here, immediately!"

She'd almost forgotten that he was still there.

Amelia turned and summoned her staff from her desk. Petals bounded off the chair and hurried to the steps in his effortless hop-step way. Joe picked up his staff and hurried to the steps as well. The three of them descended in a flourish.

Howard began marching and tapping his staff as he made his way to the back of the precinct and toward the solitary cells and interrogation rooms.

Petals picked up the pace in order to march alongside. "What did you discover, my friend?"

Howard continued to tap along with his chin tilted up and his ears guiding the way. "Wadnar, always good to see you again." He paused as he tilted his head slightly. "I fear I cannot say out loud. I'd rather not cause a panic."

That doesn't bode well.

The lot of them made it to the interrogation cells at the back of the blue coats' bullpen. The doors for those cells were solid riveted iron and framed in glowing arcane runes. Spell users or violent offenders were often thrown into those cells.

Whenever a cell was empty, the door remained open. Only one cell was shut. They didn't often have violent offenders or spell users thrown into holding.

Howard guided them to the one shut cell and gestured for the blue coat on guard to open it. The woman pulled a key from her belt and unlocked the door before stepping aside again.

Howard reached out and grabbed the door handle, paused, and spoke over his shoulder, "Before I open the door, I must warn you. Do not let him touch you, and do not get too close."

The hairs on the back of Amelia's neck stood on end.

This doesn't bode well in the slightest.

The senior detective grunted and heaved open the heavy door. Garrick Jenkins was inside, sitting on a chair in the middle of the room. It, however, was not the same Garrick Jenkins she had arrested that morning.

The man sitting in the room was screaming and thrashing in the chair. He was laughing, crying, cussing, and spitting. His eyes were flickering with an angry red magic, and he looked deranged.

"Oh, gods! I touched him earlier today! I arrested him!"

Howard nodded. "I know, I touched him too. I have all the blue coats that touched him in a private room. I'd suggest you join them until we can confirm you haven't been afflicted. I will join you shortly. I just wanted to bring this to the attention of Petals and Joseph."

She managed to peel her eyes off the thrashing and mouth-foaming menace that was once Jenkins and looked to Petals and Joseph. Petals was facing her and Howard. He was eyeing them both up and down with brilliantly glowing violet eyes. "There's no need to quarantine, you can release the others. There's no sign of it spreading by touch."

Howard looked like how Amelia felt: relieved. The man even let out a sigh. "Thank the gods."

"Joseph?" Petals turned to face their prisoner, placed his hands behind his back, and stood calmly.

"Yes?"

"Start praying."

"I– Uh– Why?"

"Because… he's corrupted."

Chapter 10

The term 'corrupted', in the arcane community, was never used lightly. Like a sickness, it could spread. It could move through many mediums and often circumvented conventional wards. Worse, it only ever responded to custom-made countermeasures.

Amelia's knowledge of such countermeasures was non-existent. Corruption was only vaguely mentioned in the classes she took at the Arcanum and only ever covered as a theoretical threat while at the Academy.

It was typical for Petals to act so casually while mentioning such a dreadfully frightening thing. One would find it to be irritating and think it a sign of immaturity. In truth, it meant he knew how to handle it or had experienced handling it before. Or… it meant he was trying not to cause panic and was just as terrified as the rest of them.

The air was sucked from the room as everyone within earshot immediately gasped and froze.

Amelia was no different. She gripped her staff

tighter and held her breath out of fear. Fear, that at any moment, something awful would spill out of the open cell door and damn them all.

Joe was the first to speak, and it nearly startled the life out of her. "Merciful Lord of Light!" he croaked a bit as he barked out the beginning of the prayer. Thankfully, he cleared his throat and eased into a quieter tone, "Protect us and guide us with your wisdom. Shelter us and shield us with your divine grace, and smite the wicked and cruel." He then lifted a finger and drew a circle around his chest, spread out his hand, and placed it over his heart.

She was raised in a fairly devote household and understood the nature of the gesture. Joe had drawn the sun around his heart and used his spread fingers to represent the sun's rays. It was the symbol of the god of light.

Not wanting to be left out, she did what she thought she'd never do again. Amelia drew the symbol on her chest and spread her hand out across her heart. When she looked around the room, she spotted several blue coats busy enacting their own whispered prayers and symbols of protection or copying Joe and Amelia. Howard had his eyes shut and looked deep in prayer as well. Petals was unmoving.

Mr. Jenkins continued to thrash as he had before. He spat, swore, twitched, kicked, and screamed.

"Blast it! It's not a demon!" Petals rounded on the spot while stroking his bearded chin.

Joe threw his arms up and gripped the hair atop his head. "Thundering fireballs!"

"Calm yourself, my boy!"

"Calm myself?" Rook turned his full attention on the little gnome, let go of his hair, and raised two fingers and his voice. "We only have two more possible causes of corruption and they're both worse than a demon!"

Amelia staggered back and quickly found a desk to lean against. "*Worse*? What do you mean *worse*? What could possibly be *worse* than a demon?" She lifted her staff and pointed it at Joe. "And how do you know so much about corruption?" Her heart was at a full gallop.

The implications of what they were dealing with were unreal. She never thought she'd ever deal with corruption or have a conversation in which demons were not the worst consequence.

Howard stepped between them and lowered her staff with the tip of his own. "Everyone needs to breathe, before we cause a greater panic than the one that is already started and gripping us all in terror. Rule number one!" He said it with a bit of a heavy breath. He was clearly just as frightened as the rest of them.

Joe shut his eyes tight and began murmuring something under his breath.

She remembered rule number one from her days at the Academy, it was drilled into every single cadet: *Don't panic.*

Easier said than done!

Joe took a few deep breaths and stood a bit straighter before finally answering her questions. "One of the classes I took at the Arcanum covered corruption. It was a theoretical class at best because corruption is far too organic of a problem."

He held up three fingers. "There are three source of corruption that the arcane community is aware of." He held up one finger. "Demonic corruption is the first, the most notable, and the easiest to handle. Demons require a great deal of leverage to push through into our world. Something as simple as saying the right prayer can deny them entry." Joe pointed to Mr. Jenkins. "He didn't even flinch when I prayed to the Lord of Light."

Amelia pointed her staff at the swearing and fidgeting man. "He's been doing nothing *but* flinching."

Petals interjected, "He hasn't flinched metaphysically. I've been watching. His aura hasn't changed. Whatever has him isn't demonic."

Joe pointed to Petals. "That's what I meant. If the corruption was demonic, we would have seen something much different."

"And the last two?" She didn't want to know but she had to.

He let out a deep sigh before answering under his breath, "A cursed object… or a witch."

Both possibilities caused her heart to sink. "By the gods." She sat back on the desk she had been leaning against and tried to steady her shaking.

Cursed objects were forged from the souls of the living. They were often created by powerful wizards or sorcerers that had gone mad, who invested themselves into an object. By doing so, a portion of who they were would possess the object and whoever touched it. Thankfully, cursed objects also tended to have specific weaknesses and flaws, just like people that crafted them.

Witches were walking nightmares. Their magic was not easily definable and even harder to defend against. Some in the magical community had speculated that a witch's spellcraft was somewhere between a warlock's and a wizard's.

Warlocks were little more than foolish idiots that made a pact or offering in exchange for access to the arcane. Typically, they were power hungry and lazy. They didn't bother to study the proper arts in order to best control what they were given. In truth, they usually wound up as little more than puppets to whatever entity granted them power.

It was believed that witches were somehow immune to being controlled, meaning they could make offerings or pacts in exchange for power and keep it without consequence.

Either Mr. Jenkins had touched a cursed object or he was corrupted by a witch's power. Neither possibility boded well for the man.

"We have to send out an alert to all other precincts and inform Central." Howard pulled his network box from his belt.

Petals hopped forward and put a hand on Howard's

arm. "Perhaps we should first inform the captain and allow him to utilize the proper channels. If the wrong people catch wind, it may cause the people of the city to panic."

When people panic, they tend to lose all sense of intelligence. Opportunists utilize that time of senselessness to strike. Looters and career criminals take their chances, and often get away with numerous crimes. Law enforcement gets too tied up with the panicked masses to notice purse snatchers or petty thefts. They all knew it, and it didn't need to be explained.

Howard lowered his network box and placed it back on his belt. "You're right, old friend."

Petals took charge. "Joseph, Amelia."

Joe stood a little straighter and gripped his staff as he looked down upon his training officer. Amelia slid off the desk and leaned on her staff for support.

"I need the both of you to finish up your reports and provide them to the captain. Then you are to immediately return to your domiciles and get rest. You're no good to me as drained as you are." He pointed to each in turn and gave them both stern glares.

Joe nodded, but he looked a bit more pale than he had earlier.

Amelia felt just as spooked and likely looked as pale. She desperately wanted to crawl into bed and pretend she hadn't heard anything about corruption, witches, or cursed objects. "Don't have to tell me twice."

Petals rounded on the spot and pointed at the cell. "Shut that door! I'm tired of his hollering!"

The blue coat that had mysteriously excused herself from standing anywhere near the cell jumped to attention and ran over to shut it. The screaming abruptly stopped as soon as the door slammed shut. Thankfully, it had been spelled with noise muffling.

It eased only a small portion of her terror.

"Fireballs." Joe let out a grumbling curse as he turned about.

Amelia quickly turned away from the cells to look where he was looking.

What more could possibly go wrong today?

She found herself confused by his foul outburst, as she couldn't see anything wrong. "Rook?"

He lazily lifted an arm and vaguely gestured. "We have to climb the stairs again."

~~

Despite their exhaustion, they climbed the stairs. Amelia had thankfully finished her report prior to the corruption discovery.

Joe looked sickly pale and exhausted. He slumped into his wobbly chair and breathed laboriously while hanging limp. He had been gassed by the climb. It would be a miracle if he could produce a legible report, let alone stay awake. Eventually, he got to work.

Petals and Howard went directly to the captain's office and shut the door.

Amelia cursed her luck. She had wanted to get in there first and hand over her report so that she could head home as soon as possible. Admittedly, their discussion was more important.

Thankfully, the two senior detectives didn't spend too much time with the captain. In all, they were only in there for ten minutes. As soon as they left the office, Amelia stepped inside and handed over the documentation. The captain thankfully dismissed her and told her to go home and get rest. He would review the report later.

She hurried as best she could and grabbed her coat, hat, staff, and heating container. A hearty swig of her warm tea helped reinvigorate her a small bit.

After pulling on her coat, she stuffed the container in her outer pocket. With her hair pulled free and her hat straightened, she headed for the stairs.

Petals waved at her from his desk and stopped her

momentarily. "Wait! Before you head out…"

She stopped and turned to him. "Yes?"

"Tomorrow morning, I want you to head straight to the warehouse crime scene and thaw out those corpses."

Amelia blinked and shook her head. "They're still frozen?"

Petals nodded. "Yes, the ice is apparently doing an effective job of insulating itself."

She nodded in understanding. "All right."

He lifted up a stack of heavy parchment papers on his desk. "And take these with you."

She frowned and made her way over to pick up the documents and examine them. "What are these?"

There was only a dozen, but the parchment was of a heavy weight. The top line read *Body Identification Form*. The fine print beneath the header outlined how it was to be used. Remains of the deceased were to be placed in the purple border box at the bottom of the parchment, and the arcane incantation for identification was to be read aloud.

"They are a recent addition to the law enforcement toolbox. You are to test them tomorrow and identify the frozen bodies." Petals had a half-smile. "With everything that is happening, we need all the information we can get, and as quickly as we can possibly get it." He was scared.

Who wouldn't be?

"I understand. I'll try to get these back as soon as possible."

He smiled a little more. "Very good." His attention turned to the bullpen and he frowned a little.

Amelia turned to see that Joe's head was down and tilted to the side. His hands were resting on the rune keys of his arcane mechanical typographer and there was a soft rumbling coming from his general direction. "Is he?"

Petals snapped his fingers, and Amelia jumped. She knew what it meant when that little menace snapped his fingers.

A brass horn appeared beside Joe's head, and a

bubble of water the size of a melon appeared a step above where he was seated. Amelia quickly dropped the parchment on Petals' desk and stuck her fingers in her ears.

With a second snap of the fingers, the horn began to loudly blow out the rhythmic and familiar tune of the Academy morning call. As much as she felt for the poor man, she couldn't help but stifle a snort when he screamed, comically flailed, and bolted upright to stand at attention and salute. The morning horn rhythm must have triggered some deeply-rooted memory of the Academy.

The floating melon-sized bubble of water burst over his head as he stood up into it. It drenched him in its deluge.

He gasped from the cold water and slowly turned on the spot to face them both, with a baggy-eyed glare.

Petals was outright beaming.

Amelia stifled a snort, snatched up the papers, and bolted for the stairs. As much as she loved watching him get pranked, she didn't want to be associated with those pranks. She felt that their working relationship was a little tenuous as it was.

The humorous reprieve from the dread of a witch or cursed objects being loose in the city was exceedingly short.

As soon as she began winding her way down the steps, she saw the tense state that the precinct was in. Support staff looked flustered and rushed to fulfill document requests. Blue coats were rushing out the door and shouting into their network boxes as they went. She hadn't seen it so busy or chaotic since the precinct had been besieged by an organized crime syndicate a few years prior.

Knowing that many of the precinct staff would be looking to the detectives and captain for guidance, support, and a sense of stability, Amelia did what she did best: she put on the guise of the ice queen.

Strength and confidence would help bolster those that were frightened. It didn't matter that she was just as terrified as the rest of them. She needed to show strength.

Amelia descended the rest of the steps with her

head held high, and marched out the precinct doors in order to head home.

Once she was down the block and around the corner, she sagged and prayed, "Goddess of Mercy, be with us."

She leaned more heavily on her staff and dragged her feet the remainder of the walk home.

The window in Mr. Greenthumb's Flower Boutique was boarded up, but customers stepped in and out of the shop as though it were a regular day.

At least his day is back to normal.

She stepped around a young man that was giddily marching his way out of the flower shop with a wrapped bundle of blue Stormbay dragon lilies. Clearly, he was out to surprise a lucky lady.

If only the people knew.

Not informing the public about the horrors that lurked about them every day was also a part of her job. Ignorance truly was a blessing.

By the time she made it back to her residence, it was nearing four in the afternoon. Not quite time for dinner. Blueregard might not have even returned from the grocer yet. She stepped into the entranceway of her building and slowly looked up the steps. "Blast it all."

For hopefully the last time that day, she begrudgingly climbed stairs. Her calves were burning by the time she made it to the top, and her thighs were aching. Having triumphed over the inanimate nemesis for the day, Amelia pulled her keys from her trouser pocket, unlocked, and opened the door.

Thankfully, Blueregard was home. The ever stoic man was wearing a white chef's apron and stirring something in a pot on the stovetop. "Early day, Ms. Iceheart?" He didn't bother to look in her direction. He didn't much need to, as he could clearly see her out the corner of his eye.

"Exhausting day, Blue." She leaned her staff in the corner, took off her hat, and hung it on the hook. She groaned as she shrugged off her coat. Everything ached. "I'm going to take a bath before supper." With her coat hung up, she turned to unfastening her gun holster and belt. Those too, she hung up. Once unburdened, she headed for her room.

Blueregard pulled the wooden spoon from the pot and tapped it on the edge before setting it aside. "And what of the letter?"

She'd forgotten about it. "Ugh." She stopped dead in her tracks and slowly turned to head back to her coat with her head hanging in defeat. "I had a colleague check it for traps; he said it's clean." A quick rummage through the pockets produced her heating container and the letter.

Another greedy gulp of tea proved to be a little helpful. She emptied it before handing it over to Blueregard. The letter, she took with her to her room. "I'll read this after my bath. I can't be bothered to devote my mind to it right now."

When the door to her room opened, she was greeted by a blanket of cool air. On any other day, she'd find it inviting. With damp clothes, it was slightly distressing. Amelia shivered and shut the door behind her before tossing the letter onto the bed.

Despite wanting to disrobe immediately, she needed to draw her bath. Otherwise she'd be standing naked and cold. She marched into the water closet and turned on the tap for a hot bath.

Once set, she returned to her room and pulled out dry clothes for the evening. The letter sat tauntingly on her bed. As much as she wanted to know what her family was up to, it could wait a few more minutes. Dinner wouldn't be ready for an hour or more yet, and she desperately craved warmth and cleanliness.

It didn't take long for the bath to fill, so she stripped and tossed everything but her vest into the hamper. A quick check in the mirror revealed a small bruise on her ribs. It was directly where the puppet-handed culprit and Howard had struck her. She frowned at it, but decided it was better to get into the tub and soak than stand and freeze.

The hot water was exactly what she needed from a very long day. It tingled against her flesh and gave her a happy shiver. She slid down into the waters and groaned a sigh of relief, as the day was finally almost over. At least, she hoped. There was still that damn letter.

Chapter 11

After a proper soak and wash, Amelia climbed out of the tub, toweled down, and slipped into her night gown and robe. She didn't have any intention of going out for the evening, even if Betty begged her. She tied her hair in a loose braid so that she would be ready for bed. It was going to be an early night.

She emptied her tub and went about cleaning up. Her spell-tome was returned to its lectern, and her detective's vest was hung up in the closet. The only thing that was left out of place was the damn letter.

Amelia grumbled and glared at it. Ignoring it could be just as disastrous as reading it.

After dinner.

She didn't want to spoil her appetite, and her family had a tendency to afflict her with an uneasy stomach.

Amelia snatched the letter off the bed and took it with her back to the kitchens. She opened the door and slipped out of the calm and cool sanctuary of her bedroom before shutting it behind her again. A rolling wall of cold air and mist followed her.

"Dinner shall be served shortly, Ms. Iceheart." Blueregard was busy stirring a pot on the stove and had his back to her. He didn't bother to turn his attention away from the pot or even lift his head as he spoke.

She breathed deeply through her nose to absorb the intoxicating aroma of spices. With letter in hand, she pulled out her chair and sat with a relaxed sigh. "What are we having tonight, Blue?" She placed the letter beside her place setting and crossed one leg over the other.

"Chicken and dumplings, ma'am." Blueregard made a deliberate sloshing of the spoon while stirring.

Her mouth immediately began watering. Blue made fantastic dumplings. Amelia shut her eyes and simply bathed in the aroma and calm atmosphere of the kitchen.

It's too calm.

"Where's Betty?"

"Ms. Hopper is dinning with her father this evening. Would you care for a cup of tea?"

That was odd. "Betty usually drags me to dinners with her father in hopes of introducing me to some new man she met or one of her father's newest workers. And yes, a tea would be wonderful."

Blueregard stopped stirring the pot and turned to open an overhead cupboard to grab a saucer and cup. "I informed Ms. Hopper of the letter you received and how you would appreciate a quiet evening to handle the stresses of a personal nature. Cream and sugar?"

You are a blessing of a human being.

"Thank you, Blue. And please."

Over the course of boiling the kettle, steeping the tea, and serving it, Amelia provided Blueregard with brief snippets of the difficulty of her day.

"Mr. Runewall sounds like quite the young man."

Amelia paused with the tea cup at her lips and turned a glare in Blueregard's direction. "I'm not dating

Rook. He's not my type."

He waved off the suggestion and turned around to return to stirring the pot. "Perish the thought, ma'am."

She took a sip of the honey blossom tea and let it soothe away some of the stress. She mulled over why he wasn't her type, came to a simple conclusion, and said it under her breath. "He's like the brother I would rather have had." Joseph was a saint in comparison to her brothers.

It was enough to catch Blueregard's attention, as he momentarily paused his stirring.

Wanting to shrug off and change the subject, she added in a relevant bit of gossip she had recently learned concerning the rookie. "Besides, he is dating a nurse."

That was also apparently noteworthy, as Blueregard paused from stirring for a moment. "Dinner is ready, ma'am."

Amelia set down her saucer and cup and gestured to the other end of the table. "Join me, Blue. We rarely dine together anymore." A detective often worked odd hours. She wasn't always home at a consistent hour, and it meant that Blueregard often dined with Betty or by himself.

He turned to her with a steaming bowl of soup and placed it before her. Afterward, he bowed in the style of the old court. "I would be honored."

Blueregard dished himself a bowl of soup, sat opposite Amelia where Betty usually sat, and dug in.

Amelia gave the spoonful a few happy hums and moans. The dumplings were soft, but held together well. The carrots still had a bit of snap to them, the chicken was spiced and tender, and the broth wasn't too heavy. Blueregard was even impressed enough by his own cooking to release a slight throaty grumble of appreciation.

She finished by sipping the last of her cooling tea.

"That was wonderful, Blue."

He stood from the table after dabbing his mouth, then collected her bowl, cup, and saucer to take to the sink. "Your praise is always welcomed, Ms. Iceheart."

With her place cleared, she couldn't help but dart a baleful eye to the letter. Joe had promised her that it wasn't harmful. He said he gave it a thorough examination and that it was clean of any harmful magic. He sadly wasn't aware of how harmful her family could be without magic.

Without any more time-wasting excuses, she picked up the letter, held it between her two hands, and snapped the wax seal. The crisp sound of breaking the seal was loud enough that it caused Blueregard to pause in his cleaning. He even glanced over his shoulder before returning to his duties.

The magic that surrounded the wax and letter came to life. Streams of red light swirled around her hands and disappeared as quickly as they had emerged. She unfolded the parchment and watched as black ink appeared across the page. The letter was longer than standard length and mostly contained fine print and irritatingly necessary details concerning names, titles, definitions, and typical legal jargon.

It was a contract that concerned the family estate and her annual allowance. It specified that she had one day from receiving the contract to contest it. If she did not contest it, then the newly-instated conditions of her allowance would be considered accepted and binding. It specified that the conditions had been outlined in the previous letter.

I burned that letter… blast it!

The bottom of the contract was spelled to present the remaining time in red ink. She had a little less than four hours left. "Blast it all!"

The letter must have been delivered while she was drinking herself into a stupor at the Anvilhearth funeral the night before. Blueregard had accepted it, and in her family's eyes, that constituted as 'received'.

She slammed the letter down onto the table and growled out her frustration. Blueregard paused his squeaky dish cleaning to inquire, "Do I need to call a cart, ma'am?" The last few times she had received word from her family, it had resulted in an impromptu visit to the estate.

"Yes!" She snapped it a bit more harshly than she had intended. Amelia pinched the bridge of her nose and sighed, "I'm sorry." Her stomach was already protesting.

Blueregard must have dried off his hands, because a dry, warm, and comforting hand patted her shoulder. "It is quite all right, my dear."

Amelia stopped attempting to pinch away the growing headache and looked up at the old man beside her. He almost never addressed her in the informal. In that moment, she saw the man behind the formality. He looked genuinely concerned for her wellbeing, and there was even a guarded look of anger behind it as well.

She patted his hand and gave a weak smile. "Go call a cart, I'll go get dressed."

Blueregard donned the formal armor once again, nodded in the affirmative, and turned for the main door; there was a crystalline network booth in the lobby. He looked just as regal and proper as he always did.

"And Blue?"

He paused and turned on the spot to face her once again. "Yes, ma'am?"

She had a feeling. "Get the coinpurse."

Blueregard raised an eyebrow and cocked his head slightly. "The one in the lockbox?"

Amelia nodded. "That one."

~~

Amelia dressed in fresh dry clothes and her detective's garb. She always wore it when facing her family. She needed to constantly remind them that she was an officer of the law, and any form of threats or harassment would be taken as a threat against an embodiment of the law. Sadly, it hadn't always been that way.

Blueregard didn't change. He never changed. He was consistently well-dressed and always ready for anything. She loved that about him.

Thankfully, they didn't wait long for the cart to arrive. Despite it being the evening, it was still light out and the sun still had a few more hours before it set.

Amelia dropped the appropriate coin into the tray and gave the address. "Bloodstone Estate."

The driver looked into his rear mirror. "Ma'am?"

She glared right back at him. "You heard me the first time, and I am short on time and patience!"

"Yes, ma'am!" The little gnome slapped his foot on the accelerator and they took off with a bit of a jolt.

Blueregard barked from the seat beside her. "Preferably alive and in one piece!"

The driver eased off the accelerator a little, but seemed to be speeding the cart along at a faster clip than she usually experienced. It was somewhat understandable, given the destination. No driver wanted to be known for being the bearer of a late guest to a noble's estate, especially a guest of the Bloodstones.

Amelia settled in for a long ride. Her family's home was on the east end of the city, near the outskirts. It would take them an hour and a half to get there, at the very least. As long as the driver knew the best route, that was.

Fantastic, an hour and a half to rack my nerves.

Blueregard placed a stack of papers on her lap. "Today's letters of news, ma'am."

She looked to him and genuinely smiled. "Thank you, Blue."

He offered a brief nod in acceptance of her thanks.

As she expected, the cart chase involving Joe and Amelia had made it into the news. There were several letters that covered it. None of them had any of the details correct, and most of them were only guesses at best. *The Red Lightning Gazette* – a fabrication of the worst fiction – painted Joe and Amelia as renegade law enforcement officers that had deliberately lured innocent civilians into the alley so that they might attack and incapacitate the denizens of the Boulevard for some sick form of personal satisfaction. She couldn't help but audibly scoff at the absurdity of it.

The Stormbay Ledger covered the incident in a far more factual manner, with no theories or guesses as to why or what happened. It was a far more reputable source of news. It also had exclusive coverage of the first merfolk appearance in decades. Several letters covered the typical city crime bulletins.

Her arrest of a flower shop thief didn't even make the list. Yet it was possibly the most disturbing arrest that had been made that day.

Good. Word hasn't gotten out about the corruption.

She slowly made her way through each letter, engrossing herself in the city's events. "The Stormbay Thunderclouds have made it to the semi-finals, it seems."

Blueregard turned his attention to the uninteresting scenery out the passenger window. "Have they now?"

She was ribbing him; he cheered for the Pirate Captains.

A few of the letters had stock numbers circled in red ink. Blueregard had done it for her so that she might more easily spot those that she had a vested interest in. The numbers were mostly positive.

Once her perusing was finished, she checked her watch. There was still an hour left to go. "If I could sleep, I would. I'm absolutely exhausted." Having said as such, she began to yawn.

Blast it all. I need my wits about me.

"Take a nap; I shall wake you before we arrive, Ms. Iceheart."

She didn't know if she could, but as she attempted to say so, another yawn struck. "I – haaaawww – all right." Amelia curled up a bit against the side door, used her arm as a pillow, and tilted her hat over her eyes.

Surprisingly, she slept. Pure exhaustion overcame the anxiety and dread of seeing her family again. Unsurprisingly, the nap was too short.

Blueregard gently nudged her awake. "Ms. Iceheart,

we are a few minutes from the front gates." He said it in a hushed tone to not startle her.

Amelia groaned and stretched as she sat upright and fixed her hat. She blinked the weariness from her eyes. It wasn't quite sundown, but it was growing nearer. She quickly checked herself in a pocket mirror to make sure she was still presentable and not a mangled corpse.

Well enough.

Afterwards, she checked her watch.

Plenty of time left.

Amelia peered out the window to get her bearings, and noted that the cart was quietly rumbling and crunching along a long pea-gravel road. It was Goldbank Row. The richest of the rich had estates along the road. All of them faced westward toward the ocean with their gardens and stables on the back end. Each house they passed had grounds that covered two city blocks at the entrance and far more stretching back. Hedges and gates blocked the view of the houses from the road. They were traveling southbound toward her family's estate.

Due to the downward slope from east to west, the eastern homes had a better view of the city and the bay. The Goldbank Row estates had some of the best views. The only thing better was the view from the king's palace. It towered over all other structures, naturally.

Her family's estate was blocked from view by a brick wall. It was topped with iron speartips and blanketed in a thick growth of poisonous thorny vines – not uncommon. The Greenhills had animated whipping bushes guarding their grounds. None ever managed to sneak through to the main house without screaming from a sudden whipping.

The gate to the Bloodstone Estate was heavy iron painted a deep crimson. The gnome cart pulled up short of it, and the driver tipped his hat to them both. "Sir, ma'am."

Amelia took in one last deep breath before donning her icy glare and following Blueregard out of the cart. Like the gentleman he always was, he held open the door for her and offered his hand.

As soon as they were both free from the cart, it sped off. The driver didn't want to spend any more time on Goldbank Row than was necessary. The families in the high end of town could afford advocates of the best regard. That often meant injustices were disregarded as 'unfortunate accidents'. Amelia didn't begrudge the little man for wanting to make an expedient exit. She honestly wished she could do the same.

She shut her eyes and turned toward the gate entrance. When she opened them, she was immediately assaulted by the sight of a yellow-toothed grin from the other side of the gate. The man belonging to that lecherous grin looked just as grimy and detestable as the teeth.

His head was protected by a bowl of a helmet and his green long coat was made of wool with leather patches on the elbows. A long-barrel was cradled between his arms. It was not a design she had ever seen before, so she guessed it to be a custom make. The spy-glass affixed to the top suggested he was good with distance shooting. His gloves were fingerless for touch sensitivity. His trousers were padded with leather and fitted with deep pouch pockets, and his black double-button vest was lined with metal plates. A thick leather belt held a minimum of three knives and several rounds of various ammunition types. The man was a mercenary for hire.

"Open the gate. I'm expected." She wanted to get it over with and get away from Mr. Ugly Teeth.

"Well, well, well... don' you look perdy." He had an accent that placed him as having grown up near the Spineridge Mountains, far on the eastern borders of Greencoast.

"I said—"

"I heard what you said, honey bun." He looked her up and down in a leering way. It made her feel ill. "How 'bout you give us a twirl?" He lifted one hand and spun his finger about while grinning.

There was no thought process, no calm calculation or pause to threaten. There was only action.

Amelia's staff responded to her call. From a compressed wand in her vest pocket, it disintegrated into a fine crystalline dust and rematerialized in her had. She pointed the tip of it at Mr. Ugly Teeth's head and released her climbing fury with a guttural scream.

The man was violently slapped to the ground by a compressed gust of wind. She pulled back on her staff and hauled the excuse of a human up off the ground. He let out a clipped scream as Amelia yanked him toward the gate. He dropped his long-barrel and stumbled toward them on a gust of wind, stopping just short of slamming into the gate.

Amelia reached through the upright bars and gripped him by the collar in order to haul him close. "I am a detective of the Stormbay law enforcement, youngest child of the Bloodstone bloodline, and expected guest! You will step aside and allow us entry!"

Blueregard stepped to her side and placed a calming hand on her shoulder. He was warning her not to take it too far.

Amelia released the man and pushed him away from the gate. He stumbled back, tripped on his long-barrel, and fell onto his back again.

Blueregard did the honors of flipping the gate latch and pushed open one of the gates. He strode through with his hands clasped behind his back, turned on the spot, and stepped up to Mr. Ugly Teeth.

The man cowered and covered his head with his forearm as if expecting a beating.

Blueregard said nothing. He simply stood there and glared down upon the man so that Amelia could walk past uninterrupted. She made her way down the long pea-gravel path toward the house, and didn't bother to look back.

The only good thing that resulted from the encounter was that she was finally in the proper mindset to deal with her family – furiously angry.

Chapter 12

The Bloodstone Estate had been with her family for several generations. Prior to her family's ownership, it belonged to another noble house and likely another before that. It was crafted from stone and mortar and was a cool slate-gray color.

As it was with many of the older buildings in the country, the stone was brought from the Spineridge Mountain's quarry. The tile roof was modern and made from red clay. The trim and molding around the doors and windows was oil-treated red pine. The overhang from the roof was substantial and it left a brooding shadow over the front doorway. In a storm-laden country, it was common for large overhangs, but they were usually offset by welcoming lanterns.

There was no welcoming lantern; there was nothing welcoming about the Bloodstones' estate. An adult dragon's skull was mounted over the front doorway. Even as an adult, it unnerved her. That was precisely the point of it being there; it was designed to make guests feel uneasy. 'The best deals are made when the other party fears your power' was the motto of her father and his father before him.

She wished she could say that she hadn't adopted such mentalities, but they had been beaten into her, and it tended to spill out from time to time.

Prior to the front entryway, there was a pea-gravel roundabout. It was originally meant for horse-drawn wagons to pull up and out again. Carts had since replaced the wagons.

At the center of the loop was a statue of men at arms. There were six of them. Three men knelt at the front and held up shields while pointing spears at the front gate. The two behind them were archers with arrows drawn. The last man looked to be a commander, shouting some form of battle cry while pointing an outstretched sabre. All of them were adorned in ancient armor and helmets. There was no shortage of intimidation for incoming guests.

She had almost made her way past the statues when two green and leather clad mercenaries ran up to her from either side. Their long-barrels were held at the ready with the hammers pulled back. They weren't yet pointing, but the threatening nature of their stances was clear. One was a man and the other a woman. The woman raised her hand and shouted, "Halt! Ident–"

"Law enforcement!" Amelia flashed her badge at the mercenary and glared at the woman as she walked by. Thankfully, they immediately lowered their weapons and apologized.

She clipped her badge back on her belt just as she reached the stairs when Blueregard rejoined her. He had clearly finished intimidating the sniveling Mr. Ugly Teeth.

"Your family never employed mercenaries before today. Something has them on edge."

The question as to why there were mercenaries hadn't yet made it to the rational part of her mind; she'd been too busy fuming over the lecherous man at the gate.

With the question in mind, she couldn't help but divert some attention to ponder it. Had her family known about the corruption at the precinct? She knew that they were resourceful and well-informed, but it was unlikely that they would learn of such a thing and hire mercenaries so quickly.

What could they possibly fear? Me?

It only took a half moment of consideration. They could very well have hired the mercenaries to protect them from her. She had killed Father after all.

Amelia stopped before the door, and Blueregard stepped forward to push it open for her. He gave it a shove, but it refused to budge. He grunted and tried again. "They locked the doors!"

Blueregard stood straighter than she'd ever seen him stand. He puffed up his chest and hammered his fist on the door in a rhythmic thundering. She could only imagine the noise it caused within, likely loud enough to wake the dead. The slamming of his fist didn't cease until they heard shouting and the locking mechanism grinding and clacking.

When the door finally opened with a weighted flourish, a young man with a well-waxed mustache shouted, "What do you want?" He was dressed in a deep crimson jacket and slacks. His vest, shoes, and gloves were black, and his button-up shirt was starched white. Clearly the man was the newest house servant. Crimson was the color of the family crest and subsequently the servants.

Blueregard scoffed at the rudeness with which he was addressed. He took a calming breath and attempted to calm his emotions and rise above the affront. "We are expected." He fixed his vest and cuffs, then bowed and gestured to her as a means of introduction. "Ms. Amelia Iceheart."

The man quickly glanced to her, then back to Blueregard and sneered, "Am I to be impressed?"

Blueregard snapped to attention and ground his teeth. "You are to announce our arrival, you dim-witted savage!"

The man tilted his nose up and looked down upon Amelia. "Why would I announce the arrival of a lowly servant and a witch?"

SMACK!

Blueregard had stepped up and backhanded the servant with as loud a slap as any Amelia had ever heard; it even echoed off the walls of the main entryway. The strength of it nearly knocked the man off his feet.

He let out an indignant scream of pain and irritation, "You struck me!"

A voice called out from further down the hall. "Consider yourself lucky!" It was Samuel, her eldest brother.

Amelia peered past Blueregard and the servant to see her brother approaching. He was as tall as Joseph, perhaps a touch taller, but not quite as broad-shouldered. He had dark hair, cropped and cut extremely short, and haunting blue eyes. The eyes were a family trait.

The man never smiled. There were no laughs or jokes. He was as flatly serious as their father had been. He was a military man. Unfortunately, he also took to the drink, just like Father did.

Samuel was dressed in black trousers, a white button-up, and suspenders. His military jacket must have been discarded in favor of the glass he held in hand. Great care was taken to distance the military uniform from the act of imbibing. He referred to drinking as 'digging into the hole that soldiers never crawl out of'. She didn't know how many glasses deep he was, but she didn't want to stick around when he started to sound like their father.

The house hadn't changed. The same paintings hung on the walls and the same pottery and busts sat on marble pedestals. The area carpets were bright red, and the floors were dark-stained hardwood.

Samuel stepped beside Blueregard and glared down upon the servant while calming declaring, "Had you said anything worse, he may have decided to kill you." He sloshed his drink, then downed the rest of the glass before clearing his throat. "If I catch you again using such language against my sister, I'll do it myself." He was a hypocrite. He had called her such things before and worse.

Blueregard loudly cleared his throat. "Threatening a man, any man, in the presence of the law—" he gestured to Amelia, "—is an unwise decision.

Samuel calmly retorted, "Shut it, old man."

Blueregard turned and squared off against Samuel and growled, "That's 'sir' to you, boy!"

Her brother simply scoffed, turned, and headed back the way he had come. "You're not a soldier."

"Using 'sir' is a courtly courtesy, and I was defending king and kingdom when your *father* was but a boy!" She'd always presumed that Blue had been a soldier, but she'd never heard him admit it aloud before.

Samuel hollered from the other end of the hall while turning into the dining room, "And now you're an old man, old man!"

Amelia sighed and stepped into the front entryway. "Quite done shaking sticks at each other?"

Blue narrowed his eyes at the dining room doorway. "I'll never be done with that boy. There is more ego and hot air to him than common sense."

"Let's get this over with, shall we?"

The servant remained at the door and rubbed his cheek while grumbling under his breath. She could have sworn she heard him mutter "witch" once more, but he was none of her concern.

Amelia marched onward. The halls were dimly lit by candlelight. It was primitive and costly to keep such lighting, but that was the way her family preferred things.

"Magic is evil," as her father and grandfather had said endlessly. They had been anti-mage and refused any advances in the technological world. It didn't take brains to guess how her family viewed her skill and schooling.

Amelia passed the grand staircase on her right and the kitchens on her left as she walked down the hallway. The dining room was at the end of the hall on her right. It was just past the kitchens, and was large enough to seat thirty guests or more.

Blueregard trailed behind her with his head on a swivel the entire way. "Are you nervous, Blue?"

"I'm merely weary of mercenaries, Ms. Iceheart." He was often on edge whenever they visited the estate. It wasn't the first time her family had been hostile. The time before last, they had somehow *forgotten* to mention the wild wolf that had managed to *sneak* its way in through the back door.

Blast them all to the darkest of frozen hells.

She hadn't fully recovered from her exhausting day. Expending what she did on Mr. Ugly Teeth had been recklessly foolish and wasteful. There wasn't much left of her will to take on anything else that might suddenly surprise them.

Blast myself!

"Thank you, Blue."

"You're always welcome, Ms. Iceheart."

She stepped to the doorway into the dining hall and stopped to take it all in. Her mother was seated at the far end of the table, dressed in a crimson button-up dress that covered her to the chin. It was of an old fashion and did nothing to flatter her. She wore no makeup or earrings and kept her graying ebony hair in a tight bun at all times. She sat on the edge of her seat, as she always did. The woman couldn't sit still for half a minute and exhibited it in her constant scanning of the room. If something even potentially looked out of place, she glared at it, then set to fixing it.

Amelia wondered how many times her mother had stood up and fixed the positions of the antique plates that were on display in the glass cabinets that lined the room. She also wondered if that was why Samuel was drinking.

Samuel had inherited Father's habit of controlling the room. If things weren't acting or moving on his orders, then it was an irritation. Irritations were handled by beating them into submission, or drinking and then beating them into submission.

Marvin was another matter entirely. He had the same dark hair and haunting blue eyes, but he grinned at almost everything. Everything was amusing to that man. It was ever unnerving. He looked as though he could laugh while committing the most heinous of crimes. She wasn't entirely sure that he hadn't. Mother and Samuel often kept Marvin on a short leash and always seemed to fuss over something he had done.

Amelia had investigated her brother on many occasions, but he proved to be slippery as an eel. His records came back clean every time. She also never managed to find him whenever he went out at night.

Unlike their mother or Samuel, Marvin held no employment, occupation, or hobby. He dressed plainly in a tan button-up and a crimson vest and slacks. His hair was always a tussled greasy mess, and his clothes were always a bit dirty. Whenever she asked him what he did all day, he would just grin in his bone-chilling way.

Mother sat with her hands clasped, Samuel had a refilled glass in hand, and Marvin focused on cleaning his fingernails with a small knife.

Only Mother looked to her. "Sit." She said it as though Amelia was a dog that could be ordered into doing so.

"No." Their interactions usually devolved into direct conflict within the utterance of the very first word. Amelia turned her attention to the rest of the dining hall. "Where is Andrew?" Her twin brother was usually the first to arrive at family gatherings.

"He is busy." Samuel had spoken with his glass halfway to his lips.

Odd… you never speak on Andrew's behalf. You always look down on him.

"Where is he?" She didn't like being lied to.

"Busy! Get the witchery out of your ears and listen!"

Mother failed to understand anything about magic and used it as the excuse for anything she perceived that Amelia had done wrong.

As usual, she ignored the intended insult and stepped into the room. Blueregard followed her inside and took up post beside the doorway. "You sent me a binding agreement that demanded I be here if I wished to contest it. I'm here for precisely that reason. Now where is the agreement?"

Her mother smirked in the most insidious of ways. "It's not here; it's with the advocate. You're too late, and you have to suffer the consequences of your laziness." She sneered out the last of it and crossed her arms while glaring.

Amelia furiously pulled the binding document from her coat pocket and slapped it onto the table. "I still have one hour and twelve minutes left." She glanced back at the document and frowned in confusion.

That can't be right… I should have less than that.

"Incorrect."

Amelia jumped a bit and turned on the spot to face the door. Edward King Law stood in the doorway. The private advocate had a leather satchel in hand, and he looked exhausted with slumped shoulders and bags under his eyes. He was a tall man with a wire-thin mustache and well-combed and oiled hair. Usually he turned his nose up, but he looked far too tired to bother.

Oh, merciful goddess. Please not him.

She hated Edward, and often spat his name whenever he came to the precinct. The man represented some of the vilest of criminals and safe-guarded them from just punishment. Having thought that, it then made sense that he would be her family's advocate.

Mother screeched, "Why are you here?"

"I am your advocate!" He snapped it with equal measure to mother's screech. Edward turned and huffed as he straightened his dark navy blue vest over his seaweed green button-up. "Ms. Iceheart." He said it with certain iciness, but it was boxed within the frame of a respectful greeting.

Amelia raised an eyebrow and restrained herself from vomiting his name. "Edward."

He breathed in, shut his eyes, then breathed out as he opened them again. He was clearly continuing to struggle to maintain civility. "The countdown on your document ceased the moment you stepped foot on the Bloodstone Estate grounds."

That explains the discrepancy in my calculations.

"WHAT?" Mother shot up out of her seat and furiously scowled at Edward. "This is outrageous! She should be bound by the new–"

Edward slammed his leather satchel on the dining table. "NOTHING!" He flared at the nostrils and looked wild-eyed. "She will be bound by nothing until I say it is so!"

Amelia imagined her own eyes rather enlarged. She'd never seen the uptight advocate lose his calm in such a manner.

Samuel shot up out of his chair, wobbled, then steadied himself. "Watch your tone with my mother!" He pointed with his drinking glass and sloshed some of his drink onto the table. He looked down at the mess he made and grumbled, "Blast it."

Blueregard looked like he was ready to pounce at any moment and haul Amelia from the room.

Marvin sat back in his chair and grinned wickedly while playing the knife around his fingers. He was clearly enjoying everything, as he usually did.

This seems about normal.

Amelia dared to try and steer the conversation back to something productive. "What are the new conditions?"

Edward jerked his head in her direction and furrowed his brow. "Did you not receive them?"

She felt a bit sheepish for saying it, but there was no point in lying. "I purposefully burn any documents *they* send me." She pointed at her mother and two brothers upon the emphasized "they".

He turned his entire body and directed his wrath upon her in wide-eyed hysterics. "You burned a legal parcel?" His voice was nearing his mother's screech.

Amelia was not one to be shouted down upon, so she raised her finger, jabbed him in the chest, and pushed him back. "No! I never received any legal parcels! Not from *them*! Not from *you*! Not from *anyone*!"

Her mother suddenly sat down and looked distantly across the table at nobody in particular. She was caught; she was guilty, and she knew it.

Edward's eyes got even bigger. He spun on the spot and turned his full ire on the family. "You didn't send a legal parcel?" If his hysterical screaming escalated any higher, he was bound to burst and injure himself.

Mother kept her chin held high and maintained her façade of silent innocence.

Samuel stared into his glass, took a gulp to finish it, and burped under his breath.

Marvin continued to enjoy the show as little more than a spectator. He never involved himself in family affairs, but he always stuck around for the legendary shouting matches.

Edward growled, picked up his satchel in both hands, and repeatedly slammed it upon the dining table like a deranged madman. It took a minute, but he eventually vented himself of his frustration. In a breathless huff, he threw his satchel down upon the table, pulled out a seat, and slumped into it.

Amelia watched as the man took several deep breaths and gathered himself. Once he was a bit more settled, he pulled a comb out and straightened his hair. A tug here and there straightened out his vest and button-up. "Shall we?" He sounded far more relaxed than when he had stepped into the room.

"Go on." Amelia remained standing, as she didn't feel like sitting at the same table as her family or the twisted advocate.

Edward took a glance about the table and paused to count out each of them. "Where is the other brother?"

Mother replied, "Busy."

Edward turned a glare upon Mother and patiently waited.

Mother said nothing more.

Edward picked up his satchel in preparation to stand and leave.

"Fine! He's auditing a boat's ledgers!" Mother snapped it.

It wasn't uncommon for Andrew to be auditing the ledgers of the boats that their family invested in. They made the majority of their wealth on trade goods, and Andrew was good with numbers.

Edward remained standing, "Which boat?"

"Why do you care?" Mother narrowed her eyes at him and glanced at Amelia.

"I have to handle his allowances just as I handle theirs." Edward gestured to Samuel and Marvin.

Mother sneered and finally spat out the name, "*Ladysong!*"

Was that so hard, Mother?

The advocate accepted that answer, sat back down, straightened his clothes out once again, took a deep breath, and began with outlining the boring details.

Most everyone in the room ignored the fine print. None of them cared; it did little more than name people, places, and accounts.

The private advocate looked about the table to see if anyone objected to what he had iterated. Nobody did. "Very well." He thumbed through the stack and stopped once he reached a page he deemed relevant. "Section five of allowances. Ms. Amelia Iceheart."

She turned to look over the advocate's shoulder and down upon the document so that she might try and read ahead to the altered portions.

Edward's finger began running along the bottom of the newest addition as he read aloud, "In order to continue receiving your allowance, you must cease all occupational activities, reclaim your birth name, wed, and denounce all arcane activities before the next moon."

Amelia scoffed at such a ludicrous demand.

Her mother looked like a hungry wolf about to eat a scared rabbit. "We already have a suitor for you."

"And if I refuse?"

Her mother didn't flinch or look worried; she clearly expected Amelia to give into the unreasonable and bigoted demand.

Edward lowered his finger to the next paragraph and continued reading. "Should the recipient refuse the conditions provided, then they must repay all allowances that have been provided since her age-day, including interest."

"What is the total?"

Edward moved his finger and pointed to a figure in the corner of the page. "Four gold marks, three gold coins, two silver half marks, one copper mark, and fourteen copper coins, to be precise."

His mother grinned all the more.

Exactly as I had estimated. Good. I want to go home to get some sleep.

"Blue?"

Blueregard pulled the purse from his inner vest pocket and tossed it onto the dining table. It struck with a heavy, satisfying, and jingling clank of coin.

Amelia turned to Edward; he looked exhaustively unimpressed. The man casually reached across to grab the purse so that he might begin counting the contents.

Her mother looked mortified, broken, and stunned. She didn't believe what she was seeing.

Samuel wobbled to stand and kept trying to blink the drink from his eyes as he stared at the coin purse as it was upended. The exact coinage that Edward had spoken aloud dumped out onto the table.

It didn't take long for her family to realize what had happened. Amelia had just bought her freedom. The looks on their faces made the day almost worth it.

Chapter 13

Despite it being her greatest desire, she couldn't just leave. There were papers to sign. A great... many... papers.

Merciful goddess, spare me from this tedium.

Edward would place one document before her, then another. He assured her that there were no loopholes, pitfalls, or clauses that could possibly be utilized against her. The fine print was clear and nothing was hidden in it.

If there was one thing she could be assured of, it was that Edward knew the law and took it seriously. He knew how to manipulate the system in order to keep deep-pocketed criminals from seeing the inside of a cell; but he never broke the law to do it. He never took bribes, never misfiled a document, and never stepped beyond his means when representing a client. When he said the agreement was clean, she believed him.

She asked how he had known that she was at the residence; he explained that the notice Amelia had received was bound with certain incantations that would notify him of her arrival. He had arrived so quickly because he had been visiting next door.

Mother was profoundly irritated by that. She had a hatred for the neighbors. Amelia never understood why. All Mother ever said was that they were "not the right kind of people."

Amelia figured that there was no "right kind of people" as far as her mother was concerned. If she ever said there was, she feared for what kind of people they might be.

Edward remarked in a growling tone that he would have arrived earlier, but he was indisposed by a yellow-toothed ruffian that stood at the front gate.

At that pronouncement, Samuel began drunkenly marching off while slurring and hollering, "SULLY!" She could only guess that Mr. Ugly Teeth was named Sully.

Mother fumed throughout the entire signing process. She had never thought that Amelia could produce the necessary funds to pay back the allowances she had accumulated through the years.

Marvin, strangely, sat in stunned silence. He was devoid of his usual sadistic grin and looked a bit haunted. He had stopped playing with his knife and stared unblinking as Amelia signed away her rights to future allowances. He seemed to come back to life again when he noticed her staring at him. A fake grin replaced his usual one. She never understood him and didn't have any interest in trying to.

"Here." Edward pointed to a small square of arcane blue runes. With his other hand, he offered her a pin.

Amelia knew what was needed of her, but felt slightly unnerved by it nonetheless.

Fine.

She quickly pressed her thumb onto the needle and pierced the skin. Resisting the urge to suck on her thumb, she quickly mashed it into the box of blue arcane light and sealed her fate.

The blue arcane letters burst alight with new energy, then slowly faded.

"Congratulations, Ms. Iceheart. You are no longer financially dependent on funds from the Bloodstone Estate."

Amelia said nothing, nodded in acknowledgement, and turned to leave.

"Amelia!" It was her mother.

She turned and looked to the woman that had abused her throughout the earlier years of her life and raised a quizzical eyebrow.

What could you possibly say that would ever make up for all you did?

Mother looked like she was in the thralls of possibly experiencing a remorseful emotion. Her brow knitted, and her eyes were slightly watery.

A brief breath of guilt touched Amelia's heart.

Her mother breathed into steady herself and turned stone-faced, "Get out of my house, you hexing wench!"

The brief breath of guilt was dead in less than a heartbeat.

Edward collected his things and marched past Amelia and Blueregard. He was either in a hurry to leave and was tired of dealing with their family or desperately wanted to avoid the icy glares that Amelia and her mother shot at each other.

Many vile and unholy slurs came to mind, but none of them would do her any good. None of them would ever be able to truly convey how much she despised and hated the woman.

Blueregard broke the silence with a deep clearing of his throat.

Amelia glanced up at the man. He stared forward, as though he hadn't said or suggested a thing.

"And you!" Mother turned her ire upon Blueregard.

Blueregard went wide-eyed and rounded on the spot. He squared off his shoulders and puffed up his chest, "Shut it, you old bag!"

Amelia blinked a few times and repeated the words in her mind. She couldn't honestly believe that he had just uttered such a thing.

Mother gaped, "How–"

"I dare!" He growled it as he glared daggers at her. He was so worked up that his nostrils were flaring. "I served your family with distinction and honor for several decades!" The veins in his neck stood out with the intensity of his words. "I never once spoke an ill word of you or your late husband, when the gods knew I should have!"

"I–"

"I am Humboldt Thandle Blueregard! I am Oath-sworn, and you cannot sully my name with your vile tongue!" He finally took a deep and calming breath. "So says the gods."

The entire estate shook with a violent crash of thunder. It was so powerful and loud that it left her ears ringing and her whole body was quaking.

Amelia jumped and clung to the doorframe out of fear that the building might suddenly collapse about them. Her heart leapt in a full gallop. She was suddenly very terrified of the man that she could always count to be there for her and on her side, even against her own family.

Her mother had collapsed to the floor and was gripping the table leg with white-faced and wide-eyed terror.

Marvin's chair was toppled over, and all she could see of her brother was a nose and a pair of wide eyes peering over the edge of the table.

Oath-sworn! You're an Oath-sworn?

Oath-sworn were said to be those that had taken an oath – a vow – before the gods, and the gods had accepted it. Few existed, and they were usually individuals that had earned a great deal of respect and fear.

Rumor around the precinct was that Joseph had baited the gods into smiting him if he acted dishonorably. While impressive, it didn't mean the same thing. He had technically drawn a target on the top of his head, while Blueregard had sworn an oath that the gods accepted as a fact of the 'verse. They were distinctly different things.

144

Her servant and lifelong friend was an Oath-sworn, and she had no idea. By the looks of it, her mother had no idea either.

The thunderous crack that shook the house slowly rumbled off into the night, and the four of them were left in a deathly chilling silence.

Blueregard wiggled his jaw, fixed his vest, and let out a huff of a breath. He acted as though his outburst had been nothing more than a momentary lapse in decorum. He spotted Amelia hugging the wall and bowed deeply in the traditional style. "My humblest apologies, Ms. Iceheart. I truly hope you will never have to witness such a thing from me again."

She eased off from gripping the wall and tried her best to straighten herself out and shrug off the frightening display that was forever burned into her mind.

What did you swear, old man?

Blueregard straightened from his bow and lifted a hand, gesturing for her to lead.

Amelia immediately turned and marched at a brisk pace. Blueregard kept stride with his hands behind his back. They rushed past the crimson-clad servant and hurried out the open door.

Samuel was lying on the green grass, not far from the front gate; he looked too drunk to stand. One arm was flailing about in the air above his prone form and slurred mumblings emanated from him.

The two mercenaries that had tried to stop her earlier were running about the grounds and staring up at the sky. They were shouting to one another, "Where did it come from?"

"There's not a cloud in the sky!"

"Was it artillery fire?"

"It was too loud! It sounded like thunder!"

Amelia glanced out the corner of her eye and saw a touch of a smirk trying to creep its way across Blueregard's lips.

What did you swear?

She would ask him when they were safely home. She felt that such a thing, having been kept secret for so long, was not something the old man wished to discuss publically.

Sully – Mr. Ugly Teeth – stepped away from the gate and cowered near the stone wall as they approached.

Good. I don't feel like dealing with you right now.

Despite Sully's retreat, Blueregard held back a step, crossed over behind her, and made a straight line for the foul man. Sully squeaked in a most unmanly way and curled up in the fetal position on the ground by the wall.

Amelia marched out the gate and stepped out into the middle of the pea-gravel road to use her crystalline network box and hail a gnome cart.

As she stood and waited, she turned to take one last look at the home she detested. Two guards were running about staring up the sky, a third was cowering in the corner by the front gate, and her eldest brother was drunk and passed out on the grass.

"Pathetic."

~~

The ride home was eerily silent. She had a great many questions to ask but didn't know where to begin. Instead she opted for watching the street lanterns zip past. Darkness had descended, and it was well past time for her to get some rest.

Thankfully, the pure exhaustion of the day pushed her into a long nap. Blueregard nudged her awake. Unfortunately, his earlier display had left her on edge, and it caused her to jolt awake.

"I apologize, but we have arrived home." Blueregard was ever-polite. In that moment, she wanted to know more about the less-polite side, and didn't at the same time.

"Thank you, Blue."

The gnome cart pulled up to the front door of their

residence. Amelia climbed out first, quickly followed by Blueregard. "Blue?"

He stood and lifted a hand to halt her. "Another night, Amelia." He almost never used her first name. When he did, he was being as serious as one could be. He truly didn't want to talk about it, at least not that night.

She accepted his request, nodded, and headed in so that she might head to bed. That was when she remembered she lived on the second floor, and there were steps between her and bed.

Stairs... I have grown to loath you.

Thankfully, she had recovered enough from earlier in the day that the steps hadn't proved to be as laborious as before. Her bed still called to her. She had bathed and her clothes were still clean, as she hadn't sweated through them. All she needed to do was slip into her nightgown and rest.

Amelia and Blueregard crept into the residence and hung up their coats. Betty was likely already home and in bed, and they didn't want to wake her. They whispered their good-nights to one another, and headed to their separate rooms.

Her bedroom door released a froth of cold air as she opened it. It was pleasantly cool inside. She gently pushed the door shut with her boot as she unbuttoned her vest.

"Amelia?"

She jumped, dropped into a crouch, and brought her hands up, ready to grapple with whomever had spoken. A look around the dark room revealed that nobody was there.

Did I just imagine that?

"Promise you won't scream, love?" It was Detective William Windwalker's voice.

"William!" She whisper-shouted, "What are you doing in my room?" She didn't want to wake anyone or alarm Blueregard.

A wavering in the air caught her eye. It came from the water-closet doorway. It could barely be made out in the darkness, but she was certain he was there. "Show yourself, immediately!" She maintained a low shouting whisper.

The wavering intensified, and colors bled into the air. A form appeared in a matter of seconds – a young and handsome man with tousles of blonde locks. He wore the traditional detective's garb, had eyes that were bright silver like Joseph's, and he had a slightly darker tone to his skin. He had an apologetic smile on his face and both his hands up in surrender. "Evenin'."

"How did you get in? How long have you been waiting? Did you watch me get undressed earlier?" Each question she asked brought her voice higher and closer to actual shouting instead of the hushed and angry whispering.

William looked heartily offended. "Never! I only just arrived... and I'm a Windwalker." He said it as thought it was the only necessary answer.

Amelia clawed her hands out in front of her as though she were preparing to strangle him. "Why are you in my room?"

He let out a heavily exhausted breath. "You haven' seen Kane, have you?"

Merciful goddess, smite him now!

She whimpered, squeezed her eyes shut, and tried to breathe through the tears that threatened to overwhelm her.

I just want to go to bed!

"No, William, I have not seen Kane. Why would you think to look in my bedroom for him?" Julian 'The Fireball' Kane was William's superior on the night shift. He was also a self-destructive drunkard and had his head crammed full of idiotic conspiracies.

William reached into his exterior trench coat pocket and removed a glowing red rod of a wand. It lit up his body in ominous shades. "Found his staff." A wizard never went anywhere without their staff. The implications were disastrously alarming – they had a missing detective that was potentially dead.

Amelia eased over to her bed in order to sit down

and think. "Why did you come to me with this? Why didn't you go directly to the captain or Petals? This is clearly serious." Nothing of what he was doing was making any sense.

"Quite the mess over at the ol' warehouses today... Don't ye' think?"

She was tired and didn't have time for run-around conversations. "Out with it William."

"Fire and ice clashed at those warehouses, love."

So that's it.

Kane wasn't nicknamed The Fireball because of his explosive temperament, though it did fit him. He had the name because of his talent with the fire element. Amelia pinched the bridge of her nose and sat silently for a while. "You think Kane and I had it out, is that it?"

William stood stone still. The brightly-glowing red wand was gripped in his right fist; it made him look quite menacing. He slowly lifted his left hand and conjured a thin swirling pillar of distortions – his staff. It was made from pure wind and crafted by ancient elementals. Few had wielded it before him. "You often clashed whenever you met... it's not an unreasonable possibility."

Amelia shook her head. "No. I'm not strong enough to beat Kane. He would have killed me, and it would have been me you would be looking for, not him."

He didn't take her word immediately, but she could see the doubt flash across his face and the thoughts going through his mind. "I thought that too... at first." He looked to her again with a renewed resolve. "But you could be a sorceress."

Wow.

Amelia shook her head again. "No. Not even close." She turned and crawled up onto her bed. She couldn't be bothered to change into her nightgown any more, or argue with him. If she had been a sorceress, she would never have been able to pick out her staff from the precinct vault on her first day as a detective. Wizards and sorcerers have different magic that just don't work together.

A thought tickled the back of her mind. Something about what she had just thought. Sadly, she was far too tired to pluck at that string.

"Either get busy killing me or arresting me or whatever it is you intended to do, or go away so I can sleep." She grabbed her pillow, jammed it under her head and against her shoulder, and curled up to sleep.

William was still standing in the doorway of her water-closet, and the red rod lit up the right half of his body and most of her room. "I'm sorry, love. I just needed to hear you say it to be sure. I needed to see it in your eyes and hear it in your voice." He shook his head. "You didn't do this... I'll go chat with the captain."

"Good! Go do that!" She shut her eyes and waved toward her bedroom door. "Now get out so I can sleep."

She waited for the door to open and close but heard nothing. She opened an eye and saw nothing but the darkness of her room. There was no red light and no looming form of a man. "William?"

There was nothing but silence. She glared at the room in general, then let out an irritated throaty growl. He had earned the name Windwalker – he clearly could get in and out of anywhere like the damnable wind.

Amelia summoned her staff from the front door and spent the next ten minutes examining every corner of her room. She compressed it into a wand, released billows of cold air, and dropped the temperature significantly.

If William had been there, his teeth would have been chattering. She heard nothing, and the hairs on the back of her neck were only standing on end because she was getting a slight chill. Nobody was watching. Having determined that the irritatingly soundless detective had left, she set about changing into her nightgown and crawling into bed.

Thankfully, she had regained enough strength to draw a great deal of the cold air back into her wand. With that done, she slid into the sheets of her bed, curled up, and lazily tossed the wand onto the floor.

With no other thoughts or worries at hand, Amelia was immediately taken into a dreamless sleep.

~~

Morning arrived too quickly. Her mind and body protested being awakened. The alarm clock beside her bed incessantly rang until she stirred enough to turn and blindly swat at it. She managed to smack it on her third try and finally silence it.

She lay in bed for a while and rubbed the grit from her eyes while stretching. Her muscles didn't ache nearly as badly as they had the day before, and her side didn't hurt where the puppet-man and Howard had both struck her.

A brief thought and twitch of a finger made her ice wand materialize in hand.

"Thank the merciful goddess." Her powers felt like they had fully restored.

Please don't let today be like yesterday.

Chapter 14

As though the man had read her mind, Blueregard prepared a hearty breakfast of bacon, eggs, toast, and a potato patty. She needed it. Amelia was starving, and something substantial was just what the doc would have ordered.

Betty was up and about and just as full of honey and goodness as she usually was. "You had a rough night, sweetie?"

Amelia took another large bite of her preserve-slathered toast and nodded while chewing. She didn't feel like talking about it, but she never reprimanded the sweet girl for asking.

Betty shook her head before sipping from her tea. "Your family always seems to get the better of you."

A smirk managed to escape the confines of her grasp. She quashed it, but not before Betty spotted it.

"What was that?" She leaned forward in her chair and absolutely beamed. "Did you get the better of your family last night?"

Amelia finished chewing and wiped her mouth with her napkin. "I don't think I'll be seeing them again anytime soon." She took a greedy gulp of her tea to cleanse her palate.

"What happened?" Betty looked genuinely concerned.

She waved it off. "Nothing terrible. They tried to corner me with unreasonable choices. I saw it coming, prepared for it, and took the choice they didn't expect." She broke a piece of bacon into two pieces and used the longer of the two to gesture to Betty. "If it wasn't for your father buying the designs of my invention, I never would have been able to pay off that debt. Make sure to thank him for me next time you see him."

Betty beamed again and sat proudly. "Papa always tells me to thank you for bringing the designs to him when I see him. I think the business arrangement that you two made worked out for the best for both of you." After a moment, she frowned. "What were the unreasonable choices?"

Amelia had hoped that Betty wouldn't ask, but she knew better than to expect she wouldn't. Betty was a little bit of a gossip. "Marriage," she spat it out testily.

Betty clapped excitedly, "Well that's—"

"To a man of their choosing."

She stopped clapping and frowned. "—awful." Betty had a fanciful dream that Amelia would one day find a man and settle down, but she always insisted that it be a marriage of love, not duty.

Amelia continued to pile on the horrific details. "I'd also have to quit my job as a detective, reclaim my former name, and renounce any and all arcane activities... before the next moon."

With each addition, Betty looked more and more disgusted. Upon the final proclamation that it all had to be done before the next moon, the poor woman looked aghast. "That's only three days from now!"

Amelia raised an eyebrow and glanced at her watch. "Is it?"

Blueregard spoke over his shoulder while scrubbing a pan. "I believe it is, Ms. Iceheart."

She looked over her shoulder to a lunar chart that was pinned to the wall by the kitchen window and squinted. "Huh, so it is." She turned back around to find Betty staring at her own plate in contemplative silence. Amelia reached across the table and gently took Betty's hand.

The girl shook free and offered a sad smile before returning to her breakfast. Amelia rarely spoke about her family. There was no point in disturbing others with the details.

Having popped the last bit of toast into her mouth and having cleared her plate, Amelia set to cleaning herself up and readying for work. "Thank you, Blue. Breakfast was wonderful."

"You're welcome, as always, Ms. Iceheart."

She went back into her room and changed out of her house robe into her detective's garb. The spell-tome was shrunk and stuffed into her trouser pocket, and her staff responded to her call and appeared in her hand as a wand.

By the time she emerged, Betty was finished her breakfast and back in her room. "Blue?"

"Another time, Ms. Iceheart."

She scowled and put her hands on her hips. "Can you read minds too?"

Blue turned to face her. He was drying a pan with the dish towel and a half-hearted smile. "Nothing of the sort. I merely heard the tone in your voice. It was the same as it was from last night. It wasn't hard to guess what you intended to ask."

Amelia didn't let up on the scowl. "When?"

For the first time in her life, she saw the man hesitate. There was a distance in his gaze and a slight furrowing of his brow. His hands continued working to dry the pan, but his mouth was silent. It was uncharacteristic for

Blueregard to be without an answer.

He turned his eyes to her and slowly shook his head. "I do not know, my dear. When I feel ready to tell you, I will let you know."

It didn't feel like she was going to get a better answer. He genuinely seemed to struggle with what to tell her and how. Amelia eased off the scowl and rested her hands at her sides. "Thank you, Blue."

He silently nodded in acceptance and turned back around to continue cleaning the dishes.

Amelia went about collecting her things and prepared to leave for work. She buckled on her gun holster and belt and shrugged on her trench coat. Her wand went into a vest pocket, and lastly, she picked up her hat.

A thought occurred to her as she grabbed the door handle. "Blue?"

"Yes, Ms. Iceheart?"

"Be mindful today."

The pot cleaning abruptly stopped. Amelia looked over her shoulder to see Blueregard cocking an eyebrow at her. He had a plate in hand and a dish scrubber in the other.

Neither of them said anything, but the message was communicated clearly. The streets were less safe than they usually were.

Blueregard squared his shoulders a bit more, breathed deeply, and nodded in the affirmative. "Understood, Ms. Iceheart."

Amelia felt that the vague warning wasn't nearly enough to impart the true dangers they could potentially be facing in the coming days, but it would have to do for the time being. She opened the door and headed on out to face whatever new horror the day had planned for her.

~~

As instructed, she headed directly for the ice field from the day before. She had stuffed the body identification forms into her spell-tome like a stack of bookmarks.

While riding in the gnome cart, she took to reviewing the basics of elemental magic and the typical frameworks associated with it. As much as she prided herself on being an ice queen, she was little more than a peasant in comparison to the ice magic displayed at the warehouse crime scene. Brushing up on the basics and lesser-utilized frameworks and forms may be required in order to properly dismantle the ice field.

The gnome cart stopped at a distance from the warehouse. Blue coats had roped off the area in a greater perimeter than the day before. They didn't need gossip of frozen and skewered corpses going about the city.

Amelia thanked the driver, exited the cart, and made her way to the roped barrier. Blue coats were on guard and keeping nosy citizens at bay.

"No, sir. We can't let you 'just have a peek'. It's roped off for a reason." It was Hank. His red mustache was bunched up as he crinkled his nose and scowled down at the man that was trying to dance around him.

The man that was trying to peer around Hank had a slight frame, a stylus and pad of paper in hand, and a badge tucked into the band of his wide-brim. He seemed familiar.

As she approached, she was able to make out the symbol on the badge. The man worked for *The Stormbay Ledger*. He was undoubtedly trying to dig up more on why the warehouses were roped off.

Like a detective, those that worked for the letters of news often had a keen mind for digging up details and facts. The young man rounded on the spot as soon as he heard Amelia approaching.

Fireballs!

It was William Knight, the pride and joy of *The Stormbay Ledger*. He was also the only man that Betty had managed to convince Amelia to attempt to go out to dinner with – it was a disaster.

"Amelia!" He was absolutely beaming at her.

Gods… smite me and end it all now.

She let out an exasperated sigh and sagged in the shoulders. "Willy."

He hurried over to stand by her side, wise to not block her path. "It's William or Will, and I wouldn't mind buying you a cup of tea some time, just like the old days. You know, talk about stuff."

She couldn't help but notice that Officer Redbell, Hank, was suddenly focusing very intently on something other than her. Despite his blatant attempts to try and avoid listening, she could almost see his ears growing into points.

I officially hate today.

Amelia marched her way over to Hank and barked, "Rope!"

He jumped to attention and lifted it so that she could duck under.

William was hot on her heels, but only made it as far as the barrier. "So what is it that the good old Stormbay authorities are hiding in among– hrmph!" He was likely stopped by Hank by that point. It didn't stop him from continuing the question. "What's among the warehouses that needs to be hidden for two days in a row?"

She continued her hasty retreat to the safety of the crime scene.

"I'll talk to you later, shall I?"

She refused to answer. Saying anything to investigators from a news organization concerning an ongoing crime was against policy.

"Over some tea?" he called after her as she quickened her pace and rounded the corner.

The jagged peaks of ice were exactly as she remembered them from the day before. Just as Petals had said, they weren't melting very quickly at all. The cobblestones beneath her feet were darkened with water, but there was barely more than a trickle of a stream rolling away from the ice field. "Good gods." If things continued as they were, the ice field would persist until winter.

Amelia sighed heavily and approached the frozen graves. The man that had been pierced and hung from above was still there. She could also catch a slight whiff of decay; he was likely the most thawed of the corpses. It meant she'd be able to get a cleaner sample from him than from any of the frozen and shattered bodies. The problem she faced was collecting the sample.

It would be easy enough to rise up and collect it while standing atop an ice sheet, but she also needed to dismantle the ice field so that the other corpses could be collected and sampled as well.

The day before had taught her a valuable lesson in expending unnecessary energy. Amelia slowly walked toward the ice field and pondered possible methods of breaking it down without causing further damage to evidence.

A blue coat she didn't recognize was stationed nearby and reclined against a warehouse wall, seated on a three-legged wooden stool. He didn't appear to be sleeping, but he was certainly not taking his position very seriously. He must be a rookie.

She looked to the ground around him and noted that there were several smoke stubs and a few empty soup canisters. By the looks of it, there had been a night shift, and the blue coats on duty were likely exhausted and drained.

"Shift almost over?"

The man jolted from his reclined position and nearly fell off his stool. He was quick to get to his feet, fix his vest and shirt, and clear his throat. "Ahem! Yes, ma'am."

"Did anything out of the ordinary take place during the night?" She was genuinely curious and wasn't badgering the officer. It was entirely possible that the puppet-man had returned under the cover of darkness.

"Well… uh… maybe."

"Maybe?" She pulled her notepad and stylus. "Describe 'maybe' to me."

"Well… my superior told me to ignore it, but I thought it was odd."

"Your superior?" She used the butt of her stylus to point back over her shoulder to the roped area where she had arrived. "Hank? Officer Redbell?"

"Yes, ma'am." He pulled of his hat and held it in hand as he nodded fervently.

"Tell me anyway."

"At one-oh-five last night, Detective Windwalker appeared and asked us if anyone had seen anything."

"Windwalker?"

What were you doing here, William?

"Yes, ma'am. He came and seemed particularly interested in the warehouse over there." He pointed to the one that Joseph had been examining the other day. It was the same one where the bodies had been incinerated.

Amelia didn't take any notes. Something was off about William's behaviour. She would talk to Petals about it when she got back. "Thank you, Officer. Go help Hank with securing the ropes. I have it from here."

He quickly put his hat back on. "Yes, ma'am." He hurried off down the road toward where Hank was stationed.

Amelia eyed the stool that had been left behind, then decided it was better to sit and examine the ice than stand and wear herself out. She picked up the stool and moved it over to the center of the cobblestone road, directly before the jagged ice spires.

The brief review she had done while riding in the gnome cart had given her some ideas. Instead of sitting and reading some more, she decided to do some prodding and examining.

She pulled the spell-tome from her pocket, expanded it to full size, and sat it down on the stool. She gently pulled one of the body identification parchments a little further out than the rest so that she could grab it in a hurry if needed. Turning back to the wall of ice, she took a deep breath and calmed her mind so that she could open herself to the greater world of the 'verse.

As she had done countless times before, she opened her eyes and beheld the arcane energies that made up the living world. Colors turned to shades. The hotter something was, the brighter; the colder something was, the darker. Surprisingly, the facets and faces of the ice field before her that faced the sun were bright hot. Far hotter than they should have been.

Amelia frowned and stepped closer for a better examination. She knew not to touch the surface out of fear of shredding her fingers on the barbed snowflakes, but she needed a better look.

As she drew closer, the truth became clearer. The surface of the ice was redirecting the heat. Like a million little mirrors, the endless facets of ice were redirecting the light. With the aid of some magic, the ice barely absorbed any of the heat and instead reflected it back up into the sky.

No wonder this has barely melted.

The problem was that she needed to deconstruct it with as little effort as possible, otherwise she'd be exhausting herself before she was even halfway done. She blinked away her arcane vision and let out an irritated huff.

Amelia turned and picked up her spell-tome in order to sit and ponder. She crossed one leg over the other and balanced the white leather binding on her thigh. She couldn't focus or concentrate any heat upon it, as the mirror effect would just reflect most of it and waste time. Her infused breath had melted a small section when she was examining it earlier the day before, but she didn't have the lung capacity or the energy to do it to the entire ice field, and that had been a tiny concentrated area. However, it did give her a brief idea of utilizing steam. The hot moisture of her breath had effectively melted the miniature ice razors, but she didn't know how to implement it on a grand scale.

Her thoughts continued to spiral and lead toward the same deadends. After a few minutes of fruitless pondering, she turned to her tome and opened it to the first few pages. A fresh perspective was needed.

She started skimming over the section she had written on fundamental frameworks when a thought started pricking at the back of her mind.

I've never seen Rook use a spell-tome.

It bothered her for half a minute. Eventually she tried to shake it off. She never read her spell-tome in front of other detectives, so it stood to reason that he didn't either. It still bothered her.

She returned to reading with her finger still fixed on whatever passage she had last been focusing on. It was pointing directly at the word 'framework'. The word was written a good several dozen times throughout the tome, but it stood out to her for some reason.

Amelia lifted her head and looked at the jagged ice before her. She looked down again at the word 'framework'. It hit her, and she nearly slapped herself for not having thought of it sooner. "Good gods, I'm an idiot." She slammed the spell-tome shut, stood, and dropped it on the small wooden stool. "Idiot!" she continued to rebuke herself as she prepared the necessary incantation in her mind.

Ice was nothing more than crystalized water. Crystals – while hard – don't stand up well against oscillation or vibration. They can't compress or flex like other materials can, so they shatter. She'd been too focused on melting the ice with heat. What she needed to do was shake things up a bit, literally.

Detective Windwalker would have been better suited for the job, but she had a strong enough understanding of wind magic and was confident in her ability to pull off the spell she had in mind.

In preparation, she took in a deep lungful of air and breathed out slowly. She repeated the process several times in order to stretch and fill her lungs to capacity and coat her throat in a healthy layer of protective magic.

The arcane energy began building within her, and her heart pumped a bit harder with the sudden influx of oxygen. She flexed her fingers and began the appropriate gestures so that she could manipulate the energies and create a concentrated cone. A tethering of hat to head would help to keep it from flying off and protect her ears from the upcoming assault.

She took one last deep breath before shutting her eyes, cupping her hands around her mouth, and releasing the scream.

The wave of compressed air that resulted from the sudden expulsion blew her hair back and nearly snapped the tether that kept her hat on. Her trench coat snapped in the wind behind her as she released the full force of a Shattering Screech spell.

At first, her scream sounded like nothing more than the high-pitched wail of a woman's scream. It lasted for little more than a fraction of a second before it elevated and transformed into something otherworldly and inhuman. It rose in pitch until it was a whistling hum. A second after that, all she could hear was the deafening harmonic wave of overpowering silence.

The jagged ice spires rumbled.

Amelia opened her eyes in order to watch in triumph, only to be horrified by what she'd done.

The ice spires were shattering into countless pieces and collapsing in a thunderous avalanche. Every single one of them was crumbling and falling into piles. She realized she was about to be buried alive.

Amelia clipped her spell short, snatched up the stool and her spell-tome, and bolted in the opposite direction. Her Shattering Screech spell quickly devolved into a plain old panicked scream.

"AHHH!"

I didn't think this through!

Chapter 15

She made it three steps. Despite her panic-induced flight, the avalanche of shattered ice overtook her in a fraction of a second.

The wave struck her in the back of the legs and knocked her down. Mid-fall, she tossed the stool out in front of her. She didn't want it battering her if she were to be tossed about.

Cold and darkness overtook her, and the miniscule shards of ice covered her entire body from hat to boots. It sounded like shattered glass bits were being shoveled and scraped along the cobblestones as she was buried alive. Thankfully, the wave was short-lived.

Everything settled into grave silence. She could hear the *tink-tink-tink* of icicles shifting and settling as well as her own heart in her ears, but she couldn't hear anything else. There was no wind or the sounds of distant traffic or city life. There was just unnerving silence. She was truly buried alive. It felt sickeningly ironic that she should die being buried beneath a mountain of ice.

I'm not going to die here!

She tried to push herself up and out, but the weight of all of it on top of her pressed her hard down against the cobblestones, and trapped her one arm and spell-tome beneath her. She wanted her tome to be safe, but she didn't want it to be the object of her undoing.

In the awkward state she was in, she couldn't shrink or compress the spell-tome. It was pressing against her chest and ribs as the ice weighed down heavily upon her back and shoulders.

The fingers of her right hand were going numb, as her arm was trapped between the cobblestones and the tome. Neither of which would give before her arm did. She wasn't entirely certain that it wasn't already broken.

Out! I need out!

Panic was starting to set in, as she could barely draw a breath.

Don't panic! Think!

Panic didn't respond to rational thought, but years of training with the Arcanum and Academy did.

I'm an ice queen, damn blast it!

Amelia flexed her control of the elemental forces and pushed the pile of ice away from her back. Unfortunately, the push was far more panic-fueled than she had intended it to be.

Ice shards erupted into the air and burst in all directions, raining down upon the chaotic scene around her. The world came back in a life-affirming rush: the wind, the city, and the hollering and cursing of her fellow officers.

"Gods blasted thundering icicles!" It sounded like Officer Redbell.

Amelia pushed herself up and out of the hole she had just made. Feeling immediately returned to her arm, and her fingers wiggled without any pain or hindrance.

At least it's not broken.

With the weight of the ice off her back, and finally able to breathe deeply, she compressed her spell-tome and stuffed it into a pocket. Her hands were shaking slightly, but it was mostly due to the lack of air and panic.

"Ms. Iceheart?"

Amelia looked to Officer Redbell but kept standing where she was – she couldn't trust her legs in the moment. "Yes?"

The man was looking at the ground all around them and shuffling knee deep through the ice shards. His hands were held out before him as though he were expecting an answer to be dropped into them. "What in the blazes was that?"

The other officer that she had sent to help Hank was standing nearby and looked just as bewildered.

"Magic." She didn't feel like going into the details.

Hank dropped his hands and scowled at her. It was usually quite humorous when the man scowled, as his mustache was quite expressive. It drooped into a bright red frown. "I guessed that much!"

She still didn't feel like going into the specifics of it. "I shattered the ice… with magic."

She figured that Hank had deduced that as well. He said nothing, glared at her for several more moments, then turned on the spot to head back the way he came. The moment he turned, he jumped to attention. "You!"

William Knight jumped from the corner where he had been hiding, flipped closed his notepad, and bolted down the road and out of Amelia's sight. The officer that had been assisting Hank took off at a full sprint in order to capture the trespasser.

"Get back here!" Hank sloughed his way through the ice shards with high-kneed stomping before he could take off at a run. Citizens, even news organization investigators, were forbidden from entering a crime scene; there was the possibility that they could tamper with or damage evidence.

She didn't feel that any harm had been done, but it didn't bode well that the rope had been left unattended. The rookie blue coat would likely get the heavier reprimand. Such was the way of things.

Her job wasn't to catch irritating news investigators, it was to identify the bodies. Amelia turned to look back upon the sea of ice shards and cursed herself again for not fully thinking the plan through. She couldn't see the bodies.

Growling in irritation, she sent a touch of magic down through her legs and stepped across the ice shards. With her skills, she could walk on top of the pile of ice without sinking in and having to slough through.

Amelia drew her wand from her pocket and released it into a staff. She began poking through the mounds in hope that it would find some resistance and a body. It didn't take long for her to find the one that had been pierced by the largest ice spire. It was very close to where she last remembered it hanging in the sky.

A touch of levitation magic was all she needed in order to pull the body free from the depths of the ice. As she had long suspected, it hadn't shattered or fallen to pieces like the other bodies had.

The thought then occurred to her: she had just shattered the remaining bodies.

"Gods blasted thundering fireballs!" She roared her frustration. A headache was building, so she pressed two fingers to the side of her head and tried to rub away the stress that was building there.

I seriously didn't think this through.

She used her staff as a guide, walked the floating corpse closer to the incinerated warehouse, and pushed the ice shards aside with a wave of her hand so that she could set the body down on the cobblestones. Amelia breathed a heavy sigh, then turned to go look through the mountain of ice to try and find the pieces of the remaining bodies.

It took her an hour, but she did it. She pulled out her spell-tome and reviewed the formulas and structures of tracking, tethering, and mending spells. Within twenty minutes, she had devised a means by which to track down blood amongst the ice. Once she found a piece, she would combine a tethering and mending spell to gather all the like pieces and puzzle the body back together.

The reconstruction was rather easy, as the magic did all the work. The majority of her time was spent fishing through the massive pile of ice shards in order to find a piece of a body. The tracking spell helped, but there were so many pieces spread over such a large area that she would often get conflicting signals. Her arcane vision didn't help either; the pieces were simply far too scattered.

Due to her investigation from the day prior, she knew exactly how many bodies she was looking for and vaguely remembered where they had been located. Once all the corpses were accounted for, she went about setting down the body identification forms. She had two to spare and stuffed them back into her spell-tome.

The bodies were lined up and she was ready to begin identifying them. Knowing that the doc would want them for further examination, she pulled out her crystalline network box and called for two body carts. Dispatch informed her that they would be along shortly.

She turned back to the stiffs and prepared to begin identifying them. However, the looks of horror and excruciating pain that were quite literally frozen on their faces unnerved her. A few handfuls of ice shards placed over each face helped her slightly.

Amelia pulled on her silk gloves and drew a long pair of tweezers from one of her vest pockets. Carefully, she plucked a frozen bit of hair from one of the bodies, and then placed it inside the purple border box at the bottom of the parchment. Once situated, she cleared her throat and spoke aloud the incantation that was outlined at the top of the parchment. The magic took effect, and the bit of hair melted and vaporized into particles of light as it was consumed.

While the magic went to work, she stood and turned

her attention to visually examining the bodies. It was never something she could do while they were frozen, as her arcane vision wasn't that precise.

They were all men, and each one of them had been wearing long and heavy leather coats and boots. Their appearances were jagged at best, as they had all been shattered, but based on the clothing, she guessed them to be deck hands or dock workers.

Ink was already appearing on the body identification form, but it would take a minute for it to fully appear and dry based on how slowly it was forming. Not wanting to waste time, she went about collecting hair or skin samples from the remaining corpses and activating each identification form in turn. Once she had activated the last in the line, she headed back to the first and picked up the parchment for examination.

It was garbled. "Blasted, stupid magic." The ink was everywhere and there wasn't a single legible word or letter.

She put it down and went to the next form. It too was garbled and illegible, but less so than the first. The third didn't have anything on the page at all, and the purple-bordered box was filled with a smoking hole. She let out an irritated sigh and continued to look at each parchment in turn.

They were all illegible except for the one man that had only been pierced. His form was perfectly legible. Her frustration at the documents may have been misplaced.

Instead of a frozen bit of hair or skin, she had taken a drop of blood from the thawed out hole in the man's chest. It was plausible that the frozen samples were simply too damaged to identify, or the magic within the ice was corrupting the identification.

Either outcome didn't bode well for the usability of the identification forms. She quickly made a note of it with her stylus and turned to reading the one form that she could.

As suspected, the man was a deck hand. It listed his name, age, profession, and registration numbers with the port authorities. "Hello, Mr. Caspian Smiley." It also listed his employer and the ship he was last employed upon. The employer was common enough that it wasn't even worthy of note. Many sailors utilized the exact same company, or an equivalent rival. The boat, however, caught her eye.

"*Ladysong*?" She knew the name. It danced in her mind for half a moment before she remembered where she'd heard it from. Amelia let out a long groaning sigh.

It had to be dragged out of her, but Mother had finally revealed that Andrew, her twin brother, wasn't present at last night's gathering because he was busy auditing the ledgers of a boat. That boat just happened to be the *Ladysong*.

She shut her eyes and mumbled a hopeless prayer. "Maybe it's a coincidence." Opening her eyes, she lifted the parchment and scanned for the listed date of departure from the *Ladysong*. She found it. "Damn it all!" It was listed as the day before.

Andrew had removed the deck hand from the ship's roster. Her family was trying to cover up their involvement. It was no longer much of a wonder as to why they had hired the mercenaries. They weren't scared of her; they were scared of whomever they had gotten involved with.

There was a brief glimmer of hope that Andrew had just been doing what he needed to do as per his duties as an auditor. It was possible that the deck hands had been missing for several days, and the boat had taken on new crew and needed to depart.

That didn't explain the mercenaries, unless her original theory was correct and the family was truly just afraid of her. She didn't like coincidences, and there were far too many of them. The only way to be certain would be to talk to Andrew. Before that, she would need to return to the precinct and speak with Petals. He would understand the delicacy of the situation.

~~

"Certainly not." Petals said it with his typical cheery grin.

"What? Why not?"

The little man smiled and declared, "It is against policy." She had caught him on the steps of the precinct, returning from somewhere.

"But... this is *my family*." She said it in slightly hushed tone but made sure to emphasize the importance.

"That was made quite clear at the beginning of your request, my dear. The fact remains that they are *your* family, and you cannot be listed as the investigating detective when it comes to questioning them." Petals knew about her past. He knew about the incident with her father.

She was about to object when he raised one of his terrifyingly powerful stubby little fingers. "I assure you, the utmost discretion shall be taken when investigating." He added in a much quieter tone, "Your secret is safe, my dear."

I still hate it.

Amelia clutched her fists and ground her teeth through the frustration. She couldn't argue with him. He was her superior and his word was final. It was also policy.

"Did you clean up the ice field?"

"Yes." She didn't feel like having a lengthy discussion.

"Completely gone?" He raised an inquisitive brow.

"Shattered and melted."

"Huh!" He seemed impressed. "And the bodies?"

"Carts picked them up before I left."

The trickster gnome gave her a satisfied grin, turned, and hopped up the long steps to the doors. "Excellent."

It took her a moment, but she wrestled her anger under control and followed him up the steps with a few questions of her own. "Why are you just returning? Where were you this morning?"

Petals spoke over his shoulder as he reached the doors and pushed them open. "I was at a meeting at the

Central precinct."

That doesn't bode well.

Senior detectives were never called to meetings unless there was something greatly concerning taking place.

"About the…" She gestured to the back of the precinct where the corrupted man was confined.

Petals held open the door for her as she stepped inside. "That, and our missing hot-headed conspiracy theorist." His tone was far less jovial.

She'd almost forgotten about Julian missing. "And?"

"*Everyone* is on high alert, and Detective Windwalker has been supplying the captain and I with regular reports."

A meeting of senior detectives that resulted in a city-wide collaborative investigation would have people asking questions. It wouldn't take much longer for fear and panic to set in. She wasn't worried about William any longer, not if he was reporting directly to senior staff.

"Uh… I have some bad news."

Petals cocked an eyebrow up at her. "Oh?"

She chewed on her bottom lip while contemplating the best way to go about saying it. As they neared the spiral stairs, she opted for simply saying it. "An investigator from *The Stormbay Ledger* saw the ice field after I shattered it."

"Oh dear… did he see the bodies?"

"No, those were buried. I'm certain he missed them."

"Well we at least have that much. At worst he'll think a detective caused a spell to go awry." The little man hopped his way up the steps.

She hadn't thought of it that way. She supposed it wasn't as bad as she had originally thought. With how things were going recently, the worst plausible outcome was frequently coming to mind.

Shouting from above caught her attention and broke her train of thought. "How was I supposed to know?" yelled John.

Amelia took to the steps and hurried her way up.

Petals – in his ever-graceful way – was already at the top. As soon as she rounded the last corner, she found herself confused by the sight before her.

There was a block of stone sitting in the middle of the detectives' bullpen. Joe and John were standing on either side of it. Their staffs were out, and they were shouting at each other. "Well you could have asked me first!" Joe was throwing his arms up in the air.

John angrily pointed across the stone at Joe. "You were the one who asked me to help you!"

"That was before!"

"So the asking of help just suddenly vanishes after a certain amount of time?" John looked thoroughly irritated.

Joe looked absolutely confused by the angrily posed question. "I– What? No!"

Petals skipped over and effortlessly hopped up onto the stone block between them and shouted, "Boys!"

The two of them immediately jumped to attention, shut their mouths, and turned wide-eyed frightened looks upon their superior. They were just as equally frightened by the power of the tiny gnome as Amelia was.

The little man took a calming breath and turned to each in turn. "Mind explaining to me what this argument is about?"

John diverted his eyes, cleared his throat loudly, and waved it off. "Not important."

Joe shook his head vigorously. "Not important." He looked embarrassed.

Ooh… now I want to know.

Amelia stepped a bit closer so that she might better hear the conversation and also get a quick glance at the monstrous stone curiosity that nobody seemed bothered to discuss.

Petals leveled a pint-sized stink-eye upon each in turn. "Out with it."

Joe vaguely gestured at John. "He tried to do something nice for me… it backfired."

Petals' stink-eye morphed into confusion. "Pardon?"

John compressed his staff to a wand and angrily stuffed it into a pocket. "You have any idea how many favors I pulled?"

Petals hopped on the spot in order to turn around and look at John. "You pulled favors? What favors? What are the two of you talking about?"

John glared directly at Joe. "You owe me. I used up some good favors *and* lost a bet cause of you."

Joe sighed and sagged in the shoulders. "Yeah, I know… offer her my apologies?"

Oh… I think I know what happened.

Petals stood straight and slowly turned to face Joe again with a knowing grin. "Her?"

Joe nodded and shut his eyes. "Detective Vinethorn."

Amelia was thoroughly impressed. Ms. Vinethorn was one of the most sought-after single women in the Southeastern precinct. Having fey heritage tended to offer a certain natural beauty that was beyond human standards.

John threw up his arms and headed back for the stairs. "The next time you start dating a woman, warn me!"

I knew it.

Petals whipped his head around to John, then looked back and barked at Joe. "Dating?"

Joe looked to take offense to the outburst. "Yes! You have a problem with me being happy?"

Amelia finally stepped forward, confident that she wouldn't get caught in any crossfire. "A nurse, from what I hear."

"The nurse?" Petals stomped his little foot. "Dang blast it!"

Joe looked hurt. "Don't tell me you bet against me too!"

Petals squeezed his eyes shut. "I apologize, my boy, but you have cost me some coin… yet again."

The captain's rumbling voice startled the lot of them. "What is with all the yelling?" It wasn't yelled, as it never needed to be. Amelia turned to see the captain peering out of his office.

Petals hopped down and hop-skipped over to deliver the unbelievable news. "The boy has found himself a lovely young nurse to court."

The captain turned his massive head to eyeball Joseph. "Truly?"

Joe shrunk a little on the spot. "Yes, sir."

The captain stared for a moment or two before grumbling, "Blast" under his breath and slowly retreating back into his office.

Joe straightened. "Seriously! Did anyone bet in my favor?"

Chapter 16

Petals left the two of them to examine the chunk of stone while he discussed matters with the captain. John had left to continue investigating wherever it was that they had picked up the stone from.

Not wanting to work in her trench coat and hat, Amelia headed over to her desk and hung them both up. Afterward, she turned her attention to the oddity in the room and gave it a good once-over. It was two and a half paces long, one and a half wide, and the same again tall; it was almost big enough to be a stone coffin. It looked to be carved from something akin to marble or slate and had a thundercloud gray color to it. There did not appear to be any hinges or seams.

As she walked about it, she took note of the etchings and chisel-work. Each face had a set of raised runes completely foreign to her. "Where in the name of the gods did you find this?" She turned to look toward the narrow spiraling staircase. "And how did you get it up here?"

Joe spoke over his shoulder as he headed to his desk to hang up his coat and hat. "We found it at the Wayside Inn, and we levitated it up and over the railing from the main floor."

Amelia had a hard time believing the second part of his answer. "Levitated? That?" She pointed at it in complete disbelief. Even with John's expertise in the earth element, there was no way that the both of them could have levitated it. It looked far too heavy.

Joe nodded as he returned with his wand in hand. "Yep. When we went to attempt to lift it the first time, some runes automatically synchronized with our wands. Watch." He pointed the head of his wand at one end of the stone chest and twisted his wrist.

The stone chest jumped to life and the end that Joe was pointing at suddenly began lifting away from the ground. Amelia jumped a little from the surprisingly easy movement. "It's designed for transportation?"

He shrugged. "Seems that way." Joe twisted his wrist back in the opposite direction and lowered his wand.

Surprisingly, the chest didn't drop like a sack of bricks. It lowered to the ground and settled slowly and softly. "You said you found this at the Wayside Inn? Why were you there?"

"John searched the puppet-man's cart the other day and found a registration certificate."

"If they were staying at the Wayside then they likely didn't have any residence in town."

Joe frowned and nodded in thought. "That would be my guess as well. Apparently the more expensive suites come with the privilege of renting a cart for the day."

She was familiar with the practice.

"They also didn't seem to understand the value of the coin that they were carrying."

Amelia knelt down and leaned in closer to better examine the stone and runes. "What makes you say that?"

Joe leaned over and examined the same bit of runes

she was studying; the only difference was that he was using his arcane vision. She could tell because his eyes were polished silver orbs of light. He glanced to her briefly and answered her question, "Puppet-man tipped one of the bell hops with a gold coin."

Amelia had to shake her head in disbelief. "A gold coin?"

Joe nodded. "A whole gold coin." He shook his head in disbelief as well.

A gold coin, if spent properly, could sustain someone for years. She could only fathom three plausible reasons why someone would so easily expend a gold coin in that fashion: either the individual handing out the coin had an abundance of it and didn't care how much they tossed away, had a specific agenda in mind that required buying the bell hop, or they truly didn't understand the currency they were holding. "Did you question the bell hop?"

He shook his head. "The kid quit his job as soon as he had the coin in hand. The Southeast precinct is tracking him down so that they can get his statement. John is returning to give the room a second look and see if he can stir up some more witnesses."

She breathed deep and let out a puff. "So... what are we looking at?"

Joe blinked and returned his eyes to normal, then stood. "Well, this was in the puppet-man's room. It was open, and there were two empty square slots."

That only raised more questions. "You shut it in order to transport it here?"

"We had to. The levitation runes for the box won't engage unless the lid is on."

Amelia frowned at that. "Why would they design it that way?" She looked closer at the strange stone carvings and drew a complete blank. "Whoever it was that designed this had some strange ideas."

"I can't translate a damn word of the runes on the outside, but it doesn't take a genius to tell that they are designed to ward people from breaking into it." Joe tapped the side of the chest with his wand.

Amelia brushed some hair out of her eyes and looked up at him. "And how do you know that?"

"Except for the levitation rune on either end, the entire box shows up as a dark nothingness if you try to look at it with magic."

She looked back at the chest, shut her eyes, and took several deep breaths. When she opened herself to the 'verse and looked at the stone chest, she nearly wet herself.

Amelia barked out a scream and fell on to her rear as she tried to push herself away from it. There was nothing there. As it was whenever she used her arcane vision, she could see Joseph, the bullpen, and everyone in it; they were bodies of light and shades of warmth. The energies of magic that flowed throughout the room stood out like beacons of light, but the chest was nothing. It was a void in the world, as if someone had taken that very object and ripped it from her vision. It was hair-raisingly unnerving and eerie.

As Joe had suggested, there was a pinprick of light nestled in amongst the nothingness. It was a touch of magic free-floating in the air. If she narrowed her eyes and focused on it, she could make out the glowing runes that made up the framework of the levitation spell. It was all in an arcane language she had never seen before, but it was evident what it was used for.

She blinked several times and cleared the arcane vision so that she could see normally again. The runes vanished, as did the nothingness. The world returned to normal, and the stone chest was exactly as she had last seen it. "That…"

"Creepy, isn't it?" Joe seemed perfectly calm, and that unnerved her even more.

"Just a bit."

He offered her a hand up, and she took it. Joe hauled her to her feet with ease.

"You going to open it up and share what's inside?"

Joe nodded and headed back to his coat rack to rummage through the trench coat pockets. He turned back to her with a wooden puppet hand. "We need this."

Amelia stood a bit straighter. "Did you–?"

"No, no." Joe waved off the thought. "We found a wood and leather travel trunk that had spare feet and hands. If we had run into our attacker again, we would have told you."

It was only slightly comforting. "So you just put one of its hands in your pocket? What if the hand came alive and attacked you?" She couldn't help but shiver at the thought of a disembodied hand crawling all over her and trying to strangle her to death.

Joe frowned as he stared at the wooden hand he was holding. "I thought of that too." He gave a whole-body shiver and shook his head. "I gave it a thorough once-over to make sure nothing like that could happen. There aren't any remote tetherings or strings of magic attached to it." Joe manipulated the hand and bent the fingers so only the pointer finger was outstretched. Once appropriately positioned, Joe reached out across the chest with the puppet hand and tapped specific runes along the surface.

Amelia was immediately alarmed as each touched rune began to glow, and a hum emanated from the stone chest. "Joe!"

He paused to reassure her. "It's all right." He wiggled the wooden hand. "This thing is the key that opens it." He returned to tapping the runes with the puppet finger. With each tap the hum got louder, and the thrumming vibrated through the floorboards. "I got a good look at the framework of runes that built the lid. There's an exact match built into this finger." He continued to tap the keys until there was a loud *clack*.

Amelia jumped and shut her eyes. She hadn't been expecting it, and there was a legitimate fear that the rookie had just triggered a trap.

Thankfully, there was no thunderous explosion of

sound, heat, or light; there was only the sound of the bullpen. After a moment of calm, she peered out one eye.

Joe was looking at her with a raised eyebrow, and the lid to the chest was raised. "You good?" She released the breath that she had been holding, then waved him on.

He gestured to the chest. "I triple-checked to make sure we wouldn't set off any traps." He pushed on the raised lid, and it slid aside with ease. It didn't move far, but it was enough to peer inside.

She was hesitant. "No traps?"

He shook his head. "None."

That's odd. Something like this should have plenty of traps.

Amelia relented and stepped toward the chest to look through the opening he had made. Just as he had said, there was a square empty space carved into the bottom of the chest. She could only see the one closest to her, but if they fully removed the lid, she was certain she'd see the second. The interior walls of the chest had inset runes carved into the faces. From what she could see, there wasn't a single space that wasn't utilized. The inner walls had a prismatic crystalline sheen, as if it was painted with magic dust. She still had no idea what the runes meant. "I think we need a linguist."

Joe breathed out a heavy sigh through his nose. "Agreed." He gestured to the end he was closer to. "Mind giving me a hand with the lid? It has levitation runes as well."

She nodded and stepped back so that she might draw her wand and pointed it at her end. "Ready."

He stood at his end, raised his wand, and cocked an eyebrow while smiling. "On three?"

Amelia rolled her eyes. "Fine. We do it *on* three."

Joe smiled like a happy idiot. "Got it."

They did get it, and on the first try. Amelia and Joe aimed their wands at their respective sides and levitated the lid up, off, and to the floor beside the chest. It was surprisingly light.

"This seems far too easy." She put her hands on the

edge and leaned over to get a good look inside. It definitely had a second empty square space, just as Joe said. What it was meant for, she had no idea. "It's a glorified travel trunk. It levitates with ease and there aren't any traps. Why is this thing so special, and why did they bring it?"

"Oh, no, it definitely has traps."

Amelia jumped back and pulled her hands away. "You told me there were no traps!"

He shook his head. "No, I said I triple-checked to make sure we wouldn't *set off* any traps." He lifted the puppet hand and wiggled it. "This deactivated all the traps when I unlocked the lid."

She gaped as she took another step back from it, "Are you insane? What if we accidentally triggered a trap while examining the box?"

Joe waved it off. "If anyone was going to set it off, it would be me. I poked and prodded this box for a good hour back at the Wayside."

That makes me feel slightly better.

Despite the assurance, she narrowed her eyes at him and kept her distance from the box. "You promise?"

Joe sagged a bit in the shoulders and let out an irritable sigh. "Trust me, if any idiot is going to trigger a trap, it's likely to be me."

A bit more than slightly.

"Ha!" Petals barked joyously from the door to the captain's office. "My boy, as much as it pains you to hear it, I would be delighted to see you get smacked by another lightning bolt."

"Another? When did you get hit by a lightning bolt?"

Joe furiously waved off their comments, then pointed with both fingers at the chest. "Let's get back to examining this thing!"

As much as they needed to understand what the box was for, she left the majority of the examinations to the Fate's personal bullseye. He had the experience when it came to understanding wards and traps, and all they knew about the chest was that it was warded and trapped.

With Petals free, she took the time to show him the body identification forms she had collected.

"Yes. These are quite messy. Finish your report and I'll send a copy to Central along with the tainted forms."

She accepted her assignment and was happy to not have to deal with the stone chest anymore. By the time she had finished her report and handed a copy to Petals, it was a little after noon.

The rookie stopped fiddling with the stone chest long enough to generate a letter of request for a linguist to examine it. Petals sent that off with the tainted forms.

Shortly after the forms were sent, he was back at it. He didn't stop to grab a bite to eat; he just went right back to work. The moron even went as far as sitting cross-legged inside of it so that he could "get a better angle" on the runes. It set her on edge. It was like he was taunting the Fates to swat him.

Blueregard sent her some leftover chicken and dumplings. It was just as delicious the second time and filled her stomach. However, the stress of watching Joe sit in the box made her scrawl out a quick note, tear the page out of her notepad, and stuff it into her arcane delivery box. It didn't take long for Blueregard to come through. Within a few moments, she had a parchment-wrapped bar of iced cream. It was also her favorite: chocolate and raspberry.

I don't care if you're fatty, I earned you.

She took a hearty bite and blew out a thick froth of cold air. It was amazingly delicious and settled her nerves.

"Hey? Anybody there?" Joe's voice echoed out from stone chest.

I'll blame him. He drove me to chocolate.

She swallowed the bite she'd been chewing on. "Yeah, Rook?"

"Come take a look at this."

"I'd really rather not. I'm quite happy where I am."

She took another big bite of her treat and put her feet up on her desk.

Joe slowly turned his head and peered out of the box in order to give her a less than impressed look. It quickly turned to that of intrigue when he saw what she was eating. "Where did you get that from?"

She smirked, swallowed, and licked her lips. "A woman doesn't reveal such secrets." She liked teasing him and watching him squirm.

The frown returned and he grumbled as he slowly turned back to his work.

Shortly after she finished her iced cream, a ruckus rose from the main floor. There was shouting, swearing, growling, and grunting; it sounded like the same sort of ruckus from when the corrupted Jenkins was loose.

Oh no.

They all must have been thinking the same thing, as Joe, Amelia, and Petals all bolted for the railing with staffs in hand. As she thought, it was the corrupted man. What she was not expecting was a small gathering of robed men and women. All of them were garbed in starburst patterns from the Temple of Light, and looked to be a few years younger than she. Some may not have even been of age. Mr. Jenkins was in their custody on a stretcher.

One of the robed men was not much smaller in stature than Joseph. He had massive broad shoulders and an athletic frame, if aged. He hobbled alongside the stretcher that the corrupted man was strapped to, and his hand glowed from within. That hand was placed on the corrupted man's forehead and looked to be holding the thrashing outbursts at bay.

It was astounding and awe-inspiring. She'd never seen divine power at work.

Petals broke the silence but spoke softly. "The Calming Hand. It is a powerful tool granted to the devoted."

Amelia kept her voice low as well. "They came to take Mr. Jenkins for safekeeping? Or are they going to try and cleanse him?"

"They'll do what they can." She had asked Petals, but Joseph had answered. She had forgotten that Joe had grown up at the temple and was probably far better versed in what they would attempt to do. "He's in good hands."

The procession of robed men and women began to softly chant and sing in a harmonious choir. She couldn't make out anything of what was being sung, as the notes were far too high or far too low. Whatever it was, it was beautifully moving.

The singing caused Mr. Jenkins to calm even more. He was barely thrashing or twitching. The light that spilled in through the front entryway grew brighter, as if a cloud had just blown aside and let the sun out in all its glory. It made her feel strangely warm inside.

"Ah, the power of the divine." Petals grinned happily with his hands behind his back. "I believe that poor corrupted fellow might soon prove to be a valuable witness and a source of many answers."

Finally, we get some good news.

The procession slowly moved toward the front entryway and the bright light of the sun. Their rhythm was slow, and they all swayed the same amount from foot to foot as they sang. Blue coats opened the doors and stepped aside for them as the temple procession made their way to the exit. It was serenely quiet as the entire precinct stopped to watch.

Mr. Jenkins appeared to have been cast into a light sleep, as he twitched only sporadically.

They were all gone out the door and were little more than sunlit shadows when she heard it — the unmistakable roar of an oncoming Fireball.

Chapter 17

To utter 'fireball' was considered poor form and foul language. All were aware that it was the name of a spell, but fewer and fewer outside the arcane community remembered why it was considered such a thing. Fireballs were only cast by the most skilled of users. It was not easy to compress air, ignite the exterior, and throw it without it prematurely exploding. Many apprentices were killed throughout the centuries as they attempted to master it. Many more innocents were consumed by those failures.

Warring nations would hire mercenary wizards to rain Fireballs down upon unsuspecting villages. The devastation it caused was unparalleled in the old world. If someone were to hear the howling and roaring scream of a lobbed Fireball, it usually meant they didn't have long to live and would soon be greeted by the god of death.

To make matters worse, jugs of oil were sometimes held in the core of compressed air. It made the explosions bigger and the flames stick to whatever was caught in the blast. There was no forgiving anyone that utilized such tactics.

Amelia had seen a Fireball demonstrated only once before, while studying combative elements. The instructor that generated it was deemed the best in the city and had produced a Fireball about as big as a small gnome cart. It devastated a large chunk of land in the distance and left a crater two steps deep and twenty steps across.

Every student that had witnessed the destructive power was easily divided into one of two groups: those in awe of the power and devastation of the spell, and those that were terrified by it. Amelia was one of the latter. Just thinking of the potential devastation it would cause in a populated city left her dizzy and sick to her stomach.

When she heard it approaching the singing procession, the bottom of her stomach dropped out and her legs nearly turned to jelly. The screams came first. Choir singing devolved to maddened panic. Panic was then drowned out by the harrowing roar of flames and the near-deafening impact.

Despite the brick and mortar of the precinct being infused with arcane wards and barriers, the building trembled. The doors burst inward and sent splinters rocketing into the lobby. Flames followed and belched out from the entrance in a massive red-hot pillar that turned black with smoke.

Nobody had enough warning; it all happened in a moment. Amelia only had enough time to recognize the sound and draw in a breath that she might shout, but it was too late.

The billowing black clouds rose to the roof and the detectives' bullpen. It choked them all and blinded them from seeing the damage below.

For a brief few seconds, there was quiet shock. Bits were still falling and clattering to the floor, flames were still crackling and popping, but nobody was speaking. Cries for help began to ring out from the dark cloud, and screams of pain and sorrow followed. That was the beginning of the chaos.

Amelia coughed violently and tried to expel the smoke from her lungs and wave it away from her face. Her eyes were burning, and she couldn't see more than a few paces.

Don't panic!

She reached into her vest pocket, pulled her handkerchief, and covered her mouth so that she might breathe easier. Petals and Joseph were coughing as well.

Amelia gripped her staff tight, pointed it at the ceiling, and began swirling the tip in a wide circle. It didn't take long for the wind to answer her call and begin to swirl about. The miniature vortex she created pulled the black smoke up and away from her, and it soon started drawing in more and more.

"Nathaniel!" A soot-covered Joseph raggedly yelled while diving over the railing. She wouldn't have believed it if she hadn't seen it at the last moment, but through her bleary and teary eyes, she witnessed the fully-grown reckless idiot diving over the railing. He had enough magical skill to slow his fall or float, but It still was damned reckless. What if he miscalculated where he was jumping and hit the iron stairs?

Petals staggered about and coughed heartily. He too was covered in a healthy blanket of smoke and rubbing his eyes while holding his spectacles.

Amelia kept her handkerchief tight around her mouth and nose and did her best to breathe through the cloth. It helped, but only just. She could still taste the smoke in the air as she breathed. Her lungs felt thick with it.

The captain's office door flung open, and the massive dragon kin roared in anger and frustration, causing a bloom of ash to jet away from him.

Amelia tried to pull greater winds to her aid and made broader circular motions of her staff, but it was only able to pull away so much at a time, and she wasn't that gifted with wind magic.

The captain, however, had a talent all his own. A loud echoing snap filled the room. All the hair on her head suddenly stood on end as the room became highly charged. The power was so jarring that she could have sworn her teeth were vibrating. All the black smoke that had been filling the room, including what was swirling above her head, suddenly jumped to a point directly in front of the dragon kin's outstretched claw; a dense black ball of smoke hovered just before the tip.

She could see again, clear across the precinct and down into the lobby below. Her eyes still watered, but the air was clear.

The captain immediately bellowed orders with his thunderous voice. "Secure the precinct!" It carried throughout the building and shook her down to her bones. The lightning-charged mythical beast didn't need to yell; he never needed to yell. His voice could carry across a field on a whisper, yet he was yelling. "All available blue coats to the lobby!"

The intense energetic feeling quickly dissipated from the room, and her hair began to settle. With that unnerving sensation set aside, she took a deep breath in order to clear out her lungs with a hearty cough, then spat out the offending black phlegm. She pocketed her handkerchief, pointed to her coat rack with her staff, and summoned her trench coat and hat. Petals had the same thoughts as her and bounded over to his desk in order to snatch up his attire as well.

The two of them pulled on their coats and donned their hats as they descended the iron railing in a hurry. Blue coats were running forward with six-shooters drawn and taking up flanking positions on either side of the scorched and debris-ridden doorway. There were some bits still aflame, and when one could, a blue coat kicked it aside or stomped it out.

She could hear wailing coming from the desk of the lobby clerk.

Oh no... Maggie!

Amelia bolted to the lobby and surveyed the damage as she approached. Bits of wood and glass peppered the front of the desk and were embedded into it. When she peered over the side, she nearly lost her lunch. The poor woman had been just as similarly struck by glass and flecks of wood. It was strewn through her hair and several splinters poked out of her cheek. She was covered in a blanket of sweat and ash, and her arm was burned and lacerated; she had probably tried to cover her head while ducking for cover.

Amelia turned to look back through the precinct and screamed, "Doc! We have wounded!"

Petals' small hand touched her leg, causing her to turn and look back. The little man was looking to the entrance, and he was removing his hat.

Amelia didn't want to face it, but she knew she had to. She turned and saw what she hoped she would never witness in her lifetime. Her stomach turned, and she couldn't stop it; dropping to her knees, she became sick and lost her lunch on the lobby floor.

She wasn't the only one. A blue coat was in the corner with his hands on the walls, emptying his stomach as well.

Piles of ash and debris littered the entryway and steps. Everything was charred and black, and skeletal hands reached up from the floor, clawed and reaching for the sky, as if begging for help. There were bodies everywhere, at least a dozen of them.

Joseph was standing before all of it, and he wasn't moving.

Those blue coats that could stand it shuffled further out to begin containing the scene. With each step they took, they checked for survivors. None of them stopped, not even over the blue coats covered in ash.

Doctor Broom soon arrived with his black bag in tow. He stepped up beside Petals and took in the chaos before all of them. He dropped his bag and swore under his breath. The man took off his hat and muttered.

Maggie whimpered again. That got Amelia to thinking and pulled her from the shock of what she was witnessing. She staggered to her feet and gripped the Doc's white coat. "Maggie." She used the sleeve of her trench coat to wipe her mouth and pointed behind the desk where the poor woman was cowering and trembling in pain and fear.

The doctor thanked her and got to work. "Are there any others?"

Amelia turned and looked back to the doorway where Joseph stood and shook her head. "No... I don't think so."

A sputtering cough erupted from a pile of ash that had blown up against the frame of one of the charred and blasted doors. It caused everyone, including Joe, to gasp and start. The entire ash pile suddenly moved and a person sat up out of the ashes.

"Goddess of Mercy!" The Fates delighted in proving her wrong in that brief moment, and she was truly delighted that they did.

Joseph jumped to life. "Nathaniel!" It was the man that he had been screaming for while diving head first over the railing. The rookie threw himself into the corner and began digging out the man that had emerged from the dust pile.

Amelia immediately noticed that the man's clothes were gone and turned away instead of approaching. "Joe! Clothes!"

"On it!"

She heard the whipping of cloth on the wind and looked up just in time to see a trench coat fly over the bullpen railing from above.

Petals didn't need to share her sensibilities and marched forth, asking the very thing she was dying to know. "Dear sir, how did you survive that Fireball?"

Nathaniel coughed heartily and spat. "The Lord of

Light must need me alive." His voice was unsurprisingly ragged, but it also sounded weathered and old. There was even a soft whistle on the 's'.

She heard sniffing and a shuttering breath. "But these children…" His voice was choked, and she could tell he was crying. "They deserved better than this."

She glanced over her shoulder and saw Nathaniel wearing Joseph's trench coat, buttoned shut. It fit him fairly well; the two of them were close enough in size. In contrast to Joe, the man looked very old and very tired. He was shaking in the shoulders, and she could see the lines of tears cutting through the soot that covered his face.

The rookie spoke in harsh whispers. "I'll find the one who did this." There were no tears on his face; there was, however, a very cold stare. It chilled her a bit.

"No! No, Joseph!" The old man turned and gripped Joe by the shoulders and shook him. "Vengeance is not the answer! I've been down that road!" He shook Joe again. "I'll not have you making my mistakes!"

"Detective Runewall!" The captain's thundering voice came from everywhere.

Joe's head snapped to attention, and he looked up at the railing. "Sir!"

"Barricade the entryway!" Their ever-calm captain barked, "Now!"

Even Petals cowered from the outburst.

Nathaniel let go, and Joe clenched his jaw and shook, but he eventually marched out the front door. He headed past the charred remnants of his brothers and sisters, raised his staff above his head, and savagely roared before slamming the butt of his staff against the stone steps of the precinct.

Sparks of light shot off from the stone, and the resident rookie released an impressive amount of power. The air warped, wavered, and shimmered with a silver hue. A bubble grew out from the point he struck. Within a few moments, the front entryway was covered by a quarter dome of pure arcane energy. Lines of white light grew out from the ground and intersected until an octagonal network ran along the inside of the bubble and arched from the steps to the wall above the doors.

Amelia could feel the power vibrating through the stone floor of the precinct. Nothing was getting past that barrier short of a siege… or perhaps another Fireball.

They were locked in.

~~

The captain quickly established order. Fires were put out; the remains and the ashes were bagged for evidence. Blue coats were sent out to canvas the area to find out where the Fireball was launched from. Reports were generated by those that witnessed the event, and Joseph was ordered to be their sentinel. He checked everyone entering and exiting the building and granted them the freedom to pass through the barrier. Amelia was left to check on Maggie, and Petals took Nathaniel's statement.

"He's as heartless as he is dimwitted." Maggie sounded absolutely outraged. She squeezed Amelia's hand and whimpered when a splinter was pulled from her arm.

Doctor Broom apologized and tenderly brushed the wound with a bit of healing cream on a soft makeup brush. "This should help you recover without scarring." Maggie only winced a few times from the brushing.

"Why do you think he's heartless?" Amelia glanced back to the square-shouldered silhouette standing guard on the stairs. The man wasn't shifting weight, swaying, or doing anything else a man might do while performing a monotonous task. He was rigidly still, and it unnerved her. She couldn't imagine the range of emotions he must be feeling.

"He didn't come to check on me!" she growled under her breath.

Doctor Broom plucked out another splinter of

wood with a long pair of tweezers. She whimpered again and squeezed Amelia's hand.

Amelia shook her head and gently patted the back of Maggie's hand. "No, dear, he was worried about his family is all."

"What?" Her brow furrowed. "I thought he was an orphan?"

Amelia nodded a little and kept her voice down. "He is." She made a slight nod of her head to gesture over her shoulder. "He grew up at the Temple of Light. He considers all those that pass through their doors to be his family, and he just lost a dozen brothers and sisters today." She didn't know the official count yet, but it was close enough.

Maggie glanced to the trench coat-clad old man that was sitting by the iron spiral stairs. "Like him?" She said it more softly.

Amelia confirmed, "Like him."

Their lobby clerk stared at the man for a long moment. "How... how did he live through that? The heat burned me," she lifted her reddened arm to show, "and the fire hadn't even reached me yet... and he was standing in the middle of it all."

"Divine protection, my dear." Doctor Broom answered. He kept his voice respectably low. The man continued his work without pause. His steady hands and soft touch expertly plucked and pulled the smallest of splinters from Maggie's arm. "That is Nathaniel. He is a Paladin and bringer of the Greater Light." He paused his plucking. "And he is a terribly haunted man." Both women turned their eyes to the doctor, and he glanced at them before returning to his work. "You never heard it from me."

Amelia gave Maggie's hand a reassuring squeeze, then left her in the doctor's care to head toward Petals and Nathaniel.

As soon as the little gnome saw her coming, he loudly cleared his throat and spoke above the whisper he was utilizing before. "Your statement has been most helpful."

Nathaniel seemed to come a bit more alive and noted Amelia's approach as well.

Nice try, but not subtle enough.

"Something you care to share with the rest of us?" Amelia didn't feel like being subtle and leveled a fair glare at her superior.

The little gnome offered a weak smile and waved it off. "It is of a very personal nature and not related to our case."

I don't like secrets.

Her glare soured into a stink-eye. She was about to press for more details when Officer Johnson marched on up to the lot of them from the entranceway.

"I was on patrol and heard about the Fireball. Blasted hells, I *heard* the Fireball hit. I got back here as soon as I could." He was huffing and darting looks back over his shoulder. "And I know that this was an attack on the precinct, but what's got the boy all riled up? He looks like a bottled hurricane about to unleash some unholy fury!" He had a wild-eyed look to him.

Petals waved old Johnson aside. "I'll explain."

Amelia took the opportunity to turn to Nathaniel. "Can you tell me what you told Petals?"

The old man coughed to clear his throat and gave exacting details of what he witnessed. It wasn't what she meant, but she did her duty and took her notes.

The Fireball had been lobbed from over top of the buildings from the north end of the street. He didn't know how far away it had been launched from, and he didn't see anything to suggest who had launched it. He desperately tried to protect everyone and teared up when he sorrowfully admitted that his Lord would only grant *him* the grace of life.

She rarely saw grown men cry outside of those that had been cuffed and were being dragged to jail. The idea of being tough and strong was too well-ingrained in them. To see the old Crusader breaking down in regret and survivor's guilt tore at her heart.

"Whoever did this, I feel a great swell of sorrow in my heart. If they survive, they won't have an easy time dealing with the guilt of what they've done, especially when they were forced to do it against their will."

Amelia frowned and stopped scribbling notes in her pad. "What makes you say they did it against their will?"

Nathaniel coughed, cleared his throat, and wiped his tears away. "Whoever did this was being controlled by a cursed object."

What did Petals tell you?

"Who said anything about a cursed object?"

The old man waved off her prodding question. "It was evident from the start."

"How so?"

Nathaniel pointed to where the Fireball struck. "The man we were taking for purification was corrupted and still alive." He loudly cleared out his lungs again. "I've spent a great many years battling such evils. It certainly wasn't demonic. And I can tell you that this was not done by a witch. Witches don't let their corrupted pawns walk away."

Amelia was thoroughly impressed by how much the old man knew from experience. She gestured with her stylus to the char-stained floor. "He didn't walk away. What makes this different?"

Nathaniel shook his head. "No. The corruption cast by a witch is different than this. Also, witches don't have the skill to cast a Fireball. Trust me, I've met some of the nastiest ones you've ever heard of, and they don't have the ability. A Fireball is strictly within the realm of a wizard or sorcerer."

She feared witches a little less.

The old man cleared his throat and continued, "Instead, a witch forces their pawn to hold onto or consume something that is conditioned to release and necrotize their victim should they ever try to break free or prove to be a liability." He looked at the floor with a long-gone stare of

horror. "The poor souls literally rot before your eyes."
She feared witches a lot more.

Chapter 18

With the captain's approval, Amelia helped the old Crusader up the steps so he might examine the stone chest.

Since his cane was destroyed by the Fireball, she lent him her staff. Even with it, he needed help getting up the stairs. Surprisingly, he wasn't a bag of old bones; there was still a great deal of muscle on the man.

Paladin indeed.

Due to the dangerous nature of their calling and profession, Paladins didn't often live to a ripe old age. It made Nathaniel all that much more impressive. However, it didn't mean that he had escaped the old life. Pale scars covered every inch of exposed skin, and he winced with nearly every movement. Then there was the doctor's comment – "…he is a terribly haunted man."

She wondered if he had truly been granted a mercy by leaving the adventurous life alive.

When they reached the top of the steps, Nathaniel let out a groaned sigh of relief.

Amelia breathed a bit easier from not having the old bag of muscle and bones leaning on her smaller frame.

The captain obviously thought it best to provide a comfortable chair for their guest, for one of the chairs from the captain's office was out in the bullpen and facing the stone chest. She envied him the chair; it had cushioning.

Nathaniel hobbled his way over and groaned and huffed as he dropped into the seat. "Thank you, dear." He offered back her staff and coughed from deep within his chest. "Would you mind pouring me a cup of tea?" He cleared his throat loudly, "For my throat?" He straightened out the trench coat so that it covered him appropriately. "And perhaps something to wear?"

She looked back at the tea table at the far end of the office. "I doubt we have anything other than red leaf. Will that do?"

He nodded. "That will be fine."

Amelia made her way to the tea table and checked the kettle before flicking on the heating plate. It didn't take long for it to whistle and for her to pour the old man a cup. She returned to him and apologized, "We don't have honey or cream."

He waved it off, cupped the mug in his hands and blew on the steaming water. "I prefer it without anyway." He distantly stared at nothing in particular.

She couldn't imagine what he was feeling. All of the people that had left the temple that morning with him were dead, incinerated. There wasn't a single pinch of flesh left on any of the bones that hadn't been turned to ash. Not even the blue coats that had been holding open the doors had been spared from the fire.

Not knowing how to comfort a man in a such a state, she settled for patting his shoulder and telling him she would go look for some clothes.

Joseph is probably the right size.

She quickly made her way down the steps, across the lobby, and out the door to where Joe stood guard. "Hey,

Rook." She kept her tone a little softer than she usually did. There was no point in throwing fuel on to the fire.

He said nothing and held his ground.

Amelia cleared her throat and spoke a little louder, "Rook? Nathaniel needs to borrow some clothes. Do you–"

"Chocolate-dusted fairy drops. Bottom drawer." He didn't even bother to look back at her; he just kept staring forward. His tone was neutral, but she could tell that he was not in any mood to chat. She didn't blame him, but his words made no sense.

"Pardon?"

"Bottom drawer." He repeated himself, but she could hear a slight warning in his tone. He wasn't about to repeat himself for a third time.

"Bottom drawer. Sure." She turned around and marched right back to the bullpen.

Insufferable!

The lobby was nearly empty. Blue coats were canvassing the streets in hope of finding the one that cast the Fireball. Her bet was on the unknown assailant that incinerated the bodies in the warehouse district.

Amelia took to the stairs again. When she got near to the top, she spotted Petals having another hushed conversation with the old man.

When did he sneak up here?

Instead of climbing the last few steps and interrupting the conversation, she decided to try and listen in. With a twist of her wrist, a flick of the tip of her wand, and a small investment of energy, she produced a funnel of concentrated cold air next to her left ear.

Cold air carried sound a far greater distance than warm air did. With the funnel created, she pushed the far end out toward the hushed conversation and snaked it through the iron railing and along the floorboards.

She could almost make out what Nathaniel was whispering. "…Eye on him. He's too headstrong like–"

"Ms. Iceheart?" Petals interrupted the old man and

kept his eyes on him, but she could feel the gnome's attention on her.

She cut her connection to the cold air funnel and loudly marched her way up the remaining steps. Nathaniel peered over his shoulder to see who was arriving, then looked back to Petals and nodded in understanding. Petals continued to grin like the frighteningly irritating little trickster that he was.

"Having a secret conversation about our favorite oddball rookie?" She gave them both her best glare.

The irritating little gnome beamed all the brighter. "Well deduced, my dear."

"Care to share?"

He grinned all the more.

She knew the look. It meant "Tough luck. I'm not spilling anything." It reminded her far too much of a child withholding a secret. A very beard-laden child.

Amelia rolled her eyes and sighed in irritation as she headed to Joseph's desk.

"What are you doing?" Petals sounded genuinely concerned.

"I'm getting spare clothes out of Rook's desk so that Nathaniel doesn't have to sit naked!" She reached down and tried to pull open the bottom drawer. It didn't budge. Not only did the drawer not budge, it didn't even shake or shift. It was like the drawer was glued shut.

What is wrong with this thing?

In an attempt to loosen it up, she stood up straight and kicked the side frame of the desk, hoping it would jostle something loose. She bent down again and gave it a yank.

The entire desk shifted a smidge. "Ugh!" She stood back up and gave it two more good thumps with her boot.

"Uhh… perhaps it's locked?" Nathaniel had been the one to offer the brilliant bit of information. Seeing as how there were no locks or keyholes on any of the bottom drawers of any of the desks, she had discounted that possibility and opted for the most obvious answer; the drawer was stuck.

Amelia rounded on the spot, blew stray hair out of her face, and glared at the both of them. Nathaniel looked like he regretted his comment and returned to sipping his tea. Petals bit his bottom lip while shaking in his shoulders.

I swear to the gods if you start laughing, I'll punt you across the bullpen!

The little gnome couldn't hear her thoughts like he could Joseph's, but her face said everything it needed to. She'd perfected the dead cold stare. Petals cleared his throat loudly, wiped any hint or glimmer of laughter from his face, and waved her on.

She turned back to the desk and glared at it for answers. Unfortunately, it was just a desk and could not fear her hurting it. With her hands on her hips, she contemplated possible means of getting into that damned drawer.

That was when the dumbest thought occurred to her. She shut her eyes, eased her mind, calmed her heart, and slowed her breathing. When she opened her eyes again, she was greeted by a wire-frame of warm energy surrounding the bottom drawer. "Seriously?"

"What is the trouble, my dear?"

"He spell-locked the drawer!"

She heard a mumbled comment come from the chair behind her. It sounded an awful lot like "I told you it was locked."

Amelia shot a deathly glare over her shoulder.

Nathaniel was busy staring at the stone chest and sipping from the bloom of white hot light in place of his tea cup.

She blinked away the arcane vision, looked back at the desk, and glowered at it. Sadly, it was still just a desk, and glowering did not cause it to squirm and reveal its secrets.

"Did he not give you a key for the drawer?" Petals stepped up beside her to examine the desk as well. His violet eyes had a brilliant glow to them, so she knew he was examining the desk with his own arcane senses.

Key?

"Oh gods…" She didn't want to say it aloud, so she mumbled it. "Chocolate-dusted fairy drops." There was an inaudible snap to the air, and the bottom drawer slid open as if it had always been accessible.

Petals must have heard her because he burst out laughing.

~~

Petals thought it wise to excuse himself from the precinct and investigate her family. Joseph was stuck on sentry duty, and Amelia was ordered to wait for the linguist so they could figure out everything they could about the stone chest. Nathaniel went about washing up and changing.

Amelia generated her report concerning the Fireball while waiting for the old man. The captain had her place it on his desk; he was busy rumbling murmurs into a crystalline network box.

When Nathaniel emerged from the men's washroom, he looked slightly better than before – slightly. His eyes looked red and a little puffy, as though he'd been crying. She tried to ignore it and focus on the stone chest. If he wanted to talk about it, he would. "Does any of this look familiar to you?"

Nathaniel eyed the object as he hobbled his way back to the chair. "Somewhat…"

Amelia flipped open her notepad, ready to take notes. "What about it?"

Nathaniel grunted and groaned as he sat back down. He leaned forward a bit and pointed at the symbols on the side. "This, in general, looks familiar. I think I was in the southern Braethor mountains… yes… we were hunting an undead hound that was terrorizing a farming community. We saw markings like these on some of the ruins there."

She furiously scribbled down some notes. It wasn't much, but it was a start.

"Anything else?"

She looked away from her notes to see the old man murmuring under his breath with his eyes closed and his hand outstretched toward the stone chest.

"Sir? Are you all right?"

He raised his hand as though to suggest she wait. She waited and watched him for a moment. Eventually he got up and hobbled to the stone chest with his eyes closed. When he put his hand on the stone, his head tilted. "Ah." He said it as though he'd discovered something.

"'Ah'? What 'ah'? What did you find?" She had no idea what he was doing, but she put her stylus to notepad.

He turned to her with his eyes open and a bit of a furrow to his brow. "This is a curse box."

Curse boxes were self-explanatory. They contained cursed objects.

That was when a great many of the pieces fell together. She didn't have all the answers, but she had enough to get an idea what they were dealing with and how to find out more. "I need an index of cursed objects."

Nathaniel shook his head. "That won't do you any good. All the known cursed objects are already destroyed or under lock and key. If one of those things got loose, it'd be all over the letters of news. And they don't keep curse boxes like these."

There goes that idea.

"So how do we find out more about this cursed object?"

Someone spoke up from the stairs, "I believe that would be m-m-my field of expertise, m-m-ma'am."

Amelia turned to the source of the voice and was somewhat surprised to see a middle-aged man in slacks and suspenders. He had a tousle of ebony hair and great big spectacles that magnified his eyes many times too large. There was uneven stubble across his jaw, as if he'd been in the middle of shaving and stopped. He carried a leather case and intentionally avoided eye contact.

"Are you the linguist?" She'd been expecting him, but hadn't expected him to arrive so quickly. A glance at her watch suggested he had received the request and arrived in less than an hour. "How did you get here so quickly?"

The man stepped forward and offered his hand for a shake. "I am M-M-Mr. Patch. M-M-Mr. Teddy Patch. I am the head of the Arcanum's Symbology and Linguistics department." He still refused to make eye contact with her.

She took his hand and gently shook it. "And how did you get here so quickly?"

The man released her hand, reached into his trouser pocket, and pulled out a wand littered with glowing rune work. "I'm good with teleportation; m-m-makes it easier to run away when people get irritated."

Dislike wasn't the term she'd use; weary was higher up on the list at that moment. Her eyes darted back to his wand, as she thought she spotted a pattern amongst the chaos of mismatched runes.

Teddy noticed her interest, and he began to slowly spin the wand between his fingers, rotating on a single axis. "I carved it m-m-myself. The runes cross on four axises."

As he spun the wand, she saw it. The runes could be read vertically, horizontally, and either way diagonally.

Impressive... you would have a fun time chatting with Joseph.

"Fancy." She tried to sound unimpressed. Then she pointed her thumb over her shoulder. "Can you get to work?"

The lopsided smile spread across his face and he cowered a little as he shuffled past her to get closer to the stone chest. He ignored the chest entirely and headed for the lid lying on the floor nearby.

"What? Where are you going? The chest, we want you to examine the chest!"

His odd smile that wasn't a smile grew wider until some teeth were showing. "No," his voice was soft. He was defiant but smart enough not to be challenging about it. "Any linguistic symbologist worth their salt knows that the greatest wealth of information lies on the cover stone." The man leaned over it, chewed on his lip, and wriggled his nose back and forth as he scanned the runes.

Amelia and Nathaniel stood watching the man for a good minute. Neither of them seemed to want to interrupt him or his work. Eventually he stood and looked at the stone chest, then back to the cover.

"Figure anything out, young man?" Nathaniel spoke softly.

Teddy turned to them both and quickly darted his eyes down. "Yes. This is an ancient language that pre-dates the Braethor Kingdom."

That fit with what Nathaniel had told her. "Is there anything else? What specifically does it say?"

The odd man turned back to the stone lid and began circling it slowly. She found it odd that he wasn't staying in one place and reading it.

"What are you doing?"

He didn't take his eyes off the stone chest. "It must be read this way. The lettering is designed and chiseled so that each rune represents four different characters at the same time, depending on the angle you view it from – an ancient form of cryptic cypher."

She'd never heard of such a thing. "Why would they do that?"

"It saves on space. You can fit more stories on a page, and it prevents outsiders from being able to read it properly." He kept circling the stone lid, clockwise.

It was making her slightly dizzy, so she stopped watching him and turned her attention back to her notepad. "What is it saying?" He kept circling. Either he hadn't read enough to be able to answer, or he was too engrossed in his reading to have heard her. She decided to give it a minute before repeating herself. "Anything you would like to share with the rest of us?"

He came to an abrupt stop, and stared at the lid. "Oh dear."

Out with it, Goggles!

Amelia let out a deep breath of irritation as she stood waiting. The man started circling again without saying another word.

"Goddess of Mercy! Tell us what you discovered!"

Mr. Patch jumped, flailed, drew his wand, and madly flicked and twisted it in a state of panic. There was a grating, irritating scratching to the air, and Mr. Patch popped out of existence only to suddenly pop back in again three paces to the side of where he'd been before. He also reappeared upside down and landed on his head in a crumpled mess. "Hrngh!"

Moron!

"Nobody can teleport inside of the precinct! It's warded against that sort of thing!"

The man flailed his arms, hurriedly picked up his oversized spectacles, and pressed them back on to his face before scurrying to his feet. He hadn't dropped his leather case throughout the entire ordeal either. "I'm sorry. I don't take well to shouting. M-m-my first instinct is to teleport away."

Nathaniel placed a hand on her shoulder and gave her a sideways look. It said "Calm yourself." She took another deep breath, shut her eyes, and pinched the bridge of her nose. "We're dealing with some extreme and time-sensitive circumstances. Do you mind telling us what you've found so far?"

Amelia opened her eyes again and brought up her stylus to start taking notes.

"Of course, of course." Mr. Patch kept darting his eyes around and continued to purposefully avoid eye contact. He stuffed his wand back in his pocket and squared off with Amelia. "I think the lid tells a story of warning. I haven't gotten far, but the few words I have translated suggest the contents of this box m-m-may have caused the fall of the kingdom that pre-dates Braethor."

Lovely.

Chapter 19

"A kingdom?" Nathaniel didn't sound convinced.

"Yes." Mr. Patch turned to the old Paladin in response but kept his eyes diverted.

"A whole kingdom?" She didn't believe it herself.

"Yes." The linguist turned his attention to her, but still kept his eyes focused on something else entirely. The odd man raised a finger in point. "M-m-mind you, this is only what m-m-my initial impression of a m-m-minute piece of the lid has suggested. In order to confirm that hypothesis, I would need to further decipher the rest of the text."

Amelia put her hands on her hips and let out a huff. "How long?" She hated waiting.

"Time."

She didn't know why he needed to know the time of day, but she checked her watch anyway. "Two seventeen."

The lop-sided smile returned.

"What are you grinning at?"

His odd grin vanished immediately. "I wasn't asking

for the time. I was telling you it would take time."

"Time isn't an answer to my question. I figured it would take time. I want to know *how much* time." Her patience was wearing thin.

Mr. Patch twisted his mouth to the same side he grinned from and lowered his eyes so that he was almost looking directly at the floor. "I don't like to tell people how m-m-much time I think it will take, because they either get upset and tell m-m-me to do it faster, or they expect it to be done in exactly that m-m-much time when it could take longer. That is why I tell people it will take time."

Nathaniel let out a soft grunt and nodded in understanding. "Your way of telling people to bugger off so that you can do what you need to do, and it will take you as long as it takes to get it done."

The corner of his mouth threatened to turn into that lop-sided smile again.

Amelia was put off by the grin and waved the man on. "Get it done."

Mr. Patch knelt down, opened his leather case, and began removing stationery and a tome. Satisfied that the man was busy, she turned her attention to Nathaniel. "Do you need me to get you anything?"

He hobbled a few steps to the cushioned chair and grunted as he sat down into it. "No no, dear. Thank you, but I think I will rest for a minute before heading back to the temple." His voice shook a little as he looked at his hands. "There are friends to bury."

She felt a pang in her heart for the poor man, so she rested a comforting hand on his shoulder. He didn't lift his head, but he did offer a sad smile.

"Shall I call you a gnome cart?"

The soul-sick old crusader took a deep shuddering breath and nodded. "That would be very kind of you."

She stepped aside, pulled her network box, and called for a gnome cart. Upon returning, she saw that the old man was calmly observing Mr. Patch from his cushioned chair.

"Your cart will be here shortly." Amelia offered up her staff again.

The old crusader offered another sad smile and gripped her staff with both hands as he heaved himself up and out of the chair with a laborious grunt and weary groan. "I apologize for being such a burden."

"Nonsense, you remind me of my mother's father. He grunted a lot too. He creaked more than a ship at sea." It wasn't often that she attempted to use humor, but she understood that there were times when light-hearted banter was necessary.

A throaty chuckle emanated from deep within the Paladin, and he cracked a bit of a smile. "Such is the price of old age."

She helped him down the spiral iron steps to the main floor. The debris had been swept away, and the charred frame that had once been the entrance had been pulled down in preparation for the new doors. There was nothing but a breezy stone-and-mortar hole in the front of the precinct. Joseph was the only thing standing between them and another attack. Unfortunately, Joseph didn't look all that sentry-like.

Earlier, he had been a lone silhouette of strength and resolve. In this moment, he was sagging in the shoulders and hugging a woman to his side. She had both arms around his waist, and he was resting his cheek on her head as she rested her head against his chest. His one hand was still on his staff, but he didn't look like the picture of defiance or strength; if anything, it looked like she was the one propping him up.

"Who is that?" Nathaniel whispered as they slowly approached.

The figure was too tall for it to be Ruby, and he didn't think that Joe was that comfortable with hugging her in that fashion. Amelia kept her voice low, "I presume it is the woman he's courting."

She saw a big grin spread across the grizzled face. "Good man. He needs someone like that in his life."

A curious question bubbled to mind. "Have you... ever?" She left the question incomplete and allowed the context of the conversation to fill out the rest.

There were religions and deities that frowned upon coupling or marriage, or at least the highest priests within the order deemed it so. The opposite was also true, as certain deities encouraged indulgence in certain vices and pleasures. Amelia had been raised in a household that followed the 'purity' of the Lord of Light. Seeing as how Nathaniel was a Paladin of that order, she couldn't help but wonder.

The old man slowed to a stop and stared at the floor. Sadness seemed to overtake him, one that was different than the sorrow of loss he'd been experiencing since the Fireball had dropped. If she were to try and guess, it looked like a longing sadness for something long gone. It did not appear as deep-cutting as the recent loss, but it was undeniably lingering. "Once. Long ago." His words were a whisper. "When I was a fool and thought the Lord of Light would let me leave my oath."

Amelia watched as the old man coughed to clear his throat, squared his shoulders, and hobbled onwards to the entrance. She could imagine the wealth of stories he had to share but knew better than to prod a man that was grieving.

"Joseph, my boy, you must introduce me." They had made it to the entrance, and Nathaniel was gesturing to the young woman on the rookie's side.

Amelia stepped out from under the natural protection of the precinct to eye the arcane barrier that Joseph had erected. Unlike before, it was little more than a shimmering distortion to the naked eye. However, she could still hear and feel it; there was a soft hum in the air. As she neared it, her sense of alarm spiked. There was definitely some offensive magic mixed in with the defensive; she didn't feel particularly inclined to try and find out what kind. Nor did she care to open her eyes to the greater 'verse and peek.

In response to Nathaniel's sudden appearance and inquiry, the young woman stepped away from hugging Joe's side and straightened her nurse's gown.

She was a moderately attractive woman with a button nose, thin lips, a slight frame, and curly brown hair. All of it was contained within the standard uniform of a nurse: stark white with the blood-drop symbol of the medical corp. Her hair was pulled back by a white cloth, her apron was pocketed and her gown reached just below her knees. The woman was smart enough to wear sensible slips for shoes.

"Ms. Bell. Grace Bell." She offered a hand to Nathaniel.

The Paladin took her hand and gently enveloped it with his scarred and meaty one. "It is a wonderful pleasure to meet you, dear."

The nurse immediately noticed the scars and frowned. "My goodness. You have seen far too many battles, good sir."

Nathaniel took his hand back and put it to use gripping Amelia's staff for balance. He coughed and cleared his throat. "I have, my dear, but I am afraid that my cart has arrived, and I must be going." She presumed that he had had enough of sharing his horror stories for one day.

The gnome cart was just pulling up to the base of the precinct steps. Nurse Bell jumped to attention and quickly stepped forward to help the aging ex-crusader. "Let me help you."

Joseph looked like he was about to jump to attention as well, but he couldn't. The barrier he had erected required him to stand his ground with staff in hand. He looked back and forth between the old man and his staff, and he looked increasingly irritated by the fact that he couldn't help.

Nurse Bell blindly reached out and put a calming hand on Joe's arm as she stepped up to Nathaniel's side. The old man warmly accepted her offer and seemed to even melt a little at her touch as she wrapped her arm under his and gripped his hand. Joe significantly calmed.

Amelia couldn't help but nod in approval. The woman was truly a healer at heart.

A nurse and a knight; quite the fairytale romance there, Rook.

The barrier shimmered briefly as the nurse escorted the old man down the steps. They passed through it as though nothing was there. She was intrigued and wanted to experience it, but she had more important matters to deal with.

Amelia stepped up to Joseph's side and crossed her arms over her chest. "You look as though you've healed well from yesterday."

His eyes darted to her momentarily as they both watched the nurse help the old man into the gnome cart. "I have. Doc gave me a healing salve before leaving the precinct yesterday. I still have some sore ribs, but nothing I can't handle."

She looked to the humming barrier and inquired in a more sensitive and soft tone, "And how are you feeling?"

The barrier warbled and rippled for a moment before it began to hum louder. "Angry."

I don't blame you.

"Keep your head on straight, Rook."

"It is on straight. If it wasn't, I wouldn't be here. I'd be hunting down the bastard that sent that Fireball." She felt the heat of his voice. It was slightly aimed at her, but she understood the frustration.

The nurse waved goodbye as the gnome cart puttered and rumbled off down the cobblestones. She turned and headed back toward the two of them and had Amelia's staff in hand.

"As much as you want to go after them, you don't have much in the way of offensive magic." In the short time that she'd known him, she'd only ever seen him use his firearm, fists, and knife for combat. His barriers were second to none, but he had no offensive techniques. "At best, you would prove an immovable annoyance that they might exhaust themselves trying to beat."

He growled slightly and ground his hands into the wood of his staff.

Hate it all you want, I'm right.

The nurse slowed as she approached. She was looking directly at Joseph and seemed worried. Amelia waved her up the steps and put out her hand so that she could take back her staff. It was easy enough to summon it, but she didn't feel like startling the woman.

Ms. Bell hurried up the steps, passed through the barrier, and handed off the staff. Amelia took it and shrunk it down to a wand before pocketing it.

"What's wrong?" Ms. Bell stepped up directly in front of Joe and put her hands on top of his as he gripped his staff.

He put on a fake smile that did nothing to hide the anger behind it and tried to brush it off. "Nothing. I'm just frustrated."

She gave him a disapproving scowl that was worthy of praise. Joe's shoulders sagged slightly.

"Don't you give me that 'nothing' nonsense. I may not understand all of this wizard business, but you can be rest assured I know enough about people to tell when they're hiding things."

He breathed in deeply through his nose and let out a groaning sigh as he closed his eyes and leaned his head against the head of his staff. "I'm worried."

She patted his hands. "I know. I know. I'll head over to Runelore's and will stay with Ruby until you get there."

Joe breathed deeply and exhaled. "Thank you."

She gave him a beaming smile and reached up to touch his cheek. Amelia diverted her eyes in order to give them a small bit of privacy.

They whispered something to each other, and she

heard the puckering wetness of a kiss before the young woman turned and headed back down the precinct steps and through the barrier. She waved back over her shoulder and continued down the street.

Amelia turned her attention back to Joseph and watched him turn red as he stared forward with a dumb little grin on his face.

Sorry, Rook, but I have to burst your happy bubble.

"It's a cursed object."

His dumb little grin warped into a scowling frown.

She piled on, "Actually, it's more likely to be two cursed objects."

She expected to see some sort of thinking or pondering take place, but it didn't. "I came to the same conclusion."

What?

"How?"

His scowling frown turned more introspective. "I had suspicions that it might be a cursed object, but I wasn't sure until the Fireball fell."

She narrowed her eyes. "Nathaniel told you about his experience with witches, didn't he?"

He shook his head. "Not just Nathaniel. Witches are commonly discussed as heretical beings throughout the temple. I heard enough rumors and stories while growing up. Witches are subtle and enact contingencies. There was nothing subtle about this." He took a breath and paused to eyeball a blue coat coming up the steps. He nodded to the woman, and she nodded back. Joe twisted his wrist on the staff, and the barrier between them and blue coat rippled. She walked through the barrier and entered the precinct, passing by them both.

"That couldn't be the only reason."

He shook his head again. "No, there's also the stone chest. It belonged to the puppet-man. The puppet-man was at the crime scene. Elemental magic at the crime scene was undoubtedly caused by sorcerers. Only the most powerful of wizards or mad sorcerers can craft cursed objects."

It was the same line of reasoning she had drawn earlier.

"Puppet-man refused to harm us and utilized martial skills that were specifically designed to subdue magic users."

She shut her eyes and groaned. "Blasted thundering—" She was about to say 'Fireballs' but stifled herself at the last moment. It didn't feel right to say it aloud when it had been a literal cause of death that day. "This puppet is used by a warden for the damned cursed objects."

Joe chewed on his bottom lip. "It is, but I'm wondering if there is any man involved in this at all. I'm thinking the puppet may be a construct."

"A construct?" She chewed on the thought. Constructs were old world magic; they were often referred to as golems or animated guardians. They weren't very intelligent and tended to be fairly simple-minded in their approach to completing tasks. Their movements were also wooden and simplistically precise.

A puppet was the modern equivalent; they were constructs that were designed to be remotely operated. They allowed for more precise and intelligent operations to be completed while the operator remained safe and out of harm's way. However, humans were prone to making mistakes. There was also the reaction timing to consider.

The thing that they chased to the alley was undeniably skilled in hand-to-hand combat, which suggested it was a puppet being manipulated by a master, but the precise and exact movements were too inhuman. "That actually makes a lot more sense now."

"The problem is that this construct wasn't designed to understand our way of doing things and doesn't realize we're trying to accomplish the same goals. If it came to us in the first place…" Joe ground his hands and squeezed his staff. "People would still be alive."

She slapped Joe on the back. "The construct isn't the one at fault. Whoever swiped the cursed objects out from under the warden's non-existent nose is the one at fault for all of this."

The only plausible explanation was that someone had learned of the cursed objects, stolen them, and released them on the city. Why any moron would willingly release cursed objects was beyond her. Unless of course they accidentally released the objects and had no idea they were cursed. It was possible that they thought the objects were merely valuable keepsakes to be pawned on the black market.

He glanced at her and sighed. "You're right. We need to find out who stole the cursed objects."

Amelia's stomach twisted as she contemplated the possibilities.

I have a bad feeling.

There was a loud and startling *pop* to the air, and a cloud of blue sparkling smoke materialized before the barrier. The smoke dissipated quite quickly, and it left an exasperated Petals in its place. "I apologize, my dear, but I could not find your brother."

I have a very bad feeling.

"He left his last known residence in quite the hurry. It appears as though he may be on the run."

Chapter 20

Blast it all!

The possibility that her family was not involved was swiftly dwindling. Dragging out the specifics of how involved would prove exceedingly difficult; her family was as stubborn as the ocean was vast.

She looked to her superior and pleaded, "He's my twin. If anyone can find him, it's going to be me."

He offered her a tight-lipped smile and said, "No," then proceeded to pass through the barrier, walk between her and Joseph, and into the precinct.

She could hear Joe mumbling "Twin?" under his breath.

She ignored it and followed Petals. "'No'? Just no?"

"That is correct, my dear. No."

She trailed after him. Despite the man's much smaller legs, he was difficult to keep up with. She had learned long ago that he utilized magic to aid him in moving about. "We need him to answer questions!"

"We do indeed." The trickster began hopping up the spiral iron steps.

Amelia had to take to the steps almost two at a time in order to keep up. "Then someone has to find him!"

"Precisely, my dear."

"And that someone should be me!"

They were halfway up the steps when the little gnome suddenly halted. She didn't have to worry about running into him, as that would have required her to have quicker feet. He turned on the spot to face her and offered a sad smile. "I do not do this to be cruel, and I do not doubt your invaluable insight. I do this Ie they will want to speak with you. I know how they think. Also because it is policy."

Amelia blew some stray hair from her face, shut her eyes, and tried to contemplate all the potential meanings of 'they'. He clearly wasn't referring to her family; nobody knew her family as well as she did. Sadly, it was the only iteration of 'they' that she could think of. "Who is 'th–" She opened her eyes only to see an empty staircase.

Growling, she marched her way up the final steps. She looked about the bullpen to try and spot him. Mr. Patch was standing before the lid with a large leather bound tome in hand. Petals was standing on top of the edge to the stone chest and peering inside with his hands clasped behind his back.

She was tempted to shove him in. "It's really not funny when you just vanish in the middle of me asking a question."

Her superior straightened from peering inside and expertly balanced on the narrow edge as he turned about. "You had more questions?" His grin was mischievous.

"Yes!" she barked in frustration.

There was a sudden flourish of movement and a grating, irritating scratch to the air. Mr. Patch popped out of existence and the tome he had been holding flopped to the floor of the bullpen with a thunderous clap. Half a breath later, he reappeared on the other side of the stone chest, sideways and facing the other direction.

The man let out a scream of panic as he flailed and dropped to the floor. He fell from a height equal to that of the chest, so he likely didn't sustain any terrible injuries. She heard him hit with a grunt.

Petals stood baffled by the display.

Mr. Patch popped back up to his feet, fixed his spectacles, and hurried back over to his tome without uttering a single word.

The little gnome spun about on the spot and followed the curious display. He turned his attention to Amelia, then silently and subtly pointed a finger to the odd linguistic symbologist and raised an eyebrow.

Amelia sighed and lowered her voice as she approached. "I startled him."

Mr. Patch picked up his tome and began circling the stone lid once again.

Petals gestured with his eyes and tilted his head with a greater level of inquiry.

"He's deciphering. Something about angles." She couldn't be bothered to remember exactly what the man had said or how it was said. The results were what mattered to her.

The trickster shrugged and gestured for her to go on. "You had questions?"

"Yes. Who is 'they'?"

He offered a sad smile. "Internal Investigations."

Oh. That 'they.'

She had been investigated by them once before when she was first applying to the Academy. It wasn't normal for applicants to be investigated, but it wasn't every day that an applicant had killed their own father. They wanted to make sure that she was sound of mind and not someone with murderous inclinations. Clearly, she wasn't.

"Why would Internal Investigations get involved?"

He grinned knowingly. "Why indeed?"

She hated when he did that. It suggested that he

knew something and wanted her to figure it out. "Out with it; today isn't a day for games."

He effortlessly balanced his way along the edge and paced back and forth. "Games keep the mind sharp, my dear. Besides, we have plenty of time to expend."

Amelia couldn't help but rise to the comment. "It's getting more and more chaotic out there." She blindly pointed to the front entryway. "Who knows how many more bodies are piling up! All while we stand up here and wait for a translation that may or may not provide us with useful information when we should be hitting the cobblestones and shaking down every lead we can find! What time could we possibly have to 'expend' on stupid games?"

There was a twitch to the little man's eye, and his usual smile faded to a tight line. "Amelia." He only ever used her first name when he was driving home a very important point or he wasn't very happy. "We have all available blue coats 'hitting the cobblestones', and they have yet to find a shred of evidence as to who launched the Fireball or where it was launched from." His tone was devoid of joy. "All available detectives from all precincts are strangling information from informants." He slowly balanced along the edge of the stone chest to come face to face with her. "The people of the city are in a state of panic. As soon as word got out that a precinct was attacked, they all ran to their homes and locked their doors. The streets are empty; businesses are closed. They heard that blue blood had been spilled." He paused for an intended punctuation of the point: "They don't feel safe anymore." The trickster gnome's voice fell lower and lower into an angry growl. "And *you*," he pointed at her with a stubby little finger and glared her down with his brilliant violet eyes, "are directly related to our only suspect."

Amelia stood transfixed. Mr. Patch had halted his circling and was cowering with his nose buried in his tome and his back to them both.

The little gnome must have taken note, because he straightened out his vest, cleared his throat, and breathed deeply in order to calm himself before continuing. "With all of that said, I invite you to contemplate what it is you think you could possibly be doing at this moment. Unless of course you have a lead you think we should follow, one that you haven't informed me of?" His eyes narrowed in challenge.

She shook her head vigorously.

"Wonderful!" He barked it joyously and hopped on the spot.

Amelia jumped from the outburst, and so did Mr. Patch. The man flailed and popped out of existence at the same moment. There was the familiar grating scratch in the air. He took his tome with him that time.

The jumpy man popped back into existence and bounced off the captain's door before falling to his rear. He had his tome wrapped tightly in his arms.

Petals gave Mr. Patch the same questioning frown of befuddlement that he usually reserved for the spontaneously-combustible precinct quartermaster. It was a look that expressed an exasperated and frustrated "Why?"

Amelia was about to turn her attention back to her superior and attempt to re-ask her original question when the captain's door opened. The massive dragon kin filled the doorway with his imposing frame. He didn't look agitated, as his eyes didn't have that fire to them. The scales and protruding horns didn't allow for much movement when it came to facial muscles or expressions. Much of his mood was present in his actions and the intensity of his eyes.

Nonetheless, Mr. Patch only glanced up once. The remainder of the spindly man's encounter with the captain involved staring very intently at the floorboards between his outstretched legs. She half expected the little man to wet himself.

Amelia nodded in respect. "Captain."

Petals beamed and inclined his head.

Captain Bolt looked down upon the tiny man before him and rumbled out, "Did you need something?"

Mr. Patch vigorously shook his head.

"He bumped into your door." Amelia offered the quickest explanation. The captain let out a deep rumble of understanding before slowly shutting his office door.

Mr. Patch quickly scurried to his feet and marched over to the both of them with his eyes glued to the floor. "W-w-where are the facilities?"

Amelia pointed to the men's washroom, and the odd man hurried on over to them with his tome tightly clutched in his arms. With the door firmly shut behind him, Amelia murmured under her breath, "I believe the captain scared his bladder loose."

"A fair assessment, my dear."

She turned her attention back to her superior and eyed him down. "I seriously don't have time for games."

He returned to pacing the edge of the stone chest. "I insist that you play. A good detective must have their mind tested at all times, and as I already explained, we have time to expend." As he rounded the corner of the chest, she noted that he wasn't grinning or smiling. Petals was eyeballing the runes inside of the curse box in a deep state of concentration.

Fine, we'll play your dumb game.

Amelia pondered the possible reasons why Internal Investigations would want to speak with her. She had followed all standard protocols so far. Petals went alone to try and question her twin brother, and she hadn't spoken with her family since the night prior.

I'm an idiot.

She sighed heavily and sagged slightly in the shoulders. "I went and saw my family last night."

Petals smiled a little as he continued to investigate the interior of the stone chest. "Precisely."

"Wait... how did you know I visited my family last night?" Besides her family, Blueregard and Betty were the only ones that knew about it.

Petals halted, looked up to her, and grinned

mischievously. "Our ever-vigilant rookie expressed his concern for you."

Blast it all!

She had Joseph examine the letter. "It was that stupid letter, wasn't it?"

He beamed and continued to walk along the edge. "It was."

The only plausible explanation that would follow the letter was that Petals had investigated and discovered she had visited her family. "Who told you?"

Petals paused his pacing to lean in and investigate a piece of the undeciphered runes a bit more closely. "A kindly and respectable Oath-sworn man."

Amelia was shaken. "Blueregard?"

Petals straightened and turned to her with raised eyebrows. "Do you know of other Oath-sworn men in your life?" She couldn't tell if the question was rhetorical or genuine.

That only made her question if there were more. "I don't know!"

His raised eyebrows dropped into a furrow. "What do you mean you don't know? Surely you would know if they were Oath-sworn."

She narrowed her eyes at him. "I never knew Blueregard was Oath-sworn until last night. He kept that a secret for my entire life."

Petals eyebrows leaped up again, and he turned away from her and focused his attention back on the chest. "I see."

"Do you know what oath he swore?"

The trickster lifted a hand to halt her. "If he has not told you, then it is not my place to say. Besides, it is extremely rare for a living Oath-sworn to boast of their oath. To do so often results in a dead Oath-sworn."

She felt her mind twisting into knots. "How? Why?"

Petals continued to pace. "Let us say for a moment that I swore an oath to protect all cats."

Amelia shut her eyes, rubbed them, and cleared her head of all questions. "All right, let's play this game."

"Wonderful! As an Oath-sworn, I would be considered by the gods to be the finest protector of cats that anyone had ever seen."

That was generally how Oath-sworn worked, so she didn't find it to be in any way surprising or educational. "I got that much."

Petals lifted a finger as he continued to walk about the edge of the chest. "One could then easily lay a trap by threatening to harm a cat."

Amelia shrugged. "Wouldn't that be part of your daily life of being the protector of cats?"

He beamed. "No, my dear. If I was an intelligent Oath-sworn, I would never have told anyone that I swore to protect cats."

She had to try and wrap her mind around the concept and found it full of holes. "Wouldn't someone eventually figure out that you're the protector of cats because you're always running about saving them?"

He waved off the comment with a flourish of his hand. "Yes, but this is merely a mental exercise."

The whole concept was only slightly less confusing.

"Let us begin again and instead select a more realistic example."

She didn't feel like beginning again and felt like they were far off topic. "It's fine. I'll ask Blue when I get the chance. I get that things are a bit more questionable now that you throw in the fact I visited my family, but how would Internal Investigations know about it?"

Petals halted his pacing and turned a single raised eyebrow to her. "How would they not?"

Amelia was a bit taken aback, "Are you telling me that they're constantly investigating everything that we do?"

He shook his head and waved off the comment. "Absolutely not." He returned to pacing. "They merely investigate after the fact and would find your visit to be rather circumspect."

That makes more sense.

Having finally gotten to the point, she could understand where Petals was coming from. "My family's involvement and my visit last night is starting to check off some suspicion boxes."

He beamed. "Precisely."

She understood the protocols were in place for a reason, but she couldn't help but want to find out exactly what her brother was up to.

The door to the facilities opened and Mr. Patch marched out with his lopsided smile and his eyes focused on the floor in front of him. "They're called the Twin Crowns."

"What are?" Her mind was desperately trying to switch the conversation again and redirect it to whatever Mr. Patch was talking about. It took her a brief moment to catch on. "The cursed objects?"

He nodded vigorously as he made a wide circle around her and Petals and bee-lined for the lid. "Yes. I was having some difficulty with one particular symbol. A quiet refreshing read of my tome helped m-m-me to figure it out." The man immediately began circling the lid again. "It's written in poetic prose, as m-m-many grand stories were told in the ancient days. It tells of twin siblings, born with m-m-magical powers over ice and fire."

Finally! Some answers!

Amelia and Petals stood quietly and watched as the odd man walked circles around the stone lid.

"There's still a great deal m-m-more to translate, but it effectively reads as a warning."

A curse box with a warning on it, who would have guessed.

"Entombed within are the Twin Crowns of hot and cold. The destroyers of the kingdom." He paused and glanced in their general direction.

"Is that it?"

He nodded.

"It has taken you this entire time to decipher that

small amount of text?"

Mr. Patch gave a deep shrug and kept his eyes focused elsewhere. "Time."

Petals frowned and looked at his watch.

Amelia waved him off. "He's saying it will take time."

"Ah." Petals continued to look at his watch anyway. "It is mid-afternoon, and there is still much to do."

~~

Amelia generated a report concerning what they had so far learned from the lid of the curse box, and what they presumed the cursed objects to be. The captain immediately approved the documentation and conveyed the information through the crystalline network to the other precincts.

Petals updated Joseph on what they had learned and spent much of the afternoon chatting with him. She could only guess at what was discussed as she was stuck monitoring the translation process. More accurately, she was stuck watching an oddball walk in circles.

Sadly, most of what was translated that afternoon was a recounting of how the kingdom fell. Much of it simply detailed the aftermath and the devastation. Any potential information that covered the Crowns had yet to be uncovered.

Petals returned near the end of the working day. He led an older woman up the iron steps. She was of moderate height, pale, thin, and wiry. Deep wrinkles framed her eyes and mouth, but despite her apparent age, she walked with a youthful confidence and bounce to her step. Her eyes were a rich brown and stood out in stark contrast to her silvery gray hair. Miniscule spectacles were balanced on her nose, and the woman wore a deep purple vest over a white blouse and long black skirts. Tucked under one arm was a massive tome, and she could see the tip of a wand in the vest pocket. She was from the Arcanum.

She looked about the place and noted Mr. Patch. "Professor, wonderful to be working with you again." Her voice was clear and the words enunciated.

Mr. Patch paused his circling to lift his head and glance in the old woman's direction. He smiled a little out one corner of his mouth and nodded his head. "Always nice to work with you again, M-M-Mrs. Spellocke."

The woman continued forth, stepped up to Amelia, and nodded her head in greeting. "Professor Aurora Spellocke, at your service."

Amelia nodded her head in turn. "Detective Iceheart. And what service is it you provide?"

The professor gave her a warm toothless smile, turned to the stone chest, and gestured to it. "I am a professor of Protective Runes. I'm here to help find the means by which to subdue and contain these cursed objects."

Finally!

Amelia perked up a bit. She had hoped to get some sort of information from the translations, but a means by which to combat and contain a cursed object was far more appealing. She gestured for Mrs. Spellocke to go ahead.

The professor stepped up, immediately began examining the stone chest, and opened her tome. "When I first caught word that a cursed object was loose, I was understandably shaken by the news." She shuddered and flipped through pages. "When my presence was requested at the precinct that had been hit by the Fireball... I dreaded undertaking the journey." She paused and spoke over her shoulder. "I mean no offense, Detective. I am certain you are all capable in your own rights..." she paused before speaking in a grave hush, "but a Fireball thrown by someone under the influence of a cursed object is something else altogether."

Amelia turned to look for Petals, only to find he wasn't present. "What was it that alleviated your fears?" She turned about and eventually found her superior sitting at his desk. The gnome was generating a report with his arcane mechanical typographer. She crossed her arms and promised herself for the unknown-numbered time that she would find a way to put a bell on the trickster.

The professor offered a relaxed chuckle. "My fears were set aside when Detective Pettlebottom came to the Arcanum."

"He offered to teleport you here so that you didn't have to traverse the city?"

"Yes. I was also convinced of the safety of my visit when I was informed that my star pupil, Mr. Runewall, was stationed here and holding up an arcane barrier."

Amelia turned on the spot and uncrossed her arms. "Star pupil?"

Professor Spellocke offered up another light-hearted chuckle. "Oh yes, unnaturally gifted. I'd almost swear he had fey ancestry."

Amelia wheeled back around to see Petals looking directly at her with a bit of a surprised look on his face. He had heard as well.

Chapter 21

The professor continued to talk while examining the stone chest. "Of course, my theory proved to be incorrect." She sounded rather disappointed.

Amelia turned back to the professor. "He isn't?"

"Sadly, no. I would have been delighted to have a sorcerer amongst my students."

She wasn't convinced. "How do you know he isn't?" She turned and looked back at Petals; he wasn't there, and he wasn't anywhere to be seen.

Blasted gnome! You need a bell!

"Well…" The woman cleared her throat and side-stepped a bit so that she might examine a different portion of the stone chest. "I may have tested his blood."

"May have?" Testing blood without permission was technically illegal, but the Arcanum sat in a legal gray zone. It bothered her on more than one occasion.

She glanced at Amelia with pressed lips. "I may have helped myself to a sample of his presented blood when he asked me to check his work."

"A lineage spell?" It was the most obvious reason for Joe to have drawn his own blood and used it in a spell. He was an orphan and wanted to know who his parents were. She almost envied him.

She offered a sad smile and nodded. "Yes."

"And what exactly did you do with this sample that you helped yourself to?" Depending on how the blood was used, the professor might see the inside of a prison.

The professor pulled a violet-shaded monocle from her vest pocket and peered through it. Amelia presumed that the monocle was utilized to examine the magical framework of the box.

"Alchemical testing," the professor said in a very matter-of-fact way.

"Pardon?" She'd never heard of anyone using alchemy to determine a bloodline.

The professor slowly shuffled her way about the chest, examining it. "Yes. A friend and fellow professor at the Arcanum has discovered a means by which to discern whether or not someone has mixed blood."

"How?" Amelia had never been that stellar of an alchemy student.

"Certain minerals, metals, and herbs react differently to different races." She continued to circle the stone chest but stopped for a moment. She frowned, peered closer, then continued on her way again. "Dwarves, for example, have a hearty resilience to toxins."

Despite her blurred memory of Anvilhearth's funeral, she did recall that the dwarves in attendance were able to withstand staggering amounts of ale. Mindfully, a good portion of that overpowering drink wound up in beards and on the floor of the grand hall. Drunken dwarves enjoyed telling drunken tales with their hands.

Nodding in agreement, she waved the professor on. "And fey?"

She got a twinkle in her eye. "Fey blood revitalizes

dried-out leaves."

"And Joseph?"

Professor Spellocke scrunched her nose. "Not a damned thing. He's wholly human."

Blast.

"Could a human be a sorcerer without fey lineage?"

The professor's eyebrows raised a little as she continued her examination and conversation. "Of course. They are extremely rare, but there are individuals that are bestowed powers by greater beings–" she stood straight and gestured with both hands to the stone chest before them, "– or an item."

It explained the sorcerer spellwork at the ice field. Whoever had been possessed by the cursed object had been turned into a conduit for the contained entity.

Amelia couldn't recall seeing any particular odd items or trinkets that Joe carried about with him. "How else can you possibly determine if someone is a sorcerer other than blood or an item?" She was genuinely curious and hoped she might find some other method by which to test the newest member of their precinct.

The professor bent back down and rounded the last bit of the stone chest and tracked her way back toward Amelia. "Physical appearance is the most obvious. Horns, claws, tails, wings, and any other number of various oddities would surely point toward an individual being a sorcerer."

Amelia was already familiar with such things and Joseph didn't have any outstandingly odd physical features.

Blast.

"Why do you ask?" The professor turned a quizzical eye upon her.

"Wanted to know how I might recognize one."

She grinned a little. "They're interesting folk, aren't they?"

She glanced over her shoulder to find Petals had returned to his desk and was tapping away at his typographer. "Interesting indeed."

What were you doing?

The professor loudly cleared her throat. "Pardon me, dear."

Amelia turned back around to find that the professor was shuffling toward her and gesturing to the part of the stone chest that Amelia was standing directly in front of. She apologized and immediately stepped back and out of the way.

"When it comes to cursed objects, you want to keep an eye out for odd behavior and an item that can only be seen with arcane vision."

A thought occurred to her. "Like a crown?"

The professor nodded as she continued to eye the chest. "That would certainly be an oddity in this era." She stopped as she finally made a full circle and returned to her opened tome.

Amelia turned on the spot and headed to Petals. "We–"

One of his hands shot up and suggested she stop. His other hand continued to tap away at the rune keys as his eyes remained fixed on the page. "I heard. I will inform the captain. A city-wide notice will go out to all detectives to use their secondary eyes to see if they can spot anything out of the ordinary."

She felt utterly and irritatingly useless. "What–"

His hand shot up a little higher than the first time. "The translation and counter-spells will take time to decipher and formulate, the front door is covered, and we have plenty of officers and detectives on the streets." He finally stopped tapping the rune keys on his typesetter, clasped his hands before him on his desk, and looked to her with a warm smile. "Go home and get rest. There will be plenty of work to do tomorrow and plenty of exhausted detectives and officers wanting a reprieve."

The idea was both lovely and demeaning. Seeing as how she lost her lunch and had seen enough death and destruction for one day, she opted for taking the advice. She also wanted a bath.

"Fine." Despite giving in, she wasn't about to let one thing go. "But I still have a few questions left."

Amelia turned back to face the professor and inquired, "Why would Detective Runewall put you at ease? You were his instructor; surely you can craft wards and barriers that are superior to his?" She felt she knew the answer, but she wanted to hear it spoken aloud.

Professor Spellocke released a tittering laugh of amusement. "Hahaha!" She clearly found the question to be absurd. The woman turned to Amelia, shaking her head. "That boy can create barriers *far* stronger than mine."

Knew it.

The woman continued and gave her a knowing smile. "My expertise in barriers, wards, locks, and the like is mostly academic. I am fascinated by them and study them relentlessly. For that reason, I am skilled in crafting and deconstructing complex designs." She paused briefly to catch her breath. "Mr. Runewall, on the other hand, is driven by an unflinching need to protect. His magic is driven by sheer force of will. Combine that with his schooling, and he is a formidable protector."

It made sense. The foundational principal of magic was that the intensity and strength of magic was based on the will of the caster. Half-hearted or lackluster attempts would not succeed. Joseph was one of those 'knight in shining armor' types. He would throw himself into the path of any danger if it meant protecting an innocent. That sort of determination would undoubtedly lead to stronger magic.

Amelia had one last question. "You truly believe he is capable of stopping a Fireball with one of his barriers?"

The professor clasped her hands before herself and looked down in thought. Eventually she smiled and looked up at Amelia. "If there is anyone in this city that can, it is him."

It was high praise. She only hoped that the professor was right. Knowing how volatile and dangerous cursed objects were, she feared Joseph would be tested on that very premise. There was plenty to contemplate, so she decided on calling it a night. She thanked the professor for all of her insights and wished her a good night.

She turned to Mr. Patch and surprisingly found the man sitting cross-legged on the floor with his tome open and a piece of parchment covered in scribbles. The odd man had clearly been listening in on the conversation, as he had been looking directly at them. He immediately diverted his eyes back to his work and returned to his deciphering. Having no thoughts or words for the odd behavior, she simply shook her head and bid him a good night.

Petals assured her that if anything occurred that required her attention, she would be alerted of it. The assurance was only mildly comforting. A quick check confirmed that she had all her things, and with a farewell to her superior, she headed down the stairs toward the entrance.

There were men in sawdust-coated leather aprons and jumpsuits installing new wooden framing. The wood was rust red-stained maple. There was also a utility cart parked out front of the entrance with Oak Brothers' Furnishings painted across the side in bright red lettering. She only hoped that whatever they installed would also be infused with the necessary wards to prevent it from being blown to bits by another Fireball.

The rookie was still there, but he looked less stalwart than before. He was leaning quite a bit more on his staff and sagged heavily in the shoulders with his head bowed forward.

"You best not be sleeping on the job again, Rook."

His head slowly turned, and his ear was directed toward her. His head didn't snap to attention though.

Not quite yet sleeping.

She walked past the men that were busy measuring out and hammering in the wooden frames and stepped up to Joseph's side. He had bags under his eyes and a grumpy glower.

"Did you have a chance to speak with your old professor?"

He shook his head in response. "Just quick pleasantries. Not exactly the time to put on a pot of tea and chat."

The idea of tea made her glance at her watch. She couldn't imagine standing at attention for so long without a break. "You must be exhausted."

He shut his eyes and let out a deep sigh. "I feel like I'm back at the Academy and just spent an entire day at attention."

In a way, he had done exactly that. Feeling daring, she decided to push it. "How... how do you manage to keep up a barrier of this power all day?"

He slowly turned his head back to staring out onto the street. "Tell me your secret and I'll tell you mine."

My secret?

"What secret?"

He gave her a sideways glare that gave her a bit of gooseflesh.

No... you couldn't possibly know about my father.

"You know exactly what secret." He growled it at her.

Panic and anger drove her heart into a gallop. "Who told you?" She needed to know who betrayed her.

His brow tightened even further. "What? Nobody told me anything, you just refuse to talk."

Did you look at my file? You couldn't have guessed.

There was a pause between them as she tried to find the words.

He clearly didn't have the patience for it and finally barked, "Fine! Keep your damned clothes-changing and iced cream-conjuring secrets to yourself!" He straightened a bit from his slouch and the near-invisible barrier warbled with his outburst.

What?

The realization hit her, and the panic-induced anger immediately subsided. She did her best to hide it because she didn't want to lead on that there was anything else she wasn't saying. Trying to play it off as nothing important, she played to his tantrum and swatted his arm. "Don't be such a child about it!"

That must have angered him even further because his hands ground into his staff and the warbling intensified to a soft hum.

Not wanting to be hit by pure arcane energy when she attempted to leave the precinct, she thought it best to tone it down. "Sorry, Rook." A pat on the arm was the best she was willing to offer. The warbling slowed and the humming vanished as Joe took in a deep breath and released it out his nose.

How do you still have this much power?

"I have trouble trusting others." She was of the mindset that you cannot be disappointed or hurt if you never let anyone in.

She could see him roll his eyes.

"I have my family to thank for that."

He glanced at her, and there was an immediate softening to his posture. His shoulders started to sag again.

Amelia pretended to relent and gave him what he wanted. "Fine. The secret to my clothes changing is a simple spell I devised that involves a slightly complex two-way recall. I wear my detective's outfit as the first part of the spell, then change into the other and set it as the second part. Whenever I need to switch, I simply activate the trigger and my clothes change near instantaneously. Happy?"

His brow furrowed deeply as he stared at nothing in particular. A grumble of a curse slipped out under his breath. He then asked, "And what of the iced cream?"

"Lunch box." She didn't think it was relevant to specify that it was a magical lunch box. There were plenty of regular ones that kept items hot or cold.

He tilted his head back and groaned in self-rebuke.

"Your turn, Rook. Out with it. How do you have this much power?" She felt it was her turn to glare and gave him the best she could muster.

He let out an agitated sigh. "I'm not using anywhere near as much as you think I am. At first, certainly, I threw everything I had into the barrier. I was angry... I still am angry, but I quickly realized I wouldn't be able to maintain it. So I adjusted it and I tapped into the natural protective barriers of the precinct." He pointed his thumb up over his shoulder to the face of the precinct. "I'm effectively just a conduit at this point. If I hadn't adjusted my spellwork earlier this afternoon, I would have exhausted myself into a spell sleep hours ago."

Amelia stood for a moment and absorbed his answer. She eventually concluded that it was sound.

Blast you and your damned reasonable explanations.

~~

Strangely, her step through Joseph's barrier was underwhelming and anti-climactic. She had expected some sort of tingling across her flesh or rising of the hairs on her neck, but there had been nothing more than a gentle pressure difference. It was like pushing through a thin wall of water. She supposed it was better than having her skin crawl or being singed.

The walk home was quiet – eerily quiet. Nobody was out and about except for the odd citizen, and they were moving along in a hurry.

It wasn't late. The sun was still high in the sky, and dinner likely hadn't been served in most households. Stores were shut, doors were barred, and the odd curtain or shade moved in the window. People were terrified.

She couldn't blame them. The very symbol of law and peace in the neighborhood was struck by an ancient and powerful siege spell. Worst of all, brothers and sisters of a religious order and two blue coats had been killed in the attack.

Fear was a palpable force, and it would soon spread and escalate into hysterics and looting. If it got that far, it would grow all the more difficult to find the people that were possessed by the cursed objects. They needed more leads, and fast.

She had keys in hand and was about to reach for the door handle of her home when she inexplicably found herself lying on the ground and staring up at the sky. There must have been a violent collision, as there was no memory of the hit, or even of experiencing any pain. All she could recall was that she had once been standing, and then wasn't. The world blurred and spun as though she were drunk. A solid hit to the head tended to cause that sort of reaction.

A face peered into view, and it looked vaguely masculine. There was no telling for certain whether it was or wasn't, because the hair on top of the head could have possibly been the beard. Everything was spinning too quickly for her to be able to focus.

You are fine.

She felt immediately better. The spinning ceased and the face was immediately recognizable as that of a man's. He had curled brown and gray hair, a blue sweater coat, heavy sailor's trousers, and a blue flat cap. "Ma'am? You all right?"

"I'm fine!" Amelia heaved herself to her feet and began brushing and dusting off her trousers and trench coat. Her hat, however, was lying on the ground.

The middle-aged sea-farer offered up her wide-brim as an apology. "I'm terribly sorry for running into you like that. I was reading the letters of news and wasn't looking where I was going." He pointed to the scattered letters all about their feet.

She snatched her hat back and tried to put it on. It didn't quite fit right and felt slightly off.

Blast it all!

Amelia quickly examined her hat and didn't see anything in particular that was wrong with it. She likely just had a bump on her head from smacking it against the cobblestones.

She rounded on the man and was about to give him an earful, when a thought intruded upon her.

He is not worth it.

It was an accident and not worth the time to give the man a dressing down. "Just be more careful next time."

A momentary flair of pain in the back of her head and a ringing in her ears caused her to grit her teeth and shut her eyes. It only lasted a moment, but when she opened her eyes again, she noted the man had collected his letters of news and was bidding her farewell, offering his apologies once again.

She waved him off and told him to go home and be more mindful of his surroundings.

You are hungry.

She was starving.

Chapter 22

Amelia headed up the steps to the second floor and paused just before her door. The yeasty aroma of freshly-baked bread was wafting out from her residence. A moment was taken to breath in the intoxicating scent.

When she opened the door, she was happy to find Blueregard standing at the stovetop wearing a pair of oven mitts and a baking sheet loaded with dinner rolls in hand. "Good afternoon, Ms. Iceheart." He looked at her worryingly.

"Afternoon, Blue." She hung up her hat and began removing her trench coat as she looked about the residence, listening intently. The residence was silent except for the steady hum of the oven. "Is Betty with her father again?"

Blueregard put the baking sheet down and turned a nob to shut off the oven. "She is. The news of the Fireball had her father quite upset. He didn't want his daughter anywhere near the Southwest district."

She wasn't surprised. Betty's father was rather

protective of his youngest child. "Just you and me again then?"

He offered her a slight smile. "Precisely." He looked her up and down. "May I suggest a bath and a change of clothes?"

Amelia looked down and remembered that her usually white blouse and trousers were an ashen gray. She had managed to clean off her face and hands while at the precinct, but she didn't have a spare change of clothes. "I believe I will."

"Dinner will be ready in a few hours." The man set aside his oven mitts and pulled a spatula from his white apron so that he might begin transferring the dinner buns to a cooling rack.

Secrets can hurt us. He holds secrets.

She continued to unburden herself and unbuckled the belt and gun holster to set them both up on the rack. "What oath did you swear?"

Blueregard paused with his fingertips atop a dinner bun, holding the bun aloft with the spatula. He didn't turn to look at her. He simply resumed moving the bun to the cooling rack and cleared his throat. "I informed you that I would speak of it when I felt ready. That hasn't changed." There was slight disapproval in his tone.

Demand the truth.

The thought that intruded into her mind felt wrong to her. She tried to shove it aside and ignore it, but couldn't. Instead, she reasoned with it. Blueregard had been with her family for decades; the man had even swaddled her as a babe. He had more than earned her trust. If he felt it necessary to not speak of personal things, then it was not her place to pry and push.

A rumbling of the voice remained. It continued to demand that the truth be given. There was no disagreeing with it. The truth needed to be found. She assuaged that side of her mind with the idea of letting Blueregard provide the details when he felt ready. Pushing would undoubtedly result in Blueregard clamming up and not speaking of it at all.

Instead of standing ground and attempting to have it out with the only man she truly trusted, she opted for a bath.

Amelia reached into her vest pocket and began to pull out her wand. That was when the flair of pain in the back of her head returned. It was brief, but it was enough to throw her off and cause her wand to prematurely release into a staff. It jolted up and out of her pocket and pierced the ceiling of their abode.

Blueregard was startled by the sudden display and accidentally lobbed a dinner roll up into the air. Thankfully, the man had the reflexes to catch the dinner roll when it came back down. He put it on the cooling rack with the others, glanced to her staff as it hung from the ceiling, and then to her. "Are you all right, Ms. Iceheart?"

You are fine.

She shook her head. "I'm fine. It's just been a stressful day at work with the Fireball and all."

A twitch and wiggle of her fingers should have caused her staff to disintegrate and rematerialize, but it didn't. Amelia frowned as she stared up at it. She wasn't entirely certain, but she thought that the many facets of the staff looked slightly duller. It was perhaps a trick of the light or the bump to the head. She didn't feel disoriented, but it was possible that her collision had thrown her off enough that her magic wasn't responding properly. Bed rest would fix the issue.

Instead of pulling the staff out with magic, she did it the old-fashioned way, with a hearty two-handed tug. It came loose easily enough and dropped into her hands, along with some ceiling plaster.

Blueregard jumped to cover the dinner rolls with his body as he eyed the hole in the ceiling and falling bits of dust and plaster.

Good man, I don't want dust and plaster in my dinner rolls.

Amelia coughed and waved the dust away from her

face. With a bit of clearer air, she could see where the damage had been done. A simple mending spell would resolve the issue. She lifted her staff and pointed the tip at the ceiling where the hole had been made. The magic flowed through from the core of her body and down her arms to her staff, but that is where it stopped dead.

She huffed and set her staff down and leaned it against the wall.

Fine, I'll fix you without the staff.

The appropriate energy alignments jumped to her mind and her outstretched fingers connected the pieces effortlessly. Plaster bits and dust that had fallen to the floor or landed in her hair or on her shoulders leaped up and floated toward the ceiling. The spider-web cracks began filling in and the hole began to vanish as each piece that had broken free found its home again. It only took a moment for it all to come together and return to what it had once been. There wasn't any evidence that the ceiling had ever been pierced or broken.

Blueregard watched all of it unfold with a certain look of awe, wonder, and... confusion? "When did you learn to do that without your wand?"

She frowned as she thought upon it and stared at the ceiling, examining the results of her work. "I've always been able to. The wand just makes it easier."

It was undeniably true. A wizard was always capable of the spells they cast; a staff, wand, or implemental item merely helped to focus their energies and concentrate the spellwork so that it wasn't as taxing. She'd never done it before without her wand, but also hadn't tried in some years.

Ignore it.

She ignored the brief oddity and headed to her room. "I'm going to have a bath and clean up." She was about to open the door to her room when she decided to take her staff with her. Amelia turned on the spot and used a touch of tethering to grasp her staff from the corner and summon it to her. It didn't take.

Stupid stubborn staff.

She huffed, marched to the corner, picked up her staff, and took it to her room.

Once happily secured within the confines of her private domicile, she tossed her obstinate staff on the floor beside the bed.

Strangely enough, the room didn't feel all that cool. A deep breath and a long exhale helped to drop the temperature. It was plausible that Blueregard had left the door open for too long while cleaning her room and handling her laundry. It wasn't entirely his fault. Her room routinely warmed up throughout the day during the warmer months. Her magic was the only thing that brought the temperature down. Standard interior climate controls consisted of overhead fans.

She turned the taps on for the bath and proceeded to strip down and toss her dirty clothes into the hamper.

The thought then occurred to her to ask Joseph for help in locking the bottom drawer of her office desk so that she might too hide a spare change of clothes at work.

He is dangerous and hides secrets! We cannot trust him!

A momentary splitting headache followed the sudden panicked thoughts. It quickly subsided, but it was enough to stagger her and force her to seek solace on the edge of her bathtub. She sat and cradled her head for a moment while the pain faded.

It dissipated quickly and left her a little light-headed. When she looked up, she was momentarily startled by her reflection in the full-body mirror. She thought she saw a different face in the reflection. Thankfully it was just her eyes returning to their pale blue from the ghostly white they usually were whenever she utilized magic. The hit to the head was proving more troublesome by the minute.

She decided that once she was done her bath, she would peer through her medicine cabinet for any pain tablets. One of those before bed would help to settle her headache and provide her with an invigorating night's sleep.

The thought that preceded the headache also proved to be troublesome. Joseph wasn't someone she could count on for anything at the moment. He was hiding too much.

The oath-keeper hides secrets as well.

The thought railed against her mind, but she had already reasoned out against nagging Blueregard for an answer.

With the tub near to full, she turned off the taps and slipped into the water. At first the water felt like it might scald her, but she quickly adjusted and slid into it with a satisfying groan. From there, she began scrubbing away the ash and grit with a stiff brush and berry-scented soap.

The soak did her some good. A deep sense of calm must have overtaken her, as she woke with a bit of a startle when there was a knocking on her bedroom door.

"Ms. Iceheart, dinner will be served shortly." It was Blueregard.

Had she slept the entire time? "Coming!"

Amelia went about giving herself one last scrub down before pulling the plug, standing, and freezing all the water off her skin. It flaked and fell off as little bits of ice and snow.

Needing only a bath robe, she quickly headed to the kitchens and dinner. Opening the door immediately created a thick wall of steam; the temperature differential must have been substantial. She quickly shut the door and stood in great discomfort at the heat the stove and oven released upon the kitchens. "Merciful goddess."

Blueregard stood with a fry pan in hand and a quizzical look upon his face. "Ms. Iceheart?" He wasn't sweating at all.

She waved him off and sat. "What is for dinner?"

He seemed to ignore her behavior and proceeded to dish up on her plate a filet of cod and a layer of scalloped potatoes. The dinner bun was already waiting.

It smelled marvelous, and she didn't bother to wait

for Blueregard to sit before she picked up her fork and began devouring.

Again, he gave her a quizzical look. "Are you all right, Ms. Iceheart?"

It was the second time he had asked her.

You are fine.

She worked her tongue around the hot potatoes for a moment before finally being able to chew, swallow, then answer. "I'm fine. I lost my lunch earlier today following the Fireball."

He sat after having dished up his own meal, but his eyes remained locked on her and her apparent appetite. "I would have sent you some bitters had I known."

Oddly enough, the mention of it and the memory of the scorched bodies didn't upheave her stomach as it should have.

I must be too hungry.

The reasoning wasn't entirely sound, but she also had never smelled any corpses; the smell usually did her in. The fire had been so powerfully hot that it had flash-fired and burned everything too quickly for there to be any scent in the air other than ash. It felt like the better answer, but it still left her feeling a bit off. She should be more disturbed by the deaths of those people.

Amelia sat in contemplation as she stared at her forkful of butter-seared cod.

What is wrong with me? This can't be just the hit to the head.

You are fine.

She was wrong. The head injury had her connection to her staff all muddled and had her mind in a bit of a twist, that was all. A good night's rest would resolve the issue.

Amelia looked up from her cod and saw a look of genuine worry upon Blueregard's face. "It's all right, Blue. It's been a rough day all around. A good night's sleep will do me some good."

He eased up slightly and nodded in acceptance.

They sat in silence for a time as Amelia devoured most of her plate. She didn't slow down until almost all of her meal was gone. Eventually she sat back and let her stomach settle a bit as it greedily accepted the offering she had attempted to placate it with.

Her twin randomly sprang to mind. "Blue, have you heard from Andrew lately?"

Blueregard wiped his mouth with a napkin and cleared his throat before speaking. "I haven't, why do you ask?"

"It seems that he's moved out of his former residence. Did he send any letters with a different address or forward notices?"

A deep contemplative rumble escaped Blueregard's throat as he looked off in thought. "I do not believe so, no, but I shall double check recent letters before bed tonight."

"Thank you, Blue." Amelia picked up the last bits of her dinner roll, picked it apart, and wiped up the butter that covered her plate. She happily devoured the last bits of potatoes and cod while cleaning up the rest with her bun.

Her stray thoughts were interrupted when Blueregard cleared his throat and said, "It was to your family."

Amelia frowned and looked to the family servant. "What was?"

"My oath."

She frowned even more. "Your oath was to my family?" It was not what she had been expecting. She figured the words that had been sworn to the gods had to be grander in scale and worthy of some legendary tale.

The old man took in a deep breath through his nose and slowly nodded in affirmation while exhaling. "Yes, and I was a damned fool to make it."

Her frown almost turned to a scowl. "What do you mean?"

He let out a slight bark. "Ha! Do I really need to tell *you* of all people what kind of family you have?" The man grunted as he stood and set about clearing the table.

"You can't just tell me your oath was to my family and not go into greater detail!" She felt cheated.

Blueregard bobbed his head as she expressed her grievance. "I know, I know. Please allow me to gather my thoughts on the matter as I clean the dishes. Once these are done, I will tell you all of it.

She didn't have the patience to wait, so she stood and stepped to his side. "You wash, and I'll dry."

Blueregard glowered at her slightly. "Cleaning the dishes quicker won't make my head think faster." His glower softened a little. "But it would be nice to have you standing beside me and drying the dishes again." He turned to the sink, lowered the dishes in, and turned on the tap. "It will be like when you were little."

She vaguely remembered being a very young girl and standing on a stool beside the sink with a dish towel in her tiny hands. "If I remember correctly, I dropped a plate, and mother swatted me for an hour."

There was brief stiffening to the old man's posture. He paused his scrubbing and grumbled, "I remember that as well."

Something that Blueregard had said while they were at the Bloodstone Estate popped into her mind. "You said that you were in the military when my father was a boy?"

He let out a deep grumble before answering, "Yes. I joined the military as my father before me, and his father before him." He paused scrubbing. "I was only sixteen and a damned fool as well." The scrubbing continued a bit more aggressively than before.

There was a pause in his storytelling as he focused on a bit of burned cod stuck to the frying pan. She figured he wasn't really that focused on the burned bit as he was gathering his thoughts.

He picked at the bit with a fingernail until it broke loose. "Your father's father, your grandfather, was my commanding officer."

Amelia had never really gotten to know her paternal grandfather. He had died when she was little. He had been one of the victims of what the letters of news had referred to as The Noble Killings. Following his death, her father had inherited the Bloodstone family fortune and the estate.

"We were sent out to the Spineridge Mountains." He finished scrubbing the pan and offered it to her. Amelia took the offered pan and began to dry it off as he continued his story. "There were reports suggesting orc scouts were pecking at our defenses, testing the perimeter."

She'd rarely heard tales concerning orcs. Not many veterans survived close encounters or were too traumatized to speak of their experiences. "Were the reports correct?"

"Yes." He paused and looked down into the sink for a while.

Amelia saw the same long-gone stare that she had seen on Nathaniel. She'd never seen it on Blueregard's face before that night; it scared her.

She put a comforting hand on his arm, and he seemed to come back to her as he began to talk again. "Those brutish monstrosities were just as savage and destructive as the stories told." He glanced at her, then returned to scrubbing with a focused intensity. "We were set upon by scouts. If it wasn't for your grandfather, I would be a dead man. He saved my life. In return, I swore to the gods that I owed your family a life debt." He looked at her out of the corner of his eye. "Little did I know that the life debt would be decided by your family."

She had a sinking feeling in her gut.

"I went on to risk my life and soul to save your grandfather from certain death." He lifted three shaking fingers. "Three times. I saved your grandfather's life three times. I even took a poisoned arrow for him, and I didn't get a single 'thanks' for it. He lorded my oath to him over me! He demanded that I serve him and his family!" The veins on the old man's neck rose as he gripped the countertop.

Amelia almost felt like that terrified little girl that

was about to be swatted all over again. Her family had wronged an Oath-sworn man.

"I argued that my debt was paid, but he held me to my word and grinned like a sadistic demon while doing it." He looked away from the dishes; his eyes held hers with fierce and unwavering determination. "I decided then, that if I was to be stuck with your family until my dying days, then I would make an honest soul out of one of his children." He broke the eye contact and visibly flexed and gripped the countertop edge as he growled, "But that thundering blasted child turned out to be exactly like his father!" She'd never heard him swear so openly before.

No wonder you didn't want to talk about all of this.

Her father had been a monster, but she had a feeling that there was far more to him than what she had seen. The reason behind Blueregard's unflinching devotion to her became much clearer. "And then I was born." She remembered the night that her father had come for her. It was the same night that Blueregard had taken her away from the Bloodstone Estate and to her maternal grandparents. It was the night she had killed her father.

Blueregard looked to her with tears streaming down his face. He was barely holding it together. "And then you were born." It was barely whispered, but it was said with a genuine smile.

They both knew the rest of the story, and nothing more needed to be said. She could trust him with her life.

He can be trusted.

She put down the pan and dish cloth, wrapped her arms up around his neck, and hugged him as tightly as she could. "I release you from your oath, Humboldt Thandle Blueregard."

He wrapped his arms around her and nearly squeezed the life from her in return. "My dear Amelia… if only it were that easy."

Chapter 23

The two of them finished cleaning up the kitchen before calling it a night. Blueregard double-checked the letters they had received throughout the last few moons and noted that nothing had been recently sent by Andrew. Anything they did have was marked with the old address.

Amelia found a pain tablet in her medicine cabinet and took it before bed. Unfortunately, she had one last dizzying headache. She experienced it when she went to pick up her staff and lean it against the wall. It was a fairly disorienting and painful headache, but it was thankfully brief. With her staff set in the corner, she crawled into bed and closed her eyes.

The pain tablet must have been stronger than she thought, for it caused the strangest of dreams. Children's laughter echoed through her mind as she swam through a tipsy and blurred world of brilliant sunlight, grassy hilltops, and carpeted hallways. A blink or a blur of light would transition her from one setting to the next, and in each instance, Andrew was running ahead of her. They were children, no older than four or five, and they were chasing each other while playing some sort of game.

The strangest part about the dream was that her twin brother routinely changed hair and eye color. One moment, he would have jet black hair and blue eyes, exactly as he always did. The next moment his eyes would be amber and his hair a brilliant shade of red.

She too changed throughout the dream. Following the giggling merry chase, she jarringly transitioned to a near-white room of stone and mortar. Amelia stood before a full-length oval mirror that was lined with gold. It was symmetrically decorated with vines and leaves.

Half of the time spent in the mirror, her reflection was not her own. She started out as a little girl in a pink dress with black hair and blue eyes; she looked exactly as she had as a little girl. A shifting of the light or the blink of an eye would have her staring at a reflection of a pale-eyed and white-haired little girl. The cheekbones were higher than Amelia's, and her chin was softer. They shifted back and forth, and the differences between the two of them were apparent.

Another blink of the eye and Amelia stood as an adult before the mirror. Her hair was white and her detective's garb replaced her little pink dress. The woman in the reflection shifted. She appeared to Amelia as a woman that hailed from Braethor. Despite being from a warmer climate, her skin was pale instead of warm. The cheekbones and soft chin were also evident of that heritage. Her eyes were ghostly pale and her hair was stark and pulled back, pinned, and braided in the elven style. The woman wore an elegant white gown that was buttoned to the neck.

Dream turned to nightmare when the lights went out in the world, and the room turned as pitch as a starless night. She turned about, fearful that something was hiding behind her. Her skin crawled and the hairs on the back of her neck stood on end. The haze and blur of a dream was immediately replaced with cold and frightening clarity. She couldn't see through the dark, but she was oddly certain that nobody was out in it. The fear was momentarily abated.

Something was behind her again; she could feel its hot breath on her neck. Terror overcame her, and she wasn't able to move. Despite that paralyzation, she began to turn.

As a graduate of the Academy, Amelia had been exposed to many nightmarish things. She hadn't been hazed or tortured, she had simply been shown the horrors of the criminal world in hopes that it would prepare her. None of what she had been shown scared her enough to cause her any real terror.

The panic of losing control of her body and having that haunting hot breath on the back of her neck sent a chill down her spine that made her toes curl and the little girl inside of her scream like a wailing banshee.

Not wanting to see what was watching her, and in an attempt to break herself free from the nightmare, she shut her eyes. Unfortunately, the nightmare didn't allow her to quit so easily. Shutting her eyes resulted in nothing more than a fraction of a reprieve.

In the mirror's reflection, she saw the panic and terror of the other woman. The room grew hotter, and a reddish glow grew behind the mirror. She still couldn't move. Amelia felt her heart hammering harder in her chest and the need to wake grew all the more desperate.

Bubbles began to appear on the surface of the mirror. Distortions warped the reflection, and soon enough, the glass began melting, along with the frame of the mirror.

Her panic was taking her dangerously near to hysteria. She was panting and gasping for air as the heat grew unbearably intense.

She was startled near to death when a fist burst through the melting glass; the skin was cracked with veins of throbbing red light. The hand reached out to her and swiped at the air as though it was trying to grab her. Thankfully, she was finally able to move, but only enough to pull her face away.

The fingertips of the hand turned to ash, and smoke trailed the arm as it flailed and swiped through the air. A face peered through the melting glass and metal, and the eyes looked maddened and deranged while burning like red hot coals.

Every swipe brought the hand closer and closer to her face, causing her heart to skip in fear. She felt that she knew the sensation of her skin burning and blistering at the touch of those hands. It was as familiar to her as breathing.

"No!" Words finally managed to escape her heaving lungs.

The hand swiped again, and the head and shoulders of the deranged man pushed through the melting mirror. It was the same red-haired boy she had seen before, the boy that had been swapping places with her brother Andrew. He was now a full-grown man. The sickening look on his face told her all she needed to know. She wanted out – she didn't want to be touched by him.

"NO!" She screeched it.

Scalding, searing pain ripped up her arm as the fire-infused madman snatched her wrist in an iron grip. Amelia wailed with the pain of it and used the sudden surge of energy to lash out.

Unsatisfyingly, she woke before she could throw a javelin of ice into the frighteningly mad grin. Amelia bolted upright in bed and clutched the bedsheets to her chest.

Thankfully, she was in her room. She was alone, and it was still the middle of the night. Cool air kissed her bare skin and eased away the ghostly pain that was quickly vanishing from her wrist.

Despite all that, she shook. Waking when she did had been a blessing. The thought of the nightmare continuing had her nearly in tears. Instinctively, she reached out to the corner of the room and summoned her staff. Like a good friend, it answered. The familiar facets of her ice staff slapped into the palm of her hand. Amelia gripped it tight for a moment, then let it go. It lazily drifted back to the corner. The assurance that it would answer her call was enough for her. She lay back down, curled up tight, and cried for a while.

She presumed that the events of the previous days had prompted the bizarre dream. With a prayer whispered to the Goddess of Mercy, she closed her eyes and hoped the night would be devoid of any more nightmares.

~~

Thankfully, there were no more dreams for the rest of the night. Though she didn't sleep quite as heavily as hoped.

Amelia awoke shortly before the alarm was set for. To prevent it from ringing and startling her, she flicked the toggle to turn it off. Her staff responded to her call and floated across the room to her outstretched hand. Satisfied, she set it to lean against her bedside table and got up for the day.

Her bath wasn't as warm as usual. Heat of any kind didn't appeal to her. Her wrist didn't hurt, but she lingered on it. She scrubbed vigorously as the nightmare played itself out repeatedly in her mind. It wasn't until she had braided and pinned her hair in the elvish style – much like the girl in the mirror – that she realized she had spent most of her morning in a frightened daze.

I'm a god's blasted detective! Before that I was a blue coat!

Frustrated with her own childishness, she furiously pulled her hair out of the braids and combed it all straight. The nightmare wasn't anything more than a bad dream, and there was no reason to linger upon it.

Fear the Crown of Fire.

She felt a very real shiver crawl its way up her spine, and it wasn't because of the cooler bath and cold air. There was someone out in the city that was possessed by a cursed Crown, and they were gifted with the ability to launch

Fireballs. Amelia shook her head, pushed aside the thoughts, and finished preparing for the day.

Blueregard prepared a hearty breakfast for her. The plate was piled with scrambled eggs, sausage patties, and a sweet cake drizzled in honey. He even provided her with a small vial of stomach bitters "just in case."

Despite the knowledge that she needed the hearty meal, she didn't feel all that hungry.

Blasted nightmare.

She forced herself to finish the sweet cakes and eggs and asked that the sausages be saved for lunch. Of course, Blueregard obliged her and saved them in the chill cabinet. "Will that be all, Ms. Iceheart?"

"That will be all, thank you, Blue." She hugged the old man and told him to stay safe inside the residence unless there was no other choice. He hugged her back and promised that no unnecessary risks would be taken.

With the pleasantries out of the way, she set to buckling on her belt and holster and donned her trench coat and hat. Thankfully, the hat fit her just fine. She had been worried the day before, but realized that in her daze, she had probably attempted to put on her hat the wrong way.

There was an undeniable clarity to her thoughts. She didn't feel as hazy as she did from the night before, and her magic staff responded to her call. It rematerialized in hand as a wand and didn't give her any fuss when she stuffed it into her vest pocket.

Set and armed, she exchanged "good day"s with Blueregard, and headed out the door and down the stairs to the street level.

By the looks of the sporadic cloud cover and the wet streets, it had rained during the night. When she stepped out the front door and caught a whiff of the air, she could smell the storm that was brewing.

A few people were out and about, but they huddled together and hurried to get to wherever it was they were going. Most of them carried grocers' bags.

Chill cabinets were a recent enough invention and not all residences had them installed. As a result, many had to go out and collect their foodstuffs in the morning in order to cover them for the day's meals and the following day's breakfast.

It was also possible that they had chill cabinets, and they had simply run out of food just following the Fireball hitting the precinct. She couldn't blame them. They needed to eat, and the idea of being stuck inside all day while they waiting for news had to be nerve-racking. Some people stress-ate. She understood the need. Many bars of chocolate and raspberry iced cream had been devoured during her last moons at the Arcanum. Final exams were stressful.

Amelia crossed the street and walked to the intersection so that she might look down the cobblestone road to the waterfront and the horizon. It was a fair distance away, but she was certain she could see storm clouds approaching from the west.

Good. A solid storm will hamper the accursed Crown of Fire.

She had no doubt that someone capable of summoning a Fireball was also capable of adapting to the rain. However, water was what she needed in order to combat fire. It would even the playing field for her if she ever came across them. Sadly, it also amplified the other Crown, the one she presumed represented ice.

The Crown of the Ice Queen.

The thought appealed to her. Then it immediately unnerved her. She was referred to as the ice queen because she often gave the cold shoulder. There was no desire to claim the title.

You are noble born. You could be.

Being of noble birth, it was plausible that she might somehow catch the eye of the king of Greencoast and become his queen. The memory of the king bubbled to mind, and she immediately remembered how repulsive she had found the man.

Unlike Braethor, the kingdom of Greencoast had a

stale royal bloodline. There weren't many direct descendants left, and the current ruler was a pot-bellied snore. The man had long greasy hair ringing a balding cap and a patchy unkept beard. He slouched, scratched himself, and routinely whined about whatever small and unreasonable inconvenience had prevented him from existing like a slovenly snail.

They had met only once, during her graduation ceremony from the Academy. It was apparently the duty of the king to attend such civil events. She truly hoped she would never meet the man again.

Amelia's morning walk to work was interrupted by a sudden and startling sensation. Much like how one would jump and turn to the source of a loud noise, she lifted her head and snapped free of the thoughts of his royal repulsiveness. Her attention was drawn directly toward the precinct, but she heard no noise and saw no commotion. There was only the knowing.

Whatever had startled her was not immediately in front of her. Nobody was walking down the street, and there were no carts driving by. There was a sense of danger to whatever had grabbed her attention, but it was distant.

She pulled her crystalline network box from her belt and was about to depress the button to speak and inquire whether there was anything odd taking place near the precinct, when she felt the danger grow stronger.

When she was a little girl exploring the back gardens and forest of the family estate, she was frightened by the appearance of a yellow-eyed wolf. At first, it had just been the snapping of a twig that caught her attention; that scared her a little. Then she spotted the wolf, and it was staring directly at her. That terrified her to the core.

The sensation she felt now was the same as when the wolf locked eyes with her. Whatever she had sensed, had sensed her.

Run!

No! Rule number one! Don't panic!

She needed to know what she was dealing with, and the only way to do that was to gather information on what was taking place at the precinct. Amelia lifted the network box back to her mouth and was about to depress the talk button when it sprang to life. Joseph's voice rang through loud and clear, "All officers southwest of the precinct, report in."

She was stunned. It was *him*. She had sensed *him*.

RUN!

There was no time to contemplate or question. Action needed to be taken, and she needed to put distance between herself and the 'eyes' of the enemy. With her network box back on her belt, Amelia turned around and took off at a full sprint.

No! Not back home! We can't endanger Blue!

A quick glance over her shoulder told her that no carts were approaching, so she darted across the cobblestones to the other side of the street and headed for the nearest intersection to take her north.

The thought to use ice magic and glide across the cobblestones came to mind. It was quickly followed by the thought that Joseph might somehow sense her use of magic. It also posed the problem of grabbing too much attention and expending too much energy. She opted for good old-fashioned panic-fueled running.

By the time she rounded the corner, the sensation of being observed had lessened significantly. It was also entirely possible that she was being paranoid. Amelia paused and looked back around the corner to make sure nobody was following her. There wasn't anyone on the street, and nobody seemed to be looking in her direction.

Thank the merciful goddess.

She let out a brief sigh of relief.

"Detective?"

"AH!" Amelia jumped and whirled on the spot while drawing her firearm.

"AH!" Officer Johnson ducked and covered his

head with his hands. "Blasted woman, what you trying to do? Kill an old sea-dog?"

Realizing who she had nearly shot, she quickly tilted her six-shooter skyward and sighed in relief. "Thank the gods, it's just you."

Old Bob straightened and scowled at her. "What do you mean 'Thank the gods, it's just you'? Who were you expecting, a masked menace pointing a piece at you? What idiotic criminal approaches a detective and attempts to get her attention with the expectation of being shot?" He waved his arms about in an exaggerated show of exasperation to point out the ridiculousness of her reaction.

"I thought you might have been Joe."

Bob's scowl turned to a deep frown that curled his white bushy mustache. "The boy?" He said it in a whisper. He seemed deeply hurt by the possibility that she might shoot Joseph.

"It's not what you think."

"I think you spend far too much time with Ms. Mistwind."

She quickly holstered her weapon and put up her hands to try and stop him from jumping to conclusions. "No. No, it's not like that."

"That boy wouldn't hurt a fly!" Bob was getting more and more worked up about it.

Fear the Crown of Fire.

She reached out and grasped Bob by the trench coat and hauled him in so that she could keep her voice low and harshly whisper in his ear, "Cursed objects don't give a damned as to how polite or courteous you are!"

Bob's white eyebrows shot up in surprise. He looked to her, then looked to the cobblestone road. "By the spirits, I hope it's not true." She hoped it as well, but she couldn't ignore what her wizardly senses had warned her about.

The old man looked down at his trench coat and swatted her hand off so that he might brush away the ice and bits of snow that had been deposited there. "You're even colder than usual, my dear."

Amelia shook her hand free of the ice that had built up on her skin. She hadn't even realized she'd done it until she saw it.

There was a startling *pop* to the air. Amelia jumped a little and whirled on the spot to see a large cloud of blue sparkling smoke on the street corner just behind her. The sensation of being watched returned with a furious slap to the face.

A trench coat-covered arm took large sweeps of the air in order to clear the smoke away. Instinctively, Amelia shut her eyes and opened herself to the greater 'verse. When she opened them, she was greeted by two plumes of heat. One was tall, and the other was short. Joseph and Petals had arrived.

Horrifyingly, her worst fears had been realized. The taller of the two bodies had a crown of flames around its head.

Amelia quickly blinked away her arcane vision, and looked directly into the eyes of the rookie. He was staring directly back at her, and his eyes were molten iron instead of their usual cool silver.

RUN!

Chapter 24

She didn't know how, but Joseph had been possessed by the Crown of Fire. Strangest of all, she could sense it. It must have been after she last saw him, because he wasn't possessed when she left the precinct the day before... was he? The thought left her mind as quickly as it entered. Joseph was undeniably keeping secrets from her, but there was no way he could have possibly launched a Fireball at the precinct while standing within it.

Her thoughts must have played out across her face, for Joseph's eyes widened and his body stiffened in preparation to attack.

Thankfully, her heightened sense of alarm had granted her the quicker reaction time. Amelia pulled up every bit of energy that she could and threw her hands skyward. As she did, she broke eye contact and glanced to Petals. The little gnome had a glimmer of red energy in his eyes. He was corrupted and couldn't provide her with any aid. He too needed to be subdued.

No words were exchanged throughout the brief encounter, as the time between arrival and reaction lasted half a moment at most. Shouts of surprise didn't count.

The water from the cobblestone street and the moisture in the air aided her as she summoned a wall of ice between them. Amelia let out a heaving scream of effort as she drew the water up from the ground. Surprisingly, it proved far more effective than she could have ever hoped.

Joseph and Petals vanished from sight as a massive wall of dark blue ice erupted between them. It jutted toward the sky with ragged white peaks that were easily a story tall, and the wall stretched halfway across the street. She rarely fueled her magic with panic, so the results were impressively surprising.

Officer Johnson barked out a scream and reeled back. "Blasted storms!"

She knew how powerful Joe and Petals could be and didn't waste any time utilizing the moment of surprise in order to escape. Amelia turned, gripped Bob's sleeve, and hauled him along. "Run!"

"Confounded woman!" He stumbled as she dragged him along at a full sprint. "What is in your head!"

"Joe is possessed and Petals is corrupted!" She gasped between breaths as she put every bit of effort into building distance between them and the ice wall.

"Briny barnacles!" Officer Johnson caught his footing and put boot to cobblestone faster than she could. Shockingly, the old man could run when properly incentivized.

Between labored breaths, she yelled out, "Right!" Bob turned at the alley, and Amelia followed right on his heels. It led them into an alley; one would think it a terrible idea to corner oneself, but the alley wasn't a dead end, and she knew better than to stay out in the open where Petals could spot them and enact his trickery.

She jumped over a small crate lying in the middle of the alley. Bob simply ran around it, as it didn't block his path. "Left." She kept her voice low and quickly checked over her shoulder as they rounded the next corner. Nobody seemed to be following. Hopefully her ice wall had not only blocked them from view but also caught them up in some of it. She wasn't worried about them freezing to death, as Petals was far superior to her in skill and would easily break the both of them free in no time at all.

"Keep going." The two of them kept low and ran to the mouth of the alley. With a check for the all clear, they quickly darted across the cobblestone street behind a rumbling gnome cart. Once safe on the other side, they ducked into the next alley.

They made two more turns through back alleys before they eventually slowed to a stop. She immediately pulled her crystalline network box from her belt and wiggled her fingers for Bob to hand over his. "Give me... yours." She breathed heavily as she impatiently waved him to hurry.

"What?" He huffed and puffed and his white mustache wiggled with his exhales. "Why?" He took a few more quick breaths. "Is yours broken?"

"No!" She puffed a bit from the brief but sudden sprint. "Just give it!" She kept her voice low but maintained a panicked level of urgency.

The old man pulled his network box and handed it to her. Amelia held both together, drew her wand from her pocket, and pointed the wand at the base of both of them. Ice began to build up on the bottom of the boxes until a small boat of ice was formed.

"What are you doing?" Bob kept his voice low, but he looked like he was about to pull his hat off and hair out.

"Shh!" She quickly did a turnabout in the alley and pointed to a nearby storm grate. "Open that!"

Bob looked like he might protest, but he scrunched up his mustache and did as requested. The wiry old man marched over to the storm grate and bent to lift it. He stopped, pointed to some grungy lump amongst the cobblestones, and whispered loudly. "Padlock!"

She cursed her luck, but quickly remembered she had memorized the key that the city workers used to open the storm grates; she had gotten a good look during their storm drain search back in the spring.

Amelia dropped to a knee, pointed her wand at the padlock, and summoned the necessary magic to craft the key from ice. Sadly, the padlock keyhole was gummed up with something she didn't want to think about or touch. "Geh!"

Having lost all patience, she opted for breaking the lock. There was more than enough moisture in the locking mechanism for her to freeze it. Metal did not handle cold temperatures very well. All she needed to do was sap enough heat out of the metal and it would turn brittle enough to shatter.

It only took a minute, and the padlock did exactly as she expected it to. One good thump with her boot smashed the lock into pieces. "Now can you open it?"

Bob nodded in approval and got to work grunting and lifting the rusted storm grate. She put a hand on his arm to stop him as soon as the rusted hinge squealed. Thankfully, the grate was opened wide enough for her to do what she needed to.

Getting down on to her belly, she was able to reach in through the opening and drop the crystalline-network-box-ice-boat down into the waters. It immediately floated away.

Certain that it would do as intended, she pulled her arm out and told him to drop it. Thankfully, he didn't just drop it like some numbskull. The old man bit his lip, groaned in his throat, and eased the heavy metal back down instead of dropping it with a clang that might have given away their position.

As she predicted, the little ice boat carried their crystalline network boxes to the south. If they were being tracked by any mystical means, it would have been through the network boxes.

Amelia got up, brushed off her clothes, took one

last peek around the corner they came from, and silently waved Bob to follow her in the opposite direction.

When they reached the mouth of the alley, she let out a small sigh of relief, as she didn't see any sign of Joe, Petals, or any nearby blue coats on patrol.

She stepped out into the daylight and waved Bob to follow her. They quickly made their way eastward for a few storefronts. When Amelia spotted an open tea shop, she checked over her shoulder, tugged on Bob's sleeve, and gestured to the shop.

He got the message. The old sailor diverged toward the open door and stepped inside. Amelia quickly followed.

The interior had a warm and cozy atmosphere. The walls were rustic and bare to the brick, the floor was polished hardwood, and the countertops were a red-stained mahogany. Upholstered wooden chairs surrounded small circular tables where lantern lights hung from brass chains.

There was only one customer in the shop. A middle-aged woman sat at a table by the east-most window. She wore well-ironed floral white skirts and a blush-shaded blouse with a daisy yellow sun hat. She noted Bob and Amelia's arrival with slight alarm. It wasn't every day that a detective and a blue coat rushed into a store with such a flourish.

Unfortunately, the clerk behind the counter looked far less impressed. He had thinning hair, a protruding gut that strained the apron he wore, and a glowering face that belonged on a troll. There was even a wart on his bulbous nose.

Amelia ignored the man and shut the door behind her. A quick flick of the wand locked the top, middle, and bottom deadbolts.

"Hey! We're still open! Open up that door!" He even sounded like a troll. The man either smoked a pipe every day of his life, or he regularly gargled razors and sandpaper.

She flicked her wand at the storefront shades. All

the blinds dropped and covered the windows in a quick flourish. It startled the lone patron, but Amelia didn't have time to warn the poor woman.

"What are you, deaf and stupid? Open my door and get out!"

Amelia peered through the blinds and ignored the store owner.

Bob snapped, "Sir! This is a delicate situation and we need you to remain silent!" As much as Bob was an old sea dog, he still had some tact in him.

"I'll not have you so-called officers of the *law* shutting down my business because of some wizard kerfuffle!"

The lone patron gasped in shock. "Charles! A kerfuffle?"

Oh lovely, I'm in Chuck's Tea Parlor.

She hadn't exactly had the time to look up at the storefront sign when she noted the open door.

"There was a Fireball, and it killed innocents!" The woman was truly shocked and offended by Chuck's outburst.

Amelia wasn't surprised. The man was well-known for the outrageous dribble he spat; he was also known for having a good selection of tea. Amelia focused on keeping her eyes on the street.

"Nothing but lies and propaganda, I tell you!"

Bob straightened and scoffed, and the lady in the corner gasped even more from the insinuation.

"Nobody really died!" the lardy disgrace angrily shouted as he pointed fingers at Bob and Amelia. "They just want you to think people died!"

He is not welcome in our kingdom.

Amelia didn't have time for the idiocy or loud noise. She turned and angrily flicked her wand at the man.

"It's all– Hngh!"

He went wide-eyed and stiffened on the spot. His skin flashed a brief shade of blue, then he toppled backward. There was no crumpling; he fell back as stiff as a wooden plank and hit the floor with a meaty and weighty *thump!*

The woman that had been arguing with Charles let out a clipped scream of surprise when Chuck hit the floor. "OH!"

"Detective!" Bob wheeled on her with a shocked look on his face. He looked to be outright gobsmacked by the fact that she had done such a thing.

A moment of shame overtook her.

Officers died in that attack.

The feeling was quickly replaced by determined anger. "No… we lost two of our own yesterday."

Bob's look of disapproval softened a bit, but it didn't altogether vanish. "I still don't approve."

"Do or don't, we have bigger problems on our hands." She lowered her voice and pointed with her thumb out the window. "Like a cursed object that is after us."

He continued to level her a disapproving glare. "I'm still not letting this go."

The woman that had been sitting by the window got up and hurried around the countertop to check on the unconscious moron. "Charlie? Charles? You okay? Wake up!"

Guilt began to creep in alongside the realization of what she had done. She had stunned an unarmed innocent.

He was too loud and not our primary concern.

The guilt vanished as she thought of how he might have endangered them all. With her determination renewed, she turned to look back out the window and peered through the blinds. The way looked clear.

She turned back to grab Bob and noticed he wasn't there. He was behind the counter, looking over the woman's shoulder at the prone form. "He'll be all right. Just stunned is all."

She sniffled and whimpered, "Are you sure?"

"Of course I am, dear." He patted the woman on the shoulder and shot Amelia a nasty glare.

Again, the ugly and nauseating feeling of guilt began

to wash over her.

Not our concern.

It ebbed away as quickly as it had washed over her, like a retreating wave on the beach.

Bob quietly made his way back over to her and berated her in hushed tones. "As much as I would enjoy forcefully silencing this blobbing fish-mouth, it's not something *we* do. *We* are better than that."

Amelia reflexively squeezed her eyes shut as a small headache and a brief moment of dizziness overtook her. Thankfully it was momentary, and she was easily able to shake it off.

She opened her eyes and tried to blink away the pain. When she did, Bob looked at her with a great deal of concern and placed a hand on her shoulder. "You all right, Ice Queen?"

"I'm fine." She waved off the concern. "It's probably nothing more than an after-effect of exerting my powers to make that ice wall earlier."

"Of course, of course." Bob looked about the tea shop and quickly snatched a biscuit from the countertop. "Here. Eat. I'll take care of the unconscious idiot."

She hadn't paid for it, but she couldn't ignore her waning strength. Amelia took the proffered tea biscuit and bit off a piece before turning back to the window and peering through the blinds. "Keep an eye on the back door, will you, Bob?"

"On it!" She heard him shuffle and grunt as he vaulted the countertop and headed into the back.

Irritatingly, the woman continued to sniffle and sob. It proved distracting, but she wasn't about to stun her for being upset. At least she wasn't making a racket that would draw attention to their location.

The next steps would be crucial. They needed to make an expedient retreat and figure out how to deal with the cursed object that had possessed Joe while not getting caught in an arcane throwdown.

They'll figure out the decoy soon enough.

Amelia took another bite of the tea biscuit and grimaced. It was dry and stale. The precinct had better biscuits, and they were on a city budget.

The precinct is not safe.

The thought occurred to her that if Petals was corrupted, then there was no telling how many others at the precinct were corrupted as well. She couldn't go there for answers.

That complicates things.

The cursed chest was at the precinct, and so were the two professors that were studying and deciphering it. If she couldn't get there, then she needed to get her answers elsewhere.

Amelia tried to piece together all the clues and formulate a backup plan as she nibbled on the awful biscuit and stared out the window. The occasional gnome cart would drive by or a pedestrian would hurry past; otherwise, the streets were empty and silent.

She looked back to talk to Bob but found that he wasn't there. Her state of alarm rose when she realized she couldn't hear the sobbing of the woman looking after Charles.

Another glance out the window showed that the street was empty and nobody had passed by in at least a full minute. Amelia took a step away from the windows, turned to the countertop, and leaned a bit to her left to peer into the back. That was when she spotted Bob's prone form in the back storage room. He was face down, and the only movement was his slow and steady breathing. The woman and Charles were also nowhere to be seen.

Where did they go?

The hairs on the back of her neck stood on end as the sensation of being observed struck. She instinctively turned to the windows and the sensation came from the north, directly out the front of the shop. He had found her again.

Chapter 25

Had it not been for her heightened alarm, Amelia wouldn't have heard the scuffing of shoe on tile.

Amelia threw herself to the floor and twisted during the fall to land on her back. Her wand erupted into a full staff, and the Guardian of the cursed Crowns was struck square in the chest.

Like the day before, the puppet-man wore a dark trench coat, dark slacks, gloves, vest, and a hat. All the apparel was a deep shade of brown, well-tailored, and designed to fit a human man of thin and short stature.

It had undoubtedly snuck in through the back and been the one to knock out Bob. She didn't know how it had managed to get the stunned Charles and the sobbing woman out without making a noise, but that was not her concern at the moment.

Since she had caught it mid-jump, the Guardian was thrown back by the sudden impact of her extending staff. Unsurprisingly, she could not hold the weight of the

Guardian with just her hands. The butt end of her staff jammed into the crevice between the wall and the floor just beneath her right armpit.

Piling onto the small victory, she pushed her staff harder and extended it even more. The length of ice *clinked* and *cracked* with the sounds of expansion and pushed her attacker off the ground until it was slammed and pinned to the ceiling.

Once she had it against the ceiling, she piled on again. Ice spread out from the point of impact and began engulfing the constructed body so that it was spread out, flattened, and unable to attack her with its martial skills.

The windows directly above her burst inward and showered her in a rain of razor sharp glass. Thankfully, she turned away from it in time and tilted her hat to cover her face. Her detective's garb protected her with its enchantments and only two of her exposed fingers were mildly scraped.

Knowing that more was coming, she quickly pushed to her feet, shook off the glass debris, and stood in the middle of the store. Petals stood in the middle of the street with both his hands raised, and he looked like he was about to snap his fingers. There was no joviality upon his face; he was truly taken by the corruption.

Amelia drew as much strength as she could muster and swiped the air with her hand. The lantern lights in the store warbled, popped, or flickered out while the transactional station *pinged* open with a flourish behind her. She had doused the air with as powerful of a jinx as she could conjure in a pinch. Her magic would still work, but the jinx would hopefully be enough to muffle whatever anyone else threw at her.

Petals snapped his fingers. There was a hefty *thump* to the air and two sources of violet sparks erupted only a step and a half before her face. The jinx prevented the magical assault from getting to her, but not by much. A few more like that and the jinx would be chewed up and expended. She needed to act fast. Amelia quickly recalled the necessary spell framework, mumbled the incantation to strengthen the binding, and pointed at her intended target.

Half a dozen purple sparks and *thumps* assaulted the air around her. She hadn't expected her spellwork to hold that well against Petals.

The moisture was pulled from the room and the warmth pushed out into the street with a violent cough of hot air. The temperature dropped so dramatically that the tea pots *pinged*, *panged*, and *popped* as the water inside expanded and cracked or warped the metal. A wall of ice immediately shot up and out the window and door, creating a spiked wall of ice between her and her superior. It would hopefully hold for a short while.

Hissing and the sounds of dripping water drew her attention back to the ceiling. The Guardian was somehow melting the ice with its palms. Red plumes of heat were emanating from inside the gloved hands of the Guardian.

Why are you after me?

You are the bait.

The realization hit her at the same moment she heard the *pop* behind her. Amelia dove over the countertop of the transactional station and shoulder-rolled to her feet. She was just shy of stepping on the unconscious Bob.

A large cloud of blue sparkling smoke lingered right by where she had been standing just a moment before. Had Petals sent the teleportation just a step to the left, then Joe would have appeared on top of her.

Her jinx hadn't held out at all. Petals had aimlessly launched magic into the store in order to chew up all of her jinx and activate a successful teleport.

Blasted trickster!

Joe stepped clear of the cloud with his staff held out before him. She couldn't see it, but she could feel the magic he was pushing out between them.

Fantastic, the only person in the city that is potentially capable of defending against a Fireball is now possessed by the very thing creating the Fireballs.

That simple realization made the situation that much more terrifying. Joseph was amongst the strongest offensive and defensive wizards she knew. He could hold out against just about any attack and throw out one of the most powerful.

Her only hope was to release the Guardian. However, that meant taking time to summon her staff, and it was currently occupied. It would take too much time and leave her open to attack. She suddenly regretted freezing it to the ceiling.

The ice that had been holding up the Guardian shattered and great chunks of it fell to the tea shop floor beside Joe. Sadly, the Guardian didn't fall free with the ice chunks.

That was when Joe did the one thing she never expected, or thought possible – he freed the Guardian.

Joe wheeled on the spot, swung his staff like a club, and struck the ice pillar that was her staff. It snapped in half and erupted in a burst of freezing cold air that filled the entire shop and covered everything in a blanket of frost, temporarily blinding her. Her staff was broken… so was her understanding of the situation.

RUN!

Amelia turned, jumped over Bob's prone form, and looked around the storage room for the back exit. It took her half a second to find it, but Petals occupied the doorway.

She reflexively swiped her arm through the air and flooded the back room with a powerful jinx. Violet sparks burst from Petals fingers as he snapped them. He barked out a curse and shook out his hand. "Blast it!"

A dark iron manacle zipped toward her from out of the mist and struck her left arm. The pain was immediate and severe, causing her to scream and cradle her arm to her chest. She hoped it wasn't broken.

The odds were stacked against her, and the only exit was blocked. Amelia retreated to the very back of the storage room. Certain there were no more doors around her and only brick wall on three of the four sides, she used her other hand to gather all the cold air and moisture and erected a wall of ice between them. It didn't take much as the room was already below freezing.

In the last moments as the ice wall rose from the floor, she saw Joe jump into the back room. He spotted her and hurled his staff at her like a javelin. Amelia pushed harder, shut her eyes, and tilted her head back in hopes of evading the weapon being lobbed at her.

She opened her eyes and stumbled back a step. The staff had stopped dead with the head of it pointed just above her head and only a scant eighth of a step from touching her. It was frozen in layers of the ice and wasn't about to go anywhere quickly.

Panic and relief threatened to overtake her in a combined wave.

No time to panic! I have to think!

Momentarily separated from her pursuers, she had time to formulate an escape; it was the only option left. The problem was trying to think of a way to escape that didn't make it obvious where she had gone.

Teleportation spells could be tracked. The runes that were left in the wake of such an event could be read and duplicated. It was possible to create layers of encryption around the runes, but that required preparation and practice. She had none of that. There was also the added difficulty of making it so complex that even Joseph couldn't figure it out; she highly doubted that she could. He had gone from irritating rookie to absolute nightmare within a single night.

There was a hefty thump to the ice. They were already trying to break in, or they were being thrown about by the Guardian. She hoped it was the latter but didn't plan on sticking around to find out.

Amelia cradled her sore arm to her chest and checked her immediate surroundings. There was shelving to her right, stacked with preservation canisters of tea leaves and biscuits; a tea shop typically didn't need much else. None of it was going to help her, so she continued to look. There was an arcane box behind her that fed the store with energy. It would light the lanterns and heat the heating plates. If she had more time to plan, it might have been some use to her.

There was a hefty thump to the ice wall and she heard a loud popping crack.

Running out of time!

Amelia shut her eyes as she ran a mental tally of what she had in her pockets and what she could possibly do. Her jinx wouldn't last long, and they would soon be smashing through her ice wall with greater efficiency. Setting off an anti-magic incendiary seemed highly appealing at the moment, but it wasn't something one just had lying around.

That was when the solution came to her. She opened her eyes and quickly dug through her belt to draw an anti-magic bullet.

There was a significant thump against the ice wall, and she saw some cracks starting to spider out on her side.

Time's up!

Amelia lifted the bullet above her head and held it horizontally. A quick tethering made it float; secure and steady, she quickly linked a trigger to the tethers. With the bullet in place, she shut her eyes and solidified the destination in mind. She drew a circle of ice around her feet by pointing at the floor with the fingers of her good arm. She knew it was completed when she felt the connection to her destination strengthen. From there, she drew in and built as much arcane energy as her body could muster.

That was when the arcane box suddenly became useful. Amelia slapped her hand against the box and pulled in as much raw power as her body could take. It was invigorating and dangerous. If she didn't properly regulate the flow of energy into her body, she could burn herself out and permanently lose her connection to the arcane.

There was a wall-shaking smash, and bits of ice

struck her boots.

They're breaking through!

Do not panic.

Her fear sank as quickly as it had risen. Confidence and a clear head would save her.

She kept her eyes shut and focused on where it was she wanted to go. The magic was near to a palpable apex. Her skin and bones felt like they were beginning to hum with the power of it. Not wanting to take any more chances, she drew her hand back from the arcane box and focused on concentrating what she had drawn in.

Something smashed through the wall. She could tell because there was a sudden *woomph* of air as the pressure changed and things suddenly became louder, as if a door were opened. She was also struck in the knee with a chunk of ice; it nearly toppled her in pain.

Focus!

Her mind was perfectly clear, and there was no place in the world that she knew as well as where she intended on going; she just wished she didn't have to go there.

There was finally enough focused magic to complete the teleportation, and she released it all in a single burst.

If unpracticed or unskilled in the art of teleportation, one could be killed, maimed, disfigured, or any other number of horrible things. Thankfully, Amelia had practiced enough times at the Arcanum to survive a teleportation event without causing herself any harm. Her stomach, however, hated it.

Amelia snapped her eyes open when she felt her stomach lurch. There was a momentary weightlessness, and the world went black. It was as if she'd just been dropped off a cliff into the darkest abyss. She knew to expect it, but it never ceased to cause her a great deal of terror and unease.

Shutting her eyes and solidifying the image of the destination slammed her back into the world with both feet striking hard against the wooden floorboards of her childhood bedroom.

Morning breakfast decided to greet her. She doubled over and wretched as she emptied her stomach onto the dusty floorboards. The little girl's bed, upon which she put her hand for stability, was covered in a thick layer of dry dust.

With her stomach emptied, she spat out the offending taste and took a look about while wiping her mouth on the back of her coat sleeve. Her bed wasn't the only thing covered in dust; the entire room was one large blanket of gray. The air was thick with it. The teleportation event had also kicked up a great deal of it, causing her to sneeze violently and cover her mouth with the other sleeve of her jacket.

A look around revealed a great deal more. The room was bleak and dark. The curtains were open, but the window had been boarded shut. The door to her room was gone and replaced with wooden slats and plaster. Instead of boxing up her things, burning them, or whatever else they could think of to destroy their memory of her, they had simply opted to board up her room and pretend she had never existed in the household.

You were always petty, Mother.

The four-poster bed was just as she had left it that fateful night all those years ago. The dresser drawers had been pulled and upended, just as she remembered doing while packing to leave. Everything seemed so much smaller to her.

Do not reminisce.

Amelia shook her head clear of the memories and focused on what needed to be done. Hopefully, Andrew never boarded up their secret.

The closet at the far end of the room, near the bay window, shared a wall with Andrew's closet. Being that they were twins, the family had decided to put them side by side. It hadn't always been that way; as children, they often ran between each other's rooms in order to play. It didn't matter how far apart the rooms were.

Their parents gave up on separating them and stuck them beside one another. It had cost nothing, as all the children's rooms were of the same size and layout. She never understood the point in attempting to drive that wedge in the first place. They were twins and likely to be inseparable, as all twins were.

The memory of that fateful night bubbled to the forefront of her mind again, and she remembered all too well what drove them apart.

Focus!

Amelia again pulled her head from the past, shook the memories from her mind, and hobbled over to the closet. Her knee hurt something fierce.

There were still a few dresses hanging up in the closet, exactly as she had left them. They were disgustingly garish and she hated them, even as a child. The only time she ever wore them was when her parents wanted to parade their 'perfect' children before others.

Ha! Perfect!

If only Father could see the mess that was the Bloodstone Estate. She hoped he was writhing and suffering in the afterlife from that disgrace alone.

Before sneaking through to her brother's old room, she decided it was best to give it a quick look. Amelia shut her eyes, calmed her still hammering heart, and opened herself to the greater 'verse. Upon opening her eyes, she saw the world through shades of hot and cold. While the wall blocked her vision from seeing anything specific, she could tell that there weren't any large clouds of heat on the other side. She also couldn't hear anyone moving about. Satisfied that the room was empty, she blinked her eyes clear and proceeded.

With her good arm, she shoved aside a good dozen dresses and painfully knelt on the floorboards before her closet floor. The bottom section of paneling nearest the left wall of her closet was secretly a door. Amelia pushed against it in order to open it, but it didn't give. Thankfully, a hearty shove did the job. The panel receded and slid aside as if on tracks. It likely hadn't been used in quite some time.

The house had been built with a few secret entrances and exits. The closet tunnel, as she called it, was one of a few she had discovered. Unfortunately, the hole looked a great deal smaller than she remembered it, and she wasn't sure she could fit.

Ah, blast it!

It didn't look as though it was wide enough for her shoulders or hips. Amelia let out an aggravated sigh, took off her hat and belt and tossed them in. The only way to know for certain was to try.

Staying inside of her bedroom was out of the question. There was no telling if Joe and Petals might show up.

The anti-magic bullet casing that she had set up to float above her head was triggered to pull open the instant she teleported out. With any luck, the anti-magic dust and gunpowder would have released, fallen, and erased any possible runes left behind by her teleportation event. However, the ice that had been knocked inside and hit her in the knee could have potentially covered up enough of the runes to protect it and preserve the bits about her intended destination.

Sitting around and waiting to find out was not the smartest idea. In spite of her aches, she crawled through one arm at a time. She was able to squeeze her shoulders through, but her chest didn't fit; something was snagging.

Looking down and under to investigate, she spotted her gun holster hitting the frame of the secret passage. Irritatingly, no amount of sucking it in would collapse her rib cage enough to squeeze it through. "Ugh!"

Amelia backed out and took off her jacket and gun holster. She tossed them to the other side and began wiggling her way back through.

She could have easily frozen the wall and smashed it to bits, but that would have made too much noise and garnered unwanted attention. Sneaking away was her main goal. Some noise was acceptable, as the house was often empty and the flooring was solid enough and insulated to muffle most activities. Still, she wasn't about to go knocking down walls. Despite teleporting to the other side of the city, law enforcement could show up in record time if they were tipped off to her presence, especially if Joe and Petals caught wind of it.

It took a little wiggling, and her trousers rubbed a bit roughly against the frame, but she managed to squeeze her hips through. She couldn't help but think about how much bigger everything seemed when she was a child.

Amelia crawled out of the closet and quickly dusted herself off. Her trousers and blouse were dusty but unscathed.

She peered through the secret doorway to glance at her old room one last time before shutting it behind her. Joe and Petals weren't anywhere to be seen.

Good.

Andrew's room was spotless except for the area where she had crawled in and caked the floor with dust.

You deserve it for being a coward.

Amelia felt a bit petty at that thought.

Find him.

Her brother had answers, and she was going to drag them out of him. She turned to the closet and quickly began looking over the old shirts and vests until she found what she was looking for.

With her eyes on the prize, Amelia blindly reached into her vest pocket, drew out long metal tweezers, and plucked a length of jet black hair from one of Andrew's dark vests.

I'm coming for you.

Chapter 26

Tracking spells are simple in concept but require a bit of finesse and specificity; one cannot simply repeat a name and know the person's location. Unrelated individuals may have the same name. William is a popular name in the kingdom of Greencoast; the last name of Smith is also quite common. The most recent annual report suggested that there were seventeen William Smiths within the kingdom, and none of them were related. More were likely to exist within the greater world. In order to track down a specific William Smith, one would have to know more about the one they wanted to track. What was their profession? How old were they? Knowing those things would undoubtedly aid in narrowing the search, but it would still be too vague. Adding components to the spell such as familiar objects or keepsakes would help stabilize and narrow it down to a single individual. Hair and blood worked best.

Amelia hobbled to the writing desk by the window and set down the tweezers and hair. Unlike her old room,

Andrew's was well-lit. The curtains were open and the window wasn't boarded up, providing her with ample sunlight.

Her sore arm still felt numb, and wiggling her fingers only caused more pain. It was possibly broken, which meant she would have to work one-handed.

If only I still had my staff.

The fact that Joseph had smashed it to bits still shocked her. It didn't seem possible for an object so heavily imbued with magic to shatter so easily.

She dragged her belt over to the desk and pulled the necessary tools from one of her left-hand belt pouches. It took a little bit of work since she was working one-handed, but she managed to get it all out onto the writing desk. Alongside the tweezers and hair, she placed a miniscule vial of magic dust, a leather pouch of sewing pins, and a folded map of the city.

The map was invested with magic of its own. The parchment was resistant to tearing and was designed to work in conjunction with the pins. Amelia picked up the map and unfolded it with one hand. It took a bit of work and was an irritatingly slow process because the folds and creases caused it to try and fold shut again. Eventually she was able to flick out the map and spread it across the wooden desk.

Next, she picked up the little leather pouch and used her thumb to push back the flap; there were several pins inside. She always carried more than one just in case she had to track multiple targets. Since her arm was of no use and it still hurt to wiggle her fingers, she lifted the pouch to her mouth and used her teeth to find the head of a pin and pull it from the pouch.

Amelia dropped the pouch onto the desk, took the pin from her mouth, and pointed the head of it at the hair. The tweezers and hair leapt off the desk, and one end of the hair attached itself to the pin head as though it were charged. With the hair attached to the pin, she dropped the pin to the desk and released the tweezers from the hair; it would interfere with the tracking spell if she left it attached.

Picking up the hair, she held it between two fingers and dangled the pin above the map. It immediately snapped to attention and pulled toward the map. She lowered her hand until the hair loosened a bit and the pin floated a finger-width above the parchment. It was almost ready.

There was only enough magic dust to complete the spell once, so she took her time and carefully wiggled the stopper out with her teeth. She spat the cork out onto the desk, held the vial above the map, and closed her eyes.

She couldn't partition her mind like Joseph could, but she could at least use it to remember things with a fair amount of accuracy. The appropriate incantation came to mind, and she spoke it under her breath as she slowly poured the magic dust.

When she opened her eyes, she was nearly blinded by the brilliant white glow of the ink lines on the map. The pin was circling and slowly narrowing, and there was a soft humming sound emanating from the desk.

It only took a moment for the circling pin to narrow down to a single point on the map. When the vial was entirely tipped over and the dust was gone, the ink lines settled and the hum faded out.

With the brightness gone, she leaned in for a closer look and frowned in confusion. The pin was pointed at Goldbank Row, at the Bloodstone Estate. Either her brother was hiding somewhere other than his room, or she had plucked one of her old hairs off his vest. Unfortunately, the only way to know for certain was to search the estate.

Blast it!

She was hoping to sneak out the window and avoid the family altogether. Hobbling around in front of them with a potentially broken arm didn't sit well with her either.

Not wanting to leave her detective's tools lying about for mother to find and toss in the trash, she quickly and neatly folded up and stored away the map, pins, and vial.

Amelia dug around in the rear-most belt pouch and

pulled free her medical tin. It was time to deal with her arm and knee. Her knee was fine mechanically, but it hurt something awful; there would undoubtedly be a sizeable bruise on it. A quick search through the tightly-packed container revealed a much smaller tin. She hadn't used it in a while, so she quickly flipped it over to read the bottom and the dosages.

She mumbled to herself as she quickly skimmed, "'Take one tablet for mild injuries, two for severe. Three if you are out of danger and able to sleep soundly for four uninterrupted hours.' One tablet it is." She popped the top, wet the tip of her small finger with her tongue, and tapped one of the miniscule tablets with the finger. It stuck and she quickly lifted it free from the tiny tin, popped it into her mouth, and swallowed it.

The gag was nearly immediate; it was strong enough to cause an involuntary convulsion of her facial muscles. "*Hagh! Ack!*" Thankfully, the tablet went down, but she shook violently in revulsion. Never before had she tasted something so bitter and vile. A few deep breaths helped her to stabilize her gag reflex. "Oh gods... never again."

How can something so small have such a strong taste?

Fortunately, the tablet kicked in immediately, and made her skin feel fuzzy and slightly numb. That numbness included her sense of taste; the bitterness left immediately. The other good news was that she didn't have to hobble anymore. She walked a circle in order to test the pain killers. It worked. She only hoped that there wasn't any permanent damage that may be aggravated by walking on the leg.

The arm was a different story. It still throbbed a bit, but the pain was significantly reduced. A snub-nosed bone wand was included in every medical kit. It sat on the table beside some bandages she had taken out while searching for the pain killers.

Bone wands have one purpose – to set bones. If there aren't any broken bones to set, they do nothing. They are made from bone and have the necessary spellwork carved into the surface. It unnerved her that it was made from bone, but she didn't have much of a choice.

Amelia picked up the tiny stub of a wand that was no longer than her pointer finger and cautiously moved the tip toward her left arm. She shut her eyes, grit her teeth, and inhaled sharply in anticipation. Unfortunately, something happened; fortunately, she didn't hear any cracking or feel any grinding, but something definitely shifted. Wiggling her fingers didn't cause any more pain. Hopefully it would hold up until she could get to the doc, supposing he wasn't possessed.

Ready to take on whatever challenges or obstacles the family would throw at her, Amelia packed up her medical kit and put on her belt, gun holster, hat and coat before heading for the door.

As she crossed the room, she couldn't help but take a quick look about. The bed was a four poster, like her own childhood bed, but it didn't look like it had been slept in for some time. The room was dusted and clean, but much of the upholstery looked as though it still belonged to an adolescent. The only conclusion she could draw was that Andrew hadn't returned to his old room. Or, at least, he hadn't yet moved in his new things.

Amelia eased up on her steps as she neared the door and leaned into listen. The hallway beyond was deathly silent. With the aid of her arcane vision, she confirmed that there were no large body-shaped sources of heat near the door.

It was possible that Mother wasn't home. Marvin lived somewhere off on his own; Amelia could never figure out where. Samuel spent most of his days at the military barracks. Andrew, prior to recently abandoning his dwelling, lived close to the seaside docks so he could more easily commute and audit the ledgers. Mother was the only one that stayed at the estate. The only other individual she had to worry about was the offensive manservant.

A quick glance at her watch told her it was nearing mid-morning. Her stomach gurgled and growled in misery.

"I know, I know." She whispered to it and patted it in hopes of settling it into silence. Trying to sneak about on an empty stomach tended to be slightly more troublesome when the gurgles and growls of hunger gave away your location. It was also entirely possible that it was gurgling and growling in protest against the tablet she had just fed it.

I'll stop in the kitchens first. Then I'll search the house.

The door wasn't locked, so she took her time to slowly turn the handle. The hinges must have been well-kept because nothing squeaked and the door didn't creak. The floorboards were in good condition and didn't groan as she slowly stepped her way out into the hall.

The hallway was dark and bleak, as the wall sconces were unlit. Light wouldn't have done much to brighten the place as the walls were plastered with the same old dark and ugly wallpaper of maroon and gold filigree.

The only spot that wasn't wallpapered was the section where her bedroom door had been. It had been hastily plastered over and painted in an attempt to match. It looked awful and didn't match at all. There was also an obvious hump. Whoever had done the work tried to cover up the half-hearted job by hanging a large portrait painting of Grandfather Bloodstone. The patchwork looked questionable and highly circumspect at best. She could only imagine what a visitor would think of it. Then again, Mother never had visitors.

Not wanting to be caught off guard, she decided on having a more focused listen to see if she could hear anyone moving about. Amelia went to pull her wand from her vest pocket and painfully remembered that it was shattered and destroyed. She grumbled under her breath, "Blast it all," then did her best to recall the necessary hand gestures for summoning the funnel of cold air.

It took her a moment, but she was able to remember the runes associated with the task, draw them in the air with her finger, and tether the magic to her left ear. There was a brief whistling rush of air and a sudden shift in volume. The difference almost made it seem like her right ear was plugged with gunk and wax while the left was clean. That wasn't the case, but the sensation was similar.

From heel to toe, she slowly crept along the hallway and headed toward the grand staircase that led to the main floor. Her head was tilted slightly so that the left ear was pointing the way. There didn't seem to be anyone in the estate. There were no creaking floorboards and no idle hum of chatter. Despite the obvious signs and assurances that the house was empty, she took her time moving about and remained on alert.

There still hadn't been any loud pops to announce a teleportation event, so she had a strong feeling that her plan had worked, and she had gotten away clean.

Amelia peered around the corner and over the banister in order to look down upon the main hall and grand staircase. Nobody was there.

Certain that she could be a little louder, she hurried to the stairs and made her way down to the main floor. Both front and back doors were closed. The main hallway, like the floor above, was dark and dreary, as the wall sconces were unlit. The few windows that framed the front and back doors were shuttered.

Mother must not be home. And it doesn't look like Andrew is either... Blast it!

Knowing that she couldn't function well on an empty stomach, she headed to the kitchens, opposite the grand stairs.

Confident that nobody was home, she pushed open the right-hand swinging door and stepped into the white tile of the kitchen. Everything was white; the countertops were white marble, the cabinetry was painted white, and the tile and backsplash was all white. The stove and oven, built into the kitchen island, were also factory white. It was undeniably her favorite part of the old house.

It was one of the few places that she could be a child and play. Baking biscuits with Blueregard had been a highlight. Her father demanded that she "learn how to cook and bake as any woman should." As bigoted and demeaning of a sentiment and mentality as it was, she enjoyed it. The aromas were always intoxicating, and the reward at the end of the hard work was something she could eat. Her brothers had envied her for it. She couldn't imagine any child not wanting to bake.

"Hello, sister."

Amelia had been so focused on remembering better times that she had forgotten to check the breakfast nook. With a startle, she turned to look into the corner.

The breakfast nook was set into the far corner of the kitchen. It was framed with windows in order to provide ample sunlight for morning breakfast, and it was furnished with a round table and six chairs. Andrew had pulled a chair away from the table and was sitting with his back to the far corner.

So... he is here.

Strangely, Andrew was not behaving like his normal self. Typically he sat with his eyes downcast and his shoulders sagging, hands in his lap and both feet firmly together touching the ground. As he sat in the corner, he had his left leg crossing over his knee, his shoulders were square, and he leaned back in his chair while boring a hole through her soul with his hardened gaze.

There was a red glint in his eye, but it was due to the a small pine crate sitting on the breakfast table with four health potions nestled inside and packed with cotton. Health potions could easily be identified by the purple wax caps that were stamped with the insignia of certification from the Arcanum, and they gave off a distinct luminescent red glow. That red glow was lighting Andrew's face.

His blue eyes were locked on hers, and he wasn't cowering away like he always did. Despite his thin and small frame, he looked surprisingly imposing. "Not going to greet your brother?" His tone was flat and devoid of emotion as it usually was, but there was an undertone of confidence that was never there before.

"Andrew, wh–" She couldn't finish. Her mind was ravaged by a skull-splitting headache, and everything went dark.

~~

She woke in darkness to the sounds of shouting, cursing, and the roar of ocean waves. Light flooded the world, and she found herself at the bottom of a stone box.

It must have been a curse box, because the runes that were etched into the inside were identical to the ones from the stone chest back at the precinct, though this box seemed much smaller. That was when she remembered the two empty square slots. She was inside of a secondary box.

Dizzyingly, she could perceive everything around her body; except, she wasn't in a body. She was a Crown, made from ice blue metal. The face of it looked as though it were nothing more than large crystals of ice that jutted up instead of regular metal points.

The world outside the box was an officer's quarters on a boat. She could tell it was a boat because the deck was rolling and the men standing about the box swayed with the movement of the ship. There was also a second box beside the one she resided in. It, too, was open.

In a flash, the world changed, and she was seeing through someone else's eyes. Her ears were ringing and sound was muffled, but she could see Julian Kane standing over her. They were in the warehouse where the bodies had been incinerated, and the ice field was outside.

Kane was wearing the Crown of Fire where his hat should have been. His eyes were a fiery red instead of the deep burned orange they usually were, and there were bright yellow veins starting to show across his face and hands.

Oh gods... the health potions...

She was finally starting to understand.

The sadistically-grinning Kane raised one clawed

hand, ignited it in a plume of raging fire, and brought a torrent of pain screaming down upon the body that she was possessing. Amelia felt all of it, every bit of heat and blistering skin. The pain could only possibly be described as otherworldly. Maddeningly, she couldn't scream. Her voice was not her own. The Ice Crown simply accepted the defeat and gave nothing to the possessed Kane. The poor sailor that had picked up the Ice Crown from the curse box died a silent and agonizing death.

Thankfully, her awareness and essence retreated from the quickly burning body and back into the Crown.

Another flash changed the world around her, and she found herself being tossed off the eastern docks and into the freezing depths of the bay. From there, she was discovered by a curious merfolk.

If the circumstances had been different, Amelia would have found the merfolk to be one of the most interesting and breathtaking things she'd ever seen. Scales covered their body from head to fin and reflected from deep sea green to a brilliant sky blue. They had the upper torso of a female human, but her hair looked like it was made from kelp, and her eyes looked fish-like and bubbled.

That body was also possessed by the Crown. She felt the waters flowing over her body as they swam to the surface. As soon as they breached, the Crown was taken from the head and thrown at the nearest dock warden.

Again, her perception changed. She was in the body of the dock warden, the one that had gone missing. It was the exact same man that had later bumped into her and passed the Crown to her head. She watched it all play out and was unable to stop any of it. Amelia hadn't been knocked over; she hadn't even been bumped into. It had all been staged.

The dock warden, who she then knew through the knowledge of the Ice Crown was named Allard Anchors, simply took off the Crown and swapped it with her hat when her back was turned. After easing her to the ground, he tossed the letters of news into the air, then helped her back up again.

Many more things were shared with her following that point. Flashes of memories and visions were granted to her. At any moment that she had experienced a headache, it was the Crown taking control. Her staff was safe and sound and hiding under her bed. The one that Joseph had smashed had been a copy that had been crafted by the entity in the ice crown. It had done so in order to keep Amelia from becoming suspicious or discovering the truth. Keeping her in the dark and acting as normal as possible was part of the plan.

The Ice crown had wanted to go to the precinct in order to use the information gathered to find out where the other Crown was. It wanted to know where its twin was. Joseph had fouled that plan. She didn't know how, and the Crown didn't seem to want to share any knowledge on it.

Joe had never been possessed, and Petals had never been corrupted. It had all been a lie. The Guardian had been after her the entire time. She hadn't been bait; she was the one that was possessed… and the ice crown made it very clear to her.

You are the perfect vessel.

Chapter 27

The flashbacks ceased, and she was finally able to see through her own eyes again. Her mind returned to the kitchens, and Andrew hadn't moved from where she last saw him at the breakfast nook, but he stared at her with a bit more of a furrow in his brow.

"Where is my brother?" It was her voice, but it was not her words. The entity still had control.

Surprisingly, she didn't feel possessed. It seemed an odd thing to think, but she'd been fully possessed by the Ice Crown at multiple points before. At each instance, Amelia had been completely unaware. Why then did the Ice Crown allow her to think, feel, and sense everything?

Andrew narrowed his eyes at her and tilted his head slightly. "What are you talking about?"

Amelia – the entity possessing her body – removed her hat. She sensed a shift in temperature in the air.

Andrew's eyes darted to Amelia's head, and he sat a little straighter. "Ah. I see."

It was obvious that the Crown had finally revealed itself. Her best guess was that the Crown used some form of illusion spell in order to hide.

Correct.

Now that she was aware of the other voice and how it had been manipulating her, she could finally begin to distinguish it from her own internal thoughts. Not only that, but she could direct her thoughts to it as well.

I didn't have a lump on my head when my hat wouldn't fit, did I?

No.

It was you, wasn't it?

Yes.

How did my hat fit the next day then?

I shrunk to fit.

Why didn't you do that the first day?

There was an adjustment period.

Amelia was too busy directing her thoughts to the entity, she had forgotten it had asked Andrew a question. He was responding, and she hadn't been paying attention.

"He cannot be reasoned or bargained with." The entity was replying to something that Andrew had said. It was apparently something about striking a deal with the Crown of Fire.

Andrew stood with his hands clasped before him. She didn't remember seeing him get up, but that was likely while she was busy having an internal discussion with the Ice Crown. "Everyone can be bargained with, as everyone wants something." He stepped forward and placed both hands on top of the bottles that sat inside the pine box. "I've been keeping close tabs on your counterpart. He has made several attempts to start a botanical apothecary with the hopes of brewing his own health potions." He gently tapped the tops of the potion bottles. "I have what he wants."

"He will kill you and take the bottles. The moron has no foresight or sense of consequence. He is little more than a rabid dog with far too much bite. You have nothing to bargain with." The entity of the Ice Crown clearly had a low opinion of its twin.

The nightmare I shared with you is but a taste of what he truly is.

Why do you share at all?

We are stronger when united.

Amelia didn't feel like sharing anything, but had a strong suspicion that the Ice Crown had already examined every corner of her mind.

You are correct. There is nothing that I do not know about you.

"That is where you're wrong, dear sister." Andrew plucked a match from his left sleeve and quickly flicked the tip of it with his right thumb. The match ignited, and Andrew did what Amelia thought would never happen. He upturned his palm and created a floating sphere of fire out of the burning match.

It wasn't uncommon for less-skilled wizards to use consumables as a means by which to jumpstart their connection to the arcane. Andrew was a lesser-skilled wizard.

How?

How is not important at this moment. He is. Accept it.

"I offered myself as a willing host."

You idiot!

"He refused my offer and simply declared me to be a lesser-rate wizard that was unworthy of his time. He was correct in that I am a lesser-rate wizard in comparison to the fire-happy host he currently inhabits. But he was wrong when he said I was unworthy of his time." He paused momentarily to pick his words. "You were correct in your assessment. He has no foresight. I knew it as soon as we met. He threatened to kill me, and he gloated about how powerful he was with the current host." Andrew closed his hand and choked off the air that was feeding the small ball of fire. It extinguished immediately. "But he couldn't see the flaws in his own thinking. Nobody can think like I can." He said it more to himself.

"Why did he not kill you?" While the entity had asked it, Amelia was just as curious to know the answer.

"I told him I could purchase health potions, and if he killed me then he would never know where I intended to purchase them from." Andrew let out an irritated sigh. "He threatened to kill me again if I did not tell him." He closed his eyes as though he were reliving the suffering of a buffoon. "I pointed out the inherent flaw in his threat and he begrudgingly agreed to let me live for one more day so long as I was able to provide him with the health potions I said I could acquire." He gestured to the pine box crate. "I provided."

"That doesn't explain why he won't kill you when he comes to claim the potions."

Amelia came to the realization why Andrew was waiting in the breakfast nook with his back to the corner.

Shush, your thoughts are distracting.

There was the slightest hint of a smirk that crawled across Andrew's face. "By my estimates, the host will nearly be dead by the time your brother arrives. Any magic he casts will be detrimental to the continued use of that host. He will have no choice but to accept my bargain or be nothing more than an inert Crown on an ash heap." He bent down and picked up a short stock shock-barrel and placed it on the table. "I also armed myself with anti-magic rounds." He snarled as he glared at Amelia, "I'm not the coward or the fool that you think I am, sister."

I have what I need from him. My brother will be along shortly. You may speak if you wish.

Amelia found that she had control of her voice again. She couldn't look where she wanted to look or move where she wanted to move, but she could at least speak.

"How? When did you learn magic? You never went to the Arcanum." Andrew had always been a coward. He had never stood up for himself. There was no way that Mother would have ever allowed him to study magic.

"Unlike you, dear sister, I learned how to hide things from Mother."

The fact that he hadn't said "Mother and Father" gave her the impression that he didn't attempt to learn magic until after Father had died. "You're still a coward. I don't care how smart you think you are. Congratulations! You outsmarted a rabid dog! You still hid behind Mother's skirts when Father came at me with grandfather's cane sword! I still have the scar on my back where he caught me with the tip on a sweeping strike!"

"And what was I to do, Amelia?" He finally raised his voice. Andrew stood straighter and puffed out his chest. It was the first time she'd ever seen him stand up and show some spine. "Hm? What was I to do? I was nothing more than a spindly boy. I'm still spindly!" He gestured to himself with angry fervor. "I didn't have the power that you possessed!"

She couldn't argue against it. He would likely have died if he had tried to protect her. The inaction still hurt. "And what of the years that followed? What of the years in which I wrote to you and you said nothing? At every family gathering that I was forced to attend, you avoided me like I was some pox, plague, or witch!"

"A calculated deception." His answer was swift, cold, and calm. "A deception that I still despise to this day." He looked down and away from her.

She recognized the look of shame. It was the same look of shame he wore every day of his life that followed that fateful night, the night that she had clawed at her father's chest and froze his beating heart.

"Why this?" She nearly choked on the words. She couldn't believe her cowardly brother was committing such crimes.

"The Bloodstone Estate is nearly bankrupt." It explained why there was a sudden and unnecessary change in the allowances and why the household hadn't changed in the many years since she last lived in it. "Mother has expensive tastes and poor business skills. When I took control of the family finances two years ago, I noticed the inevitable end was approaching."

"You knew I could pay off my allowance... didn't you?"

"Yes." Andrew lifted his head and met her gaze with a slight glint of pride. "I had calculated your earnings from the patent you had developed and determined that you were more than capable of injecting the family estate with an influx. I also knew that you would rather pay out your debt than bend to Mother's ridiculous demands. I even helped her concoct some of them just to be certain you would repay your allowance." He seemed a little too smug about it. "The influx was desperately needed and had the potential to stave off the collectors for another moon, maybe two."

"So... what? You planned on selling off cursed items on the black market in order to uphold a family estate that is doomed to shrivel and die in these modern times?"

Andrew scowled and barked, "Ha! I wouldn't dare sell something so valuable to ruffians. I had plans on using the powers of the Crowns to craft my own inventions and patent them for the wealth, just as you had." His features hardened a bit. "And this family can be damned!" He frowned as he looked down at the pine box of bottles. "Mind you, I had no idea that the Crowns were cursed."

"And instead you released death and mayhem upon the city. Fantastic job, Andrew."

"I can salvage this!" He barked it with a ferocity that she would have expected from Samuel or Father.

The Ice Crown took control once again and raised a hand so as to silence Andrew. Her head turned toward the east wall of the kitchens. She looked to the stove, oven and sink, but the entity was sensing beyond it.

Amelia felt a growing sense of danger coming from that general direction. The hairs on the back of her neck stood on end as she could feel something or someone approaching.

He nears.

Her body marched toward the swinging doors of the kitchen, pushed through them, and headed for the front entryway.

She heard Andrew scuffle about in the kitchens and begin shouting after her, "Wait! WAIT!" His voice was cut off and muffled as the doors swung back and forth.

The Crown of Fire was quickly approaching. Just like Joseph, she could sense it sensing her.

How could I – we – you – sense Joseph?

When we corrupt him, we can ask him and finally know.

How do you corrupt people?

I share my essence with them.

Just as her body was about to reach the front door and turn the lock, Amelia was struck with a memory.

She was back in Chuck's Tea Parlor. Bob had been giving her a stern word about using magic against the tea shop owner. It was then the headache had struck, the Ice Crown took control, and her body did the one thing she was mortified to see.

Amelia gripped Bob by the face and pressed her open mouth to his. They weren't kissing, but she could taste his breath. Through that proximity, the Ice Crown pushed out its influence and infected Bob's mind. A cold bluish light passed from Amelia to Bob.

The corruption was why he had called her Ice Queen so readily. While it was a nickname that she had earned amongst the blue coats, it was also an appropriate title for the entity that possessed her body. Despite having gained that relevant information, it was horribly embarrassing to witness.

Please never do this to Joseph, or ever show me that memory again.

You are a prude, child. He is valuable and must bend to my will, as must all others. They will all be willing allies or corrupted servants.

Gods, please no.

Up until that point, she had been willing to think of the Ice Crown as mostly reasonable. It hadn't killed anyone with wanton abandon, and it had given Amelia a great deal of free reign up to that point. It even allowed her to have a conversation with her brother. In the end, the entity was still a tyrant, and she desperately needed to find a way to fight it.

There is no fighting my control.

A loud metallic click caught her ear and brought her sight back to the present. Her head turned to look back over the shoulder.

Andrew was standing with the shock-barrel in hand and the pine box at his feet. Despite his chest-puffing and smart talk, he looked rather ridiculous holding the shock-barrel. He wasn't even holding it properly and was barely able to hold the nose up. Had he pulled the trigger, the butt end and handle would have smashed him in the chest from the recoil. He likely would have only shot the flooring as well. "You're not going anywhere until my business is concluded!"

Please don't kill him!

I promise nothing.

Amelia's hand rose from her side, and her fingers flicked toward the ground. The shock-barrel that Andrew had been trying to level at her tipped toward the ground and discharged. There was a startling and violent *kabang!* The weapon launched into the air and out of Andrew's hands.

Naturally, Andrew jumped on the spot and let out a high-pitched bark of surprise as he clapped his hands over his ears. It had been undeniably loud, but Amelia didn't experience any ringing or damage to her hearing. It was then that she noticed a subtle muffling spell had been placed over her ears, and it quickly dispersed.

The shock-barrel arced overtop of Andrew and clattered to the floor behind him. The floor had a saucer-sized hole in it and crimson smoke lingered in the air. He truly had armed himself with anti-magic rounds.

Andrew danced about on the spot, checked his body for holes, then looked down at his intact pine box before letting out a heavy breath of relief. It was almost comical.

The entity turned her attention back to the door, twisted the door lock, and yanked open the front door. The entryway was as she remembered it from a few nights previous. Sully – Mr. Ugly Teeth – wasn't anywhere to be seen, nor were his mercenary accomplices.

Storm clouds were rolling in from the east, hung low in the sky. Earlier, Amelia had praised the arrival of the storm clouds, for they would grant her an environmental advantage against the Crown of Fire. At that point, she feared how much of an advantage it would grant. If Julian was as depleted and as near to death as Andrew predicted, then the Ice Crown would easily be able to defeat him, if not outright kill him.

My brother will never submit to anyone, especially not me. He will use the host of Julian until the body turns to ash or is near enough to it.

A brief queasiness overtook her as she stepped out the door and levitated into the air and out over top of the statue that sat before the front doors of the house. Naturally and irritatingly, the Ice Crown had completed the levitation without the aid of a platform of ice about the feet. In answer to her thought, her body lifted her right hand in order to show a ring of ice that had erected around her forearm. A brief glance showed that there was one around her waist and more around her boots.

Show off.

Unite with me and your simple understandings will be broadened.

No!

It is a shame, but it is inconsequential to me. In a few days, I will envelope your mind and take full control of this body. If we had merged, we would have been more powerful.

The answer is still no.

Petulant child.

The entity seemed exasperated.

As soon as they reached the top of the statue, they stopped and settled atop the arm and shoulder of the army commander. There was nothing to grasp for balance, so she was immediately anxious about falling.

Ice Queen, or whatever her name used to be, didn't seem to be bothered by the height and stood tall atop the statue. Like her father, the being saw the strategic importance of appearances and positions of power. Amelia couldn't help but feel that it was a foolish vantage point. As much as she gained in visibility, it also made her a blatant target.

"Sister!" The voice was distinctly Julian's, but it sounded more rough and hoarse than usual.

Her head tilted down, and she spotted a figure hiding in the shadows by the main gate. They stayed out of sight and only half-peered around the brick and mortar of the outer wall. Despite trying to hide, he gave off a warm glow of fire. Due to the distance between them, she couldn't make out individual features, but there were definite signs of cracked skin glowing hot. The Crown informed Amelia that the host wouldn't survive much longer. It looked like Andrew had guessed correctly.

He must not be allowed to continue.

You cannot kill a man of the law in cold blood!

He is possessed, and you don't seem all that broken up about him dying. I know your thoughts on this man. You cannot hide them from me.

Blast you!

Julian was a drunkard and a mess of a detective that constantly lost his calm and barely managed to do his job correctly. She had no love for the man, and wouldn't miss him if he was gone, but it didn't mean she wished him dead.

Amelia's right hand rose to rest beside her right ear, and a spear of ice began to materialize. Water was easily pulled from the air, and it would soon become easier. She was about to tether the spear to the wall that Julian was hiding behind when there was a hearty explosion from behind. *Kabang!*

A split-second reaction on the part of the Ice Crown resulted in a hastily-erected barrier of ice. It stopped most of the pellets from hitting her, and those it couldn't were easily stopped by her trench coat. Most went wide and chipped tiny bits of stone off the statues or simply arced into the air to land elsewhere.

She looked back to the front entryway and spotted Andrew holding the shock-barrel as though he'd fired from the hip. Black smoke curled away from the tip; he'd clearly had only one anti-magic shell.

At least he didn't hurt himself.

His efforts were pointless. The weapon is ineffective at this range.

Andrew knows that.

The Ice Crown whipped her head back around to the front gate and she growled in irritation. The gate was open and Julian – the Crown of Fire – wasn't anywhere to be seen.

She could sense him. She knew he was there, she just wasn't able to narrow it down to where specifically. Her head darted about and she quickly scanned the expansive grounds of the estate, but she still couldn't see him; the statues were in her way.

Her body floated up off of the arm and she continued to scan the grounds from a greater vantage point, one that wasn't obscured by the stone figures. Fearing that they had attempted to circle around her and out of her sight, she checked to the left. There was nothing.

A labored grunt pulled her attention around and down. Julian was face-down on the ground right beside the base of the statue. He must have rushed in and used the shield-baring soldiers to hide his approach. She was horrified to notice that he wasn't wearing a Crown.

Time seemed to slow as she tracked toward Andrew

and the front steps. She didn't want it to be true, but there it was. Spiraling through the air was the inert Crown of Fire. It had a reddish-gold hue and wavy little spikes. There was no grand design to it; it looked like something a child would have designed, and yet it held a monster.

NO!

Andrew reached out and caught the Crown. Flames erupted from the wavy little spikes, and her brother grinned madly while placing the Crown atop his head. "Dear sister! I think it's time we had ourselves some family fun!"

Chapter 28

Andrew – the Crown of Fire – aimed the shock-barrel at Amelia once again and pulled the trigger. *Click!* The entity that possessed her brother looked to the firearm with confusion, then furiously shook it with both hands while grumbling something in a language she wasn't familiar with. Unsurprisingly, the Ice Crown understood the words and roughly translated it into a foul curse.

"Idiot." Amelia dropped from where she had been floating and took up position behind the makeshift wall of ice that she had erected when deflecting the first volley of pellets moments ago. Once safely behind cover, she tethered the ice spear to the stone steps directly behind her twin brother.

NO!

The slightest effort was all that was needed in order to launch the shaft of frothing ice. The magic did most of the work. It flew through the air with deadly speed and pinpoint accuracy.

Andrew dodged the attack with little to no effort. He simply stepped back with one foot and leaned a little to the side. The lance of ice struck the steps and sheared directly into the stone.

This is not the first time my brother has played this game. Now, be quiet.

Her twin was too busy fumbling with the shock-barrel to look up at Amelia. It was odd; if he possessed Andrew, then he should have known how to utilize the weapon.

My brother does not care to listen to anyone for any reason. He refuses to learn from others. He sees others as inferior to him. That is why he is little more than a rabid dog. He must be put down.

Amelia agreed that the cursed Crown of Fire was something that needed to be dealt with, but she didn't agree with it costing her brother's life.

The man threw a fit upon the steps and banged the weapon against the ground as though it would somehow make it work.

Another lance of ice was prepared and released.

Andrew didn't dodge the second one. Instead, he turned bloodshot crazed eyes upon the hurtling ice and swung the shock-barrel like a club. The entire metal shaft and wooden stock erupted in flames, and the spear exploded into a burst of steam that enveloped him in a thick cloud.

"Ha, ha!" He laughed as though he'd finally discovered how to use the weapon. It clearly did not hold her brother's interest, as she heard it clatter to the stone steps, discarded.

The brief cover of the steam cloud obscured her vision and allowed her brother to launch into the air and fly directly toward her in an outright surprise attack. He was propelled into the air by concentrated streams of fire that erupted from the soles of his feet. He came roaring, "GRAAHHH!"

Amelia was terrified by the sudden bull-rush. The

Ice Queen wasn't. Her body twisted and she shifted into a braced stance as both hands slapped the back of the ice barrier.

Water was quickly pulled from the air and pushed to solidify over the first ice wall. Along with the additional structural support, a row of spines protruded from the front. While all of it was impressively quick, Amelia couldn't help but feel that they were blatantly exposed on all other sides. The wall was solidly connected to the head and shoulders of the statue and couldn't be maneuvered in case they were suddenly attacked from the side.

You give him too much credit.

He can't be this dumb.

There was a *woomph* to the air and a roar of fire. Steam immediately followed, then the heavy and meaty impact of body striking ice.

I can't believe he's this dumb.

Ice cracked and popped with the steady barrage of meaty thumps against the barrier.

Rabid. Dog.

Her hands retreated from the ice as a red glow began to push through the core of the wall. Amelia stood straight and raised her left arm. Ice gathered about the back of her wrist and slowly grew outward in an expanding circle of ice.

A flaming fist punched through the ice wall, then a second soon followed. The knuckles were scratched, torn, and bloodied.

He cares nothing for the body he uses.

Her right hand clenched into a tight fist, and a duplicate fist developed out of the water that was melting away from the ice wall. It slowly solidified into an ice ball as big as her head.

The Crown of Fire burst through the ice wall, quickly followed by an unnatural sadistic grin. "Hello, si–" He stopped as he realized what was about to happen to him.

Amelia shifted and grunted with the force of

punching the air with her first. The ice fist followed her exact movements and lurched forward at bone-breaking speed.

Andrew heaved back in order to duck out in time. The ice fist collided with the wall and continued on through it. The deafening crack was near thunderous. Stone bits flew in every direction, and the ice exploded in a rain of glittering shards and water. It all crashed down onto the pea-gravel and front steps.

Andrew, both fortunately and unfortunately, was able to divert his fall and land some ways away so he didn't get crushed by the falling debris. He did have a bloodied face; his nose looked crooked, and there were some scratches across his forehead.

"Unlike you, *brother*, I learn from my hosts," she said with absolute disgust. A sword of ice slowly grew out of her hand.

Your combat training is illuminating and freeing.

Andrew stood for a moment and seethed. His cheeks puffed with his quickening breath, as his bloodshot eyes stood out in stark contrast against his reddening and bloodied face. At first, the madness looked to be anger, but the frown twisted upward into a wild grin.

He is going to launch a Fireball.

Can —

No.

She was about to ask if the Crown had the power or knowledge to deflect it, but the thought was obviously quicker than her trying to push it. Instead of running, they stood their ground, and remained on the arm of the statue.

We should run!

Not yet.

Why?

He will tire quicker this way.

She couldn't help but think that he would also burn through her brother's body quicker as well.

Andrew continued his unwavering psychotic grin and upturned both palms before his chest. Amelia could sense the sudden snap of energy and she could see the air distort in a sphere above Andrew's upturned palms.

It was the barrier. A brief gust and a fluttering of Andrew's clothes suggested that air had been pulled into the barrier and compressed.

We could have attacked him by now!

No. We wait.

The knowing returned. It was quick and sudden, like a cold splash of water to the face. Surprisingly, they both turned to look toward the road and the front gate.

Amelia knew what the sudden knowing meant. Joseph had arrived. Andrew, on the other hand, looked completely confused. "What is–" Andrew's question was interrupted by an explosive release of compressed air. The sphere that was the precursor to the Fireball had popped. His head whipped back and his clothes fluttered. His words were also garbled by the gust of wind.

Her twin brother staggered from his failed spell, but didn't topple or lose focus. The rabid dog shook off the momentary discombobulation and focused all his attention to the front gate. "Who is that? How? How can I feel them?" He turned his attention back to her and roared, "This is *our* thing!"

She focused on the gate but kept her brother in the periphery.

"Answer me!" He spat as he roared.

Neither Amelia nor the Ice Queen had one to give. She could tell that the Crown was just as confused because it was silent on the matter.

Her eyes darted skyward momentarily. The storm clouds were almost overhead, and the world was darkening. A great shadow was creeping across the city and growing nearer by the moment.

Soon.

Her eyes lowered just in time to spot a figure darting

across the road to hide on the other side of the gate entrance. It looked like a pale grayish-green trench coat; a Southeast detective had arrived with Joseph.

Andrew was yelling and spitting again, "You did this! You ruined our thing!" A brilliant ball of fire erupted in his hand, and he lobbed it up at her.

Turning and swatting at the sphere of fire with the flat tip of her constructed ice blade resulted in another burst of steam. Sadly, half her sword melted in the process, but at least the fire didn't get any nearer to her. The heat from the ball of fire had been exceedingly uncomfortable.

Look.

She couldn't not look, as her eyes were no longer her own. With her attention and focus forcefully directed at Andrew, she couldn't help but notice that bright lines were starting to appear on his face and hands.

It's beginning.

Blast it all! Can't you just stop him?

No. He is still stronger.

We are smarter than him!

We are. That is why we wait, hold the high ground, and let him tire himself out. Like the tantruming child that he is.

More water was drawn from the increasingly muggy air. It was pushed down into the half-melted sword, and the tip regrew.

Her attention was immediately drawn back to the gate when she heard a metallic whirring. One of Joseph's manacles was screaming through the air and directly toward her head. She could only guess that he had plans to knock the Crown off. The second manacle headed for Andrew.

Amelia's hand and sword came up, and a quick backhanded swipe of the ice blade batted the manacle aside. It bounced off the stone statue and fell to the pea-gravel below.

Andrew screamed in rage and ignited both hands. He threw all the fire at the ground in front of him. There was an audible *thump* and a significant amount of sod and dirt was kicked up into the air. The second manacle collided with the dirt and fell to the ground.

Real smart there, Rook. Could you be more obvious?

It was clearly a distraction.

Her attention turned to the side wall that bordered the Bloodstone Estate. In the blink of an eye, her arcane vision was fully realized and sharper than ever. She could see bodies of heat rushing along the far wall. Her head turned to look to the other side, and she could see similar masses of heat moving along that side as well.

We are being surrounded.

Real smart there, Rook.

The arcane vision vanished as quickly as it had appeared, and the world returned to normal. The looming shadow of the storm clouds began to blot out the sun, and with it, the direct warmth. She turned her full attention back toward Andrew, pulled together all of the cold air, and breathed out the heat.

Ice began to form on her skin and across her body. The statue beneath her crackled and popped as the tiny imperfections in its surface were filled with bits of water that froze and expanded.

Amelia lifted herself up off the statue's arm as it crumbled, and she floated up into the air.

Winds began to howl as the storm drew closer. Her hair whipped up and blew to the east as the winds came from the west.

Andrew darted his eyes skyward, then glanced to Amelia. He clearly understood that the tides had turned. The coward turned, bolted for the house, and fueled his steps by throwing fire out behind him. It propelled him slightly.

It wasn't fast enough. Amelia eyed the target and pointed with her ice sword.

Rain began to fall at nearly the exact moment she pointed. As soon as it entered her aura, she froze the droplets and sent them rocketing toward Andrew.

He flinched and turned his head away as he was inundated with a torrential wall of ice pellets. They wouldn't kill him, but they would hurt and slow him down.

Her twin raised his right arm and covered his head as he fled into the house.

Health potions!

That is not my concern.

How can it not be your concern?

The front entryway of the house spontaneously erupted into roaring flames.

That is my concern.

Oh.

The Crown of Fire had created itself a source of fire to draw upon and combat the rain.

Based upon the depth and weight of the clouds, she predicted that the storm would last longer than the fire would, especially with how hot the Crown of Fire seemed to burn.

Her body reflexively twisted in the air in order to look back upon the front gate, and her ice blade flicked through the air twice more. Two manacles bounced off the flat of the blade. Joe was persistent.

While the lack of imagination was slightly irritating, she couldn't argue with the potential results. If the Ice Crown was adequately distracted, she could easily see it getting caught by the manacles. There was no telling whether that would result in anything, but it was better than nothing.

A roar of fire had her turn back around and point her ice blade at the oncoming belch of flame. The rain that had begun falling turned and focused itself upon the fire plume. Unfortunately, it wasn't enough. The fire was too concentrated and too hot. It ate the water droplets and reached up into the sky in an attempt to engulf her.

Amelia retreated further in the air while continuing to point her sword down, but it was no use. The fire was simply too much, and there wasn't enough time to gather more water to hinder the flames.

That was when it all suddenly stopped. The burning mass flattened and spread as if it had struck an invisible wall.

A quick glance over her right shoulder informed her that Joseph had finally come out from hiding. He was standing on the pea-gravel road and pointing his staff up at the reaching inferno.

He will make an excellent Guardian.

With some time to regroup, she lifted her sword skyward and began to gather as much rain as she could. A sphere of water formed and grew exponentially. As soon as there was a sizeable enough mass prepared, she swung her blade and pointed it at the entrance of the family estate. The massive ball of water rumbled through the air as it passed her. She couldn't begin to estimate how much was in it, but it looked enough to fill her tub dozens of times over.

The barrier must have dropped, because the fire that had been advancing toward her suddenly lurched forward. It was struck by the massive sphere of water and burst into a cloud of hissing and screaming steam.

The shield on her left arm did well to protect her from the scalding effects. While she couldn't see, she could hear as the sphere continued to chew through the fire and descend like a giant hammer. It was only a few seconds before she heard the calamitous crash, and the steam grew again by a giant burst and the deafening hiss of fire being extinguished. The world grew darker as a result.

Her body twisted around once more and her sword swung down in order to swat away the manacles that had been rocketing up toward her feet.

He is persistent.

Irritating, isn't he?

Amelia reached out with her shield-covered hand and pulled back while drawing her fist closed. The steam pulled away and quickly condensed into another sphere of water. A thrust of her fist caused it to lurch forth and barrel through the front doors of what was once her family home.

Amelia began to descend again in order to follow

and take pursuit, when the front doors erupted, and a pillar of white hot fire slammed into the base of the statue. She quickly ascended in retreat. That which had been extinguished was burning once again.

He's irritating too.

Amelia dropped the sword behind her back, and she suddenly sensed it as a separate presence, yet still within her control. It darted through the air, and she could hear two distinct clashes and ringing of steel against ice.

Never give up, Rook.

Her free hand turned palm up, and a small and tightly-concentrated sphere of ice began to grow. It wasn't until the exterior frosted over and a runic iris appeared that she knew what was being created.

The Seeing Eye was crafted in a matter of seconds. It usually took Amelia several minutes to construct it. The tethering was completed with a brief touch of her forehead to the Seeing Eye. A gentle tug between her eyebrows was all she felt. She experienced something completely altogether new when the eye activated; she could see through it and her own eyes at the same time.

As much as she wanted to blink and make it go away, she couldn't. The secondary vision almost overlapped her regular vision. Had it been Amelia, and not the Crown controlling it, she was certain she would have already lost her breakfast.

I'm going to be very hungry after all of this.

Be silent, you're distracting.

A wild swipe to the air brought her attention back to the sword. It had missed. Two more frantic swings resulted in two more loud *clangs* of ice and metal.

Fire roared from inside the mansion and it brought her attention back to the forefront. The eye was moving, and she couldn't blink away the nauseating vision. It had covered half the roof and was quickly accelerating toward the back.

Windows shattered as the fires within the mansion grew wildly out of control. Light was starting to illuminate to the second floor.

The Seeing Eye reached the other side of the household and quickly descended toward the back entryway. Licking flames were flailing out the door and windows. They were scorching the exterior walls. Thankfully, the rain was falling in blanketing waves and dousing the flames that tried to escape. Nothing was catching... yet.

That was about to change. As she dropped the Seeing Eye to standard eye level, she could see clear through the back door and into the center of the house. Andrew was standing before the grand staircase, and the interior of the household was lit by the glow of a bright white and yellow sphere of raging fire.

Andrew had prepared a Fireball.

Chapter 29

Neither Amelia nor the Crown wanted to be on the receiving end of a Fireball. Her shield hand turned to the sky, and she floated out over the steaming roof of the household.

The Crown quickly informed her that its brother was capable of sensing body heat, just as she was. By floating over the roof, they would better mask their presence and wouldn't be spotted by any available windows or doorways.

In order to maintain a higher moisture level, Amelia pulled down more rain from the overhead clouds. Waves of droplets turned into a steady torrential downpour, not a drop of which touched her.

Any other storm on any other day wouldn't have been a concern for the Bloodstone Estate. The clay tiles were replaced when broken, and the roofing was appropriately engineered and slanted with multiple drainage gutters. The fire damage that was stressing the interior would undoubtedly hinder the integrity. The Ice Crown was counting on it failing, as that would expose the internal flames to the downpour and weaken the available source of heat for the Crown of Fire.

Sadly, the Seeing Eye informed them that Andrew wasn't moving toward either exit, and he wasn't looking for Amelia through doors or windows. He was looking straight up and grinning.

He sees us!

It took a moment for her to release her spell hold on the storm clouds and focus on climbing skyward.

That moment was what Andrew needed in order to launch his Fireball. Like heaving something heavy above his head, Andrew crouched and bent at the knee, dropped his hands to his shoulders, then pushed up with his knees and arms with a visceral grunt. "Grah!"

The Fireball dropped momentarily as Andrew did, then it launched toward the ceiling as it was thrown. It flew up through the open air of the grand stairwell and screamed toward the ceiling.

Amelia released the tether that connected her to the Seeing Eye and focused entirely on climbing. It wasn't going to be enough. She only had two dozen steps of clearance from the rooftop, perhaps a little more. She should have flown sideways, but the thought wasn't quick enough.

They were caught in the explosion. The world shook with a deafening and concussive thump. Normally when she was hit by something, she'd feel the pain of it immediately or after a brief moment of shock. Amelia felt nothing, saw nothing, and heard only a piercing ringing in her ears.

After an unknown amount of time, she began to feel again. Of all things, it had to be her stomach. It lurched up and down in a steady and nauseating rhythm. Rain was no longer being deflected and battered her from front to back in the same rhythm as her flipping stomach. Without any further context, she could only guess that she was tumbling and falling.

The world came back to her when she had a

cushioned landing and ceased to tumble. Whatever it was that she landed on, it was soft and hummed against her body.

After a second of lying against that something, she dropped. The drop was brief and her feet and back hit something solid. An arm wrapped around her midsection and held her upright.

At first there was a brief moment of panic; the concern was that Andrew had caught her. The Ice Crown immediately informed her that whoever had caught her, it had not been her brother – the Crown of Fire was not so gentle.

With the concern gone, she gripped the arm and used it as a base for steadying herself. Thankfully, she couldn't vomit. She wanted to, but her stomach was entirely empty. Her vision eventually returned, but everything still tilted and rolled. A few blinks fixed it and she was able to orientate herself.

A quick glance over her shoulder revealed that Joe had caught her and was holding her back against his chest.

She quickly looked around her in order to get her bearings again. They were high up in the air, and the roof of the Bloodstone Estate was gone. There wasn't a single red clay tile to be seen. Flaming debris littered the estate grounds and neighboring grounds. The torrential downpour had softened to a hard rainfall, and Andrew was floating above a massive pyre of fire. She was wrong; flying sideways would not have gotten her out of harm's way.

Her eyes darted down, and she saw that Joseph was standing on one of his manacles. It had expanded in size to accommodate a shoulder-width stance. Bridging the empty space in the middle was a mild field of energy that was strong enough to hold their weight.

With his other hand, Joe was pointing his staff out in front of them and had it aimed directly at her brother. The second manacle was centered upon the point of the staff and was stretched as wide across as Joe was tall. The space inside the ring was filled with a loudly humming and vibrating field of energy. It looked concave, and it distorted the air. That barrier must have been how Joe caught her. She recognized the hum.

Her brother must have seen the catch, because he was screaming in rage. The fires surrounding him flared and burned all the brighter. It was almost blinding.

He is a possessive and rabid dog.

The Crown sounded irritated and weary. Amelia absolutely understood the irritation and felt the weariness. Her hands were red and small bits of skin were blistering and peeling off. She'd been burned, and she was finally noticing the throbbing pain that covered every bit of uncovered skin. A combination of her detective's garb, the rain, the roof, and the Ice Crown's evasive efforts had narrowly spared her from incineration. Joe had saved her from being scraped off the ground with a shovel.

The bright light of the pyre dimmed significantly. It looked as though the fire was receding or being smothered by the rain. She knew that the rain wasn't falling hard enough to dampen the flames. Andrew was up to something.

He is channeling the heat and is going to send it at us. I've seen him use it to cut through metal.

Amelia felt a quivering fear, a child's fear emanating from the Crown.

We must go on the offensive.

No.

Yes! If we don't take the fight to him, then he'll incinerate my body and you'll be without a host again. Do you want to get thrown back into the dark depths of the ocean?

Amazingly, it worked. She felt fully in control again. She could move her hands and turn her head and eyes as she pleased.

"Can you stand?" Joe spoke calmly into her left ear, and a puff of cold air followed his words.

Having control again also meant that she couldn't stave off all the pain. It hit her and left her shaking from exhaustion, hunger, frustration, fear, and the thrill of battle. Despite that, there was more than enough left for her to continue. She grabbed his arm and pulled it away from her waist. "Yes." He released her without hesitation. "He's about to throw a line of fire up at us."

"Good to know." Joseph leaned into his staff a little, and she could hear the hum of his barriers grow steadier and louder.

Hold off the pain.

The Ice Crown didn't project any thoughts in response, but the pain was significantly dampened. It made it easier for her to fight down the shakes.

Joe kept his voice to nearly a whisper. "Get him to the ground. We have a surprise waiting for him."

Andrew pointed one hand up at them and released all of the heat that he had pulled from the fires around him.

Something akin to sunlight struck Joe's shield barrier. The impact nearly knocked both of them off the makeshift manacle platform. Amelia had to drop low and bend at the knee in order to keep her balance.

Unsurprisingly, Joe's barrier held. The sunlight spread like a sunburst upon impact and blocked their vision from anything but a wall of blaring heat and fire.

"Keep him distracted!" Amelia had to yell it over the reverberating roar of the colliding energies.

Joe patted her shoulder twice in confirmation. Having received the acknowledgement, she leaned over and dove off the side of the platform. Clear from the heat of the lance of fire, ice immediately gathered about her outstretched wrists, ankles, and waist.

With the ice sufficiently formed, she leveled out and got her bearings. While the drop had only lasted perhaps two seconds, it was enough to place her just below the roof level of the estate. Before the drop, she had been at twice the height of the house; a lot of distance could be covered in only a few seconds of falling.

She was near the southwest corner of the estate

grounds and a good ways from the house. The explosion from the fireball had tossed her quite the distance.

Andrew was still floating over the remnants of their old home, but she couldn't look directly at him, as the beam of light that erupted from his hands was far too bright. The only hope was that it was too bright for him to see anything either.

Clear of the heat, she could gather up some rainwater. With so much moisture on the grass below and still falling from the clouds above, it only took her half a moment to gather a blanket of water and wrap it around her body. Breathing out, she was able to immediately freeze the outer layer, creating a shell of protection.

What are you doing?

Read my thoughts!

She didn't have time to explain.

This is madness! He will catch us!

That's the idea!

NO! I refuse!

The fear was palpable. She could feel and hear the panic in the thoughts of the Crown.

Then the cycle of abuse will never end! Stop being a coward and stand up!

An eerie familiarity came with the words. They were the same words that she had yelled at Andrew more than once before. The two of them routinely fell into a shouting match about why Amelia despised her siblings. None of them had bothered to try and stand up for her whenever their parents had been misogynistic or unjustly berated her. She had to stand up for herself, and it cost their father his life.

No more thoughts came from the Crown. No objections and no wrestling for control either.

Amelia continued with her plan and lowered to ground level as she skirted around flaming debris and made her way for the ember-glowing entrance of the front entryway. In order to evade any possible detection, she took a wide approach and circled to the northwest, around the lump of stone that had once been the grand statue.

She flew with her hands stretched out before her in preparation to defend or attack in case Andrew caught wind of what she was up to. As she flew by, she couldn't help but glance to see if she could spot Julian's body. There was too much burning ruble scattering the grounds, and she was moving too quickly to tell for certain, but she couldn't spot any prone forms near the statue. Odds were against him surviving anyway.

Amelia rounded the statue and made a straight shot for the fire-belching entrance. Black smoke was pouring out the doors and windows; she would be rendered blind once inside.

Knowing that it would only be for a moment, she charged forth. The ice barrier that surrounded her began to crack, sizzle, and scream with the unbearable heat being thrown against her. Visibility reduced to nothing as the black smoke enveloped everything. Thankfully, the bubble of water protected her face and lungs from the excruciating heat and ash. It didn't last long, as the raging inferno quickly began melting away the layers of protection.

She closed her eyes and focused on the feel of the building. So long as none of the structure began to give way or alter in any significant fashion, she could find the grand stairwell. It was always to the right of the front entryway.

It only took a moment for her to find the open sky and her brother floating above. He had stopped channeling the lance of scorching heat and was hurtling fistfuls of fire up at Joseph. His well-tailored shirt and vest had burned away, leaving his upper torso bare. He'd never been an athletic young man, but there was enough muscle for her to be surprised. More surprising was that his skin was brightly marked with yellow veins. He looked like a wild man as he screamed and hurled fire. The deterioration was advancing.

The rookie – in all his brilliant glory – was darting around and providing ample target practice for her brother to throw a tantrum at.

Good job, Rook.

With the last bits of water starting to evaporate and the heat turning unbearably painful against her burned skin, Amelia leaped up into the air and aimed straight at Andrew's back. Sadly, he sensed her coming. Thankfully, he sensed her too late.

All Andrew managed to do was turn his head as she rocketed toward him. She passed the remnants of the charred rafter ends and slammed shoulder-first into his back and right side.

There was an explosive hissing scream as the ice that she had wrapped around her ankles, wrists, and waist blew off her body and evaporated. To say it stung would have been a horrific understatement; it felt as if though someone had taken a club to those specific parts of her body.

Both of them let out winded grunts, and they tumbled through the air and out over the southern grounds of the estate. She successfully removed Andrew from the flaming household and his source of fire.

As suspected, the Crown of Fire didn't give in so easily. Andrew clawed at her wrists and fingers as he spun about and tried to throw her off. "Get off. Get off! GET OFF!" He started to hammer at her hands with his fists.

While he busied himself hammering away at her hands, she pulled from the rain and the wet grass below, and drew up a sizeable amount of water. Ice reformed around her legs and waist and calmed the throbbing pain.

Amelia released her grip, snatched his wrist, spun him about, and jabbed him in the nose. Andrew's head whipped back and she felt the soft crunch of his twice-broken nose against her knuckles. He let out a bloodied and nasally gurgle of a scream before wildly swinging for her head. Fire arched through the air in the wake of his fist.

Amelia ducked the attack and flicked a gesture of her own. The massive orb that floated behind her released a solid bucketful of water. It arced over top of her head and slapped Andrew in the face, throwing him off balance. The jets of flame that erupted from his feet sputtered and coughed.

"You think you're smart and all powerful." Amelia was speaking to both Crowns and her brother.

Andrew wheeled his arms and regained his balance. He shook off the disorientation and came back swinging hammer fists.

Amelia stayed low, shifted to the side, spun about, and brought her elbow into Andrew's stomach with a forceful grunt and a stiff strike. Her bother went wide-eyed as the air was driven from him. The fire that held him aloft died out, and he dropped from the sky.

"You might be stronger than me..." they had natural talent that she would never have, "and you may have outsmarted me today." Andrew had gotten the better of her, and the Ice Crown had kept her in the dark. "But I have something that you don't!"

Amelia clawed her left hand and brought it up to her chest. The sphere of water that she had kept behind her darted toward the ground and scooped back up under Andrew in order to catch him before he hit the grass.

Her brother looked as though he had caught enough of his breath to attempt to throw some fire, but when the water hit him from behind it shocked him and knocked the wind from him a second time. She also noticed with great relief that the burning veins of yellow dimmed significantly.

Finally encapsulated, she pushed down with her right hand and slammed Andrew and the water sphere against the waterlogged grass. They both hit with a loud *clap*.

A wave of the hand cleared the water from her brother's mouth and nose. He choked, spat up bloodied water, and gasped for air. As he gargled and coughed, she clenched her fists and hardened the water around his body into solid ice. The only part she had left exposed was his face and the Crown on his head. She wanted it removed, and she had a guess that joe had a plan for it.

Andrew gasped and immediately began to shiver and turn blue from the sudden shocking cold.

Amelia slowly lowered down so she floated a dozen steps from the ground. It was entirely possible that Andrew, or more accurately the Crown of Fire, would suddenly break free and attack again. She wanted to have enough of a view to see the attack coming, and she wanted to remain airborn in order to execute evasive maneuvers if required. She ground her teeth and growled at them all, "I have proper training!"

It shouldn't have been a surprise that the Guardian appeared, but it was. The Guardian, along with a Southeast detective, appeared out of a block of stone debris. They hadn't been hiding behind it, they had *been* the block of stone.

Illusion magic.

She couldn't help but be slightly impressed.

The darkly-clad figure darted and dove for Andrew.

In her brief moment of distracted surprise, the Crown of Fire attempted to flare up and break free. Light was growing from inside her brother's body, concentrated within his right hand. His face was contorted in rage, and he was focused entirely on her.

Unfortunately for the Crown of Fire, the Guardian got there first. A single finger poked the top of her brother's head, and the growing light and heat winked out as quickly as a snuffed candle. The Crown fell freely from her brother's head into the hand of the Guardian. It was over. Whatever the Guardian had done, it hadn't killed her brother, and it had safely removed the cursed object.

Thank the merciful goddess.

Pain shot through her skull and the Ice Crown took control of her body once again. Amelia was shoved to the back where the outside world felt as though it were being viewed through a distant tunnel or a window.

Amelia – the Ice Crown – summoned a javelin of ice and hurled it at the Guardian. It rolled to the side and evaded the first throw. The next three struck true and pinned the construct to the soil with javelins piercing the torso, left thigh, and right arm.

Her body turned toward the detective that had utilized the illusion magic. The young woman looked no older than Amelia but slightly taller, and her hair was light brown. There wasn't much more she could see, as they were bathed only in the flickering light of dying fires. From what she could see, the woman was terrified.

"Illusions shall prove amusing. Bow to me and I won't have to corrupt you."

The poor woman staggered back a step, and her eyes grew wider in terror.

As much as she wanted to, she couldn't even rail against the Ice Crown. It had taken full control of her body, and she couldn't even force her thoughts against it. She tried. She tried repeatedly.

Something caught her attention, and her body twisted on the spot and threw her hand out toward the northern sky above the collapsing mansion. Water leaped to her command and snatched a manacle from the air.

Amelia could feel a twinge of disappointment emanating from the Crown.

You were wrong before... it is not over. My reign as Queen has yet to begin.

Chapter 30

Her vision momentarily changed to one that focused on heat. The Bloodstone Estate was a massive block of bright light, and the world around it was a dark shadow. She panned across the estate grounds and focused on small bits of flaming debris that were big enough for a body to hide behind.

Joe was hiding behind the fire, and the Ice Crown was looking for him. Her vision snapped back to normal as she spoke, "I am giving you a choice. Bow to me now and give up this pitiful resistance…" The Crown paused for dramatic effect. "Or I shall enslave you. Choose!"

The manacle that she had caught inside the bubble of water was trying to pull away from her and escape its confines. Amelia's fist clenched and the sphere of water turned into a rock of ice. She threw her hand down toward the ground and the block of ice thumped and buried itself into the soil. There was little chance that Joe would be able to pull it free without giving it some effort.

Both of her hands turned palm up and slowly rose from hips to shoulders. As they did, symmetrical triangular-shaped ice plates formed around her to create a free-floating icosahedron barrier. They were solid, thin, and clear; she could see through them with ease.

One would think the barrier a pitiful form of protection, but Amelia could see the magic runes that ran along the edges of every pane. She didn't know what it would take to break them, but she had a feeling that they wouldn't break easily and could be fixed or replaced quite quickly.

The Crown was losing its patience. "Despite your earlier aid–"

"The answer is no!" Joe's voice seemed to come from all directions. He had empowered it so that it enveloped the entire area. It made it impossible to locate him by sound. "I will never bow to someone that hurts the innocent!"

The Crown scoffed in annoyance before responding, "I have harmed no innocents."

Amelia disagreed with that sentiment, but she couldn't exactly speak against it.

"Lies! You enslave the innocent, and that is harm!" As much as she agreed with Joe's outrage, he had put too much emotion into his words. A small part of his yelling could be heard emanating from the other side of the burning estate.

Her body darted around the front side of the house and careened over the rubble that had once been the grand statue. She turned wide of the corner with her right hand outstretched, one of the triangular tiles ready to shatter and launch razor sharp shards.

A blink of the eye caused her vision to switch to arcane thermal. There were a few bits of debris that were still on fire large enough to mask a body, but the ever-increasing downpour of rain was starting to choke those out.

Joe wasn't there. There were no bodies of heat, and

the Ice Crown was growing weary of the hunt. "Come out of hiding!" Her body circled the north end of the estate and headed for the east. There were no sources of heat hiding amongst the hedges and gardens.

It was possible that he was just matching her movements in order to keep the roaring fire of the crumbling house between them. Figuring it was a possibility, the Crown reached toward the sky and halted the rain above the house.

The downpour quickly accumulated, and a massive sheet of water began to pool over the house. Her hand immediately began shaking, and a second hand was needed in order to focus. Black smoke billowed up into the water pool and tainted the color of it.

The effort of holding up so much water was too much for even the Crown. Her arms dropped and the body of water that she had been holding aloft plummeted in a tidal wave.

Whatever had once been left standing of the Bloodstone Estate was immediately disintegrated under the mass of water that was dropped upon it. Fires were instantly snuffed in a momentary hiss. Walls crumbled and burst outward as the water dispersed upon impact and the floors gave way down to the cellar. Brick, wood, and stone collapsed in every direction in a cacophony of noise. At the end of it all, there was nothing more than a pile of rubble.

Joe couldn't hide anymore, and she could see him clearly on the other side of the estate. He was hiding behind the remnants of the statue.

Amelia quickly darted over the destroyed house and briefly passed through the cloud of ash and smoke that continued to rise into the air. Her right hand came up and made a clawing motion as she saw Joe's body heat attempt to make a dash away from the statue base.

Her vision returned to normal with a quick blink.

Joe let out a scream of surprise as the water that covered the ground shot up to grab him.

Amelia's body slowed as it passed over the statue remnants, and she turned to look down upon the rookie. His staff had been pulled aside and was slowly being encased in a jagged spire of ice. He was pressed hard against the statue, his body was pinned by water slowly freezing from the ground up.

Halting the water had been a calculated risk. Amelia's body was tired, injured, and hungry. The Ice Crown couldn't cast much more magic without harming her and drawing upon her soul. The Crown of Fire didn't seem to care about that, which was why Julian's body had been so badly burned and used up; Andrew would have been next. The Ice Crown didn't seem to share that recklessness.

For that reason, the ice was slower to freeze. Controlling water was easy. Anyone with a bucket or a ladle could technically control water. Changing the temperature of water took a great deal more effort and energy. The Ice Crown was running out of that energy.

Joe took in gasping breaths as he looked at his feet wide-eyed. "Oh gods! That's cold!"

Amelia descended to the ground in order to ease off her energy exertion and get close enough to corrupt Joe. He was struggling, but there wasn't much he could do against the water that was slowly freezing over his body. The ice was crawling up past his waist, and he would soon be fully encompassed but for his head.

She didn't want to watch, but she couldn't exactly turn away or close her eyes. "Do you have any last words before I take your freedom?" Her body stepped up to Joe, and she floated a small breadth off the ground so that she was even in height with the rookie. Her face was only a step away from his, and she could see the silver light draining from his eyes. He was growing weaker as he grew colder.

His teeth started to chatter as he began to freeze. "Y-y-y-yes!"

"Out with it then." The Ice Crown wasn't entirely merciless.

Joe's lips were turning blue and he struggled to get a full lungful of air. He puffed and strained and took deeper, ragged breaths. With one final pull, he tilted his head back a bit and let loose the strangest noise. It sounded like he was trying to gobble like a turkey, but it was strangled and deranged.

Her brow scrunched in confusion. Both she and the Ice Crown had no idea what the point was. Irritation bubbled to the surface. Both she and the Crown were annoyed, but for different reasons. The Crown felt insulted; Amelia was disappointed.

"Are you mock—"

A trilling whistle pierced the air. It wasn't a call that someone might utilize to get attention in a crowded room; it was a sustained note of ear-splitting pitch. Her hands instinctively went to her ears, but it wasn't good enough. The sound went from a whistle to a ringing that drove her to her knees.

She couldn't concentrate or focus on casting any magic to cover her ears. Bits of ice and snow fell down upon her as she felt the icosahedron barrier shatter.

They were destroying the Ice Crown's magical constructs and her ability to cast magic by using the exact same methods that Amelia had used to shatter the ice field.

Her world was nothing but an endless deafening ring. It changed when there was a sudden and excruciating ripping sensation inside both ears. The pain was so awful that even the Crown cried out. Not surprisingly, she couldn't hear her own voice. She couldn't hear anything. There was nothing but deafening silence.

Something warm ran down her palms. Amelia took her hands from her ears and looked down in horror as blood covered her hands.

The Ice Crown looked about in confusion and tried to piece together what had just happened. Joe was to her left and no longer frozen to the statue. He was kneeling beside her, rubbing his arms, and shivering with an idiotic grin on his face. The rookie still had his hat on, which explained why he hadn't been affected by the whistling. He smiled and pointed to her right.

Her head turned, and she was greeted by the sight of William Windwalker. His lips were pursed. If anyone could have possibly been that dangerous with a whistle, it was a wizard that had mastered the element of air.

William twiddled the fingers of one hand as if to say "Hello", and with the other he flicked something at her face.

A powder-laden ball of cotton bounced off her nose and caused her eyes to instinctively shut. Naturally the powder tickled her nose and throat. She didn't know whether she would cough or sneeze. The reflexive inhale that would have preceded one of the two actions was the last thing she remembered.

Darkness immediately enveloped her, and the Crown screamed inside her mind as she drifted into nothingness.

~~

Her world was first filled with echoes. Brief recollections of voices filled her mind. She couldn't think straight, and everything was clouded in a deep haze. Worries and anxieties would briefly rise only to vanish and wash away again.

Pain was the first sensation to stabilize her thoughts. Everything hurt. Smell was the second sensation to return. The air was slightly musty, and damp. But there was the scent of burning candle wax. Knowing better than to open her eyes, she kept them shut and tried to listen. Unfortunately, she could only hear the softest of hums.

That was when everything came back to her. The first thing she realized was that she had full control again. She could feel and sense most things, but her hearing was still nothing more than a muffle. Every twitch of her toe or flex of the finger or hand was of her own volition. When she attempted to lift her hand to check to see if the Crown was gone, her arm abruptly stopped, as her wrist had been strapped down.

Peering out one eye proved to not be so terrible. The room was fairly dark, and there was a small bit of candlelight in the far corner. She was centered in the room with the headboard against the wall. All of the walls were stone and mortar – it wasn't the hospital.

To the left on the far wall was an iron door with a small barred window.

Am I in a dungeon?

The lack of response from anyone or anything was reassuring, but that didn't mean the Crown was gone; it had hid itself before.

She lifted her head a bit in order to try and examine what was going on. Wide leather straps held her down against the bed. One strap covered her legs, another over her hips, and a third across her chest. Her hands were bound at the wrists. The leather didn't rub directly against her skin; it felt like warm lambskin on the inside.

Out of the corner of her eye, she could see that her hair was braided over her right shoulder, and scrunching her chin down, she could see that she was in her favorite nightgown. That immediately calmed her. Only one person knew which nightgown was her favorite and braided her hair over her right shoulder.

Amelia cleared her throat and found it parched and sore. Despite that, she called out, "Blue?" Surprisingly, she could hear her own voice, if muffled. Turning her head a bit resulted in an odd scratching sound and sensation. There was cotton stuffed into her ears.

There was some brief shuffling outside the door, followed by an inexplicably loud clacking of metal. It was painful enough to cause her to wince. Screeching hinges caused her to squeeze her eyes shut and bunch up her shoulders in an attempt to cover her ears. The iron door swung open and shut again with a loud and echoing *bang!*

Boots loudly scraped against the stone as though they were dragging tiny stones. "Gods! The noise!"

The scraping footfalls stopped, and the grating sound of the gravel on stone made one last crawl up and down her skin and spine. A woman's voice loudly bounced off of all the walls. "I apologize." A warbling pin drop sounded in the room. It was the magic signifier that was easily recognized as a muffling effect.

The woman's voice came again, but far softer. "Your eardrums had to be regrown. They will be quite sensitive for a few days."

Amelia opened one eye, and watched as a woman clad in black sat down on something at the foot of her bed. She didn't remember seeing any chairs or stools, so she could only guess the woman had brought it in with her.

It only took her a moment to eye the woman up and down. Since she was sitting and it was dark, Amelia could only make out a few distinct features. Firstly, she was from Internal Investigations.

This doesn't bode well.

With any and all investigations, they never introduced themselves. They appeared, they asked their questions, and they vanished. To that end, Amelia did as much as she could to memorize the woman. She was dressed in the typical detective's garb, except it was all in black. A blue badge hung from the left coat pocket, and the hat was tilted down to hide her features.

A distinct pink line cut through the skin of the left side of her face. As far as Amelia could tell, it went all the way up. The hat hid the eyes so she couldn't see where the scar ended. She had a soft chin, pale skin, and some fine age lines. Her lips were uncolored, and her nose was slightly off-center. The woman crossed her legs and set a notepad down on top of her thigh. She immediately began scribbling down notes and didn't bother to look up.

After a few moments of silent scribbling, Amelia dared to ask, "Water?" Her throat was still hoarse and dry, and she couldn't exactly go find any on her own. In fact, she couldn't feel any in the air, though she knew it was there. They likely had her in anti-magic bindings.

"In a minute." The woman scribbled a few last notes before lifting her head and looking Amelia in the eye. The candlelight lit the left side of her face; that was when she saw the extent of the scarring. It went all the way to the hairline and cut through the eyebrow. The eye was the most unnerving, made from polished obsidian and had a glowing red crosshair of runes for an iris. With the better lighting, she was also able to see that the woman kept her hair short. It was cut like a man's, and it was peppered gray and black. "I have some questions first."

Amelia felt like sinking deeper into the bed, but knew that the best option was to cooperate.

"I'll start by answering the questions that you undoubtedly want answered but haven't yet asked." She uncrossed her legs and switched sides. "You've been out for two days. You're in the dungeons beneath the Temple of Light. You no longer wear the Crown thanks to the efforts of…" She looked down and flipped a page to check her notes, "the 'Guardian', and you were cured of the corruption that followed the removal of the Crown. The second removal was done at the hands of Nathaniel, an ex-crusader. I understand you're familiar with him."

Amelia nodded, cleared her throat, and said, "Yes."

The woman opened her notepad and made a quick scribble before continuing, "Your brother is alive, uncorrupted, and being treated for his wounds." She paused and narrowed her red crosshair of an eye on Amelia. "It is still uncertain as to whether or not Detective Kane will live."

I can't believe he wasn't already dead.

She had a great many more questions but decided on letting the woman from Internal Investigations lead the discussion.

"Let us begin, shall we?"

Again, Amelia nodded and said, "Yes."

The interrogation began with her family, as suspected. They covered the payment she had made to her family, their activities, known whereabouts, and the reasoning behind the cursed Crowns. Amelia answered as best she could while continuing to clear her strained throat.

Partway through the interrogation, the investigator asked, "Do you not remember being corrupted?"

Amelia shook her head and tried her best to swallow and speak, but couldn't. Her throat was too sore.

The woman nodded. "You did quite a bit of screaming during the cleansing. I will let you rest for a minute while I get you something."

She watched as the woman left, then slumped back into the bed and tried to focus through the pain. When the woman returned, she brought an old iron-wrought key with her and a tea cup on a saucer. The tea was set aside, and the iron key was used to unfasten the leather bindings.

Finally free, her hands first went to her head. It was clear; there was no Crown. She didn't think the Internal Investigator had been lying, but the self-reassurance was calming. Amelia tried to play it off by pulling the cotton from her ears and gently pulled on her braid before taking the offered tea.

"It's over. The cursed objects have been safely contained." The woman sat back down upon the wooden chair at the foot of the bed.

Amelia said nothing and greedily drank from the steaming tea. It smelled of mint and tasted of honey. Despite the hot water, it cooled and soothed her throat.

"Now the nightmares will start."

Amelia looked up at that.

The woman wasn't smiling, teasing, or taunting. "At first you won't be able to sleep. Everything is too fresh in your mind. You'll try to put it off and make excuses... but sleep will inevitably come."

She didn't know what to say to all of that.

"If I were you..."

Amelia kept her attention focused on the more experienced officer, eager to hear any suggestions.

"Practice your partitioning. Those that are good enough can will themselves into a dreamless sleep. It's not a cure, but it will help you to rest."

She didn't feel like testing her voice at that moment, and instead nodded in acceptance of the advice and drank more of the tea.

The woman let out a deep sigh and crossed her legs again, "If you need someone to teach you, send a letter to the Central precinct. Address it to Detective Voidmind."

Amelia frowned a little and swallowed before testing her voice. "Is that your name?" She had never heard of Internal Investigators revealing their identities.

Detective Voidmind raised an eyebrow. "I didn't say that." The briefest glint of a smile tugged at one corner of her mouth.

She couldn't help but feel comforted. The woman gave off a stern grandmotherly impression.

Blue would like you.

"Are you ready to finish this?" Any hint of a smile immediately vanished.

Amelia downed the last of the tea and nodded with a bit more confidence. "Yes."

Chapter 31

The questioning continued for several hours. Most of it was spent answering the same questions; lies tended to fall apart under intense scrutiny. Amelia didn't mind. There were no secrets to hide. She also saw the intense and thorough scrutiny as a solid signifier of professionalism.

It wasn't all one-sided. She was able to ask some questions of her own, and received honest answers. They had found Andrew's new residence in the Northeast district. He had signed under a false identity. That bothered her; false identities were rare, expensive, and only available through black market dealings.

Amelia asked about her brother's magical talents. The woman had an answer for that as well. Andrew had secretly been studying with their maternal grandmother. The Arcanum didn't officially recognize students taught outside of the school, but they also couldn't stop one generation from teaching the next.

While searching through his personal effects, they

found ledgers, journals, and maps relating to a 'hidden power' on an abandoned isle off the south coast of the dwarven empire. One journal in particular had belonged to a first mate that had passed away the year before.

Part of Andrew's responsibilities as an auditor included cataloguing of personal effects for trade company employees. The deceased first mate had no living relatives, so nobody would notice a missing journal. It contained a map and an entry that spoke of an island inhabited by a non-speaking construct. It saved his life when his ship was thrown on the rocks during a storm at sea. The journal went on to describe ancient symbols that were not dwarven in nature. Poor translations hinted at a 'great power'.

Amelia inquired as to how a first mate on a trading vessel was able to translate ancient runes. Detective Voidmind shrugged.

With the family fortune dwindling, her brother hired the captain and crew of the *Ladysong* to go out on an expedition and recover the 'great power' so that he could use it to rekindle the family investments. Obviously, the captain and crew thought that they could horde that power for themselves. Everyone knew how well that turned out.

They still didn't know how Julian got the Crown of Fire. If he survived, he would likely be interrogated about it.

Professors Teddy Patch and Aurora Spellocke had managed to decipher the language that had been inscribed on the lid. By doing so, they were able to learn that the Guardian was not only designed to incapacitate wizards and open the curse box, but also capable of removing and safely handling the Crowns. That resulted in the construct becoming a greater priority.

Simultaneously, John managed to pick up the Guardian's trail from the Wayside and follow it to a warehouse. He was also very lucky and able to convince it that he meant no harm; John didn't feel like being disabled like Amelia and Joe had. Of course, the damnable thing couldn't speak. Despite the communication barrier, John was able to convey the necessities, and it followed him back to the precinct in the early hours of the morning.

Up to that morning, nobody had heard or seen anything concerning cursed Crowns or any violent magical offenses utilizing ice or fire. It looked as though they would have to wait for another incident, until Amelia and Joe sensed one another.

When Voidmind inquired, Amelia answered honestly. She didn't understand how they were able to sense one another, or how the Crown of Fire was connected. Joe had apparently provided the explanation that he could sense the wards the Crowns were using to try and conceal themselves. Amelia thought that answer was a heaping pile of goblin shite.

From there, she understood everything that had happened up until Joe and the others had started arriving at the estate. Apparently William had found Julian and followed him across the city. When he arrived at the family estate and saw Amelia with the Ice Crown, he called it in.

Windwalker proved to be the savior of the day. He had found and followed the Crown of Fire and reported on all of Kane's activities. Which included the illegal apothecary he was attempting to build. Corrupted men were discovered and rounded up for purification.

Captain Bolt also had a hand in things when he sensed something drastically wrong with the storm front. It had apparently been summoned and wasn't a natural weather front.

The Ice Crown had corrupted a handful of individuals as well, and they had constructed a ritual circle. They too were quickly discovered, rounded up, and sent to the Temple for purification. She didn't envy Nathaniel. The poor man must be exhausted.

William had been the one to collect Detective Kane and remove him from harm's way once the Crown had left him. The illusion wizard, Junior Detective Runeveil, had snuck into the estate and stole the health potions, while also providing cover for the Guardian to approach undetected.

With all the questions asked and answered, Amelia was free to go. Detective Voidmind reminded her once more about the partitioning practice and the inevitable nightmares. She thanked the woman and accepted the offer. Training would begin the next night.

Blueregard marched into the room with a tea platter the instant that Detective Voidmind left. "Ms. Iceheart, I have prepared some tea for you." He looked as prim and proper as always, but there seemed to be a bit of a hurry to his movements, and his voice didn't sound as steady as it usually did.

"Hello, Blue."

He immediately set the platter down on the far table by the candle and hurriedly began pouring tea. Blueregard never sloshed, and yet she could distinctly hear it.

"Blue?"

The man didn't turn to her. He maintained his ever-stoic composure and stirred her tea with a bit of a flourish. "Ma'am?"

"I'm okay, Blue."

The stirring halted, and he turned perfectly still. "You almost weren't." His voice was barely above a whisper.

"That's no different than any other day, Blue."

For the first time in a great many years, she saw him sag in the shoulders. A long and shaky sigh escaped him and he hung his head a bit. "All of my adult life has been spent serving your family. I never once had a chance to seek out anything for myself." There was a long pause where he took in a deep breath and shakily breathed it out. "I have no wife or children." Blueregard looked to her over his shoulder with a pained look upon his face. She'd never seen him in such a way before.

While unspoken, the message was clearly conveyed. She had never thought of it or put words to it before, but Blueregard had truly acted as a surrogate father, and she was his adopted daughter.

"I'll be more careful, Blue." She offered a soft smile.

He didn't smile or grin. Instead, he breathed deeply, straightened himself, and donned the armor of propriety that he wore at all hours of the day. With steady hands, the man brought her a saucer of tea.

They talked, mostly about the events of the last few days. John, Joe, and Petals had all visited to check on her recovery.

Amelia specifically wanted to know about Joe. When she inquired as to what exactly he had been doing, Blueregard drew a small envelope from his vest pocket. "That reminds me. This is for you, Ms. Iceheart."

The envelope was exquisitely cut in a style of lace roses. She only ever saw that method of print cut on celebratory invitations. The wax was white, which also suggested a celebration. Frowning, she broke the wax seal and opened the envelope. It was indeed an invitation.

She was invited to Ms. Ruby Moonberry's age day celebration. "Blue, what day is it?"

"It is the fourteenth day of the second waning moon of summer."

The celebration was in two days. "Why was I invited to her age day?" Such celebrations were usually held by family and friends. She wasn't either of those things.

"Mr. Runewall insisted and stated that it would be an enlightening affair."

She looked to Blueregard, and he regarded her with a raised eyebrow.

Ah… he'll answer my questions at the celebration.

"Thank you, Blue." She shut her eyes for a moment and nearly fell asleep where she sat. Exhaustion was setting in, and she didn't feel like spending any more time in the dark and damp dungeon. "Can we go home now?"

"Of course, Ms. Iceheart. I was informed that once you awoke and spoke with the Investigator that you would be allowed to leave. You were cleared by Doctor Broom and your superiors. I have a change of clothes prepared for you and shall request a gnome cart as soon as I pack up the tea set."

The man was a blessing from the gods.

~~

Betty greeted her with the same overly-excited enthusiasm she always did. Most of it involved crying, hugging, and exclamations of how worried she had been. Amelia thanked her for the concern but promised to talk about it in the morning. Happily, Betty understood and helped her to bed. The first night was free of any dreams or nightmares, as she was simply too exhausted.

The next day was rather difficult. Betty was delightful, and the breakfast that Blue had prepared was hearty enough to fill her growling pit of a stomach.

It was the precinct that gave her the greatest grievance. Margaret Mistwind wasn't at the lobby clerk's station. She had apparently transferred to another precinct. The woman cited 'emotional distress' as her reason for transfer.

According to the transfer request, the Fireball wasn't the reason for the distress. Her lack of attention from Joseph, then John had caused her to feel unwanted. That needed to be explained by John; he *had* been courting Ms. Mistwind. She broke it off with him because he didn't give her enough attention. He described her as being too needy. It understandably left John in a bad mood.

She didn't know who or how much to believe, and left it as none of her business.

The new lobby clerk was a young man with spectacles named Egbert Willows. He was tall, lanky, and nervous. Papers were scattered everywhere across the lobby desk, and he looked like he might explode from the amount of stuttering, shaking, and confusion he put himself through trying to locate a single file.

Bob was another problem altogether. He spotted

her coming up the steps to the station and immediately turned and headed in the other direction. She could pull rank, yell at him, and tell him to face her, but that felt like it would only make the situation worse.

Thanks for making this more awkward than it needs to be, Bob.

Joe wasn't anywhere to be seen, and Petals greeted her with his typical mischievous grin. Her desk greeted her with a giant stack of reports to be filed. Petals suggested she do some paperwork for the next few days while she recovered.

Naturally, there were two summons amongst the papers. The first was from Chuck's Tea Parlor, the second was from her mother. They both cited damages. She could understand how both of them would seek recompense, especially Mother.

Petals reassured her that both grievances would be settled and all the blame would be shifted to Andrew. He had brought the cause of the damages to the city. She couldn't be held accountable for her own actions while under the influence of a cursed object. There was even a law concerning it. It didn't make her feel any less guilty.

Worst of all, she had forgotten her favorite travel heating container at home, and the precinct was out of tea. It was dear to her, not only because it provided her with much-needed tea, but also because it was the prototype that she and Mr. Hopper designed together. From it, Mr. Hopper's factory produced an array of travel heating containers. It was the symbol of her freedom from her deranged family.

In all, it wasn't an awful day, just a difficult one, and the end of it didn't come fast enough. Her march home was more of a shuffling trudge. Halfway to the residence, she was greeted by a man she desperately did not want to talk to.

"Hello, Amelia!" It was William Knight. He ran across the road and dodged a rumbling gnome cart that rang its bell fervently. "I heard that the family estate was razed to the ground the other night. Any comments?"

Amelia halted, turned her attention to the man, and glowered down upon him. "Hello, Willy." He was only slightly shorter than she, but his slight frame made him look even smaller. He didn't cower, cringe, or back-pedal. The man held his ground against her glower, kept his eyes open, and stylus at the ready in case she said anything of interest.

"It's William or Will. Do you have any comments about the destruction of your childhood home?"

I hate you.

She narrowed her eyes at him and imagined socking him in the nose. It helped, but only a little bit. "No." Amelia picked up her feet and marched to her residence.

The irritating little nuisance followed her like a sick puppy. "Do you have any comments concerning the Fireball that struck the Southwest precinct?"

"No!" She picked up the pace in the hopes of leaving him behind.

He matched her speed with ease.

Blast it all!

"Multiple sources are suggesting that the storm on the night of the estate fire was unnatural and had been summoned; are we certain that the merfolk sighting isn't somehow connected?"

The man was desperately grasping at straws. "No comment!"

She rounded the last corner and crossed the cobblestone road without even bothering to look. Gnome carts screeched to a halt and furiously rang their bells as she crossed. Her residence was in sight, and she couldn't wait for the traffic to clear before crossing. Waiting meant being hounded, and she didn't know how much more she could take before losing her temper.

Amelia drew her wand from her pocket and flicked it at the door to the residence. The door unlocked and swung open. Usually she would use her key, but she had taken a page out of Joe's non-existent spell-tome and began memorizing her keys so that she could apply them to familiar locks. It was handy.

"One more question?" He was hurrying behind her.

Amelia turned on the spot, which caused the man to grind to a halt. "NO!" She stepped through the doorway and slammed it shut behind her.

Safely within the confines of the lobby, she let out an exasperated sigh and looked to the stairs that led to the second floor. "I hate you too." Thankfully, the climb didn't prove to be as horrible as she thought it might be.

When she reached the door to the residence, she heard lively chatter coming from the other side. Betty was talking up a storm. It was followed by the throaty chuckle of another woman. Betty's mother passed away some years ago, and Amelia's mother never laughed.

Amelia unlocked and opened the door and groaned in misery. Detective Voidmind was sitting at the kitchen table, drinking a cup of tea. Betty was seated across from her, and Blue was standing in the kitchens preparing supper. She'd completely forgotten about the partitioning lessons and was far too tired to try.

Betty turned to greet Amelia with a smile but quickly pouted. "Aw, puddin', what's wrong?"

Amelia put up her hand and lazily waved it off. "I'm sorry, detective. I don't have the strength to train my mind tonight." Despite how much she needed it, she didn't have the focus or strength.

The elder woman sipped from her tea and eyed Amelia with that unnerving prosthetic. "There won't be any training tonight."

She couldn't help but frown in confusion. "Isn't that what we said we would be doing?"

The older woman nodded. "Yes. But you're clearly not in any shape for it. Tonight, I'm simply going to force you to sleep. Tomorrow night, we'll train."

Amelia raised an eyebrow. "You're going to put me to bed?"

The woman narrowed both her eyes. "I prefer to

look at it as me thoroughly knocking you out cold." She paused momentarily. "I haven't yet decided if it will be with my fist or my mind."

She couldn't help but smile at that.

I like you.

The briefest smirk crossed the older detective's lips. "I like you too, kid."

Amelia stopped smiling. "Wait. Did–"

The woman nodded with her chin to the door. "Someone is about to knock."

There was a knock, and it made her and Betty jump. Amelia turned and opened the door.

William had his stylus at the ready and stepped forward with one foot. "I just–"

CRACK! Amelia interrupted his words with her fist in his nose. The man dropped like a sack of bricks.

The ensuing silence was at first gratifying. When she realized what she'd done, the silence turned deafening.

That was when she noticed that William wasn't alone in the hallway. Blue Coat officer Argen Tannen was standing just outside of the doorway and had seen everything. He was looking down upon the unconscious man. Even worse, a detective from Internal Investigations was sipping tea in her kitchen and had also witnessed the entire interaction.

Well if I wasn't in trouble before, I am now.

"What an idiot." Officer Tannen had been the one to speak, looking down upon William Knight.

"Pardon?" Amelia wasn't entirely sure if he was talking to her or William.

He stood straight, pointed at the unconscious William, and said, "He told me he was expected. Based on your reaction, I'm guessing he wasn't."

Amelia scowled. "I would *never* invite that man into my home!"

Tannen nodded in acceptance. "All right." He bent down with a grunt and pulled out a pair of manacles. "Sir, I understand that you probably can't hear me at the moment, but you're under arrest for the attempted invasion of a detective's residence."

Detective Voidmind spoke up from the kitchens. "I'll sign as witness."

Amelia had to shake her head and rethink what all had just happened. Based on the sequence of events, they were right. William had lied about being welcomed into the building and hadn't bothered to ask if he could enter her private residence; he had simply tried to enter. She hadn't been thinking about all of that when she punched him. She'd simply been thinking about how good it would feel to teach the man a lesson in the meaning of the word "no".

Tannen grunted and heaved the man into a sitting position against the wall, dusted off his hands, and stood straight. "Now," he turned to Amelia, "I'm here concerning a payment?"

Amelia frowned. "Payment?"

Tannen pulled out a coin purse, jingled it, and cleared his throat. "Uh, yes, ma'am. There is an outstanding payment concerning the rookie betting pool." The young man had won the bet concerning whether or not Joe would ever find a date, and if he did, when.

As much as she appreciated him standing up for her and arresting the unconscious idiot in her hallway, she scowled in irritation. "I already paid!"

He nodded. "Uh, yes. Yes, ma'am, you did."

When something began to move past her shoulder, she jumped yet again. It was Blueregard's arm. He was reaching over in order to drop two copper pieces into Tannen's coin purse. His face, as always, was entirely neutral and showed no hint of guilt or remorse.

Tannen thanked Blue for the coins, then turned to tend to the unconscious William. Blue said nothing, pulled the door closed, and made his way back to the kitchens to finish preparing supper.

Amelia watched in stunned silence.

Chapter 32

The four of them shared dinner and Betty regaled them with the tale of her latest courtship disaster. Voidmind never really outright giggled or barked in laughter, but she would occasionally chuckle at the stories of their youthful exploits. She was very much like Blueregard in that manner, tightly controlled and always reserved.

After a late night tea, Amelia thanked them for the pleasant evening. It was a welcome respite from the terrors and stresses of her daily life. Betty wished them all good night, and Blueregard excused himself to focus on the laundry.

Detective Voidmind suggested that Amelia prepare for bed and get comfortable, because once she applied her mind magic, there wouldn't be any waking until the morning. It wouldn't be like the slow and gentle drowsiness that came from a sleep tonic. Voidmind wasn't quite that talented and informed Amelia that she usually applied her mind magic like a hammer to a nail.

The thought of having her mental faculties smashed into unconsciousness wasn't appealing, but the alternative was to try and sleep while fretting about being possessed again. Only the gods knew what sorts of nightmares her mind would concoct.

Amelia thanked the detective and prepared for bed. Her hair was brushed, clothes were folded, teeth were brushed, and she had found a comfortable spot in bed.

She was about to call out to the detective when darkness struck her mind.

~~

The woman hadn't been joking. Amelia woke in the exact same position she had laid down in and only after Blueregard had entered her bedroom in order to deactivate the blaring bedside alarm. She'd never slept so heavily in her life; there was even a bit of drool running down the side of her mouth.

Since Blueregard was the only one to witness that brief embarrassment, it didn't prove to be all that terrible of a thing. She was refreshed, and that was what truly mattered.

Her morning bath was invigorating. A spot check in the mirror showed that all of her bruises had healed over well enough, and a thorough brushing of her hair routinely proved that there was no Crown.

Breakfast was hearty, and Betty's enthusiastic spirits were encouraging. Not only was it a good start to the day, but she also remembered to fill her favorite travel heating container and take it along to the precinct, which was still out of tea.

The day proved to be another dreary adventure in sorting files and generating reports. Joe and John were out investigating a series of arsons and fires. Bob still avoided her like she was infected with the pox.

In all, the silence suited her just fine. It made for a quiet day. At the end of her shift, Joe returned to the precinct covered in a heavy coating of soot.

When she gave him a quizzical eyebrow, he replied with a deep and weary sigh, "Fire fairy."

That only raised more questions and caused her to frown in confusion. He shook his head. "You can read my report in the morning."

I definitely will.

She turned to leave when he called after her, "Ruby is expecting you at the party."

Amelia stopped and called back over her shoulder, "I'll be there… but you'll be late if you don't hurry and wash up."

He blindly shooed her away as he shuffled through the reports on his desk. "I won't be late."

~~

He was late.

It was irritating but not unexpected. Since Amelia had never been to the store before, she spent the time exploring all the goods that were on display. Most of what was presented would be considered delights and treats for children. There were a few oddities that adults would find amusing or desirable. There were some self-folding napkins and mood candles for sale. Romantic parties would be interested in such things. She wasn't, but the appeal was there, and business appeared to be good.

Despite being an orphan, Ruby had invited quite a few friends to her age day. Most of them were Ruby's age, and they filled the store with chatter and laughter. It felt good to be surrounded by high spirits.

A celebratory banner had been erected over the transactional station, and sparkling candles had been lit around the store. Sugar biscuits and fruit tarts were served alongside tart cider. Trumpeting music played on a wind-up, and many of the girls danced along with the tune.

On occasion, some of them huddled together,

whispered something, glanced in Amelia's direction, and giggled endlessly. It made her horribly uncomfortable, but she was willing to stick through it if it meant getting answers out of the rookie.

It didn't take long for Ruby to hop on over with unbound joy in her step. "Hi! Glad you could make it!" Ruby was dressed in a green skirt stitched with vines and flowers and wore a blush blouse. The young woman was distinctive with her bright strawberry blonde hair and the bright scaring that ran along the left side of her face. Wide, pale lines ran down from her temple and ear, across her cheek, and over the bridge of her nose. They had darkened since last she saw the poor woman; restorative creams must have been applied. Despite the scaring, she was a beautiful young woman and didn't use her hair as a curtain to hide the scars.

You're a brave girl.

Amelia gave a curt nod, and tried to respond in kind. "I'm... glad... I was invited."

Ruby absolutely beamed. "It was my idea."

"To invite me?"

"Yes."

"But why?"

Ruby shuffled a little closer and lowered her voice, "So you could talk to him without suspicion."

"Suspicion?"

"Yes. He's very secretive and worries too much. So I told him I would invite you to my party, and that way, the two of you could talk and it wouldn't look suspicious."

Amelia saw a flaw in that plan. "Wouldn't it look suspicious that you invited me to your age day celebration? We don't exactly know each other all that well, and I'm a bit older than your friends."

Ruby shook her head. "Not really. Joe needs you to act as a witness as he signs over my dad's shop to me."

She stood a bit straighter at that. "He's signing over the shop to you?"

The young woman looked up at Amelia and

grinned. "Yes. He's going to surprise me with it."

"Oh. Then how did you find out?"

She shrugged. "He's not very good at keeping his secrets."

Amelia couldn't help but bark out a laugh at that. It was far too true. If the idiot was any good at keeping secrets, she wouldn't have caught onto the fact that he was hiding something.

The door jingled, and Joe and Nurse Bell stepped into the store. He was clean for once and not wearing his detective's garb. He wore a grey flat cap, a jacket that was patched at the elbows, and a dull brown vest. His button-up was white and his trousers were ragged and beige. Nurse Bell, however, looked stunning. She held his hand and followed him into the store while wearing a cream-colored silk dress that fit comfortably around the chest and shoulders and flared out from the waist.

Joe drew up short when he noticed that he was the only man in the store. He looked around, cleared his throat, and gestured for Grace to lead the way. She did, and she immediately gathered some of the girls for a quick chat.

With the way cleared, Joe squeezed passed the girls, made his way toward Amelia, and kept his voice low. "We can talk in the basement."

Ruby continued to smile as though it were all part of the plan. "You have thirty minutes. Then I want you back here to celebrate."

Joe nodded in understanding. "It should only take a few minutes."

Amelia quickly downed the last of the tart cider that she had been drinking and put the cup down beside Ruby before waving him on. "Let's get going."

Joe quickly led them through a hallway into the back. They walked passed a stairwell that led to the residence above the store and into a back storage room. From there, Joe turned left and walked to a locked door that led under the stairwell. He drew his wand from a vest pocket and pointed it at the door.

A quick blink allowed her to see the door with her arcane senses; that caused her to jump in alarm. The door was almost humming with power. There were so many wards, shields, triggers, and alarms. It might as well have been the entrance to a damned vault. "Merciful goddess, what are you hiding behind that door?"

Joe shrugged and tapped the padlock on the door; it clicked open and hung freely. "Store supplies." He then tapped the door, and all the wards that she had been sensing suddenly dropped.

Amelia blinked twice to return her vision to normal and shook her head clear to make sure she hadn't just imagined it. Once she was certain that it had happened, she turned to Joe and scowled. "This better be a damn good chat."

He frowned at her for a moment before opening the door and gesturing to the flight of stairs that lead into the store cellar. "Ladies first."

Amelia continued to scowl at him and crossed her arms.

Joe rolled his eyes and his head. "Oh gods, I don't have time for this." He turned his attention back on her and emphasized, "I need to reactivate the wards once we go through. Would you rather I squeeze past you on the stairs, or would you like to go first?"

She didn't like it because she didn't fully trust him, but it was the preferable choice. Amelia headed down the stairs first. Joe followed, shut the door, and flicked a switch that turned on a lantern light at the bottom of the stairs.

Amelia made her way down to the landing and peered out into a small makeshift workshop. There was some metal shelving holding an array of magical reagents and components and a wooden countertop off to the left with small tools scattered across it.

Joe squeezed passed her, wound his way through the shelving units, and stepped into the furthest corner of the room. Once there, he turned, put his back to the wall, and waved her over.

She didn't like it. Something was off about the behavior. "Why are you all the way over there?"

He rolled his head and eyes again. "Please, humor me!"

Amelia glowered at him but slowly made her way closer. As she neared, she could see that there was a small amount of space set aside in the far corner he was standing in. There were no shelving units and nothing within arm's reach.

She rounded the last shelf and stopped a few steps short of him. "Can we talk now?"

He shook his head. "Now you make a choice."

"What choice?"

"The choice to hear what I have to say or ignore all of this and go back to pretending I have no secrets."

Amelia frowned and threw up her arms. "Why in all creation would I come all this way to just turn around and pretend not to know you're hiding something?"

Joe gave her a level look. "Because of how dangerous this information is."

That gave her pause. "Are you being serious?"

"Deadly."

"I'm not kidding."

"Neither am I."

"You swear?"

"You want to feel the world shake?" Joe wasn't bluffing. He had invoked the gods once before, and the reports said that it sounded like the loudest thunder anyone had ever heard had just crashed through. Amelia knew what that was like. She felt it when Blueregard had sworn in the name of the gods.

Amelia took a minute to process that. She had just dealt with being corrupted and she didn't want to hear any more terrible or terrifying news. The flip side was that she didn't want to be hit by something that she couldn't see coming. "I want to know."

Joe let out a deep sigh and nodded his head in acceptance. "All right." He reached into his trouser pocket and pulled out a beat-up old silver ring, "Best get over here then."

Amelia took a tentative step closer while eyeing the ring he had pulled. "What's that for?"

"It's a key. If I put it on, I activate the teleportation runes in this corner."

She looked at the cement flooring and saw nothing. She breathed for a moment and blinked to switch to her arcane vision. There was still nothing there. "I don't see any runes."

"That's because they're hidden... like how Ta'at's warding stone was hidden."

Amelia blinked away the arcane vision and turned her attention back to Joe. He was still hitting her with that level stare. She didn't like it, but she had no other choice. "Fine." She took a step closer and folded her arms.

He shook his head. "Closer."

They were only one pace away from each other. Amelia glared up at him and took a smaller step closer. "Good enough?" They were a step away from being toe-to-toe. She was close enough to smell his aftershave. It was similar to Blueregard's and pleasantly non-offensive.

He looked around her, to the side, and sighed before nodding. "Yeah, that should be good enough." Joe lifted his hand and showed her putting the silver ring on his finger. Nothing happened. He started taking off the ring, stepped away from her, and out into an open expanse of a cobblestone room.

Amelia darted her head back and forth and turned full circle. They were in an entirely different place. She hadn't even felt the transportation spell take effect. She had blinked and missed it.

Looking down nearly blinded her. She was standing on a giant recall circle. It had to be two dozen paces across, and the runes of power were so bright that they left spots in her vision. "Joseph! Where are we?"

Joe pulled her attention to him by flicking on an old portable sun lantern. He was in the corner of the room. Amelia stumbled toward him and continued to blink away the spots in her vision. "Blast it all! I asked you a question!"

"I know… the problem is that I don't know how to answer it."

She caught herself on a nearby stone pillar and steadied her vision. "The beginning tends to be a fantastic place to start!"

"The beginning, right." He looked to the table he was standing beside and idly ran his fingers over a notebook that was laying upon it. "I'm not normal."

"Oh, really? I never would have guessed!" Amelia rubbed one eye at a time as she leaned back against the pillar.

Joe turned an irritated scowl upon her as though to tell her to watch her tone.

She didn't feel like it, but she had no idea where she was and didn't know how to get back, so she rubbed her eyes one last time and gestured for him to get on with it.

He turned his attention back to the notebook and continued to talk. "I'm not a wizard."

I had a feeling that might be the case.

"I think I might be a sorcerer."

You think?

"I'm fairly certain that's why I could sense the Crowns. The entities within them were sorcerers as well. My best guess is that sorcerers might be able to sense one another."

She couldn't think of a better answer and she didn't know enough about sorcerers to refute it.

"But to be honest, I have no idea what I am." He shook his head and paused before continuing, "I do know that I share the *exact* same magic as my family." He looked to something else that was on the table and tossed it to her.

Amelia adjusted for the arc of the object and caught

whatever he had tossed. Bringing it up into the light a bit, she could finally see that it was the amulet of Ta'at. "How–"

"It's the fake one that John made. The real one is still in the museum vault." Possessing the fake was far more plausible, as it was nothing more than a carved bar of soap. "The reason I was able to find the original is because it looked like my spellwork, *exactly* like my spellwork. It was as if I had designed it myself."

She had never heard of such a bloodline. "Okay, so your family is weird. What does that have to do with danger?"

Joe gestured to the room they were standing in. "This is a reception room." He let his arms drop and he spoke a bit softer. "Or at least I think it is." He clearly wasn't confident in anything he was saying. "It was designed by my family. All the wards match the spellwork I usually use, but it's far more complex and advanced. As far as I can tell, it's been here for generations."

She started getting a sickening feeling. Where were all the other members of his family?

As if he had read her mind, he answered, "I think they're all gone." He held up the beaten silver ring and gestured to the room again. "This is all that's left." He dropped the ring on to the notebook. "All of this and a letter that was sent to me... from my dead mother." He put both his hands on the table and hung his head. "She was likely murdered by the people that she referred to as 'them'. I have no idea who 'them' Is."

The danger was starting to make a little more sense.

"My ancestral family was capable of crafting an amulet that could banish a god from the mortal realm." He looked back at her. "If they could do that, imagine what it took to kill them to the last."

The danger made a great deal more sense at that moment, but one thing still bothered her. "Why hide all of this? Why not ask for help from your superiors?"

Joe blindly reached down and picked up the

notebook. He opened it to where a fold of parchment bookmarked the page. "This is my mother's journal. The last entry is dated twenty-three years ago. It's the exact same summer as the Noble Killings." He held it out to her so she could read it.

She was intimately familiar with the Noble Killings; her grandfather was one of the victims. She palmed the amulet, stepped closer, and took the notebook. The looping script was immaculate and definitely belonged to a woman's hand. She read and listened as Joe quoted the entry, word for word. He had clearly memorized it.

"'My husband may be dead, but my child is at least safe. I fear that the organization that seeks to destroy us is the same one that is killing the nobles of Stormbay.'"

Amelia kept pace with his words.

"'I go now to seek out a contact within the law enforcement's Internal Investigation division. If I make no further entries, one thing can be verified as certain. They have found me, and the law enforcement cannot be trusted.'"

There was nothing left on the page, and Joe was silent.

The entry was hopeful and disheartening in the same breath. It clearly read 'seeks to destroy us'. The 'us' part suggested that there was more than one still alive when Joe's mother had written the entry. The disheartening part of it was that it circumstantially suggested that the Internal Investigations division was corrupted.

With all evidence suggesting that 'they' had infiltrated city law enforcement, she couldn't help but ask, "Why do you trust me?" It was the burning question that gnawed at her since he had finally opened up.

"Two reasons. First, you'd never give up and would likely tear my life apart looking for the answers if I didn't tell you."

He isn't wrong.

"Second... an Oath-sworn man said you could be

trusted."

Bless you, Blue.

There was a brief silence as Joe allowed her to absorb it all. Eventually he broke it. "I shared my great secret. It's time to share yours. I know you have one. I saw it on your face when I asked for the secret to your clothes-switching trick." He looked a little smug with his arms crossed.

Blast you, Joe.

"Fine." After having offered up the great secret of his life, hers felt miniscule by comparison. She was also no longer afraid of it, not after her brother had released cursed objects upon the city. "I killed my father when I was a girl. He came at me with my grandfather's cane sword."

"Wait... what?"

"My parents were anti-magic, and my maternal grandparents were instructing me behind their backs."

"So you–?"

"Froze his heart. Killed him dead."

Joe stood stunned and his arms slowly uncrossed.

"You have a problem with it?"

Joe clapped his mouth shut and frowned in thought. "He came at you with a cane sword?"

"Yep."

He stared at her for a long moment. He was clearly deciding on how to answer. Eventually, his features hardened and his eyes focused. He declared with absolute conviction, "I hope he suffered."

Bless you, Joe.

To Be Continued…

Author Bio

B.T. Frost is an avid fantasy writer and a fan of Dungeons & Dragons. His writing credentials include an Applied Bachelor's Degree in Communications in Professional Writing from Grant MacEwan University and a seat as a Dungeon Master at the gaming table. He grew up in Edmonton, Alberta, Canada, devours books of the fantasy genre, and spends countless hours absorbing crime dramas and movies.

www.author-btfrost.com